HER WEREWOLF ALPHA

WEREWOLF GUARDIAN ROMANCE SERIES

JODI VAUGHN

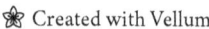

CHAPTER 1

Petit Jean State Park, Arkansas

BARRETT MIDDLETON WAS IN HELL.

Pain burned through him like white, hot lightning arcing across his nerves, his body consumed by fire.

Despite the agony and indescribable pain, it was his chest that hurt like a motherfucker.

He tried to pry open his heavy eyes but found it was impossible.

He was stuck in hell, surrounded in darkness, suspended in perpetual pain.

He tried to remember what happened and how he had journeyed into purgatory. But his mind was a black screen. He wanted to scream, to yell, but only managed to swallow. He winced in pain.

Apparently, someone had shoved shards of glass down his throat.

He tried to lift his arm, but his body wouldn't obey.

His chest clenched.

Shit. Maybe he couldn't move because he was paralyzed.

A cool hand closed around his neck and slender fingers pressed into the side of his throat.

"You really should stay still. I can tell by your elevated heart rate, you're trying to move," a feminine voice whispered near his ear.

What's wrong with me? What happened? He tried to force his lips to form the words.

"And it's no use trying to talk. Because you can't. At least not yet," she said.

Who the fuck was she, and why did she sound so fucking familiar?

"Looks like it's going to be just you and me for a while, wolf. Cozy as a bug in a rug." She pressed her lips to his ear. She sucked his earlobe into her warm mouth.

Her hand slid from his neck down between his legs. She palmed his cock.

His heart raced. For the first time in his life he was helpless and vulnerable.

"I've had my eye on you for quite a while, Barrett. While you are recovering, we'll have the chance to get to know each other a little better," she purred.

His stomach turned.

"Get away from him, witch." A dark, familiar voice rumbled.

Ryker. Thank God.

"I was just making him comfortable." She moved her hand away and stepped back, according to the sound of her footsteps.

"Making him comfortable? With your hand on his dick? I don't think so," Ryker rumbled.

"Well, until we can leave this cave, we're just going to have to learn to get along together," she drawled. "And if you play your cards right, maybe you and me can learn to play well together too."

Not hell. A cave. They were in some sort of cave.

"No way in hell. I don't fuck with psychotic witches. You'll probably make my dick fall off," Ryker snarled. "And if I see you groping Barrett again, I'll cut off your fucking hand."

"I'm not a psychopath," she shrieked. "I'm borderline personality."

Shit. He was stuck in a cave with a psychotic witch and his irritable Guardian. Hell was beginning to look better by the second.

"Whatever you are, you need to get that fucking cat under control. It clawed my leather jacket to shreds!" Ryker yelled.

"She's just bored," she said. "Besides, I don't control Nyx."

"Ella, I'm warning you. You better keep that fucking cat away from me and my stuff, or I'm going to skin her!" Ryker shouted.

Ella. Now he remembered. Now it was coming back to him. Ella, the Witch of Yazoo City. She'd escaped from the cemetery in Mississippi when he had sent Lucien to get some intel for him. She had been cursed to spend all of eternity in the cemetery until she'd worked blood magic to escape.

Brief scenes flashed behind his eyes.

Witch.

Edward Boudier.

Jaxon.

Death debt.

Nausea swamped him, and he wished he could roll over and vomit.

He remembered everything.

The Tribunal where Jaxon had been found guilty. Where he, Barrett, had taken Jaxon's debt upon himself. And paid it in his own blood.

His muscles tensed.

But that didn't make sense. If he was dead, then why was Ryker and that fucking witch with him. He didn't remember them dying too.

"How long do we have to stay here?" Ella huffed.

"You complaining?" Ryker cautioned. "Remember I could put you back in that cemetery."

"I can't help it. It's dirty and moldy, and the walls leak when it rains," she hissed. "Not to mention all this dampness makes my hair frizz."

"Tough shit. We stay here until it's safe to move Barrett out of Arkansas and somewhere no one will look for him."

"And where would that be?"

"Nowhere in the South. We've got too many werewolves that know what he looks like. We have to move him out of the Southern region."

"How about New York?" Ella said excitedly. "I've never been to New York."

"Hell, no. Barrett would hate the city. Plus, it's on the East Coast. He's originally from South Carolina. Or maybe it's North Carolina. Hell, I can't keep them straight."

"Ooohhh. I would love to go to South Carolina. I hear Charleston is lovely," she cooed.

Barrett frowned. Or at least he did in his head. It was hard to know if he was actually making any facial movements.

"No. Not Charleston," Ryker growled.

He relaxed. Ryker was right. Going to Charleston would be a deadly mistake. His family hailed from there, and someone would surely recognize him. No, it would be better to go somewhere far, far away.

"What about California?" Ella asked.

"No." Ryker let out a frustrated sigh. "We need something

surrounded by nature. Lots of places to live where people don't really look at you."

"Sounds like Missouri to me."

"Except that Missouri is a rogue state, and everyone there would recognize Barrett the minute he showed his face."

"So, you want nature, mountains, and places to be able to isolate himself if necessary." She snorted. "Sounds like Alaska."

Barrett tensed. Alaska was nice to visit but not to live. He didn't think he would be able to bear the cold winters.

"That's not a bad idea," Ryker said.

Fuck no. No way. No how. If Ryker hauled his ass to Alaska, the second Barrett was healed, Barrett was going to rip the Were a new asshole.

"But Alaska is too far away," Ryker spoke to himself.

"I thought you wanted far away," Ella groused. "Geez, you need to make up your mind."

Silence spread through the cave.

"Give me your phone," Ella demanded.

"What the fuck for?" Ryker argued.

"I need to see what I missed in the real world," Ella sighed heavily. "I feel like I'm cut off and back in that cemetery away from the living."

"Fine. But no calls. Understand?"

Barrett still didn't understand why Ella was with Ryker. Why didn't Ryker just hand her over to the Mississippi Pack Master? What about his other Guardians? What was going on with them? And what the hell was going on with the state of Arkansas? Had Boudier taken over Arkansas? Had he killed the rest of the Guardians?

"And don't be using my phone to watch those dumbass housewives shows. If one of the Guardians finds that on my phone, I'll never live it down."

Barrett wanted to grin at the distress in Ryker's voice. No

doubt they would all give him hell over that. He couldn't wait to get out of here and rat him out to the Guardians.

His heart sank.

Hopelessness washed over him.

Even if he did get out of here, he could never go back to Arkansas. If he did, then Jaxon's life would be in danger.

He'd never be Pack Master again.

Anger and regret welled inside him.

He had sacrificed himself for the Pack. He was supposed to be dead. Something must have gone wrong. Maybe the silver knife had been knocked out of his chest when he landed at the bottom of the mountain. He should be dead. Not lying paralyzed and helpless like a mortally wounded animal. They should have stuck the knife into his brain and let him die with some dignity.

He managed to crack open his eyes slightly, but it was all he needed to see his surroundings.

The walls were stone and the floor dirt. There were lit candles along the floor, and a couple of torches hung on either side entrance to their rustic dwelling.

He moved his head to the side slightly and blinked. He really was in a fucking cave which meant they were probably still at Petit Jean State Park. The place where the Tribunal had been held.

Ella squealed.

"What the fuck is wrong with you? Your favorite band coming to town or something?" Ryker groused. He cast Ella a glare and then squatted by his leather bag where he proceeded to rummage.

"No, you idiot. I'm looking at tiny houses, and there's one in my price range that's for sale."

"You want to live in a tin can? Where are you going to put all the shoes you steal."

Ella brushed her red hair away from her face and froze.

"Maybe I can get two tiny houses. One for my shoes and the other for me."

"What about me?" A black cat slinked out from the shadows and sat. It curled its long, inky tail around its legs and looked up at the witch. "Where am I going to live?"

Ella's red lips grew into a smirk. "On the roof."

A talking cat. Perfect. He'd heard of familiars before but never actually saw one.

"That's a terrible idea." The cat jumped up, swatted its paw, and knocked the phone out her hand. It landed with a soft thud on the ground.

"Watch it, cat. That's my phone," Ryker snarled.

The cat walked over to the phone and looked down. "Where is this house anyway? Looks like out in the middle of nowhere," the cat asked.

Ella picked up the phone. "Colorado." Her shoulders slumped. "That won't work. It's too far away."

"What did you say?" Ryker stilled and stood. He turned and faced the witch.

"I said it's too far to drive." Ella frowned.

"No, you said it's in Colorado."

"Yeah, so?"

"So, it's away from the South. No one really knows Barrett in that state, and it has mountains and lakes and areas where you can be isolated if you want. It's the perfect place."

"Yeah. Plus, weed is legal in Colorado. So, if someone does recognize him, they'll be too hammered to care," the black cat offered.

Colorado? Ryker wasn't seriously thinking of taking him to Colorado?

A slow smiled stretched across Ryker's face. "Colorado, it is."

Barrett tried to open his mouth, to let them both know

what he thought of their idea. But his body wouldn't cooperate.

He felt his eyelids grow heavy. Slowly his eyes closed, and he was soon drifting off once again to a dreamless sleep with no future in sight.

CHAPTER 2

"You ou don't need to babysit me. I'm a grown-ass male," Barrett snarled. He cut his eyes at Ryker who was hanging out in the kitchen of the hotel suite. "Besides, I'm sure the Guardians are starting to wonder why you've been gone so long."

Ryker shrugged. "And when they ask, I'll tell them I was mourning the loss of my esteemed leader. Though to be honest, I doubt they will even ask."

"Why is that?" Barrett had only been in Colorado for a week, and he was already antsy. He'd stayed in the cave in Arkansas for weeks, long enough to heal and make sure that no one would see them moving him out of the state. Ryker had let Ella go her own way the night they pulled out of Arkansas. Ryker had agreed not to turn her into the Mississippi Guardians in exchange for her silence on Barrett being alive. He wanted to leave earlier, but Ryker refused. He said he didn't want to take any chances of one of the Arkansas Guardians seeing him alive.

"Because they are all dealing with your loss in their own way. They think I'll be dealing too." Ryker shrugged and grabbed a beer out of the fridge. He uncapped the icy bottle, took a long drink, and followed it with a loud burp.

"Glad to see you're handling my death so well, asshole." Barrett turned away and stared out the hotel window. It was only August, and the weather in Colorado was enjoyable. It was only three in the afternoon, and he'd been holed up in the hotel for a week. Ryker only let him go out at night and never alone.

Barrett had never been one to crave someone's company. Even as a child growing up, he preferred his solitude. He liked being alone. He never understood why his Guardians were so intent on mating. He didn't think he could stand to wake up to the same female day after day after day after day.

It would suffocate him.

Much like Ryker was starting to smother the life out of him right now with his constant presence.

Ryker let out a laugh. Barrett turned.

"What's so funny?" He glared.

"That expression on your face. The one that screams you're thinking of several ways to kill me so you can be alone." Ryker eased onto the sofa and propped his biker boots on the coffee table. "Sorry, amigo. Ain't gonna happen."

"A guy can dream, can't he?" Barrett turned his attention back to the city scene out the window.

"Well, think of the positive. At least you can't mate now. You're supposed to be dead, and dead werewolves don't mate." Ryker gave him a broad smile.

"That's one thing you won't ever have to worry about concerning me. Even if I wasn't 'dead,' I still wouldn't mate," he huffed. "I don't have the temperament for it."

"That's the fucking truth," Ryker agreed.

Barrett turned and stared.

"Besides, no female could put up with you. You're too abrupt. Too stubborn. Too scary for any female to …

Barrett held up his hand. "I get it already."

Ryker shrugged and took another sip. "We'll go out after it gets dark to grab something to eat."

"Perfect." He was getting tired of eating delivery, and he longed for fresh air.

"I can't stay in a hotel forever. I need to get out." Barrett stared at the bustling city of Denver below. The cars and people were in constant motion going to and fro, never suspended in time. Unlike him. He, on the other hand, had been caged for weeks now, and he needed to be let loose.

"I wanted to talk to you about that," Ryker said.

Barrett pushed off the window and looked at his Guardian. Former Guardian. Ryker was no longer under his command and Barrett was no longer the Pack Master of Arkansas.

"I'm telling you right now, I'm not staying another fucking week in this hotel." He wasn't going to stay another night. But he wasn't going to tell Ryker that. After they grabbed something to eat, he was going to go to the bathroom and then slip out into the night. He cared for his friend, but Ryker was part of a past he could no longer associate with.

He was officially dead. He'd been stabbed with a silver knife, slicing apart the valves of his heart and then fell off the cliff at Petit Jean State park in Arkansas. He'd felt his body dying, and the last thing he remembered was the howl of a wolf standing on the ledge above him and the gruesome sound of his neck breaking when he hit the jagged rocks and boulders below.

He'd never really given much thought to the afterlife. He figured once you died that was it. But when he opened his eyes and found himself in a cave with a psychotic witch grabbing his cock, he then figured he was in hell. Then he saw Ryker. And that confirmed it.

Then they told him he wasn't dead. That they'd brought him back with the help of a witch and a Fae.

The cell phone buzzed, and Ryker pulled it out of his jeans pocket. He studied the screen and then looked up at Barrett.

"You got a hot date tonight or something?" Barrett snarked.

"You're the only date I have tonight, and you're not hot."

"That's not what Ella said," Barrett deadpanned.

"Yeah, well, she's psychotic, so I wouldn't put much stock in what she says. Not to mention, she tried to grab my ass every time I bent over."

"Well, in that case, she's definitely desperate." Barrett nodded at Ryker's phone. "Who's that on the phone?"

Ryker met his gaze. "Celeste."

"The Fae? What does she want?" A shiver went through him.

"Just checking on you. Making sure you're still breathing." Ryker settled back against the couch. "You could show a little more gratitude for her bringing you back to life. It's not like she had to."

He stared hard at Ryker. "I didn't ask her to bring me back."

"I know. I did." Ryker shrugged.

Barrett curled his fingers into fists. "How did you know that I was planning on dying instead of Jaxon? I didn't tell anyone."

"I had a very strong suspicion you were going to do something stupid. I had called Celeste to come help. Good thing she owns her own plane. She made it just in time." Ryker eyed him carefully. "I watched you give that briefcase to Jack Welbourn in the woods. When you left, I cornered him. He said he swore a blood oath to you and couldn't look inside the briefcase. I told him I swore nothing and if he didn't hand it over, I was going to gut his old ass and strangle him with his own intestines."

"I'm sure that went over really well with the Pack Master of Mississippi." Barrett arched his eyebrow.

"Better than you expected." Ryker took another drink and stood. "Anyway, after reading how you were leaving Damon in charge, I knew that you were planning on offering your life in exchange for Jaxon's. I also knew that the Council wouldn't allow it. When I saw you grab Ava, I knew how you were going to die. You were going to force Damon to kill you."

"I had no other choice." He forked his fingers through his hair. He hated thinking what he'd done to Damon.

"I understand," Ryker said.

"Do you? Then you know I didn't plan on coming back from the dead."

"That's on me." Ryker tipped his beer at him.

"What good am I now? I'm hiding in hotels, eating shitty food, and I can't contact anyone from my past to let them know I'm alive. Because if I'm alive, then that means Jaxon's life is still in danger, and he must be sentenced to death. I paid the death debt. And I thought that was the end of me." Barrett paced the small room, his footsteps landing on the carpet.

"You know I couldn't let you do that," Ryker sighed.

"What good am I now?" He felt as useless as tits on a bull. "I'm stuck here hiding."

"Not anymore."

"What do you mean?" He stopped in his tracks.

"I have found a place for you." Ryker grinned.

"No way am I going to Alaska," Barrett growled.

"It's not Alaska, dumbass. It's up in the mountains, away from Denver."

"How the fuck am I supposed to pay for this? All my

money went to Damon upon my death." Once a Pack Master died, the next in line would inherit all his money.

"Well, boss, not only is it a place to live, but it comes with a bar and grill. So, you can live there and have a way to make some income to live on." Ryker smiled.

"Run a bar? You're seriously telling me I'm going to run a bar?" He stared hard at him.

"Well, yeah. I mean you ran the Arkansas Guardians for years. You know how to put up with drunk, obstinate, unruly assholes. This is perfect for you." Ryker pointed at him with his bottle.

"You're not wrong. And I still have one unruly asshole hanging around."

Ryker laughed.

"You still haven't told me how I'm going to pay for this." Barrett propped his hands on his hips.

"You took out a loan."

"How the hell could I take out a loan when I'm technically dead?"

"It's not from a bank. It's from me. The place is something I inherited a while ago from a distant relative. I planned on living there once I retired from the Guardians." Ryker shrugged.

"Fuck." He hated owing anybody anything. It was something he always avoided. He didn't want to be indebted to anyone, even Ryker.

"You need to show a little gratitude, man. I mean you get a second chance at life."

Right. A second chance with absolutely no money, dead to everyone who knew him, and out in the middle of Colorado which was known to have horrendous snow.

"I'll be grateful when I get my ass out of this hotel." He lifted his gaze to Ryker. The rest, he wasn't so sure about.

CHAPTER 3

*J*acey Miller clutched her black canvas messenger bag against her chest like a shield and looked up at the rustic-looking bar.

She was a long way from home, and the little money she had was quickly disappearing in the way of food and cheap motels. The Mountain Top Bar and Grille was her last chance at starting a new life.

A blast of Colorado wind whipped across her skin. She shivered and burrowed down into her leather jacket. The first thing she was going to buy with her first paycheck was a warmer coat.

If she ever got a paycheck, that is.

She never imagined her life would turn out like this.

She'd taken what little cash she had and bought a one-way plane ticket as far away from Mississippi as she could get.

That one-way ticket had taken her to Denver, Colorado.

For the first time in her life, she was completely on her own. Fear had nearly swallowed her up on that plane ride.

Urgency to survive had taken over, and she quickly made plans to start looking for a job the second she landed.

When she got to the hotel in Denver, she used the business office computer to search for jobs.

She knew it was going to be virtually impossible to find something she could do since she had zero experience in the work force.

When she had spotted a help wanted ad for a bar and grill in the small town of Silverton, a tiny bubble of hope began to blossom in her chest.

She needed a job. And she didn't care what it was, as long as it wasn't illegal.

Now standing in front of The Mountain Top Bar and Grille, she began to wonder if she had made a mistake. Silverton was smaller than she imagined and sat buried on top of the mountain away from civilization. She had taken a bus to get up the mountain since the train had stopped its route for the season due to snow. There were only a handful of shops and even less houses on the wide streets of the small town. For a town once known for its vast amounts of silver hauled out of the mountains, it looked like a ghost town covered in snow. A place with no future, only memories of the past.

She rallied what little bit of courage she had and opened the door.

She was slapped in the face with the music of a band playing an eighties rock song and dim lighting. She slid further inside the bar and let the door close behind her.

The interior didn't look much better than the outside. There were black booths around the walls and tables arranged in the middle of the room. Behind the bar sat rows and rows of bottles of every kind of alcohol imaginable. An old-fashioned cash register sat behind the bar where there wasn't a bartender in sight.

It was only nine, and the place was already crowded. Her hopes soared. A busy place meant they needed help and might hire her despite her lack of professional experience.

"Honey, you need a table or are you going to sit at the bar?" An older lady in her midsixties gave her a frown. In her right hand, she balanced a tray of drinks over her shoulder.

"I'm not here to eat."

"That's good. Cause the food sucks," the waitress retorted.

She shook her head. "I mean, I'm here to apply for the position in the want ads. I saw it online, and it didn't specify what it was. I wasn't sure if it was a waitress position or cook position." Jacey cleared her throat.

"Well, we need both. But first you'll need to talk to the boss. He's in the back making a mess of things as usual." She nodded her head toward the double doors near the bar. "Just head on through those double doors."

"Ah, what does he look like?" Jacey glanced from the double doors back to the waitress.

The waitress grinned broadly. "Honey, you can't miss him."

Jacey nodded and glanced around. Although Colorado was lenient about smoking cigarettes or weed, the inside of the bar was smoke-free. Her gaze landed on a 'No Smoking – Of Anything' sign over the bar.

If there was one thing she hated, it was cigarette smoke. Werewolves had a heightened sense of smell, and smoke was one thing all Weres hated.

She wasn't sure what kind of person this owner was, but so far it was a good sign.

She clutched her messenger bag to her chest and made her way through the crowd and toward the kitchen.

She pushed hard against the swaying door and immediately hit against resistance.

A loud crash followed by loud cursing came from the other side of the doors.

With her heart in her throat, she peeked her head behind the door. A very large male was bent down picking up the white shards of what used to be plates and the remnants of a hamburger and fries.

"Oh, God. I'm so sorry," she muttered. She stepped into the kitchen and immediately began helping with the clean-up process.

"What the hell are you doing back here?" The broad-shouldered man glared at her from under his lashes. "The bathroom is on the other side of the bar."

She nearly froze at the sight of him. He was larger than any human she'd ever seen. His eyes were a startling shade of turquoise and so intense they were lethal, and his lips were curled into a snarl.

His dark-blonde hair framed his chiseled face that looked like it belonged on Greek god.

"I'm sorry. I was looking for the owner." She swallowed.

He stood. Her gaze traveled up his large body. If he was intimidating to look at crouched, he was terrifying at his full six-feet-five height.

"I'm the owner. What do you want?" he snarled.

She blinked. His wolf scent hit her like a ton of bricks. He, like her, was a werewolf.

"I, ah, am here in response to the ad you placed for help." She stood and forced her shoulders back. Looking like a wimp wasn't going to get her hired. She needed to present a confident front. Not act like some scared mouse.

"I didn't put an ad in the paper," he growled.

"Actually, it was on the internet. I was searching for work and came across it." She lifted her chin.

He narrowed his hard-blue eyes at her. "Helen, get in here!" he bellowed.

Jacey flinched at the noise and resisted the urge to stick her finger in her ear to shake out the ringing from his loud voice.

"Quit your screaming. Sounds like a banshee in here." Helen slid through the free-swinging doors and stood in front of the large Were with her hands on her hips. "What is it? And how is that burger order coming?"

His gaze slid over to Jacey and rested. "It's not coming. The food ended up on the floor."

"Don't think it would matter anyway. Only people who get drunk order the food here anyway."

Jacey bit her lip to keep from verbally striking out. "It was an accident. There are no signs indicating which door is in and which door is out."

The owner ignored her attempt at an apology and stared hard at the waitress.

"Did you put an ad for help on some website?"

"Sure did. My grandson helped." Helen brightened and then slapped him on the chest. Jacey held her breath.

"Why?" he asked.

"Because we need help. Especially in the kitchen. If you want to start making some real money, you've got to keep your drunk customers fed. Drunk people like to eat. And they like to eat a lot. That's why I had to stop drinking wine." She patted her hips. "Couldn't have wine without chocolate. Was getting a little hippy so I cut all alcohol out."

The owner grimaced. Like it was too much information.

"Look, I don't have all night to chat you up, Barrett. I've got to get back to work. Apparently, all the money I'm earning around here is my tips. And even that ain't so hot." Helen looked over at Jacey. "Why not give her a shot. Her cooking can't be any worse than yours." Helen turned and headed back out into the bar.

Barrett propped his hands on his hips and stared at her,

like he was looking into her soul. He cocked his head. "You're a Were."

"So are you," she countered.

He shoved his hands through his hair and looked down at her.

He waved his hand over the floor where fries were still scattered. "Since this is your fault, you need to fix it."

Was that a job offer? Was it a test? She wasn't sure so she bent down to pick up the rest of the food.

He grabbed her by the elbow and pulled her up. "No. I didn't mean for you to clean it up. I meant let's see how your cooking skills are. I'll look over your resume later." He didn't give her a chance to answer but darted out the double doors into the bar.

She didn't have a resume. Hell, she didn't have a single reference. All she had was the clothes on her back and what she had in her bag.

Barrett seemed like the kind of male that she would have to prove herself to. He wasn't going to give her a job on her good looks alone.

She had to make this work. More than that, she had to make a great impression on a male who was hard to impress.

This was her last chance.

CHAPTER 4

For the rest of the night, Barrett stayed behind the bar filling drink orders and closing out customers' tabs. It was mindless busy work. Exactly what he needed. He wasn't about to go back into the kitchen. Not when … hell, he didn't even know her name … was back there doing God knows what to his kitchen.

The second he'd looked down into her caramel-brown eyes, something had shot through him like electricity. Maybe he had reacted to her because his instincts were telling him to stay away, that she was dangerous.

She was trouble, and he didn't need trouble.

"Barrett, this burger is amazing," Abraham gushed from his seated position at the bar. He took another bite and continued to talk. "I mean this is the best thing I've ever put in my mouth.

Did you hire a five-star chef?" Abraham's eyes grew big, and he wiped his white bearded mouth with a paper napkin.

Abraham was human, a long-time resident of Silverton, and a regular at the bar. He had a small motorcycle shop that stayed open during the tourist season and closed during the winter.

"No. He hired a pretty, little thing that looked like she stepped off the cover of a magazine." Helen snorted as she loaded her tray with glasses of ice-cold beer.

"I didn't hire her." He shot his waitress a warning look. The next time he saw Ryker, he was going to give the Were hell for hiring Helen. She did nothing but talk back and undermined his authority. Not to mention she reminded him of another strong-willed female back in Arkansas.

Granny.

When Ryker had set him up in The Mountain Top Bar and Grille, he'd also been the one to hire the staff. Right now, Barrett was working with a skeletal crew which consisted of Helen, who was his only waitress, and himself. He had a bartender when he first opened, but that didn't last. Mic was his name, and Barrett had caught him taking money out of the cash register and stuffing the twenties into his pocket. Barrett fired him on the spot.

That left Barrett to manage the bar in between working the grill. When he was in the back, Helen had to fix her own drinks, which she constantly griped about.

He was barely keeping his head above water but trying to get help, even part-time help in this small town was nearly impossible. He'd gone through two waitresses both who tried to sleep with him and when he rejected them, they both quit. At least he was safe from Helen. He was pretty sure, at least.

"Easy on the eyes and can cook. I say you keep her, Barrett." Abraham nodded and then took another bite of his burger.

"Abraham, when I want your opinion, I'll ask for it." Barrett glared as he filled four more glasses of beer.

Abraham frowned at Barrett's words.

"Oh, honey. Don't mind him. He's just frustrated. He needs to get out and do something other than run this bar." Helen slapped Abraham on the back and grinned.

"If I'm not here running this bar, then you don't get paid." He shook his head. The truth was he could use a day away from the place. But he wasn't telling her that.

"Well, it wouldn't hurt you to close the bar one day a week. I don't know any business that stays open seven days a week." She shrugged. "Close the bar on Sunday, and that way you can get the new girl trained."

"I'm not hiring her," he ground out.

Helen froze and gave him an icy glare. "Why the hell not? She's been keeping up with every order that we had tonight. And it was edible. That's a step above where we were."

He took a deep breath and curled his fingers into fists. He needed to keep his words calm and steady.

"I'm not hiring her because I know nothing about her," he shot back.

"Well, that's easy. Just look at her resume and check her references." Helen shrugged.

"Why do you want to adopt every stray that comes in here?" he asked.

"People need a second chance, Barrett. That poor, little thing is probably homeless, and you are her last chance at a paycheck."

"Right. Just like you talked me into hiring Mic who stole me blind." He cocked his head.

"Okay, well, maybe Mic didn't work out." She frowned. "I still can't believe he turned out so bad. I guess my instincts on him were off."

"Maybe your instinct on the girl is off too," he countered.

Helen shrugged. "Could be. But why not take a chance? You've not nothing to lose." She turned and carried her full tray of drinks to thirsty patrons.

That's where Helen was wrong. He knew if he let the wrong one in, there would be a lot to lose.

* * *

JACEY FINISHED RINSING off the last pot and turned off the water. She grabbed a dishtowel and thoroughly dried off the metal before hanging it back on the rack over the industrial island.

She glanced around the now clean kitchen. Her gaze landed on a large, white clock hanging on the wall.

Two a.m.

She'd been so busy filling orders that she hadn't noticed how much time had passed.

At first, she'd only had a few orders from Helen, a couple of hamburgers and fries and a grilled cheese sandwich. Apparently, the customers had seen the food coming out and started to comment on how great everything looked. Then the orders had piled in. She was used to cooking for Jeremy, and he ate like a horse.

Soon, she was filling orders like an assembly line.

Her stomach rumbled. She pressed her hand against her tummy.

"Looks like you missed dinner," Barrett said as he came into the kitchen. He was carrying a stack of serving trays in one hand and wearing a scowl. "You should eat something."

"I'll grab something later." Truth be told, she hadn't eaten much since she left her old life behind. Worry had consumed her thoughts along with her appetite.

"That wasn't an offer. It was an order." Barrett tossed another look at her over his shoulder.

She bit back a reply. She wasn't used to a male talking to her like that. Jeremy might be a cheater, but he never talked to her like she was a child.

She shoved her irritation away. Right now, she couldn't afford to be offended by Barrett. Right now, she needed a job.

"I'll make a hamburger. Would you like one?" She pulled out some hamburger meat and grabbed a bowl to mix up her special spices.

"That would be great. I haven't eaten since breakfast." Barrett's harsh tone led her to believe he didn't like anyone doing anything nice for him. Something about him put her on edge. Like he was dangerous. Maybe he was on the run? But that didn't make sense. Criminals on the run didn't set down roots and open a bar.

Within minutes, the ground beef was sizzling on the hot grill. She's already cleaned it once and didn't look forward to cleaning it again. But when the aroma hit her, she decided that the extra work was totally worth it.

While she cooked, she studied Barrett. He didn't stay in one place too long. He was constantly in motion. He headed back into the now closed bar. She peeked at him through the window of the swinging doors. He was busy upending chairs on tables and wiping down all the counters and booths. When he was done with that task, he proceeded to sweep up the entire place.

He looked out of place in this environment. Like he wasn't meant to be a bar owner.

He looked like he was trying to maintain order in a place that reeked of disorder.

When she finished plating the burgers, she grabbed a couple bags of chips out of the pantry and spilled them on the plate.

"It's ready," she called out.

Barrett came through the swinging doors, the muscles in his broad shoulders rippling as he moved. His blue eyes landed on the plate of food and for the first time since she met him, he didn't look like he was ready to bite her head off.

She'd take it.

"Looks good." He picked up both plates and looked at her. "Let's eat at the bar."

She didn't say a word but followed him out of the kitchen. She glanced around for the rest of the skeletal staff, but the place was empty.

"Where's Helen?" she asked as she climbed on the barstool.

"She left. She's raising her grandson, and she likes to leave around one to make sure he's at home."

"What happened to his parents?"

"They're alive. If that's what you're asking. They're both on meth. Helen had to step in and move her grandson in with her. She doesn't want him around that kind of trouble."

"No doubt. I admire someone her age stepping up to do that. These days, people only think about themselves." She felt a lump in her throat thinking about her own life.

"Helen's not a Were. But I'm guessing you knew that."

"I did." Jacey nodded.

"And from the scent of the crowd, I could tell it's a human bar. I don't think I saw one Were in the building. Other than you and me," she said and picked up her chip.

"You're right. Weres in Colorado don't like to get too high up in the mountains. Too cold."

"But you're here." She picked up her burger and looked at him.

"And so are you." He narrowed his eyes. "Tell me, what's a pretty Mississippi werewolf doing in Colorado?" He took a bite of his burger and studied her.

She dropped the chip in her hand and went still. Fear rose up in her. She had done nothing wrong by leaving her cheating mate. In fact, if anyone was at fault, it was him. But in the werewolf community, leaving your mate was disgraceful.

She was disgraceful.

He took a long drink from one of the bottles of beer he'd placed in front of them. "Relax. I'm not hitting on you."

"I didn't think you were," she said quickly.

"Good. Because that's the last thing I need. Any complications." He stared hard.

"Perfect." She swallowed the lump in her throat. "How did you know I was from Mississippi?"

He barked out a laugh. "You serious? That accent is pure Mississippi if I ever heard one. Delta region probably." He shrugged and looked away. "I used to know some Weres in Mississippi."

She let out a little laugh. "It's easy to forget that not everyone in the world sounds like you when you've never been away from home."

He looked at her and arched his eyebrow. "What part of Mississippi are you from?"

"Yazoo City," she said and picked up her burger.

"Really?" A shadow of emotion flickered across his face. "I guess you heard about that witch escaping."

"Yes." She set her burger down. "It's all anyone talks about." She turned in her seat to study him. "There's been a lot of rumors as to what became of her. Some people say she's on a murderous rampage, while others say she's left the country and living on one of the Caribbean islands." She shook her head. "You know I grew up there, and no one would talk about her much. In fact, when I was a little girl, I would always ask what she did to get cursed into that cemetery."

"What did they say?" Barrett cocked his head, clearly interested in what she had to say.

"They said it was because of a man." She shrugged and took a bite of her burger.

"Always is." Barrett shook his head and leaned back in the chair. His burger was half-eaten, and she still had to make a dent in her dinner.

"So, you found the ad on the internet."

She nodded as she slowly chewed her food.

"I don't know that you would really like it here. I mean working as a cook in a run-down bar and grill isn't exactly every woman's dream."

"Maybe it's mine," she said quickly.

"The food is good. How long have you been cooking?"

"As long as I can remember." She rubbed her hands on her jeans.

"I suppose I should look at your resume and personal character references." He took another long pull on his beer and held her gaze.

Her face heated under his astute assessment, and she wanted to fidget. She felt like this was deeper than an interview. It felt like an interrogation.

"Actually, I don't have any references."

He opened his mouth, and she knew she had to talk fast.

"And before you ask, no, I can't give you any personal references."

"Are you in some kind of trouble? Because I don't need trouble in here." He stood. Even with her being perched on the stool, he still loomed over her.

"I'm not looking for trouble. I'm looking for a job. I need a job."

He put his hands on either side of her barstool and twisted it until they were facing each other head on.

"The last person I hired without references ending up stealing from me. The other two waitresses I hired, I ended up firing because they wanted more than a paycheck."

Her eyes got wide. "I'm not a thief. Never have been. And as for the other, I don't want anything from anyone. I prefer to keep to myself."

"So do I. But it doesn't answer the question of why are you so far from Mississippi?"

She should lie. She should tell him something, anything other than the truth. But something in those hard-green eyes compelled her to tell him the real reason why she was so far from home.

"I was betrayed by my mate. And I couldn't stay there. And now I have nowhere else to go. I am disgraced."

His expression didn't change nor did he blink. Unease settled in the bottom of her stomach.

There was no way he was going to hire her now. Being associated with her in any way would bring him shame.

"Where are you living now?" he asked.

"I … I'm not living anywhere. I was staying at a motel in Denver when I first arrived. I took a bus here." She frowned. Shit. She'd not thought ahead as to where she could get a room tonight. She'd been so worried about getting a job that finding a room had left her mind.

"So, what did you plan on doing tonight?" He cocked his head.

"I guess I'll get a room." She swallowed. Her stomach felt like lead.

"At this late hour?" He stepped back and picked up his plate.

She was stuck. On a mountain. With no job and nowhere to sleep for the night. She cut her eyes over at the booth and wondered if he would just let her stay here for the night. But she knew the answer would be no.

"Come on." he said before he stepped into the kitchen.

"Where are we going?" She swallowed back the emotion rising up in her throat. Coming to Colorado was a bad mistake. She didn't even have enough money for an airline ticket.

"You can sleep at Mena's."

"Who's Mena?"

"She rents out rooms in her home whenever she can. She usually has a room available."

"Like a bed and breakfast?" she asked.

"More like a bed and you make your own damn breakfast." He turned and looked at her.

"And tomorrow?" She forced herself to ask the question.

"Tomorrow you start work."

She felt a smile stretch across her face.

"But only as a trial." He waved his finger in her face. "Let's be clear up front. If there is anything illegal or something you're not telling me and I find out about it—because I will find out—then you are fired." He glared.

"Got it." She nodded furiously. For now, she had a place to sleep, food in her stomach, and a job. She'd worry about her other problems tomorrow.

CHAPTER 5

*B*arrett lay in bed staring up at the ceiling long after he'd taken Jacey over to Mena's. Thankfully, the older woman loved to stay up late watching old black and white movies so she'd still been up when he drove over there. Mena welcomed Jacey inside and gave her a room. He didn't stick around after that. He knew Mena well enough to know the older woman would take care of her.

He'd met Mena the first night Ryker had taken him to Silverton. They'd had spent their first night there since the electricity had not been turned on at The Mountain Top Bar and Grille.

Mena lived in a Victorian home with a house full of antique furniture. She wore those silly dresses like Granny did but instead of calling them muumuus, she called them caftans. She adorned herself every day with jewelry. From large gold earrings to ropes of gold around her neck to gold bangles around her wrists to the large cocktail gold rings. Mena looked like she put every piece of jewelry she owned on her body when she woke up.

He liked the fact that Mena didn't feel the need to entertain him or any of her other guests for that matter. You paid for your room, and she left you to fend on your own.

Helen had mentioned one night that Mena only rented out her rooms because she felt safer when people were in her big house and although she probably would never admit it, she got a little lonely. Her husband had died ten years ago, leaving her with a big house and a bigger inheritance.

In a way, she saw herself being charitable by letting people stay with her for so little money. It was a win-win for everyone.

He swiped his hand down his face and thought of Jacey. Just when he'd gotten used to his routine and his crew, he'd acquired another person in his staff by the name of Jacey Miller. With eyes made of caramel and silky, blonde hair, the female was not just a looker, she was gorgeous. She tried to hide it under baggy clothes and that oversized messenger bag that she carried like a body amour, but she wasn't fooling him.

He growled and threw off the sheet stretched across his body. He stood and walked over to the window that looked down on the small town.

The Mountain Top Bar and Grille had come with an apartment above the establishment. He had expected a small building in the back of the bar but soon found out it was a loft-style apartment above the grill itself.

It wasn't a bad place to live. It had a very industrious look to it with dark brick walls and exposed duct work along the ceilings. The picture windows were old and original, the kind that when you looked through them, everything appeared wavy. The hardwood floors were also circa the building and had never been replaced or refinished. He preferred the worn look. He liked the scratches and dark spots. It reminded him of his own life, his own past of mistakes and errors, yet somehow, he endured.

The large, open space had a kitchen with updated appliances. Apparently, the previous owner that had left the place to Ryker loved to cook. There was a single oversized leather sofa in the living room facing the windows. He didn't have a TV because it didn't come with the place. He had intended on buying a new one but since he started running the bar and grill, he didn't have a free minute to spare.

The only thing he did in his spare time was sleep. Even that seemed to elude him at times.

The loft hadn't come with a bed so Ryker had one delivered. It was a king-size that sat on a low platform. Barrett could tell from the quality that the mattress was the best money could buy.

He figured if he was going to be stuck in hell, he might as well be comfortable.

He lifted his hands above his head and rested them on the window frame. He looked down at the sleepy little town. Some might describe it as romantic or charming. He guessed it could be both of those things if that's what you were looking for.

He wasn't looking for either.

Jacey Miller was trouble. He could feel it in his bones. He wasn't sure she was telling him the truth. That her mate had cheated on her and then left her for someone else.

That was impossible in the werewolf world. Mates were for life. It was a stronger bond than marriage.

Besides why would a male cheat on her? She was gorgeous with a body that killed. She looked like a Victoria Secret model.

It didn't make sense to him.

If he still had his power of Pack Master of Arkansas, then he could get some answers really quick. All he would have to do is call up Jack Welbourn and ask the Pack Master of Mississippi who Jacey Miller was.

But he couldn't do that now. He could never go back to his life as Pack Master.

If he did then his sacrifice would be void, and Jaxon's death would be required.

In order to live again, it would require the death of one of his Guardians.

He couldn't do that. He wouldn't do that.

He squinted out into the night toward Mena's house. He could make out a light in an upstairs room. He glanced over at the time on the bedside clock.

He wondered if that was Jacey's room. Was she up? What was she doing?

"Jesus. I'm acting like the whole Arkansas Guardians group. Who gives a shit what some female is doing?" He rubbed his forehead and turned from the window.

He had other things to worry about. Like how his Pack was faring and when exactly Ryker was going to drag his sorry ass back through Colorado.

Until then, he would make sure to keep his distance from the pretty female and her fucked up problems.

CHAPTER 6

*D*amon stood from behind the large desk in the Pack Master of Arkansas's office. Barrett's office. His office now.

It had been months since Barrett's death. Yet it felt as fresh as if it had happened yesterday.

Since becoming Pack Master of Arkansas, Damon had to balance the burden of gaining the position and the guilt he felt for Barrett's death.

He'd been the one to kill Barrett.

Yet no one held him responsible. He didn't plunge the knife into Barrett's chest, but he had the urge to rip out Barrett's throat when Barrett had held a knife to Damon's mate, Ava's, throat.

He hadn't realized that it was all part of what Barrett had planned. Barrett had planned on sacrificing his life to save Jaxon all along. Barrett had paid the ultimate death price.

Damon swallowed the bile rising in the back of his throat. Would he be as great a Pack

Master as Barrett had been? Was he willing to die for the sake of the Pack?

His gaze drifted to the only picture sitting on his desk.

Ava. His mate and future mother of his child.

She was his life. He would do anything to protect her, to make sure she and their unborn child were okay.

Now with the responsibility of the entire state of Arkansas resting on his shoulders, he had to figure out a way to balance both his new role as Pack Master and the impending role of father.

Father. Just the sound of it always made him grin. The other day Lucien had asked him how Ava was doing with the pregnancy. A stupid grin had broken out across Damon's face without him even feeling it.

Lucien had given him hell for being pussy-whipped.

He didn't care. He loved Ava with every fiber of his being, and he knew he was lucky as hell to have found her.

His cell phone buzzed, and his smile slid off his face. His gut tensed as he picked it up to read the text.

"No body has been found. We've searched everywhere," Jaxon's text read.

Unease settled across Damon. He'd had his Guardians out in the Petit Jean State Park every day to search for Barrett's body. As the days turned into weeks and then stretched impossibly into months, they never found anything. No body, no clothing, no bones.

He hated to say what it meant. But it was time for him to stop torturing his Guardians.

"I'm calling off the search." Damon sent the reply and took a deep breath.

In other words, he was saying without actually saying what they all feared. Barrett's body had long been eaten by wild animals and the bones probably dispersed across the whole state of Arkansas.

In the days following Barrett's death, after he'd crawled out of the emotional hell he had imposed upon himself,

Damon had ordered Barrett's body recovered. He wanted to give his Pack Master a proper burial and ceremony. He'd put off the memorial service insisting that Barrett's body would indeed be recovered. It had been his first mistake as Pack Master. Ryker was the only Guardian with the balls to tell him to stop looking and move on.

He'd been so angry that he'd hit Ryker. Ryker had rubbed his jaw and then left without saying a word. Afterward, he'd felt like a total douche for raising his hand to one of his own.

Ryker had left without waiting for an apology. He would come and go as missions came up. Lately, there'd not been much to do. He'd had his Guardians positioned neared the Louisiana border to make sure to keep the peace. The night Barrett died, Edward Boudier had been taken into custody to await a Tribunal for attempting to murder the Guardians. Barrett had gathered enough evidence and along with one of Boudier's own Assassins, Lorcan, the amount of proof was overwhelming.

Mississippi's Pack Master, Jack Welbourn, had asked the Texas Pack Master to hold Boudier since Arkansas was grieving its own loss and the other Southern states were reeling from discovering that one of its own Pack Masters would murder them.

Jack Welbourn had been voted to take control of Louisiana until a new Pack Master could be put into that position. So not only was he running his own Mississippi Guardians, he was running the Louisiana Guardians as well.

Amazingly enough, Lorcan immediately threw his loyalty behind Jack Welbourn and made sure the rest of Louisiana did as well. It didn't take long before the other two Assassins, Brutus and Killian, were loyal to Welbourn as well. But Damon knew it wouldn't last. Jack had called him on several occasions letting him know they needed to find a replacement for Louisiana and fast. He said he had his own state of

Mississippi to run and wasn't interested in having Louisiana as a new territory as well. He said he had enough shit to deal with. Like getting his Witch of Yazoo back and sealed into the cemetery.

That fucking witch. Damon curled his fingers into fists and growled. He knew that witch had a part in Barrett's death. She'd been Boudier's witness in the Tribunal against Jaxon.

He'd gone over it a million times in his head. If Ella, the witch, hadn't been a witness, Jaxon wouldn't have been found guilty. Barrett would still be alive today.

"Bitch," he growled.

"The last dude that called me a bitch is still trying to find his liver." Zane's deep voice had Damon turning.

Damon met his gaze. Zane arched his brow.

"Not you," Damon grumbled.

"Just thinking out loud, are you?" Zane ambled over to the extra chair and eased into the

seat.

"Something like that.' Damon walked around the desk and sat opposite Zane. He met the Were's gaze.

"The body has not been found. I'm calling off the search." Damon waited to see Zane's reaction.

Zane's lips parted, and he eased back in the chair. His hands slowly rubbed his jean-clad thighs. "I see." He swallowed and nodded. "It's a good call." He nodded with more confidence. "It's time."

Damon looked away. "How do we hold a memorial without a body? All Pack Masters deserve a death of honor. Not to be eaten alive by wild animals." His throat thickened with anger.

"He did die with honor," Zane said slowly. "When Barrett sacrificed his life for his own, every Guardian in all the

Southern states realized what honor really is. They all realized what a real Pack Master is."

"Not all." He gritted his teeth.

"Don't discount Louisiana. At least not all of the state. All the civilians are relieved Boudier is gone. At least he's gone for now. And even a majority of the Louisiana Guardians speak highly of Barrett. Some have approached me about wanting to leave Louisiana and join the Guardians of Arkansas."

"No. I won't ever trust Louisiana or any of their Guardians."

"Even Lorcan?" Zane arched his brow

"Especially Lorcan."

"Don't let Lucien hear you say that." Zane gave him a hard stare.

"Just because Lucien and Lorcan are brothers doesn't mean they share the same moral compass." Damon said.

"Lorcan did help us with Boudier."

"So? Was it to save his own ass? You act like I'm supposed to trust someone like Lorcan. He's been indoctrinated with Boudier's bullshit for years. That doesn't just go away because the Pack Master is locked up."

"All I'm saying is that Boudier tried to have Lorcan killed, and he did come forward after Barrett's death and testified against Boudier."

"Where was he before Barrett died?" Damon stood up from his chair and slammed his hands down on the desk.

Zane said nothing nor did the Were stand. Damon didn't need to look at his Guardian to see the pity in his eyes.

"You think I'm blaming Lorcan for Barrett's death instead of putting blame where it should be." Himself.

"Shit, Damon." Zane stood up from his chair and growled. "Listen to me and listen to me well."

Damon snarled and jerked his head toward Zane. "I'm not liking your tone, Zane."

"I don't give a shit. You're going to hear what I have to say." Zane fisted his hands at his sides and held Damon's gaze.

"You had no part in Barrett's death." Zane gave him a droll look. "Look, I don't think Barrett went into that Tribunal with the expectation he was going to get Jaxon an innocent verdict. The last few hours leading up to that, he was on edge and didn't want to talk to anyone. Hell, even Jack Welbourn knew it. The fact that Ava showed up at the last minute was the only way he could properly make you the new Pack Master. If you hadn't attacked him, then we would be out a Pack Master until the Council could assign another. You actually did him a favor."

"A favor?" Damon cringed. "Taking his life was not a favor."

"Damon, you didn't know he had that silver knife aimed at his own heart when you

lunged for him. Do you know how hard it was going to be for him to stab his own self? Not to mention he was the one who jumped off the cliff, ensuring his own death. So yeah. I think you did him a favor. No wolf wants to take his own life. It goes against our every instinct." Zane threw one last scowl over his shoulder before slamming the door behind him.

Damon sucked in a deep breath and looked around the bare room. Since becoming Pack Master, he'd not changed a thing about Barrett's former office. It was as bare as ever, only containing a laptop on the sprawling desk and a couple of chairs. The wall bore the shield with the Arkansas State flag and the words, "LEADER AND COMMANDER BORN TO UPHOLD THE LUPINE LAW."

He hated to admit that what Zane said held true. He

needed to face the fact that Barrett was gone, and it was part of his own plan to sacrifice himself for Jaxon.

He needed to stop just *existing* as Pack Master and start *being* Pack Master.

He picked up his phone. He punched in a few numbers, and Jayden immediately answered.

"Hey, boss, what's up?" Jayden, his best friend since childhood, always had a way of lightening the mood.

"I'm officially calling off the search for … Barrett's body." He straightened. "I need you to inform all the Guardians. I'm doing a memorial service in a few days, so I'll need someone to help with the logistics." He had no idea what a service like that would include.

"I'll let the Guardians know right away," Jayden's voice turned serious. It was a tone Damon rarely heard on the Were.

"Why don't we get Braxton and Kate involved. I heard Braxton said Kate has done memorial services at her B&B once or twice. The family wanted an intimate environment rather than a funeral home, and I think the person was cremated." Jayden offered.

"Yeah, I think Barrett would like to be remembered some place like that, instead of a funeral home. I don't even remember the last time a Pack Master died. I wouldn't know where they held the funeral." Grief struck his gut, and he rubbed his hand across his stomach.

"Me either, man." Jayden offered. "I'll get the Guardians together and filled in. Don't worry about the details. I'm sure Granny and the females will want to be part of this. Once I get everything together, I'll let you know, okay?"

"Thanks, Jayden." Damon cut the call and laid the phone back on his desk.

It was real now. The months of refusing to face the truth and the reality were officially over.

Barrett was dead, and Damon was now in charge over the state of Arkansas.

Despite the unease spreading across his chest, Damon knew he had to take charge and handle his shit.

After all, that's what Barrett would want.

CHAPTER 7

*J*acey clutched her pillow to her chest and snuggled down deep into the cloud-like covers. She didn't want to open her eyes. If she opened her eyes, she knew what she would find.

She would find herself in a strange and unfamiliar place where she had very little money, zero friends, and no future.

She was utterly and devastatingly alone in a large, scary world.

Tears burned the backs of her eyes, and she squeezed them tight, trying to hold them in place. She didn't want to cry. She hated crying. She'd cried enough when Jeremy had kicked her out and humiliated her in front of Wendy, his mistress. She'd cried enough when she'd confided to her friends about her situation. She'd cried enough when she had told her parents what had happened.

She should be drained of tears.

She rolled over on her back and stared up at the stark white ceiling.

When she'd arrived late last night to Mena's, she had been surprised the older woman was still up. Barrett had warned her that the old woman liked to watch old black and white movies long into the early morning while sipping on her favorite cocktail of gin and tonic.

Mena had quickly welcomed her inside and led her upstairs to her bedroom.

The house was an old Victorian and despite the age was in great shape.

Her bedroom was adorned in dark-red tones. The antique rice bed was decorated in a lush candy-apple-red comforter with matching shams. The cream-colored monogramed pillowcases were provided a nice contrast to the darker colors. The walls were covered in red, textured wallpaper reminiscent of the age of the house. The furniture in the room was sparse, yet functional. The bed sat against the wall with a nightstand on both sides. The room had two long floor-to-ceiling windows with thick, red curtains. An Edwardian-style chair and matching footstool sat near a window on the other side of the room with a standing lamp, providing the perfect place to look down on the tiny town during a cold night. The room had its own fireplace which was a nice surprise.

She's always dreamed of having a fireplace in the bedroom.

The room was cold and drafty. She'd have to ask Mena how to operate the fireplace if she were going to be spending another night.

"I don't even know how much she charges." She buried her nose into the comforter and wiped her eyes. She'd been so tired when she'd arrived last night, she hadn't even thought to ask Mena how much it was going to cost her to stay.

She wasn't off to a very good start at this new life she was supposed to be cultivating.

She turned her head and stared out the window. She

could barely make out The Mountain Top Bar and Grille from where she lay. Though she'd done her best with her cooking last night, she wasn't sure if Barrett really liked it or he was just hungry and would eat anything.

Barrett was a mystery to her. She still didn't even know his last name. He didn't seem to like cooking at all and according to Helen he couldn't make a decent grilled cheese. And when he was behind the bar making drinks, he didn't look like he enjoyed that either.

So why would he buy a bar if he hated it so much?

She snorted. "Maybe he is as desperate as me. Maybe he doesn't have a choice in what he wanted to do either."

Behind the large build and gruff expression, Barrett was very good-looking. More than just good-looking, he was drop-dead gorgeous. But in a lethal kind of way. Long, dark-blonde hair and deep-green eyes set in a face so handsome it hurt just looking at him. His dark jeans and T-shirt that was stretched within an inch of its life made him look like a bouncer. Not a bar owner.

Not that it mattered. She was here to start over. Maybe she could make it work and save her money until she figured out what she really wanted to be. Who knew? Maybe in the future, she could go to community college, get some kind of degree. She knew she could never again rely on a male. No matter how much she thought she loved him.

She rolled over and glanced at the time on the clock. Almost eight o'clock. She wanted to roll back over and go to sleep, but she couldn't. She had to get out of bed and face her new reality.

Barrett was going to be waiting on her at the bar. He'd told her last night to come back, and they would talk.

At least it was a step in the right direction.

She flung off the covers and padded over to the door. She grabbed the robe hanging on a hook and wrapped it around her body. She wasn't sure how many guests Mena had staying with her, but she wasn't taking any chances running down the hall to the bathroom half-naked.

She padded to the bathroom and closed the door behind her and flipped the lock. She noticed a small electric space heater on the floor and plugged it in. The machine purred to life and begin filling the small space with warm air.

Her gaze landed on a clawfoot tub. She smiled.

She looked under the sink and found a washcloth and a towel. Kneeling beside the tub, she turned on the water and adjusted the temperature until it was perfect. She added some powdered bubble bath she'd found beside the towels.

She peeled off last night's clothes that she'd slept in. She's been so tired when she got to the room, all she managed to do was take her jeans off and climb into bed.

She caught a glimpse of her naked reflection in the full-length mirror behind the door and froze.

Her dark-blonde hair draped across her shoulders and fell in soft waves down her slender back. She'd always been slender but since her world had been turned upside down, she'd lost weight, and it showed in the way her ribs pressed against her flesh and the concave curve of her stomach. Her hipbones jutted forward, and her legs were thin. She looked sick.

Her gaze fluttered up toward her face. Slight dark shadows hung below her brown eyes, eyes that people always said were more golden than brown. Her full lips were even more accentuated against her hollow cheeks and light complexion. She usually looked tan, golden even in the winter but since leaving Mississippi for Colorado, she'd barely spent any time out in the sun and, as a result, had grown pale.

She no longer recognized herself.

She forced her gaze away and opened the cabinet under

the sink. After a few seconds of searching for and failing to find a ponytail holder, she finally pulled out some hairpins. She twisted her hair up in a loose bun and grabbed a towel.

Turning off the water in the elegant tub, she stepped inside and disappeared into the bubbles.

Jacey stayed in the tub until the water turned cold and her fingertips pruned. She quickly dressed in some dark jeans and a cream-colored long-sleeved shirt. She added some color to her pale face by adding some brown eyeshadow to her lids and added some black mascara to her lashes. She didn't normally wear blush since she always had a healthy glow, so she never bought any. Instead she pinched her cheeks to get the desired results. She swiped some pink gloss over her lips to finish the look. She took her time brushing her hair until it glistened.

She stepped back and studied the results in the full-length mirror.

Satisfied with what she saw, she gathered her dirty clothes and robe and walked back to her room. Before she reached her room, a door swung open and someone came running out and smacked right into her.

She stumbled and dropped her clothes and makeup bag.

"Oh, gosh. I'm terribly sorry." A young man in his late twenties with blonde hair and light-blue eyes gave her a horrified look before dropping to his knees to pick up her clothes.

"It's fine," she bent down and quickly stuck her makeup back into the bag. She gave him a shaky laugh. "I should have been watching where I was going."

"It's totally my fault." He gave her a warm smile. She smiled back.

He handed her the rest of her things, and they both stood.

"I didn't know Mena had another guest staying here," he said.

"I just got in late last night." She shrugged and held out her hand. "I'm Jacey."

He took her hand and graced her with another smile. "I'm Charles."

She inhaled slightly. He was also human.

"Nice to meet you, Charles." She cradled her clothes to her chest.

"You too. If I had known Mena was going to have a guest as beautiful as you, then I would have planned to stay longer." He gave her a devilish grin.

Why did humans think that's how women wanted to be talked to?

"Well, it's a good fucking thing you're leaving." A deep, male voice growled behind her. Her stomach dropped. She knew immediately who the guttural voice belonged to.

She glanced at Charles. His smiled dropped from his face, and he paled. His gaze was looking at something very tall over her shoulder.

She turned.

"Jacey, are you ready to go?" Barrett's deep-green eyes narrowed on her and for a second she felt an enormous amount of guilt.

"Ah, yes, let me just put my clothes up and grab my bag." She hurried to her room and went inside. She didn't bother organizing her things but instead dumped them in a pile on the other side of the bed. Frantically, she looked around for her messenger bag and found it near the closet. Snatching it up and grabbing the room key off the nightstand, she made her way back into the hallway.

She froze.

Barrett was alone, his large frame dwarfing the hallway. He narrowed his gaze on her.

"Where's Charles?"

"Gone," he said. "Are you ready?"

"Yes. But I need to find Mena and pay her for last night." She opened her bag and dug around for the quickly dwindling envelope of money.

"No need. You pay at the end of the month." He turned and walked down the hallway.

She quickened her footsteps to keep up with his long stride.

"But I don't know how long I'll be here." She hooked her bag across her body and stuck her room key in the outside pocket.

"Depends on if you want the job or not."

"Of course, I want the job," she said and looked at his profile, trying to judge his expression. Barrett was very hard to read.

"Then you'll be here as long as you want." He descended the staircase two steps at a time.

She held onto the dark wood banister and followed behind him.

"So, I have a job? As a cook?" Her heart hammered in her chest. "But we never discussed pay or hours or anything."

He stopped in the middle of the stairs and turned, giving her all of his attention.

She felt her face heat, and she wasn't sure why she was so embarrassed. These were valid questions, and he should have brought them up before offering her the job. She had no idea what the going salary was for a cook.

She clasped her bag to her chest and hoped he wasn't about to screw her over.

"The bar is open seven days a week, but I may change that and close on Sundays."

"That makes sense." She nodded.

"I pay twenty dollars an hour. And you can have one day off a week. Not including Sunday so technically you get two

49

days off. You can rotate it if you want, but I'll prefer if you didn't take off Thursday, Friday or Saturday."

"They're your busiest days. Of course, I wouldn't take those days off." She looked up at him. "I have to say twenty dollars an hour is more than I was expecting."

He cocked his head and stared. "I would have paid thirty. You're not a very good negotiator. I bet people take advantage of you all the time."

She lifted her chin. "That's going to change."

"It should if you expect to survive in this world." He turned and continued down the

stairs.

She followed. "What are you doing here anyway?"

"You said you didn't have a vehicle. I'm here to drive you over to Durango to pick up some things you'll need. You only showed up with that messenger bag, so I'm guessing you'll need some clothes. Clothes more suitable for this weather." He opened the front door and waited for her to go through first.

For someone so gruff, he certainly had polite manners.

She shook her head. "I have enough clothes for now. I'll get some winter clothes once I get my first paycheck."

"You haven't looked at the forecast tonight." A slow smirk stretched across his face.

"No, I haven't." The minute she stepped outside, the cold wind shot through her thin, long-sleeved shirt. She flinched and wrapped her arms around her body.

He shrugged off his leather jacket and shoved it at her. "Here, put this on."

"No, it's okay …"

"That wasn't an offer." He glared. She reluctantly took it. "I don't need you getting sick before you had a chance to start work."

Of course. He wasn't looking out for her. He was looking out for his own self-interests.

She stuck her arms into the large jacket and tried to resist the urge to bury her nose in the collar and inhale his scent. He smelled better than any male she'd ever met. Even her mate. Ex-mate she reminded herself.

"I'm not going to have any problems with your mate, am I?" He tossed her a glance over his shoulder as he made his way to his vehicle. It was an older model Jeep with bigger tires than she'd ever seen, even in Mississippi, and the color had once been green but had patinated from the snow and cold weather in the mountains. He opened the passenger door.

She grabbed the handle and stepped on the running board. Her foot slipped. Barrett's large hands clamped down on her waist to keep her from falling.

"You okay?" he whispered hoarsely and set her easily in the seat.

Her heart beat like hummingbird wings against her ribs, and her body warmed considerably. She was no longer cold but uncomfortably hot. She swallowed, forcing herself to look straight ahead.

"Yes." She managed to squeak out the word and busied her fingers on finding and hooking the seatbelt securely.

The door slammed. She watched him across the hood of the Jeep as he walked over to the driver's seat. His expression was hard, mixed with a different emotion she couldn't place.

She pressed her cold hands to her cheeks to get her body under control. What was wrong with her anyway? Maybe she was still exhausted from everything that had happened. Maybe she was missing Jeremy and being near a male, any male was making her body crave.

She didn't know, but she did know she was going to have

to get it together if she wanted to keep her job. She didn't need to give him a reason to fire her right off the bat.

He opened the door and slid inside. His scent from his coat mingled with the scent from his body. She heated even more.

"Thank you for the coat," she said.

"You're welcome." He looked straight ahead and turned the key in the engine. The Jeep purred to life, and he threw it into drive.

He pulled onto to the main street and headed out of town and down the mountain.

"How long have you lived here?" She hoped to lessen the enormous amount of tension in the cab of the truck.

"Not long."

"If you don't mind me asking, I'm going to assume you must have inherited the bar and grill."

He shot her a look. "Why do you think that?"

She clasped her fingers in her lap and looked straight ahead. "Well, running a bar doesn't

suit you. In fact, you seem to resent it a little. You don't seem to enjoy it at all."

He cut his eyes over at her. "And what exactly do you see me doing as an occupation?"

"I don't know. Something where you are over people, telling them what to do. Like a CEO or something." She looked at him.

A slow smile crept across his face. Then he barked out a laugh.

The sound made her smile and relax.

"Telling people what to do? I used to do that. But that was in another lifetime." His grin began to fade, and then the harsh expression was back in place.

Her chest tightened. "It's not too late to do something else. I mean, if you're not happy running the bar, I'm sure you could sell it and start over." She wasn't sure her words were going to carry any weight, but for some odd reason she wanted to reassure him, give him some hope. She might not have any, but he certainly could have a better future.

He turned and looked at her, his gaze intense and truthful. "That's the thing about time. Sometimes it is too late. Some things you can't get a do-over."

CHAPTER 8

*B*arrett drove in uncomfortable silence down the mountain to the city of Durango. He needed the quiet to figure some things out in his head. He wrestled with getting his irritation under control since he found Jacey in the hallway with that male who had been openly flirting with her. He couldn't explain why it had bothered him so bad.

Maybe it was because Jacey was new to town and clearly not looking for a relationship. Maybe it was because he was going to have to spend the day getting her some clothes versus tending to the bar. Maybe it was because he hated to admit that she was a really great cook and exactly what the grill needed to start making a decent income.

He scrubbed his hand down his face and studied the road ahead of him. Jacey hit the nail on the head when she said he looked like he'd be better off bossing people around. He wanted to tell her that's exactly what he used to do, boss his Guardians around.

Being a Pack Master was part of his past, and he knew there was no going back to that now. If someone found out his true identity, then it would put the Arkansas Guardians in trouble. He didn't go through all that just to put Jaxon's life in jeopardy again.

He had a new life and was just going to have to get used to it.

"So, what did you do in Mississippi?" He looked over at Jacey.

"Housewife." She kept her gaze trained out the window.

"Until you were unmated." He studied her.

"My mate was never really my mate." She sighed and looked at him. "He claimed that he never loved me and that I wasn't his true mate. So, he kicked me out and replaced me with Wendy, another female."

"He sounds like a fucking idiot," Barrett growled. Jacey was gorgeous, and she smelled even better. Any male would fight to keep her.

She blinked and then chuckled. "Yeah. Maybe he is."

"No maybe to it. He most definitely is an idiot," Barrett said. "What if he changes his mind and comes looking for you?"

"Oh, believe me, he won't. Besides, if I ever saw him again, I wouldn't give him the time of day." She relaxed back in the seat and crossed her arms. "I met and mated Jeremy right out of high school. He wanted to go to trade school to be an electrician. He didn't want me working outside the house. He said he wanted me to keep up the house and have dinner on the table when he got home. So that's what I did."

"If you could go back and do it all over again, what would you do?"

She shook her head. "I'd go to nursing school. I used to take care of my grandmother when I was in high school. When she got sick, I would help her." She shrugged. "Too late now."

"From the woman who tells me it's not too late." He cut her a look.

She met his gaze and grinned. "I guess you got me there. If I could go back and do it over again, I would make sure and have my own job and make my own money." She shook her head. "I never thought I would be left without a dime."

"So how does that work legally? I mean once you're mated, you're supposed to be mated for life. He could come back and say he made a mistake and expect you to come home."

"No, he went before Jack Welbourn and declared his intent."

Barrett slowed the Jeep as they entered the city limits. Bringing up Jack's name sent nostalgia washing over him. "I've only heard of one case of this happening. It requires blood to break a mate bond. And it can only be broken if one of the mates was mistakenly bonded to another," he said.

"You're right. Jeremy stated he was mistakenly bonded with me. He says I bewitched him somehow." She shrugged. "I don't know. Anyway, Jack Welbourn granted the breaking of the mating bond on the condition that Jeremy spilled his blood. He cut his hand, and it was granted."

"So, you can't ever go back to him?" Barrett cut his eyes at her.

"No. I can't. And I won't." She looked out the window. "Seeing someone's real character makes you open your eyes. Jeremy lied to me so many times about loving me and then sleeping with someone else. I don't think he'll ever be happy. In a way, I guess I'm glad I found out now instead of spending the rest of my life with him."

"You're still young. Plenty of time to find your mate."

"I don't ever plan on mating again. I can live my life the way I want to. And not on anyone else's terms. And certainly not mated to a liar."

He flinched under her words. If she found out his real

identity, would she think him a liar, no better than her ex? Would she condemn him as fast as she condemned Jeremy?

He pulled into a parking space in front of a store that specialized in winter clothing.

It didn't matter. Not now. Jacey would never find out who he really was. He didn't plan on getting close enough to give her a chance.

* * *

JACEY STOOD at the counter with all the clothes that Barrett had forced her to try on in her arms.

"Did they fit?" He looked at her.

"Yes. But it doesn't matter. I don't have the money to pay for them." She eyed the coat that would certainly keep her warm from Colorado's weather, but she couldn't afford it. Not now anyhow.

"I'm buying it."

"Which one?" She frowned.

"All of it." He gathered up her clothes and laid them down on the counter. The guy at the register barely gave him a look before scanning all the merchandise.

"Wait. I can't let you do that," she said.

"Yes, you can." He ignored her and handed the cashier a wad of cash.

The cashier gave him his change and bags of clothing. Barrett grabbed the two large bags and headed for the door.

She grabbed his arm, and he turned.

"Barrett, I appreciate this, but I don't feel right about letting you buy these for me."

"Don't worry. You'll pay me back." He grinned and opened the door. He nodded for her to exit first.

Outside, she turned and looked up at him. It amazed her

how big and tall he really was. Even humans seemed to give him wide berth when he was walking down the street.

"Is this an advance on my paycheck?"

"No. This is an advance on something else I need you to do for me." He grinned.

She shivered, not liking where this conversation was headed.

He set the bags down on the sidewalk and dug out her new coat. He pulled out a knife and cut the tags off and held it out for her. "Put this on."

She obeyed and slid into the warm material. She nearly sighed as the pink, dimpled fabric molded to her body.

"Better?" He arched his eyebrow.

"Much," she admitted. She glanced up at the sky that was quickly darkening with gray clouds.

"It will snow tonight," he stated.

"How do you know that?" she asked.

"I can smell it." He looked at her.

Wolves had an incredible sense of smell. But even she hadn't picked up on that. She inhaled and still didn't smell what he was smelling.

"Come on. We've got some stuff to do before the bar and grill opens tonight." He picked up the rest of the bags and led the way back to the Jeep.

He stuck the rest of their purchases in the back seat and then opened the passenger door. She took the cue and slid inside. She fastened her seatbelt and looked at him as he got into the Jeep.

He started the engine and put the vehicle in drive.

"Where are we going?"

"You'll see."

CHAPTER 9

"*D*amon, everyone is here." Kate Devereaux stepped into the kitchen of the Bella Luna and clasped her hands together in front of her and watched him with sad eyes. She, like the other females, was dressed in black. Unlike the other females, she wore a pantsuit instead of a dress.

Damon looked up at Braxton's mate and nodded. "Thank you, Kate. And thank you for having the memorial here at your B&B."

"Of course. It's the least I could do." She smiled and walked over to him. "You know, when I first met Barrett, I have to admit I was pretty scared of him," She gave him a thoughtful look. "Actually, when I met you, I was pretty scared too. All you Guardians are very intimidating." She shrugged.

"Part of the job I suppose," Damon snorted.

Her eyes softened, and she studied the floor. "I was surprised to hear so many Weres tell me that my mating with Braxton was practically unheard of. Humans and Weres never mate. But Barrett allowed it anyway. He found a way for me to be with the only male I will ever love. I don't know that I ever properly thanked him enough." Her eyes misted over.

"You have wolf blood, even if you won't ever shift. Besides, Barrett did a lot of things that were not exactly by the book. But he always managed to do the right thing. That takes more courage than following the rules." Damon swallowed the emotion building in his throat.

"You should say that during the memorial, today." Kate walked over and squeezed his arm in an unspoken gesture of support and then headed back out into the living room.

He turned and caught a glance of his reflection in the microwave. He stopped.

He didn't normally wear a suit. He was a jeans and T-shirt kind of wolf. But not today. There had been some debate as to what the Guardians should wear. Some thought it was fitting for them all to wear their regular casual attire of jeans and T-shirts. Others wanted to show up in their wolf form. In the end, Damon went out of his comfort zone and ordered everyone to wear a suit. He wanted to honor his fallen Pack Master in every respectable way. And if that meant everyone was wearing a suit, then so fucking be it.

"Damon." Ava's voice had him turning around. His gaze roamed over her, and he stifled the urge to take her in his arms.

She wore a black dress with long sleeves and a high neckline. A single strand of pearls hung around her delicate neck, and pearl studs decorated her ears. The dress hung to every curve of her body including the growing belly bump of their unborn child.

"Ava, I was just coming out." Damon gave her a grin.

"Well, we've had some more visitors, and I don't think they're all going to fit in the Bella Luna." Ava gave him a look of uncertainty.

He frowned. "More Guardians? How many more?" He'd accepted Jack Welbourn's help of assigning some Mississippi Guardians around Arkansas for this one day of Barrett's memorial. He wanted the state safe and his men time to properly mourn their leader.

"Well, there's Alabama, Kentucky, Mississippi, and even some Louisiana Guardians. They are lining up down the road. We told them there wasn't enough space for all of them. They said they would wait their turn to offer their condolences and show their respect."

"Damn." He forked his hand through his hair and studied the ground. Barrett had a bigger impact on everyone than he ever realized.

Ava smiled and walked over to him. She raised her hand and patted down his hair where he'd obviously messed it up.

"Sorry," he mumbled and pulled her into his chest. She molded against him, filling in the void in his chest.

"I love you," she whispered against his chest.

"I love you too." He rested his hand on her rounding stomach. He felt a slight movement under his fingertips

"He's getting aggressive," he said as he stroked her back with his free hand.

"I think it's a she, not he." She looked up at him with a sparkle in her eyes.

"Shit, Ava. Don't say that." His skin prickled a little. Just the thought of having a daughter set his gut turning. He'd never get a good night's sleep trying to keep her safe in this world. A son, on the other hand, would know how to handle himself. Damon would make sure of that.

"It's time." He let go of her and nodded.

"You'll do wonderful. The state of Arkansas is very lucky to have you as Pack Master." Ava pressed a quick kiss to his cheek and made her way into the living room with the others.

Damon waited a few seconds, gathered his thoughts, then walked into the living room. His jaw nearly hit the floor when he saw the crowd gathered. His Guardians were sitting in chairs lined up across the room. The furniture had been removed to make more room. More Guardians were lined up along the wall and out the front door.

He glanced out the large window and saw a sea of Guardians from all over the Southern states. They were all dressed in suits. He bit back a ghost of a smile. Seeing a crowd of badass werewolf bikers dressed in suits and riding Harleys must have been quite the sight.

Barrett would have laughed his ass off.

Braxton, Jayden, Zane, and Lucien sat in the front rows along with their mates, Kate, Haley, Skyler and Catty. The rest of the unmated Arkansas Guardians sat in the rows behind them. Arkansas was a big state and although he hadn't met each and every Were, he had seen them around the Guardian Compound. There had to be at least fifty Weres crowded into the living room. Hundreds more out the door.

He rested his hands on the wooden podium that Kate had set up in the front of the room. She'd also baked and cooked for two days straight. But now with the arrival of so many other Guardians, there was no way it was going to be enough to feed them all.

Braxton stood and walked over to him. He leaned in.

"Jack Welbourn and the other Pack Masters have sent more food. It's in a truck parked around back. Don't worry. We'll have enough to feed everyone. The women are going to set everything up outside so the Guardians can eat buffet style."

"Good." He nodded. He would have to remember to send all the Pack Masters a thank you note along with a bottle of bourbon.

Braxton took his seat beside Kate and faced Damon.

Damon didn't make any notes for this. But he had stayed up all night thinking what he would say. A sacred hush fell across the room.

"Today, we gather for the memorial service for our fallen Pack Master Barrett Middleton. He was without question the finest Alpha I had ever met. He lived his life and ran his Pack with dignity, honor, and respect. He never failed to protect his state from attacks both foreign and domestic. And he put the well-being of his Guardians above his own." His gaze landed on Jaxon who looked at the floor. His mate, Ginny, held his arm and rested her head on his shoulder. She was pregnant and as far along as his Ava.

Barrett had saved Jaxon's life so Jaxon could father and take care of Ginny's child. The most selfless act Damon had ever seen.

"I'm sure if Barrett could see us today, he would glare at each one of his Guardians and scowl. Then he would ask why we were all dressed like a bunch of pussies," he snorted.

The crowd laughed and nodded their heads in agreement.

"He didn't show his emotions and kept his private life to himself. To some he was an enigma. To others standoffish. But when I think back to my relationship with Barrett, I realize how much he gave to his men and never asked for anything in return. Yet we all gave him back the most important thing a man can want. Respect."

All the Weres nodded their heads, and a low murmur of understanding swept across the room.

"He helped more than the state of Arkansas, he also helped his Guardians. To me that is the mark of not only a worthy Pack Master, it is a sign of a loyal brother." He felt the emotion bubble up around his throat. He didn't say as much as he thought he would, but it felt like he'd said enough. He looked across the room and cleared his throat.

"As the new Pack Master of Arkansas, my first official act

that I will present to the Council, is erecting a statue of Barrett Middleton at our Guardian Compound in Little Rock. His image and his legacy will forever be in the hearts and the minds of all who knew him."

Everyone in the room nodded and then a round of applause broke out. The Weres outside waiting to gain entrance pressed their faces against the window, trying to see what was going on.

Everyone stood from their seats and made their way to Damon.

"You did good, man." Jayden stuck out his hand and shook Damon's.

Granny whacked Jayden on the back of the head. "Address him proper, Jayden. He's your Pack Master now." The old lady shot him a glare.

"Geez, Granny." Jayden rubbed the back of his head and then turned back to Damon. "Sorry. I mean Pack Master."

"I'm pretty sure you can still call me Damon, you asswipe." He felt a smile tug on the corners of his lips.

Jayden opened his mouth to respond and then slammed it shut. He scowled. "I can't even talk back to him anymore," he cut his eyes at Braxton.

Braxton grinned. "Oh, come on now. You've got a lot of other Guardians who will give you hell."

"Yeah, and I'll be the first to volunteer." Zane elbowed his way to the front.

"I bet you will." Jayden grunted.

"You did Barrett proud, Damon." Zane stuck out his hand, and Damon accepted it.

"Thanks." He glanced away, uneasy with the looks of approval his Guardians were all shooting him.

"Damon," Ava walked over and stood at his side. "I need these guys to help me move the food outside. We're setting everything up on the picnic tables so once the Guardians come through and pay their respects, they can grab some food outside."

"Thanks, Ava." He wrapped his arm around her and pulled her into his side.

"Yes, you boys come along." Granny led the way toward the kitchen.

Ava turned to go, but he tightened his hold. "Not you, Ava."

"But I need to help."

"Let the other females do it. Besides, you're my mate, and I need you by my side today." Damon said.

Her eyes shimmered, and she smiled up at him. He didn't think it was possible, but he loved her more with each passing day.

"Okay." She took a deep breath and turned to face the crowd of Guardians that were making their way to them.

One by one, all of the Arkansas Guardians made their way to the front to say a few words to him. They all shook his hand and pledged their loyalty to him as the new Pack Master. Then they nodded respectfully at Ava. He knew without a doubt that the Arkansas Pack would do whatever he said and do it without hesitation. It was a hell of a lot of pressure and responsibility. He wasn't sure he could handle it or if he was even worthy.

"Damon." Lucien walked over to Damon with Zane, Braxton, Jayden, and Jaxon behind him.

"Since Ava has already greeted our Pack, why don't you let her go eat something. Besides," Lucien looked over his shoulder at his brothers, "we would like to stand with you to receive the other states' Guardians."

Damon's heart swelled with pride. He had a good Pack. An amazing state full of loyal and trustworthy Weres.

"I would be proud if you stood with me." Damon let his gaze land on each of them.

Ava reached up on tiptoes and brushed her lips against his cheek. "I love you." She quietly made her way to the kitchen.

Jayden stood to his left with Braxton on the other side of him. Zane, Jaxon, and Lucien stood on his right. Flanked by his men, Damon was ready to meet with the rest of the Southern Guardians.

The Pack Master of Kentucky, John Morgan, walked up first and stuck out his hand. "Damon, I'm really sorry about Barrett. He was always a fair leader."

"Thank you. He was." Damon lifted his chin. John didn't stay long and after he'd greeted the rest of the Damon's Guardians, the rest of the Kentucky Pack paid their respects as well.

"Damon," Jack Welbourn, Pack Master of Mississippi, shook his hand and looked at all the Guardians. "I guess the thing I'm going to miss most about Barrett is how he always called me out on my shit." The older man ran his hand through his hair and a wistful smile settled on his face. "I don't think I'd ever met someone who could scare someone with just one look."

"He was quite intimidating. He certainly didn't stand for nonsense."

"Except when it came to Granny," Jayden admitted.

Jack barked out a laugh. "Son, that's the only Were I'd ever met that could stand up to Barrett and make him uncomfortable. That lady has gumption." He rubbed his chin. "Tell me Jayden, is she seeing anyone?"

"No, and that's how it's going to stay." Jayden gave him a horrified look.

"Too bad," Jack said and went through the line.

All the Guardians turned to look at Jayden.

He held up his hand. "Don't fucking say it. Granny is not

going to be going out on any more dates. Let alone a date with Jack Welbourn."

Damon bit back a grin and the other Guardians broke out into laugher. It was a good sound, a sound he hadn't heard from any of them since Barrett died.

In that moment, he knew that the Arkansas Pack was going to be okay. He knew they all were going to be okay.

CHAPTER 10

*B*arrett pulled up at The Mountain Top Bar and Grille and killed the engine. If he had to spend another minute in the cab of his Jeep with Jacey's scent, he was going to lose it.

Shit, he needed to get laid.

That's why he had stayed up at night thinking about her and the color of her eyes and the smell of her hair. That's why when he had drifted off to sleep, he dreamed of taking her mouth with his and tasting every inch of her pretty, pink tongue until he burned the smell and taste of her into his brain.

He growled.

"What's wrong?" Jacey asked.

Fuck. He grabbed the door handle and jerked the door open. The crisp, cold, Colorado air stung his chest. He closed his eyes and inhaled deep and rubbed his chest. It was exactly what he needed.

"Is everything okay? You're not having a heart attack, are you?" Jacey scrambled around the Jeep and stood in front of him, those caramel eyes narrowed.

"What? No. How old do you think I am?" He knew she was younger than him, but surely, he didn't look *that* old.

"How old are you, Jacey?" He narrowed his eyes. He didn't tolerate a liar. Even a beautiful one.

She lifted her chin and held his gaze. "I'm twenty-four. How old are you?" She crossed her arms over her chest defiantly.

Shit, he was eight years older than her. Not that age mattered when it came to wolves. But still. She was too young for him.

"I'm thirty-two." He shook his head. "Come on. Let's get inside before you freeze to death." He took the steps up to the bar two at a time.

The bar and grill was a hell of a lot older than him, at least. The kitchen had been updated a few years ago but other than that, it was still in its original condition. It had three rows of long windows on either side of the entrance and a covered deck. It had been built up off the ground about five feet. Because of the amount of snow Colorado got every year, the original owner didn't want a bar that wasn't elevated. No use having a bar in the winter if people couldn't get in.

The hardwood floors were original and had seen a lot of life along with bar fights and few deaths, according to the locals.

The place was dark and lively when it was full. When closed, it felt very gloomy and oppressive.

He didn't tell Helen, but it was one of the reasons he never closed the bar for even a day.

When Ryker had driven him to Colorado, he had only stayed one day before heading back to Arkansas. He said he didn't want to give Damon any reason to start snooping around and trying to find out where he'd been.

Ryker knew if Damon found out Barrett was alive, then

word would spread and his Arkansas Guardians wouldn't be safe.

Ryker had made sure to deliver a new mattress so Barrett wouldn't have to sleep on the couch that came with the apartment. He even made sure the refrigerator was stocked with food and hired a few employees for the bar. The majority had not worked out. Except for Helen.

Helen had needed the extra income when her grandson had come to live with her. And she was a people person. She was made for waitressing.

He liked her despite the fact she was human.

He unlocked the front door to the bar and stepped aside to allow her entry. As she passed by, he caught her sweet feminine scent mixed with the scent of cold weather coming later tonight.

He shook his head and stepped inside. He needed to stop acting like a pussy. Maybe he was exhausted or maybe it was because he hadn't shifted since his death.

He had planned on shifting into wolf form when he got to Colorado. But there had been so much to do. It wasn't like he knew the territory too well and since he'd been here, he had only seen a handful of Weres that had passed through on their way to somewhere else. No Weres ever stayed long in the cold country.

He had counted it as a blessing. The less he was around other Weres, the less likely the chance someone would discover who and what he was.

With Jacey, he was going to have to be even more careful. And keep his distance as much as possible.

"You said you cooked a lot. Did you serve the same thing, or did you mix it up?" He turned and leaned against the counter of the bar and studied her. She looked pretty in her new coat and hiking boots. She needed a hat to cover her silky hair and to keep her ears warm. They were already turning red from the cold. Even though she was a Were, she was still going to have a hard time keeping warm in weather like this.

"I usually planned my menu for seven days and then went shopping once a week. Mainly on Sundays. Jeremy didn't like leftovers, not that we ever had anything left over after he was done, but he liked variety. I don't think I cooked the same meal twice in a month's time." She tilted her head. "Why do you ask?"

"If you can plan out a menu for the whole month, I'm going to let you be in charge of ordering supplies. We get a shipment in twice a month. Usually I've been cooking burgers and maybe a big pot of chili on the weekend."

"So how many customers do I need to plan for? I mean how many meals do you sell a night? That could help me figure out how much to order."

He studied her. He couldn't help but stare into her unusual brown eyes and wonder what kind of asshole had let her go. Nor could he help but wonder what the fuck had gotten into him that he was so worried about her past.

He shook his head. "Usually in a night, we sell about fifteen burgers."

"Really? That's all?" She shook her head. "That surprises me. Considering the huge number of customers last night, I would have thought you would have sold as least forty burgers, if not fifty."

"Selling fifteen burgers in a night is actually a good night." He narrowed his eyes. He knew his cooking sucked. When he was Pack Master, he always had someone dropping food by, like Granny or one of the other females. When he was younger, he always had staff that cooked for him.

Now, he had no one.

"Well, with how well you cook, I predict sales will double,

if not triple." He walked around behind the bar and picked up a clipboard with paper. He slid it across the counter to her.

"I'm not going to open the bar tonight."

Her eyes widened. "But I needed to start work right away."

"Oh, you'll start today. Just not cooking. I need you to sit down and plan out a menu. Anything you think of that you need, write it down on that order form. I'm paying you for your time."

"Okay, well, that won't take long." Her gaze flittered to the kitchen. "Do you mind if I rearrange the kitchen a little? Just to facilitate a better flow?"

He grinned. "Sweetheart, the kitchen is yours. If I never see another burned hamburger, it won't be too soon."

CHAPTER 11

*J*acey took the clipboard back into the kitchen. She wanted to check the inventory of what she had before she made Barrett order more food. There was no use in being wasteful.

She set the clipboard down on the stainless-steel counter and rummaged through the cabinets and pantries. She made quick notes of what was on hand and then checked the industrial-sized refrigerator. After jotting down what inventory the fridge contained, she went into the back and looked in both large freezers.

The place was big enough to have its own walk in freezer, but she doubted that Barrett wanted to put that much money into the place. For some reason, she got the sense that he wasn't planning on being here long. He didn't seem settled to her. He was too restless, on edge.

His dark-green eyes seemed to always be searching and scanning the room for the slightest indication of danger. She also got the feeling he wasn't one to run from danger but would rush right into it.

That scared her even more.

She took her clipboard with notes and walked back through the swinging doors. She arched her brow at the doors and made a mental note to do something about them. No use cooking a great meal if it was going to end up on the floor.

She glanced down at the floors. If she was going to be serving a lot of food out of this kitchen the whole place needed a scrubbing. She was a bit OCD when it came to where she prepared her food.

She glanced around the darkened bar, looking for Barrett. When she didn't see him, she walked over to the window and looked out. She spotted him leaning against the front of his Jeep with his boot on the front bumper. His arms were crossed over his chest, and he was talking to an older man with white hair. Though she couldn't be positive, she got the feeling the old man was human.

Barrett didn't say a word as the old man continued to animatedly talk with his hands in the air. Barrett would nod every few seconds.

She slid into a booth near the window. She glanced outside as the snow began to gently fall. She found herself mesmerized by the soothing sight and finally had to tear herself away and put her focus on the clipboard in front of her.

She pulled out a blank sheet of paper and studied the ingredients listed in front of her. She quickly wrote down menu options, drawing from the ingredients they already had.

"Looks like you've been busy." His dark voice seemed to settle across the lonely bar.

She jumped a little and looked up at him.

"Sorry. Didn't mean to scare you."

"I didn't hear you come in."

"As big as I am, you didn't hear me come in?" A slight grin

touched the corners of his mouth. Her stomach warmed and tingled, and her heart began to race.

She licked her lips and cleared her throat. She needed to keep calm. And she certainly didn't need to be getting all hot and bothered over her boss. He'd already made it clear he wasn't interested in having a relationship with someone who worked for him. Besides, she was trying to get over her ex-mate. Wasn't she?

"I have some good news." She turned the paper toward him so he could see. Before she could say anything else, he was easing his hard body into the booth beside her.

She quickly scooted over to give him room and give her body a chance to recover from how close he was.

"Damn. You have been busy." He nodded approvingly and then gave her a look of appreciation.

"This is the list of what we have in the kitchen." She handed it to him. "And this is the list of food that we need to order."

"Very efficient." He scowled. "Wait, we have turkey?"

"We have a couple of turkeys in the freezer. Not enough to make a turkey sandwich for a lot of people, but it would be great to put in some vegetable soup."

"Beautiful and smart. I wish I had found you sooner," he said.

She blinked, not sure what to say.

He slid out of the booth and placed his hands on his hips and picked up the paper with the food she needed. "I'll get this ordered tomorrow. It won't arrive until next week. We can actually go into town and pick up some food to hold us over until the shipment arrives if you don't think we'll have enough."

"I don't think that will be necessary. I know how to stretch a meal." She eased out of the booth and stood. She glanced in the direction of the kitchen. "I'd really like to start organizing the kitchen, if you don't mind." She rubbed her hands on her jeans and tried not to fidget.

"Go ahead. I've got some paperwork I need to work on anyway. If you need me, I'll be upstairs." He nodded out the front door. "My apartment is around the back and up the stairs."

"You live here?"

"Yeah. Above the bar."

"That must be convenient for work." Her gaze flittered to the ceiling. She couldn't help but wonder what his place looked like. Was it decorated in the latest style or had he left everything original to the building?

"It's hard to leave my work behind, especially when I live above it." He shrugged.

"Sounds like it's all you do. Work, I mean." She stuck her hands in her jeans pockets and felt like an idiot. She wasn't sure what compelled her to continue the conversation. Since leaving Mississippi, all she wanted to do was be left alone. She knew she was depressed and had let a lot of people down, but now standing in front of Barrett, she found herself wanting to linger a while longer.

"Is there anything else besides work?" He gave her a wry smile. "Let me know if you need me." He gave her a nod and then walked out the door.

Standing there in the empty bar alone, the temperature seemed to drop. She hadn't noticed before how much heat Barrett seemed to emit from his large frame. And there was something else about him. It wasn't just that he was drop-dead gorgeous and had a body for sin, it was something behind his eyes, and the way he looked at her. Something that made her think she wasn't the only one feeling lost in the world.

CHAPTER 12

*D*amon stuck his hands in his pockets after the last Guardian from Alabama shook his hand and expressed his sympathy. There had been so many, he couldn't remember half of their names.

He felt like he had greeted a million Guardians today.

The memorial service had turned out better than he'd expected, and he knew that Barrett would be impressed by the number of Guardians from all the Southern states who had turned out in his honor.

Jack Welbourn walked over to him with a glass of brandy in his hand. He brought with him John Morgan, the Pack Master from Kentucky; Charles Price, the Pack Master from Tennessee; and Gerald Davidson, the Pack Master from Alabama.

"Thank you for sending all that food, Jack." Damon ran his fingers through his hair. "I really wasn't expecting this many to turn out."

"Barrett meant a lot to a whole lot of werewolves." Jack gave a brief nod.

"I hate to do this, Damon, but we need to discuss some

Pack business. Something we've been putting off for a while." Gerald cocked his head.

"You're talking about Edward Boudier," Damon stated.

They all gave silent nods.

Damon had ordered the Tribunal for Edward Boudier, former Pack Master of Louisiana, but put it on hold until Barrett's body had been recovered and buried. Now that they had called off the search and held the memorial, he knew it was time for Boudier to pay for the crimes he had committed against the state of Arkansas. Boudier had ordered the capturing and killing of Heimy, one of Arkansas's Guardians. He's also ordered Guardians Mitchell and Lucien captured and tortured. If the Arkansas Guardians had not discovered their location, then there would have been two more casualties from Boudier.

"Yeah, that fucker needs to pay," Damon ground out.

"Oh, he will. He will pay with his blood," Gerald said with an evil smile on his face.

"I just don't understand why a Pack Master would intentionally kill Guardians." John Morgan frowned and shook his head.

"Because Boudier is fucked up in the head. He even killed his own Guardians. He should have been put down a long time ago. I'm sorry I didn't get involved sooner. This is bad for all the states." Charles shook his head. "Is Boudier still being held in Texas?"

"Yeah. Mason Brown, the Pack Master, reached out and volunteered to hold him until Tribunal." Damon walked over to the assortment of whiskeys and bourbons set up on the small antique table by the window. He took a crystal tumbler and poured two fingers in a glass. He tossed it back. "I'm not sure how I will ever repay Mason for offering to help. I knew I couldn't hold him in Arkansas. Every Were would have tried to kill him before the Tribunal. Including me."

"No shit," Gerald said. "I would have made the trip over to rip his head off myself. Seems like a fitting end for a piece of shit like Boudier."

"We're going to have to decide who the next Pack Master of Louisiana is going to be. Right now, there are no takers." Jack said and took a drink of his brandy. "There's always been a second-in-command. In Boudier's case, that would have been his son-in-law. But since he's dead, we don't have anyone."

"No one wants it either," Charles said. "Boudier left the state unstable."

"What about the Assassins?" Damon had been thinking a lot about the three Weres located in Louisiana whose main job was to find and kill those who committed the most heinous crimes. They all answered to the Pack Master. Right now, they were kind of on their own, left to their own devices.

Jack shook his head. "I talked to Brutus the other day. He says none of them want it. He says that the state of Louisiana is so fucked up right now, no one wants to be the next Pack Master. He says none of the civilian Weres trust the system anymore. They think the next Pack Master will be just as bad if not worse than Boudier."

"Nobody could be worse than Boudier. Not even Satan himself." Gerald took a drink of whiskey.

"Why don't we do this. Every one of us will put a list of names together. Pull it from Guardians, civilian Weres, whatever. Narrow it down and then vote on it." Charles offered.

"The money and assets of Boudier have been frozen. It will go to the next Pack Master," Jack said. "I know we were thinking it would go to his daughter, Ginny, but the Council ruled otherwise. Apparently, it's some kind of old rule that the old Pack Master assets gets passed to the next."

"I don't know that Ginny would accept Boudier's money anyway. Plus she has inherited her dead husband's money and that asshole was loaded. The money her husband had is rightfully hers. She certainly deserved it and even more after all the pain that fucker caused her." Damon curled his fingers into tight fists as he recalled the conversation he'd had with Jaxon over how her husband used to abuse her. Thankfully, she'd killed him and was forever safe from his violence.

"Ginny deserves it. And she deserves to be happy with Jaxon," Jack said.

Damon nodded.

"Damon!" Lucien came barreling out of the kitchen with his cell phone in his hand. "You need to take this."

"Who is it?" He narrowed his eyes as he took the phone.

"Lorcan. He said it's urgent. He said it's about Boudier." Lucien's uneasy expression had Damon's gut tensing.

Damon held the cell phone to his ear. "It's Damon."

"Boudier's escaped." Lorcan's deep voice seemed to vibrate across the line.

Damon felt like he'd been punched in the gut. "What do you mean Boudier's escaped?" he growled.

The other Pack Masters froze, their steely gazes locked on Damon's next words.

"I mean he pulled a Houdini and is no longer in the custody of the state of

Texas," Lorcan deadpanned.

"Why the fuck haven't I heard from Texas?" Damon thundered.

"Oh, I'm sure you will. Probably in about five seconds," Lorcan stated.

The phone buzzed in his hand. He pulled it away from his ear and glanced down at the caller ID. Texas.

"Fuck. I need to take this." Damon froze. "Wait, how the hell did you know this?"

"Being an Assassin has given me valuable connections. An Assassin is usually given a heads up before the Pack Master. In case things can't be handled at the state level." Lorcan ended the call.

His cell phone went from buzzing to ringing. He looked at the group of Pack Masters in front of him. "Boudier escaped. And this is the Pack Master of Texas about to let me know that little bit of information."

"Lorcan told you that?" Lucien cocked his head.

"He did. We'll discuss that later. Right now, I've got to take this call." He looked at Lucien. "I want you to gather our Guardians. We're going to have to find him."

Lucien nodded and hurried back into the kitchen. Damon heard the back door slam as the Weres went outside to gather the rest of the guys.

"We are in this together, Damon," Jack said. "We will all send out Guardians. Just let us know where you need them."

"Thank you, Jack." He nodded at the rest of the Pack Masters and then slid his finger across the phone to take the call.

"This is Damon."

CHAPTER 13

*A*fter Jacey had cleaned and organized the kitchen to her liking, Barrett had taken her to the diner down the street. They'd lingered over dinner, talking of everything and nothing. It was nice to have another wolf to talk to.

Standing in his apartment and looking down on the empty street below, he watched the snow continue to drift down from the sky. Since he'd arrived in Colorado, it snowed often. But tonight, looking down on the tiny town, it seemed different, more peaceful, and not so desolate.

He stepped away from the window and began to pace. Was Jacey warm enough? Did Mena keep the house at an agreeable temperature or was she miserly and kept the house cold, forcing Jacey to cover up in a blanket? Did Jacey even have a blanket? He knew she had arrived with only the clothes on her back and what was in her messenger bag. Even after buying her some winter clothes, he knew she was going to need more.

"Fuck." He ran his hand through his hair and growled. What the fuck was wrong with him? He needed to be focused on keeping a low profile and not getting too close to the girl.

Hell, with her being a Were and from the South, she posed more of a risk of finding out who he really was. He couldn't have that. He wouldn't risk it.

He needed to get laid. That's what he needed to do. He should have just headed into Durango, or hell, even Denver and picked up some pretty female at the bar. The female werewolf population were few and far between in Colorado, but he had seen a couple in the bars of Denver one evening when he was with Ryker.

He sighed. There was no getting down this mountain in this storm. His Jeep was good but not that good. Besides, by the time he got there, all the bars would be closed.

He was stuck here on the mountain thinking of Jacey Miller and getting a hard-on.

He glanced down at the tent in his jeans. He could just take care of it himself, but he always preferred a woman's touch. Besides, he had always prided himself on his self-control. Something he strived for in all areas of life.

He walked over to the window again and stopped. The street lights were off, and the snow was now coming down hard and fast.

If he couldn't have sex, then he wanted to go for a run.

It would be the perfect night to shift and run in the ice-cold snow, his paws digging into the soft powder with each step. He would run until his mind was clear and his body wasn't reacting with every thought of Jacey.

He was finally getting to run. He grinned and grabbed his keys off the kitchen counter.

* * *

JACEY HAD TRIED for hours to sleep. She had even snuck downstairs and heated up some water for some chamomile tea. Even that didn't help.

She stared up at the ceiling of the Victorian home. She threw off the covers and stood, grateful for the cool hardwood floors against her bare feet.

Mena apparently was cold-natured because she had set the thermostat to hotter than hell, and Jacey was burning up. She walked over to the window and looked out at the fast-falling snow.

That's what she needed. To feel the cold snow against her flesh … or fur.

A run. God, how long had it been since she'd had a run? Forever it seemed and never in the snow.

She grinned. The whole town would be asleep. No one would be out in this mess. Besides, the only other wolf here was Barrett.

They were already in the mountains, and there were probably plenty of places to run and stretch her legs.

Excitement tickled her stomach. She quickly changed out of her T-shirt and slipped on some jeans and a sweater. She stuck her feet into the warm boots and grabbed her coat. She grabbed her bag and the key to the room. She would ease out and head toward the back of the house and into the woods. It would be steep, but with her wolf eyesight, she would be okay.

Grinning like a kid at her birthday party, she eased out of her room and walked downstairs. Quietly, she opened the front door and headed out into the night.

The snow hit her face and quickly melted against her skin. She welcomed the tiny kisses of cold and couldn't wait to get far away from the house so she could take off her clothes and shift. The snow was falling faster now and the flakes were bigger and fluffier and sticking to her eyelashes.

She let out a laugh and then covered her mouth with her hand.

She tilted her head back and opened her mouth, letting wet snowflakes melt on her tongue.

She glanced around and spotted a large tree. She hung her bag up on a low-hanging branch and hooked her coat beside it. She quickly took her sweater off and stuffed it in her bag. She hadn't bothered with a bra since it was just one more thing to worry about. She toed off her boots and stepped into the fluffy snow. A laugh bubbled out of her. She quickly shimmied out of her jeans and stuffed all her clothes in her bag. She made a mental note where the bag was so she could retrieve it once she was done.

She crouched down, letting her hands sink into the fluffy white snow. It was dark and even the moon was hidden by the falling snow. She knew once she shifted, her eyesight would be more astute and clear. Her wolf eyes would guide her where to go and how to find her way back home.

She closed her eyes and forced her body into wolf form. Her bones shifted and tendons stretched. Soft, silky fur burst out across her body, and she felt her body shift and change into the animal deep inside.

She lifted her head back and let out a howl. The sound echoed in the night. She took off.

She sprinted, her legs carrying her fast through the snow. She pushed herself harder and farther into the deep forest. The crisp scent of pine needles and snow burned her lungs, but she liked it. It made her feel alive again. Something she'd not felt in a very long time.

The wind rushed through her fur as she raced along the snowy ground, running deeper and deeper into the woods.

She caught the scent of something strange on the wind. Something dangerous.

Something sharp clamped down on her front foot. She came to a bone-jolting stop, landing hard on the snow. She let out a howl of pain and saw a drop of crimson dotting the snow. Her blood.

Pain shot through her foot and up her leg.

She tried to pull her foot out of the snow but couldn't. She lowered her head closer to whatever had her foot. She saw metal teeth. Panic settled in her chest, and her blood ran cold.

She was caught in a trap. A trap deliberately set for an animal.

"Well, well, well. Looks like we got ourselves a wolf." A human dressed in camo stepped out of the woods and shone a flashlight in her eyes. She let out a growl and her fur bristled. He aimed a gun right at her head.

"Sam, pull the truck around here, and let's get her loaded up," the hunter said.

"But it's still alive." The second human stepped around the hunter and looked down at her.

They had dead eyes, eyes that held no goodness in them. Eyes that lusted for blood. Her blood.

"We want her alive. They pay good money for a female wolf like this," the camo hunter said.

"I don't know why. Aren't they just going to skin her for the fur?" The second human said.

Nausea settled in her stomach. Some sick psycho was going to skin her alive.

"I don't ask. And neither should you." The camo hunter shook his head. "You know how some of those guys are from the South. Hell, he probably wants to have sex with it."

"Fine. But put a dart in her first. I'm not taking chances of getting rabies from that bitch." The second hunter walked back into the darkness.

She let out a growl as loud as she could. If she were going down, she wasn't going down without a fight.

He pulled out a handgun from the waist of his pants and

aimed it at her. She growled just as he shot. A sharp, shooting pain raced through her shoulder. Her vision blurred, and her strength seemed to seep out of her body and soak into the ground. She stumbled before crumbling to the ground. She tried to move, but her mind was groggy and her body limp.

Fear washed over her before her eyes slammed shut in an abyss of darkness and horror.

CHAPTER 14

*B*arrett didn't have to drive far before pulling off the snow-covered road. He got out of the Jeep and quickly divested himself of all his clothing. Ice-cold flakes landed on his bare skin and quickly melted against the heat of his flesh. He closed his eyes, lifted his head to the darkened sky, and inhaled.

His breathing increased, and his body prickled with excitement.

This is exactly what he wanted. What he needed. A run through the snow where all his problems melted away in the dark night, never to be found again.

He closed his eyes and called out to the wolf lying dormant inside. His body tightened, and the twinge of pain shot through his nervous system. It had been too long since he'd allowed the wolf side of him free. He sucked in a breath at the pain of his bones lengthening and tendons shifting to accommodate his wolf form. He embraced the bite of pain as he shifted into a different body and merged with the beast that lay just beneath his flesh.

He lifted his wolf head to the sky, taking in the night and the snow and the quiet.

A howl ripped through the night, chilling him to his marrow.

It was the distinct howl of a wolf. This howl was different; it was a howl born of pain.

He jerked his head in the direction of the sound. Every hair on his body stood on end, and he let out a low growl.

He sprinted toward the sound, his mind racing a million miles a second.

Two lights were bobbing along the ground in the distance. He caught the scent of humans, and of a female wolf.

His heart jerked in his chest. The wolf scent was distinctly familiar.

Jacey.

He ran hard toward the lights. A hunter in camo aimed a gun toward Jacey. He ran harder, trying to make it to her before …

The gun went off, splintering the silent snowy night. His world went deaf. Jacey stumbled and fell to the white ground.

Fear and revulsion clawed at his gut. It streaked thought his chest and spread to his fingers and toes. Engulfed in white-hot rage, he let out a vicious growl, leaped in the air, and landed on the hunter with the gun.

They both tumbled to the earth. Barrett sunk his teeth into the human's shoulder. The human screamed in pain. He wanted to rip out his fucking throat, wanted to watch his life blood stain the white snow until it became a crimson blanket.

"Jesus!" A second human came out of the tree line and into view. Barrett lifted his head and growled.

The second human pulled a handgun out of the waistband of his pants. He aimed for Barrett. But Barrett was quicker. He released his hold on the human on the ground and jumped through the air. He landed on the second hunter, pinning him to the ground.

He stared down into the eyes of his prey. The human's gaze grew wide with terror, and Barrett could feel him trembling under his paws.

"Please, please, please." The human shook with fear. The repulsive scent of urine hung heavy in the air. The hunter had pissed himself.

The human thought he was brave enough to inflict death but was a coward when it came to receiving pain himself.

Barrett snarled. He wanted the human to feel every inch of the pain he was going to inflict on his frail human body.

A soft whimper in the silence of the night had Barrett jerking his head over to Jacey's body.

She moaned again and attempted to lift her head but failed.

Hope fluttered in his chest. She wasn't dead.

He jumped off the human and ran to her. Skidding to a halt beside her, he lowered his nose to her face.

He felt the soft exhale of her breath on his furry snout.

She was alive.

He glanced back at the hunters who were scrambling to their feet. He let out a warning growl.

They both took off, sprinting for a truck parked near the trees.

He watched as they jumped in the pickup and tore across the snow back toward the road.

He looked back at Jacey.

She blinked her eyes slowly and tried to lift her head. He searched her body for a bullet. Instead of a bullet, he saw a tranquilizer dart sticking out of her shoulder.

He grabbed the dart in his mouth and pulled it free from her fur.

He tossed it into the snow and turned to look at her.

She was unlike any wolf he'd ever seen. Her gray fur seemed to glisten under the soft moonlight. She, like him, was a gray wolf. But unlike him, her fur was so light, it looked silvery-white.

He nuzzled her face, and she blinked lazily up at him. She tried to lift her front paw, but she let out a whimper.

His gaze dropped to her foot.

His gut twisted in pain. Her paw was caught in an animal trap, and she was bleeding.

Those fuckers had trapped her and then shot her with a dart. He should have killed them both when he had the chance.

He couldn't get her free while he was a wolf. He knew what he had to do. He lifted his head and howled as his body shifted back into human form.

Crouching on the ground, he leaned over Jacey. She was fighting the effects of the tranquilizer dart and trying to stay awake.

"Jacey, if you can hear me, I'm going to get you free," he whispered near her ear. The scent of her fear and pain washed over him. He knew how she felt: vulnerable, alone, and afraid.

He hated that she felt like that. He ran his fingertips down her leg to her trapped paw. She whimpered. He grabbed the animal trap and pulled it open. Her paw slipped out. He didn't want this trap to hurt another animal so he grabbed it in two hands and pulled until the spring broke, making it useless. He threw it up against the tree in the forest and turned his attention back to Jacey.

He lifted her bleeding paw in his hand. She whimpered.

"I'm going to have to pick you up, okay?" He wasn't sure

how she felt about him being naked, but he didn't really have a choice. He'd left his clothes back at his Jeep.

She blinked once. He took it as a yes.

He scooped his hands under her body and held her gently. He stood, holding her close to his bare chest. Her fur tickled his flesh. She had the softest fur he'd ever touched.

Holding her close to his chest, with her face lying on his shoulder, he tightened his grip on her and took off toward the road.

The snow crunched under his footsteps, but he barely felt the bite of the cold. His mind was on Jacey.

He could feel her slow, rhythmic breathing against his chest. He slowed as he approached the vehicle.

He shifted her in his arms and opened the door to the back seat. Gently, he laid her across the seat and grabbed a spare blanket out of the back and covered her body. He leaned in and picked up her wounded paw.

Her silvery-white fur was stained crimson, and her paw was at an odd angle. The fucking trap had broken the bone in her foot. Because she was wolf, she would heal in record time, but it didn't make Barrett any less angry.

He walked around, opened the glove box, and dug around for something to bandage her foot.

And found nothing. He had no bandages, not even a rag …

His eyes drifted to the driver's seat. His gaze landed on his clothes.

Still naked, the cold snow continued to fall and melt against his overheated skin. He grabbed his T-shirt off the seat and hurried around the Jeep to Jacey.

Grabbing the cotton material between two hands, he ripped the shirt in two. He did this two more times until he got the size he needed. Taking her paw in his hand, he gently wrapped up her wound and stopped the bleeding.

After securing her makeshift bandage, he leaned near her ear.

"I'm going to buckle you in. Just so you won't slip around on the drive back home."

She opened her eyes and slowly blinked and then fell back asleep.

He was glad of that. At least while she was sleeping, she wasn't in pain.

His anger flared once again, and he wanted to hunt those humans down and kill them for what they'd done to her. But right now, Jacey needed him.

His revenge would have to wait.

He leaned over her body and grabbed the seatbelt. He bucked her in, maneuvering her body so the seatbelt would be across her chest and under her arm.

He opened the driver's door and grabbed his jeans and slipped them over his hips. He put his boots on and slid into the driver's side. He cranked the engine and threw it into drive.

It didn't take him long to make the short trek back to his place. His headlights bobbed against the brick building of the grill. He killed the engine and slid out, eager to get Jacey upstairs and settled.

The decision to take her to his place was a no-brainer. He couldn't very well take her in wolf form to Mena's. The old woman would freak the hell out. His place was the only safe place for her to stay until she healed.

He took the steps to his apartment two at a time. When he reached the top step, he shifted her in his arms and unlocked the door.

Once inside, he kicked the door shut with his foot. He carried her over to his bed and laid her down on the unmade bed. Slowly, he slid his arms out from under her but not before his fingertips slipped against her silky fur.

An electric shock raced through his body, and he took a few steps back away from her.

His chest tightened, and he wanted nothing more than to curl up next to her and sleep with her against his chest.

He shook his head. He couldn't do that. Why the hell was he even thinking about that?

He looked at the time. It was almost two o'clock. He would check her bandage in another couple of hours to make sure the wound was healing.

Unable to sleep he headed into the kitchen and pulled down a mug from the cabinet. He filled the coffee maker and put the grounds in the bin. God, he missed his old coffee maker he had at the Compound. It was kept in the secret room behind his desk. He'd ordered it online, and it had cost well over a thousand dollars. But it had been worth every penny.

When he had been Pack Master, he had amassed quite an amount in the way of a fortune. Not to mention the family money that he would inherit from his relatives in South Carolina.

But now that he was dead, Damon would inherit that Pack Master money, and his family inheritance would go to the next in line.

Ryker had given him an emergency credit card and a wad of cash in the amount of ten thousand dollars in the event he had to leave suddenly. He hadn't touched the money until he bought Jacey some clothes.

Not that it mattered. He could survive where he was, living off what he made from The Mountain Top Bar and Grille. He needed enough money socked away until he could find somewhere else to live and start over. Someplace preferably warmer, like Hawaii or the Bahamas.

He filled his cup with coffee and walked around the counter. He picked up a chair and carried it over to the bed where Jacey lay. He sat and took of sip of the hot coffee, watching her for any signs of distress.

He watched the gentle rise and fall of her chest. Her soft almost-white fur trembled as she dreamed, and her back feet began to peddle.

She was dreaming.

He set his cup down and leaned over.

"It's okay. You're safe now." He ran his hand over her back and spoke to her in soothing tones.

She calmed and went back to a restful sleep.

He leaned back in the chair and wrapped his arms around his chest, his gaze never leaving her.

He couldn't explain the terror he'd felt at seeing her lying on the blood-covered snow and not moving. His gut and chest had tightened like an invisible hand had reached inside his body and clutched his heart.

Why had he been so affected by the thought of losing her? Was it because he hated to see a female hurt? Was it because as hard as it was to admit, it was kind of nice to have another wolf around to talk to? Or was it something more?

He forked his fingers through his hair and let out a low growl.

Fuck. He needed to get his shit together and get it together fast. No way in hell was he going to let someone like Jacey Miller wiggle her way into his life.

As soon as she was better, he was going to set some hard and fast boundaries with her.

And get back to his normal, boring life.

CHAPTER 15

"*I* want him found. Do you understand?" Damon growled at the Guardians standing around the gym at the Compound in Little Rock. After he'd gotten the call in Eureka Springs confirming that Boudier had escaped from the Texas Pack, Damon had ordered Jayden and Braxton to the Lone Star state to find out what had happened.

The rest of the Guardians headed back to Little Rock to change and prepare for a manhunt.

"Braxton and Jayden are headed to Texas. All the other Pack Masters offered two of their own Guardians to go with them as well." He'd taken them all up on their offer.

The more people they had on this, the quicker Boudier would be found.

"Lucien, has your brother had anything else to say?" Damon cut his eyes to the male.

"Lucien said he, Brutus, and Killian wanted to go with our men, but he wondered if Boudier wasn't going to try to head back to Louisiana to try to get some of his money."

"Tell Lorcan and the other Assassins to remain in

Louisiana. If the civilian populace finds out their Pack Master is on the loose, then all hell might break out. That state is on the brink of collapsing, and I want the Assassins to stay to keep the peace." He nodded at Lucien. "Also tell him I'll be giving him a call later to see how the Louisiana Guardians are holding up down there."

"You don't think the Louisiana Guardians would try to help Boudier, do you?" Jaxon frowned.

"I think that Boudier ruled with fear and threats. They all know they are better off without him. But they are still intimidated by him. We're going to have to settle on a Pack Master soon for that state. In fact, Lucien, tell Lorcan that we are working on establishing a new Pack Master. That should buy us some time."

"Will do." Lucien nodded and grabbed his cell phone. He stepped outside to place the call.

"How the hell did Boudier escape anyway? Doesn't make any sense." Jaxon shook his head.

"That's what Braxton and Jayden are going to find out. Right now, I want everyone in position to guard our borders in case Boudier has some kind of attack planned for Arkansas," Damon said.

"But he would have to have someone helping him to pull something like that off." Zane shook his head. "I mean after Barrett's death, I'm pretty sure all the Louisiana Guardians wouldn't piss on him if he were on fire."

"You never know. My gut tells me he has someone else helping him. Someone else we've not considered."

"The witch?" Zane offered.

"I doubt that." Ryker stepped forward and shook his head. "She signed her own death warrant after she turned on Boudier."

"Ryker. Been wondering where you've been." Damon narrowed his eyes.

"I was at the Memorial. Same as you all." He shrugged and eased over to lean against the wall by the door.

"I didn't see you," Damon stated.

"He didn't come inside," Lucien said. "He stayed outside near the woods. Like a fox, too scared to get close to anyone."

"So, you think I'm a fox. Thanks for the compliment, but I'm not into males." Ryker smirked.

"Asshole," Lucien shot back.

Damon looked around his office and then nodded. "Alright, you're all excused. Just stay available. Cell phones on at all times."

The nodded as they filed out the door.

"Ryker, I'd like a word."

Ryker took a deep breath and pushed off the wall. He waited until the last Guardian stalked out the door before walking to the chair opposite of Damon's. He eased into the seat.

"You've not been around much," Damon stated.

"But I've always managed to do my job." Ryker narrowed his eyes.

"I didn't say you haven't. Look, I know that you have been having a hard time with Barrett's death."

"We all have." Ryker looked away.

Damon nodded. "Yes. We have. But you were closer to him. Every time I came into his office, you were around. He trusted you."

"And he trusted you enough to make you Pack Master." Ryker shrugged.

Damon stilled. He jerked his head toward the male. "Ryker, are you upset that Barrett didn't make you Pack Master?" It would explain why the Guardian was never around. And when he was, he kept his distance from the rest of them.

"Hell, no." Ryker's lips curled into a horrified expression. "Why would I want that headache?"

Damon snorted. "Believe me, you wouldn't."

"I know there's a lot of shit going on, especially since Boudier escaped. But I had already put in for a week's leave starting tomorrow." Ryker looked away.

"I know." Damon reached for the folder on his desk with Ryker's information. "That's why I wanted to talk to you. Under the current circumstances, I'm halting all vacations and leave requests."

"What?" Ryker's eyes blazed. "But I already have reservations."

"Tell me what's so important that you have to leave instead of standing with your brothers to find the man who killed our Pack Master?" Damon propped his hands on his hips and glared. There was something Ryker wasn't telling him.

"It's a private matter," Ryker ground out between his clenched teeth.

Damon sighed. "If you can't tell me, then I can't let you go."

"Fuck that." Ryker slammed his hand into the solid cinder block wall. The room shook under the force, but the wall held. Barrett had the whole Compound rebuilt and reinforced after the Pack had been bombed a few years ago.

"Ryker." Damon curled his hands into fists and approached the insubordinate Were. "You better learn some respect and learn it fast."

Zane and Lucien opened the office door and peered inside. "Is everything okay in here?" Zane asked. He stepped into the doorway and looked from Ryker back to him. "Sounded like a bomb went off in here."

Lucien stepped beside Zane and waited for Damon to speak.

"Yeah. We're good. Ryker is just having a hard time adjusting to a new Pack Master. That's all." Damon glared at the Were in question.

A muscle twitched in Ryker's cheek, and Damon knew the male was having a hard time keeping his trap shut.

"Ryker?" Zane and Lucien entered the room and looked at their fellow Guardian. Their expressions narrowed.

"I'm good." Ryker looked at Zane and nodded. "We're all fucking good."

Lucien and Zane didn't move but looked at Damon. He gave them both a nod, and they stepped out of the room but didn't bother closing the door.

He could tell his Guardians were afraid that if they did, when they opened it they would find a couple of dead bodies on the other side.

Damon took a deep breath and faced Ryker. He knew if he didn't handle him correctly the first time, then he would lose his respect and authority over him. It was something he could not afford.

"Ryker, I'm giving you an order. And that order is you will not be taking a leave of absence, and you will not be taking vacation. Once Boudier is captured, then feel free to put your request in again. Until then, you're not going anywhere." Damon glared.

He could see Ryker warring with what he was going to say next. Damon's gut told him Ryker really wanted to tell Damon to fuck off, and he was going to do what he wanted to.

Instead, Ryker gave a nod and turned toward the open door and walked out.

Damon ran his hand down his face and let out a small growl. He'd never seen Ryker like this, so uptight and closed off.

He knew what it was like to be on the outside looking in,

and if Barrett hadn't come along and put him in the Arkansas Pack, Damon wasn't sure where he would have ended up.

Back then, Damon was bitter, isolated, and alone. At the time, that's how he preferred it. Until the Arkansas Pack. Until Ava. Now he was forever changed.

Looking at Ryker was like looking into a mirror from the past.

Something dark was going on in his Guardian's life, and he wanted to know what it was.

He wasn't going to stop until he uncovered the truth.

CHAPTER 16

*J*acey grimaced against the pain that pulled her out of sleep. She opened her eyes and blinked.

Her heart panicked at the strange surroundings. Her gaze darted around the room and finally rested on Barrett. He was asleep in a chair that was leaning dangerously back against the brick wall of the loft.

She relaxed. She must be in his apartment above the Mountain Top Bar and Grille.

Last night's events came flooding back into her head. Her stomach pitched.

She eased up on her elbows and sucked in a hiss of pain in her hand.

Barrett jerked awake. The chair and Barrett tumbled to the hardwood floor in a loud crash.

He scowled and quickly got to his feet.

"Are you okay?" She winced at the pain in her throat.

He scowled. "I'm not the one who got caught in a trap. How's your hand?"

The sheet slipped from her chest, and she felt the cool breeze against her bare breasts.

Shit. She was naked.

Barrett's face went red, and he quickly turned his head away. She jerked the sheet up to her chin and squeezed her eyes tight.

Of course, she was naked. She was in wolf form last night when she'd been trapped. Once she shifted back into human form, she would be naked.

"I didn't see your clothes when I found you." He cleared his throat and rubbed the back of his neck. His trained his gaze on the window.

"I left them behind at Mena's house." She shook her head and lifted her hand. "I shouldn't have gone out last night. It was stupid. I should have known better."

He spun around and pierced her with his intense green stare. "Jacey, you have nothing to apologize for. You had every right to be out there last night. Those hunters," his voice turned lethal, "are the fuckers who never should have been out there. If I ever find them again, I'm going to rip out their livers."

She froze. Somehow, she believed him.

"How's your hand?" He walked over to the bed, his gaze focused on her injury.

She swallowed as he gently lifted her hand in the air for closer inspection.

"Still sore but its healing," she managed to say.

The scent of him lingered, and she realized how intimate a situation she had found herself in with her boss.

"It's not healing as fast as it should." He frowned. "Those hunters may have poisoned the trap. That may be why you aren't healing as quick as you should." He walked into the kitchen and opened a cabinet.

"Thank you ... for ... saving me last night." She felt her face heat a thousand degrees and wasn't sure if it was because she hated to admit she had needed help or if it was because she was naked as a jaybird.

"You're welcome." He stopped what he was doing, turned, and held her gaze. Something flashed through his eyes and then, just like that, it was gone.

She looked away, too warm under his green-eyed stare. She'd never met a male who could make her feel so awkward and clumsy.

She lifted her hand and turned it this way and that. The teeth of the trap had bitten into her bone and broken tendons and cartilage. The bone had healed during the night. She tried to force her fingers into a fist and grimaced.

"You need to be gentle with yourself. Give yourself time to heal." Barrett walked over to her and handed her a cup of something hot. "Drink this."

"What is it?" She arched her brow and took the mug in her good hand.

"Something to help get rid of whatever toxins those hunters used on that trap." Instead of sitting in the chair, Barrett eased onto the bed beside her.

She inhaled the steam from the top of the hot mug and then looked at him. "Smells like a meadow full of spring flowers."

A devastating grin broke out across his handsome face. "Never heard it described like that but yes. There are some flowering herbs in that mixture."

She nodded, unable to move her gaze away from him.

He frowned. "Is everything okay? You look flushed." He reached out and put his large hand on her forehead. "You don't feel like you have a fever."

Nope. No fever. Just a big, fat idiot.

"I'm fine. Just embarrassed at having to be rescued last night." She took a sip of the tea and let the warm floral taste slide down her throat. "Trying to get my life together isn't looking so great right now." She shook her head.

"Getting your life together takes time. I should know." He snorted.

"You?"

"Yes, me." He arched his brow. "Why? Do I look like I have everything so planned out?"

She grinned at his mocking tone. "Better than most."

"It takes time." He shrugged. "You're just trying to find your footing right now. Once you are settled into a routine, then you'll float through adjusting to your new life."

"It that what you are?" She took another sip of the tea and studied his expression. "Settled?"

"For now."

"So, you don't always see yourself staying in Colorado?" She shivered and pulled the sheet up closer to her chin.

He frowned and snagged a throw off the foot of the bed and wrapped it around her bare shoulders. His fingertips skidded across her skin, and she almost forgot to breathe.

His hands lingered a little too long to be casual yet not long enough to be intimate. It didn't matter. Just the slightest touch from him sent her heart skidding into a rhythm a million miles an hour.

"Staying in Colorado?" he stepped back and looked out the window. "That's a hard question to answer." His gaze turned into longing as he looked out into the winter landscape.

"I suppose I'll go where I need to go. And if I need to stay in Colorado, then I suppose I'll stay."

"But you're free. Single. Not tied down to anything or anyone. You can come and go as you please." She shrugged. "If the bar isn't what you really want to be doing, then make a change. It's not too late."

He turned and held her gaze for a minute before looking away. But it was long enough for her to catch a glimpse of sadness wash through his eyes.

"That's where you are wrong. For me, it's too late."

hat the fuck was wrong with him? Barrett let out a low growl. His breath turned to cold smoke in the Colorado weather. He lifted the ax over his head and brought the blade down hard and fast on the log. It split clean and even all the way down.

Barrett grabbed another log with one hand and set it on end. He repeated the action and split the log in two with a single stroke of the blade.

He didn't need any more wood for the fireplace in his loft. He'd had plenty of logs split.

What he did need was an excuse to get away from Jacey.

He let out another growl and split another log. He bent and stacked the log on the ever-growing pile of firewood.

Not only was he on edge after what had happened last night to Jacey, he was overdue from hearing anything from Ryker. They had a schedule. Ryker would call him once a month on Thursday. They wouldn't use each other's names and would speak in code, talking about the weather. They had agreed before Ryker left never to talk about Pack business on the phone. Although they had secure lines, Ryker was paranoid as fuck and was afraid someone would discover that Barrett was indeed alive.

That would put his Pack in jeopardy.

Maybe Ryker had grown tired of calling him. Maybe Ryker had settled back into the new Pack now. Maybe Ryker had forgotten him.

It was probably for the best.

Besides, if Ryker knew that Jacey was in his loft upstairs, he would freak the fuck out. Ryker would see her as a threat to his safety if she found out who and what he was.

Not that he would allow that to happen. His old life was behind him. This was his life now. His burden to carry.

He growled as he brought the ax down across the wood in a hard, deadly stroke.

Why couldn't Ryker just have left him dead? Why did he think he had to bring him back? It's not like he had anything special now. He didn't have a position, a job, or a purpose.

He was just the owner of an obscure bar and grill. And the only danger he'd faced was the episode last night when he rescued Jacey.

He grinned as he thought about the look on those hunters' faces when he launched himself at them.

It felt good to get back in the game and kick some ass. If only for a little bit.

He stopped and glanced at the growing pile of split wood. He'd been out here for half an hour working nonstop and hadn't even broken a sweat.

He brought his ax down on the empty chopping block and glanced up at his loft apartment.

She'd fallen asleep after drinking her tea.

When she woke up she would be starving. He trudged through the snow and walked back to his building. He didn't have much food in his kitchen. He would stop at the bar and grill and grab some things to make them something to eat and then go retrieve Jacey's clothes. Afterwards he would call Helen and tell her not to come in. He didn't want to leave Jacey alone tonight so he would just close the bar. With the weather they were having, there wouldn't be that many customers out anyway.

Like Helen had said. He needed to start taking a break and closing the bar one night a week.

No time like the present.

* * *

JACEY HAD BEEN unable to fall back to sleep after Barrett left. She wrapped the sheet around her body and took the time to look at his apartment.

She noticed that he didn't have any pictures on the walls, and no personal items decorated his kitchen counter. On his nightstand, there was just a lamp and an old wind-up clock.

If it hadn't been for the big screen TV sitting on the wall, the loft would have looked abandoned.

Maybe this is how all males liked to live. Minimalistic.

She walked over to the small window that overlooked the back of the building. Barrett was there, bare chest and only wearing jeans and boots. He lifted the ax over his head and split the log of wood in one swipe. He put another log on the chopping block and repeated the action.

She watched unable to tear her gaze away from him. The muscles in his back rippled under the motion and she felt her stomach grow warm with desire.

He was absolutely stunning.

She took a deep breath and forced herself to step away from the window. She walked to the other side of the room where the windows looked down over the main street of the tiny town.

The snow was still falling, blanketing the street in a thick layer of white. She didn't see any tire tracks where vehicles were driving around. In weather like this, people would be snuggled up inside by a fire with a nice cup of hot chocolate.

Her stomach growled, and she placed her hand on her belly.

As much as she was starving, she desperately craved a shower. She wanted to wash the memory of last night off her flesh.

She held up her injured hand. The flesh had healed and even the dark bruises she had were now gone. She curled her hand into a fist. She smiled when she didn't feel any pain. Barrett's tea must have done the trick.

She pressed her lips together and debated whether she should wait on Barrett to come inside before she grabbed a shower.

She didn't debate long. She still caught a whiff of the hunters on her body and didn't want the reminder anymore.

Tucking her sheet under her arm she padded over to the bathroom and closed the door. She rifled under the sink cabinet and found a clean towel and washcloth. Turning to the bathtub, she turned on the shower and let the sheet fall to the floor. She spotted a black robe hanging on the back of the door. She would just have to wear that until she got her clothes.

She stepped into the spray of the hot water and sighed. Grabbing the soap, she lathered up and scrubbed her skin until it was rosy. If she could have, she would have rubbed herself raw. If it meant deleting last night's scene from her head.

Maybe coming here had been a bad idea. Maybe she should have just stayed in Mississippi and lived under the shadow of shame of being an outcast. It wouldn't have been an easy life, but it would have been safer.

No. She couldn't have stayed. If she had, she would have

died under the scrutiny of what others were saying about her and how she was found lacking.

At least here, no one knew her. At least here, she could start over. She could stay here and save enough money until she could figure out what she wanted to do and where she wanted to go next.

She was still young and practically had her whole life ahead of her.

She wasn't going to let one male destroy her forever.

She would never fall in love again.

CHAPTER 18

*R*yker looked over his shoulder, cut his eyes at Zane, and picked up his pace. After having it out with Damon, Zane had been tailing him ever since. He couldn't seem to shake the fucker.

"Ryker. Wait up," Zane called out.

Ryker groaned and turned to face Zane. "What do you want?"

"I want to talk to you."

"Yeah. Well, I got shit to do." Ryker kept walking toward his bike. He was well overdue for a call to Barrett. He knew he could only call during the day because Barrett never heard his phone over the noise of the bar at night. But every time Ryker picked up his phone to call, one of the Guardians was there, on his ass.

He didn't doubt that Damon had probably put them up to it to find out why he was being so secretive.

"I said wait up!" Zane thundered. He matched Ryker's steps and caught up to him.

He grabbed Ryker's arm. Ryker spun around and shoved Zane away. "Don't fucking touch me, dude."

Zane glared and curled his fingers into large fists. He kept them at his sides. Ryker wondered if the Were would actually hit him or if he was putting on a show. Zane prided himself on his self-control, but by the looks Ryker was getting, he didn't put it past the Guardians to try to knock him on his ass.

"What's your deal?" Zane growled. "Look, I know you were close with Barrett, but you better fucking start getting used to Damon being Pack Master."

"I've never said anything about Damon being Pack Master," Ryker countered.

"No, but everyone here knows you are still mourning Barrett." Zane took a deep breath and looked up at the sky. He lowered his gaze to him. "Look, everyone is sorry that Barrett's gone. But you need to move on. You need to accept that."

"What the fuck do you know about it, Zane?" Ryker shook his head. "Look, contrary to everyone's expert belief, I have moved on. I know that Barrett is gone."

"Do you? I mean, since he died, you're never around."

"I'm working, doing my job as a Guardian. Maybe you should try it."

"And when you're not working you keep your distance from the rest of us."

"Which is something I did long before Barrett died." That much was true.

Zane forked his fingers through his hair and shook his head. "Now everything is different. You need to make more of an effort to be part of the team. We all need you."

"Well, if I had known this was going to be some kind of sentimental movie of the week, I would have brought my Kleenex."

Zane fought a smile and lost.

"Look, just because I don't need to be around all you

fuckers twenty-four seven, doesn't mean I'm not part of the Pack. I can wipe my own ass, you know."

"Thank God for that." Zane snorted.

The tension between them lifted.

"Look, just do me a favor and go to the gym tonight. Work out with some of the other Guardians. Eat a meal with them."

"If you start singing 'Kum Ba Yah,' I'm going to punch you in your ugly face," Ryker scowled.

Zane let out a laugh. "You're just jealous of my good looks. Skylar tells me how handsome I am all the time."

"I think Skylar needs glasses," Ryker groused.

Lucien walked out of the Guardian Compound. He walked over and looked from him to Zane.

"Is everything okay here?" Lucien asked Zane.

"No. Zane is getting all mushy with me. You might want to tell Skylar her mate is swinging the other way," Ryker scowled.

Lucien grinned. "Aww. Sounds like you two need some bro time together."

"Not likely," Ryker stated.

"Sounds like you need some bro time with all the Guardians." Lucien crossed his arms over his chest and grinned like an idiot. "Why don't you come over to Granny's tonight and eat dinner?"

"Ah, no." Ryker shook his head. He knew all about Granny. He knew the old lady cooked for the Guardians and their mates. He would be the only one without a mate if he showed up. It would look weird.

"Come on, man," Zane said. "Damon will be there. Besides, if he sees you showing up, then he'll get off your ass."

Ryker arched his brow. He needed Damon to ease up. Maybe having dinner was a good idea.

"You think?" Ryker cocked his head.

"He'll get off your ass a little," Zane admitted.

"Yeah, I mean, what do you have to lose? Go have a great meal, try to be social, and don't try to hit anyone." Lucien punched him in the arm.

Going to Granny's was the last thing he wanted to be doing. Maybe Lucien was right. If he showed up, it would make it look like he was making an effort to be social. Maybe Damon would grant him some leeway after that.

He studied the two Weres and finally nodded. "Fine. But on one condition." He held his finger up to make a point.

"Sure, what it is?" Zane asked.

"Don't make me sit by Granny. The last thing I need is to have her showing me all her merchandise and trying to make a sale," Ryker grumbled.

CHAPTER 19

*R*yker walked into Granny's house and sighed. He was beginning to think he'd made a mistake by coming over.

"Ryker, I'm so glad you were able to join us for dinner." Granny gave him a big smile and patted him on the shoulder with a wrinkled hand. "And since you didn't bring a date or have a mate, you can sit by me."

Ryker glared at Lucien who was covering up his laughter with a cough.

He looked at him and mouthed the word *fucker.*

Catty elbowed Lucien hard in the ribs. He stopped laughing and rubbed his side.

Ryker grinned.

"Sit down and we can get this dinner started," Granny said.

He pulled out the only empty chair at the table and sat. He glanced around, uneasy at the tight quarters.

Damon sat opposite of him with Ava at his side. Lucien and his mate, Catty, sat next to Ava. Zane and Skyler sat next to Ryker while Jayden and his mate, Haley, sat next to Skyler.

It was a full house. Exactly what he didn't want.

Granny placed an enormous turkey on the middle of the table and clasped her hands together. "Everyone dig in."

"Granny, I thought you were saving this turkey for Christmas?" Ava asked as she passed a dish full of green beans to Damon. "Everything here looks like holiday food."

Ryker looked at the delicious assortment of food on the table. Ava was right. There was green bean casserole, sweet potato casserole, turkey, large dish of dressing, mashed potatoes and gravy, homemade cranberry sauce, and five different kinds of pie on the buffet table along the wall which, according to the scent, including apple, peach, and chocolate.

"I decided I'm not waiting to celebrate holidays anymore." The old lady gave a sad smile and a shrug. "I mean, life is meant to be lived in the moment. If I took nothing else from Barrett's death, it's that. From now on, it's china plates at every meal."

"You'd be better off skipping the china plates because someone has to wash those by hand and just go with serving your best liquor," Ryker quipped.

Everyone stopped piling food on their plates and looked at him.

"What?" he scowled. Couldn't he have an opinion?

"Ryker is right." Granny slapped her hand on the table and stood. "I have a bottle of Wild Turkey that I've had for years. Never opened it up." She scurried back into the kitchen.

"Great, Ryker. Now she's going to get sloshed." Damon arched his eyebrow. "She's hard enough to handle sober, but once she's drunk, she's like a category five hurricane."

Ryker bit back a grin and a smart-ass reply.

"She's old enough to do what she wants," Catty agreed. "Besides, I'm one of the few females at the table that can drink." She pointed her fork at Ava. "You're preggers so no hooch for you."

Ava grinned and touched her hand to her rounded stomach.

"Well, I don't drink Wild Turkey," Haley grimaced. "I've tried to get Granny to start drinking wine, but she likes the hard stuff."

"I'll take a drink with her." Skylar rolled her shoulders. "Maybe it will help me sleep. I've been so stressed these last few months."

"That's right. SKYLAR'S HOME will be opening soon," Haley said. "Are we going to have a big celebration? A ribbon cutting?"

"No." Skylar shook her head and looked around the table. "I've been talking to Zane, and I would really like to keep it quiet. I don't want a whole lot of publicity."

"Why?" Ryker asked and forked some green beans into his mouth.

"Well, because I don't want too many humans poking around. While SKYLAR'S HOME will be open to both at risk human and Were females, I'm afraid if I get too many people poking around, they are going to discover our existence."

"Why don't you just keep it for Weres? Not include humans at all." To Ryker, it didn't make sense to have a facility that would include both humans and werewolves in an intimate setting. Things happened and all they needed was one human seeing a Were shift, and they would be selling their story to any news outlet that would listen.

"Because everyone needs our help, not just female Weres," Skylar said softly and met his gaze. "I don't want to be exclusive with who I will help and who I won't."

Ryker nodded. He might not agree with her reasoning, but he could respect her opinion and integrity.

"Here we go." Granny returned with a dusty bottle of whiskey. The label was old and peeling and covered in dust.

"Eww, Granny. That thing looks like it was buried out back. Are you sure it's still good?" Jayden sneered.

"Yes, I'm sure. I had this in my secret place that nobody ever looks." Granny smiled broadly.

"Why does that make me worry?" Jayden looked horrified and worried at the same time. Ryker grinned. At least the attention was off him and on the old lady.

"Ryker, would you do me a favor and open this?" Granny passed him the bottle.

He put down his fork and twisted the cap off the bottle. He handed the bottle back to the old woman and went back to eating.

Granny went to the china cabinet and took down some crystal cut glasses. She placed them on the table and poured an equal amount into each glass.

"If you don't want yours, I'll take it," she said as she walked around table passing out the alcohol.

"No, you won't." Jayden glared. "That's the last thing you need."

"What's that supposed to mean?" Granny took her seat and glared at her grandson over her glass of Wild Turkey.

"It means, if you get drunk, there is no telling what kind of trouble you'll get yourself into," Jayden said. He sat back in his chair and waved his fork in her direction.

"Jayden Allister Parker. If you so much as bring up the whole Valentine's debacle, I'm going to take you over my knee," Granny growled the words out of her mouth.

"I'd like to see that." Damon nodded. "I'll even post a pic on Instagram for you."

"You aren't on Instagram." Jayden narrowed his eyes. "Besides, you should be on my side, whether you're Pack Master or not."

Damon shrugged. "She's your grandmother."

"She's kind of your grandmother too." Ava looked up at her mate and smiled. "I mean she did raise you when you were in Louisiana."

"Why don't you make a toast since this is your idea, Granny?" Zane lifted his glass in the air and stared at her.

"Thank you, dear." She gave him a smile and then cut her eyes at Jayden. "At least we have one gentleman at the table." She patted Ryker on the shoulder. "I want to apologize to you, Ryker, for all this foolishness. This is your first time here, and these fools are making a laughingstock out of me."

"Want me to kick their ass?" Ryker asked.

"Why, I just might take you up on that offer." Granny nodded her head.

"Hey, why are you letting him get away with bad language?" Jayden's mouth dropped open, and he looked offended.

"Because he said ass. And ass is actually a word in the Bible." She glared.

"Sweet Jesus," Jayden muttered.

"Jayden, watch your mouth!" Granny thundered.

"What? Jesus is in the Bible." Jayden stared at her with wide eyes.

Haley elbowed her mate, and he gave both her and Granny a scowl.

"You could take him out back now, Ryker." Granny huffed.

"Can I finish my turkey first?" He took another bite and chewed thoughtfully. His first time at Granny's was proving more entertaining than he'd planned.

"Sure, honey." She gave him another pat on the back, and he scooped a generous helping of sweet potato casserole onto his plate.

Damon snorted.

"Granny. The toast." Ava held up her water glass and motioned for the old lady to continue.

Granny nodded and took a deep breath. She held her glass out in front of her body and cleared her throat.

"I'd like to say, there's nothing like family. And that each one of you is special to me and to each other. As a Pack, we may not always see eye to eye, but we always have each other's back. Arkansas has suffered a difficult blow and while it may have crippled us, it certainly hasn't paralyzed us. Barrett was a good and fair leader. His memory will be with us forever." She clinked her glass to Ryker's and then the others around the table.

Ryker shifted in his seat. Talking about Barrett always made him on edge. Like someone could see into his head and see the truth.

That their leader wasn't dead at all.

Everyone clinked glasses and then tossed the whiskey or water back in a show of solidarity.

"That was a nice toast, Granny," Damon said quietly.

For the first time, Ryker studied his new Pack Master. He could see the indecision written on his face, and he knew it must be difficult to step into the shoes of someone that everyone thought so highly of.

He would hate to be in Damon's place.

"Thanks, honey." She gave him a smile and refilled everyone's glass.

She lifted her glass, and everyone followed her lead. "And this is to the new Pack Master of Arkansas. May he lead well and wise and with respect."

"Hell, yeah." Jayden smiled and tossed his whiskey back.

"Jayden … ." Granny warned.

"I'm done with my turkey. Want me to take him out back now, Granny?" Ryker asked.

"Please," Granny said with a smirk on her lips.

Everyone around the table erupted in laughter. Even Ryker cracked a smile.

Damon stood and carried his plate over to the buffet. He cut a generous slice of apple pie and walked back. Before he sat, he clapped Ryker on the shoulder.

"I knew you wouldn't regret coming here tonight. I think you're officially Granny's new favorite. Just be careful when she starts pulling out her magazines." Damon smirked.

Ryker suddenly lost his appetite and pushed his plate away. "The ones with her merchandise?" He knew the old woman sold sex toys. He wanted no part of it.

"Yeah. Those ones." Damon snorted.

Once again, the room erupted in laughter.

CHAPTER 20

*J*acey stepped out of the shower and wrapped herself in Barrett's large robe. It engulfed her, but she didn't care. It was warm and smelled like him. She buried her face in the collar of the robe and inhaled deep. Her stomach warmed.

She secured the tie on the robe and opened the door. Standing there with a look of shock was Barrett.

"I, uh … I didn't have any clothes so I borrowed your robe." Her voice cracked.

"That's fine." He nodded, licked his lips, and looked away. "I found your clothes. I put them in the dryer to get them warm. After I make you something to eat, you can get dressed. I can't take you back to Mena's dressed wearing nothing but a robe. I'm sure she'd have something to say."

He looked back at her. His gaze darkened, and suddenly she was warm, too warm.

"I'll make you something to eat." He stepped away from the door and walked into the open kitchen. She followed after him, running her hands through her still wet hair. She regretted not drying it.

"You don't have to make me anything." She sat on the barstool of the kitchen island.

He pulled a skillet off the hanging rack and grinned at her. "Despite my failure as a cook at the bar, I can make a good breakfast. Bacon and eggs. It's ingrained in my male DNA."

His smile was dazzling, and she was pretty sure it would work on any female he applied it to.

She nodded and watched as he put some sliced bacon into a skillet. The meat sizzled and popped, filling the space with a delicious aroma.

"Is it too late for coffee?" He looked at her.

"Not for me. I can drink caffeine all night and still fall asleep." She shrugged. "It doesn't have that effect on me like it does on everyone else."

He pulled down two mugs and filled them with coffee.

He placed a mug in front of her with a packet of sugar and a small container of milk.

She smiled and waved him away. "I drink it black."

"Really?" He arched a brow. "Me too."

He took a sip of his own coffee and then went back to tending to the bacon. They sat in silence as he lifted the crisp pieces and placed them on a plate covered with a paper towel. He grabbed the carton of eggs, cracked and spilled them into the skillet of bacon grease. She watched as he skillfully flipped the eggs over easy style and then put a couple of slices of bread into a toaster. He pulled out a small jar of blackberry jelly and some butter and set them both on the kitchen island.

"Are you sure you don't want me to do anything?" She crossed her arms over herself.

"No, just sit there and talk to me," he said.

"You don't have to go to all this trouble." She shifted in her seat. "I really should be getting back to ... "

She looked away.

"Were you going to say home?"

She cleared her throat. "Mena's. I should get back to Mena's."

"Too late. The eggs are done." He shrugged. "Besides, I'm starving too. What kind of host would I be if I made you cook for me?"

"Thank you," she said quietly. He went about his work in the kitchen, and she looked around at the bare apartment.

"So how long have you lived in Colorado?" She looked back at him. "You don't strike me as someone who grew up here."

"Colorado isn't my original home. I've lived here only a few months."

"Where is your original home?" She lifted the mug and took a sip of the hot coffee.

He turned and looked directly at her. "Not Colorado," he said.

What did it matter where he was from unless … unless he was hiding?

"You aren't from Missouri, are you?" Fear tightened her throat. Missouri was a rogue state. It had no governing Pack Master and was a haven for all manner of werewolves who were criminals.

"Absolutely not," he groused.

She could tell he was telling her the truth about that. So why would he not tell her where he was from?

"It's not fair, you know."

"What's not fair?" He frowned at her.

"You know more about me than I do you."

"Just because you told me you are from Mississippi and you left your unfaithful mate doesn't mean we know each other's life histories," he said.

"But it does mean you know more about me than I know about you. I mean, for all I know you could be a serial killer."

He barked out a laugh. "If I was, why are you still alive?"

She shrugged. "Maybe because you're waiting to lure me into feeling safe before you kill me."

He gave her a droll look. "Sweetheart, that sounds like a lot of time and trouble. Two things I'm in short supply of."

This time she was the one who smiled.

He served up the breakfast on two plates he pulled out of the cabinet. He set the plated meal in front of her. Her stomach rumbled, and she gave him a sheepish grin.

He grabbed his plate and sat down on the stool next to her. They both began eating.

She swallowed the tasty food and gave him a look of appreciation. "This is really good."

"I'm glad you like it." He took a bite of his bacon, chewed, and swallowed. "Want to talk about what happened last night?"

"I never should have been out there." She shook her head and set her fork down. "Nothing would have happened if I just would have stayed inside." Tears burned the backs of her eyes, and she blinked to hold them in.

"Listen to me." He reached over and smoothed a wayward strand of hair out of her eyes. "You did nothing wrong. Those humans were the ones in the wrong. They were out there hunting and capturing wolves. If I ever see them again, I'll end both of them."

His deep voice made her shiver. And not in a good way.

"I have a feeling they aren't going anywhere. They'll be back," she said softly and took a bite of her eggs.

"What makes you say that?" He froze and leaned in closer.

"From what they said. It sounded like they were trying to capture as many wolves as possible." She shrugged. "I thought it was illegal to kill wolves for their fur." The thought made her sick to her stomach.

"It is illegal." He studied his cup. "I've not had any problems with hunters since I've lived here. I've never even had them come into the bar. Maybe they were passing through."

"Maybe." Unease snaked up her spine.

He reached over and rested his hand on her arm. She looked up into intense blue eyes. "You are safe here, Jacey. And the next time you want to run, let me know. I'll go with you."

"Really?" Her eyes grew wide. "You'd run with me?"

"Sure." He moved his hand away and focused on his plate. "You're the only other wolf I've seen in these parts. It's not like I have anyone else to run with."

Her heart fell. She wasn't special. Not to him.

She lifted her head and glanced out the window. The snow had finally stopped falling and covering the tiny town in a quilt of white.

She wasn't going to stay in this place forever. She just needed to stay long enough to heal her heart and get her shit together. Once she had a little bit of money and a clear direction on where she wanted to go in life, she was going to start living her life.

She shrugged off her hurt feelings. It was good that Barrett wasn't interested in her. For her mental sanity, it was good. She didn't need to be getting involved with anyone so soon after her break up. She needed this time to focus on her and what she wanted to do.

She looked back at him and nodded. "Next Friday. After the bar closes and everyone is asleep. I'd like to go for a run then."

"Okay." He nodded.

"I didn't get to go very far this run. They captured me pretty close to Mena's."

"I know." He opened one of the doors in the kitchen and pulled her clothes out.

She let out a sigh. "I would have figured the snow would have covered them up."

"They fell out of the tree. I had to dig them out of the snow. Another plus to having a kick-ass sense of smell. I can track like a bloodhound."

She laughed. He broke into a grin.

"Thank you." She took another sip. "I look forward to our next run. I didn't want to stop running once I started. It had been so long."

"I know what you mean." He shook his head. "There are not a lot of Weres in Colorado so you need to be careful when you're out."

"The last thing I need is outing my species to the human world. If Jack Welbourn found out, he'd skin me alive."

"I doubt that. He's more of a softy than people realize." Barrett shrugged.

"You know him?" Her eyes widened.

He stiffened. His expression shuttered. "No, not personally." He grabbed his partially eaten breakfast and stuck the plate in the sink.

She'd hit an unintentional nerve.

It was time for her to leave. She could tell from his closed body language that he was shutting himself down and wasn't in the mood to talk.

"This was really great. Thank you." She stood and grabbed her folded clothes off the kitchen counter. "I'll change really quick and head on over to Mena's. I need to get ready for work tonight."

He frowned. "You think you're ready to head back to work so soon?"

"Yeah, I do." She didn't tell him that she didn't want to

spend another night alone. After what happened, she'd rather keep busy so her mind would be occupied.

"I was thinking you could take the night off …"

"Absolutely not." She shook her head. Her funds were dwindling fast, not counting the fact that she still needed to pay him back for the clothes he'd bought her. She wasn't going to be beholden to any male. Not ever again.

"Trust me. I'm tougher than I look."

He turned and faced her, and his face broke into a wicked smile. "I have no doubt about that."

Her body heated in places she'd never heated with Jeremy. But one look from Barrett and she was practically a puddle on the floor.

She nodded and scurried into the safety of the bathroom to change.

CHAPTER 21

"*F*uck it." Ryker pulled out his cell phone and dialed the number of The Mountain Top Bar and Grille. He hated calling Barrett at night. It took forever for someone to answer the fucking phone, and it usually wasn't Barrett doing the answering. It was usually that human, Helen, who wouldn't shut up.

"Hello," Barrett's gruff voice came over the line.

"You do realize that you should answer the phone 'The Mountain Top Bar and Grille,'" Ryker growled.

"Fuck off, Ryker," Barrett growled.

"Now see, that's how you're not going to grow your business." Ryker snorted.

"I'm busy as fuck right now, what do you want?"

"Well, Miss Manners, I'm calling to check on you. Like usual."

"No, not like usual. You're almost a week late. And you never called during the day."

"Aww, did you miss me?" Ryker deadpanned. He wished he could see the look on Barrett's face. He needed the entertainment. "Look, Damon's been on my ass."

"He doesn't suspect anything, does he?" He heard the urgency in Barrett's tone. The background noise got a little muffled like he had walked to a different part of the bar.

"Actually, he thinks I'm being insubordinate. He says I'm still mourning you."

"Good."

"What do you mean good? Do you know he made me go to dinner at Granny's?" Ryker groused.

Barrett let out a loud laugh.

Ryker grinned. He'd not heard Barrett laugh in ... well, forever.

"Did she try to sell you some of her merch?" Barrett asked, his tone full of amusement.

"Well, she did let me eat first." He didn't want to go over how the old lady had pulled out her catalogue full of adult toys and was asking him if he was interested in purchasing anything. He was surprised he managed to keep his dinner down after that.

Barrett let out another loud laugh.

"Jesus, man, you laugh like a fucking hyena," Ryker groused.

"Well, you do provide your own entertainment."

"Things that dull around there, huh? No excitement?" Ryker nodded. That was good. Barrett needed to stay invisible and out of any kind of trouble. His life depended on it.

"I wouldn't say that. Had some human hunters trap a female Were last night. Doubt they'll be back after they got a look at me."

"Shit. You didn't fucking shift out in front of them, did you?" Ryker tightened his fingers on the cell phone.

"Hell, no. I was already in wolf form. But I did want to rip their livers out."

"You didn't do that, did you?" Ryker's chest tightened. They didn't need dead humans on their hands.

"Didn't have a chance. I had to get the female out of there."

"Is she okay?" Ryker had a bad feeling about the direction of this conversation.

"She's healed."

"And so, she's leaving, right? When I checked out that bar and grill, I made sure there were no Weres anywhere near it. Please tell me the female is gone." Ryker narrowed his eyes.

"She's not gone. She works for me."

"Fuck, Barrett."

"Watch your tone," Barrett thundered over the phone.

"No, you listen to me, Barrett. You get that female out of there now. Fire her and tell her to keep moving. Tell her it's too dangerous. Tell her to go home."

"She has no money and nowhere else to go. Her mate broke their bond and brought another female into their house. She can't go back to Mississippi."

"Mississippi? Are you fucking kidding me?" Ryker yelled into the phone. "This just keeps getting better and better."

"She doesn't know anything. Not about me. So just calm the fuck down." Barrett murmured into the phone.

"Somehow that doesn't put me at ease, Barrett. Just one slip up. Just one and our whole Pack is in danger."

"Don't you start lecturing me about protecting the Pack, you asshole. I protected the Pack with my own life. I died for my Pack. And if you hadn't messed things up by involving that witch and that fairy, I would still be dead." Barrett growled.

"Did you want me to let you die? Is that what you wanted?" Ryker snarled. He sure as fuck felt like putting Barrett's ass in the ground right now.

"I want people to stop interfering in my life. I want to be left the fuck alone," Barrett stated.

"Fine. You got your wish." Ryker ended the call and tried to catch his breath. Rage and worry filled his chest.

Barrett was a fucking fool.

He was going to get his identity found out and put the whole Pack in danger.

He needed to get up to Colorado and fast before Barrett did something foolish.

* * *

JACEY IGNORED Barrett's command about taking the night off. She walked into the bar a little after six and headed straight for the kitchen. Barrett had taken one look at her and proceeded to follow her through the swinging double doors.

"I thought I told you to take the night off." He narrowed his gaze on her.

She grabbed a white apron and tied it around her waist.

"And I decided to come in anyway. I can use the money." She kept her hands busy, running a finger across the cold grill and making sure it was clean. She went to the industrial-sized freezer and pulled out a bag of fries and laid it on the counter.

"Jacey, you don't need to be here tonight." He gently reached for her hand and held it up.

Her breath caught in her throat at his warm touch, and she knew she needed to say something to fill the awkward silence.

How could someone so big and intimidating have such a gentle side?

His gaze landed on her injured hand, and her breathing increased. She was such a mess when she was this close to him.

"Go home. Rest. You're not ready to be back at work." Barrett narrowed his intense gaze on her.

She snatched her hand away.

"I'm not ready to be alone right now." The words blurted out like a boulder rolling down a hill. "I'd rather be working where I know it's safe than be stuck in that room thinking about what happened." She wasn't about to tell him about her nightmares she'd had during the day, that she could feel eyes on her, watching her through her second-story window. She'd woken from her nap that afternoon with a heaviness in her chest. She knew then she was safer at work surrounded by a million people than staying alone where her mind would race with dangerous thoughts.

He blinked. Yet said nothing.

"Let me stay." Her words were a whisper yet, she knew he heard them above the buzz of the bar drifting in through the door.

"I was going to close but Helen said we could manage by ourselves. I don't know how many customers we'll get but if you want to stay, it's okay." He nodded once.

Relief spread through her body.

"Thank you." Without thinking, she walked over and stood on her tiptoes. She pressed her lips to his cheek.

And then realized what she'd done. Her face heated and she stepped back, studying the floor.

Silently, he turned and left her alone in the kitchen. She looked up and let out the breath she didn't realize she'd been holding the whole time after she confessed why she wanted to stay.

The harsh glare of the overhead lights gave her a sense of security and safety.

Darkness could not hide anywhere in this room. In here, her kitchen and sanctuary, darkness could not harm her.

CHAPTER 22

*J*acey spent the rest of the night in the kitchen filling orders for a hungry crowd. The Mountain Top Bar and Grille was the only bar open during the winter on the mountain. So, after it being closed for a couple of days, the local patrons were eager to get in and get their drink and grub on.

And that was fine by her.

She fidgeted, shifting her weight from foot to foot as she glanced at the clock. The bar had closed an hour ago, and she'd long since finished washing the last dirty glass. She couldn't believe she'd kissed Barrett.

She embarrassed herself as well as him.

Groaning, she closed her eyes and wrinkled her nose.

"Are you okay, honey?" Helen frowned as she came through the double doors. She took off her waitress apron and hung it on a hook on the wall.

She cracked open an eye and looked at Helen. "I'm fine. Was just thinking about walking back to Mena's in this cold." While it had stopped snowing, the temperature was still below freezing.

"I'll give you a ride, honey." Helen smiled broadly. "Just let me grab my purse from behind the bar."

"Thanks, Helen. I appreciate it." Jacey sighed. If she rode with Helen, at least she wouldn't have to face Barrett.

Her stomach knotted as she replayed the scene of those hunters trapping her. While she'd been here cooking, her hands and mind had been busy, too busy to think about how she'd been captured.

It scared her to think about what they would have done if Barrett hadn't rescued her.

Where would they have taken her? What kind of horrors were they going to do to her? How would they have killed her?

She shook her head and took a deep breath. She needed to get a grip.

She was here. Safe. With Barrett.

Groaning, she closed her eyes.

"Are you okay?" Barrett's deep voice made her jump.

She spun around and nodded. "Yes, I'm fine. I was just waiting on Helen. She was going to give me a ride."

"I told her I could take you back home. If that's okay." He cocked his head, watching her reaction.

"Sure. I just don't want to be an imposition," she lied and untied the apron, making sure she avoided looking into his eyes.

"You're far from an imposition." He took a step closer and picked up her hand.

She sucked in a hiss.

"Did that hurt?" He frowned.

"No." How could she say that just him touching her had her heart stopping mid-beat? Or made her stomach turn to hot caramel. She would sound like an idiot.

He nodded and walked over to the freezer. He opened the door and looked inside. "We should have an order coming soon. I hadn't anticipated everyone ordering so if the supplies don't get here soon, we will run out of food."

"That sounds like a good problem to have." She nodded.

"And you are the reason for it. Not me." He turned and looked at her. "Everyone loves your cooking. Even Abraham who hates everything."

"Abraham? You mean the old man that sits at the end of the bar and never says anything but glares?" She had noticed him the first night, and every time she stuck her head out the kitchen, she cut her eyes over at him. At first, she thought he was just a miserable, mean man. But upon further assessment and the way he actually gave a little bit of a smile when Helen would stop and talk to him, she realized that he wasn't mean. He was just lonely.

She could identify.

Ever since she left her home in Mississippi, certain things had become clearer to her.

Like how lonely she had been in her marriage.

It embarrassed her to admit it. She thought she'd been in love with Jeremy. But over the last few days, she wondered if he knew what love was.

Barrett hadn't humiliated or blamed her for getting caught by those hunters. Jeremy would have.

Nor did Barrett tell her she'd done anything wrong. Jeremy certainly would have blamed her.

And Jeremy would not have cooked breakfast for her like Barrett had. In fact, Jeremy had never cooked her a meal the entire time they were together. Even on their anniversary, he expected her to have a nice meal on the table.

Barrett grinned. "Even Abraham. Sounds like you're winning a lot of people over with your cooking."

"I'm more than just a cook." She shot back, still lost in her thoughts about her former mate.

"I know that." His smile faded, and he cocked his head. "I

didn't mean to give you the impression that cooking was all you could do."

She shook her head and glanced down at the tile floor. "I'm sorry. I didn't mean to snap." She took a deep breath and looked back up at him. "It's just that, after so many years of being fit into a specific box, I finally want to do something different. Be something different." She grimaced. "That sounds weird, doesn't it?"

"No, not weird at all. Actually, it makes a lot of sense." He nodded and leaned a hip against the stainless-steel counter-top. "You are now trying to find a different way to live. Trying on a new life."

"Yeah. Exactly." Her eyes widened. "It's exciting and scary. And to be honest, when those hunters captured me, I wanted to go back to my old life in Mississippi." She sighed. "I feel like a coward for admitting that."

"Jacey, you're not a coward. You were just wanting to feel safe."

"You're being too kind." She gave him a smile.

"That's a first. I've never been told I'm too kind," he deadpanned.

She laughed.

It brought out a grin from his handsome face.

"You must have been some kind of a therapist before you moved here." She narrowed her eyes. "Now that I've told you my secret, you have to tell me yours. Were you a therapist?"

He snorted and straightened. "If herding a bunch of crazy assholes into being productive is a therapist, then yeah."

He walked over to the light switch on the wall and turned to her. "Come on. Let's get out of here. It's been a crazy night."

She nodded, wishing he had finished telling her his story. Of how he ended up in Colorado where the ratio of Weres to humans was incredibly low. He looked like a male who could be anything he wanted, go anywhere he wanted. To her, being in Colorado was the last place she would pick to live.

She had ended up here because she needed peace and distance. Once she gathered her equilibrium of her life, she was going to move on.

This was not her forever home. And Barrett was not her forever mate.

CHAPTER 23

"*W*hat's the word on Boudier?" Damon spoke into the cell phone while he looked around the activity swirling around the Guardians Compound. His Guardians–damn, that sounded weird—were hustling, getting on their Harleys as incoming Guardians were getting off work. Since Boudier escaped, Damon managed to keep his Guardians on watch twenty-four seven, with rotating shifts every twelve hours.

He knew it was hard on his men, making them work overtime, but he needed to get Edward Boudier at all costs. He wanted Boudier to pay with his blood.

"There was a lead in Nebraska. One of the Nebraska Guardians had a tip that Boudier was spotted at a truck stop off the interstate. By the time they got there, he was gone. But the civilian Were who spotted him said he got into a truck that was headed north," Zane said.

"He's going to try to get to Missouri," he murmured.

Missouri was a rogue state. There was no Pack Master, and all manner of criminal activity ran amuck in the state.

"Once he crosses into the state, we can't extradite him," Zane stated.

"Why the fuck didn't they ever put a Pack Master in Missouri?" Damon growled and tightened his hold on his phone.

"Because when the Packs were founded years and years ago, they decided there needed to be a safe haven state where falsely accused Weres could find amnesty until they could prove their case. Don't forget Braxton. That's where he was headed when he was falsely accused."

"I know, I know. But there has to be a better way to make sure the real criminals pay. It's not fair."

"Life's not fair," Zane said quietly. Damon could hear the tone in his voice, and he knew the Were was thinking about Barrett and his death.

"Stay on the trail. I'm sending Braxton and Jayden to Missouri to see if they can find anything out." Damon narrowed his eyes.

"Even if they find him there, they can't just bring him back. It's the law."

"If they find him, I guarantee you, Zane, I'll have them drag his sorry ass across the Arkansas line, and I'll serve my own justice." Damon ended the call. He didn't want to hear any more words of fair and just and law.

He wanted Boudier dead, his head on a stick.

He wasn't going to stop until the deed was done.

His eyes landed on a very sexy brunette walking down the sidewalk with a Styrofoam cup of coffee and a white bag. She met his gaze and smiled.

His chest expanded, and his heart lifted.

"Hey, baby," Ava said and snuggled into his chest.

His arms went around her back, and he held her close, inhaling her sweet scent.

She looked up at him and jiggled the bag behind his back. "I brought you something."

He hadn't eaten that morning. He had just enough time to grab a coffee on his way out the door. That was around four a.m. It was almost noon.

"Thanks, babe." He took the coffee she held out to him and took a drink. The black brew was just what he needed. He had a long day ahead of him.

"And donuts." She smiled and unwrapped the top of the white bag. She pulled out a glazed donut, and he gladly took it.

He bit into the sugary confection and groaned with delight. His stomach growled.

"Let's sit." He motioned to a decorative iron bench sitting in front of the Compound. He followed her over and sat down beside her. He finished off his donut, and she handed him another one.

She grinned and fished a jelly donut out of the bag for herself.

"I thought you said these were for me?" He arched his brow and grinned.

"They are, but I got a jelly donut. I've been craving lemon-filled." She took a bite and groaned. "Oh, God. That's good." She closed her eyes and rested her hand on her bulging stomach.

He rested his hand on top of hers. He loved how beautiful she looked, full of his child in her stomach. She bitched a little about thinking she was fat, but to him she was beautiful.

She finished off her donut and licked the icing off her fingertips. "Any word on Boudier?"

"A sighting. I've sent someone up there."

She sat up straight. "A sighting? Where?"

He narrowed his eyes. "I'm not telling you."

Her mouth dropped, and then she pressed her sexy lips into a pout. "Why not?"

"Because you'll tell Haley and Catty, and then Granny will interrogate them until she gets that information out of them. The next thing I'll know, Granny will have all the females rounded up and headed up north to capture Boudier herself." He shook her head. "So, I'm not telling you. It's for your own good."

She glared. "Fine." Ava crossed her arms over her chest.

"Don't be mad." He softened the tone of his voice. "I just don't want to see you get hurt. The thought that something could happen to you or our baby makes me insane."

Her expression softened, and she smiled. "I know, babe. I know." She sighed and laid her head against his chest. "I used to think that we were invincible. That because we were werewolves, we could do anything, and nothing could hurt us."

He nodded. He'd thought the same.

"Until Barrett," he added.

She lifted her head and looked up at him. "Yeah. Until then, I hadn't realized how many risks I had taken. I know you think I let Granny talk me into a lot of stuff, but it's not all her."

"I know," he grinned.

"You do?"

He turned and faced her. "Ava. You are the most stubborn female I have ever known in my life. You will run head first into danger without thinking."

She shook her head. "Not anymore. I've got this little one to think about." She patted her stomach. "I'm sorry, Damon."

"Sorry for what?" he frowned. What kind of trouble had she gotten herself into now?

"For being a pain in the ass."

"Ava, you're my mate. For now, and forever. I will never

say you're a pain in the ass."

She served him a look of disbelief.

"You're just hardheaded ... sometimes."

She scowled and then let out a laugh. "Alright. I'll take it."

"I'm sorry I've been so busy lately." He held her close.

"You're the Pack Master. You have to stay busy." She shrugged and burrowed into his chest.

"I feel like I'm missing out on time with you, Ava." He touched his finger to her cheek and tilted her gaze up to his. "Do you feel like I'm neglecting you?" Worry gnawed at the pit of his stomach.

She snorted. "Well, since you only give me three orgasms every single night, yeah, I totally feel neglected."

"I'm serious."

"So am I." She sat up and twisted in her seat so she could look at him head on. "No, I don't feel neglected. You bring me flowers or candy or chocolate every single night, and you can't keep your hands off me when you're home. I'm the one that needs to be apologizing to you." She looked away.

"Apologizing to me? What the hell for?" He had no idea what she was talking about.

"I'm the one that jumps you the second you walk in the door. I'm the one that demands sex all the frigging time." She shook her head. "I don't know what's wrong with me. It's like my sex drive has quadrupled. You never get any sleep because I'm on you like two rats in a wool sock."

He let his head fall back and let out a laugh. Ryker walked by and gave him a strange look. Still, he couldn't stop laughing.

"What is so funny?" She pressed her lips into a thin line and scowled.

"The fact that you think I think you're asking for too much sex is hilarious," he snorted.

"But you don't ever get any sleep. You need to get some

sleep, Damon. You need me to get off your ..." She pointed to his crotch, and her eyes got big.

"My dick?" He liked the way she was looking at him. All of him.

She slapped his arm. "This is serious."

He glanced down at the bulge in his jeans. "Yeah, I know it is. I have a little time before my next phone call if you want to step into my office for ... a meeting."

"Damon," Lucien called out to him as he parked his Harley and turned off the engine. "I've got some news."

He let out a breath and nodded. He stood and helped Ava to her feet.

"How about I bring you dinner to your office and we can play secretary and boss?" She whispered in his ear.

"Only if you wear nothing but a trench coat and glasses."

"You got it." She gave him a quick kiss and waved to Lucien as she walked back to her car.

"What's the news?" Damon asked, wasting no more time.

"I talked to Lorcan. He found out who the mole was in Texas that let Boudier out of his cell." Lucien propped his hands on his hips. "His name is Bubba. Not even from Texas. Originally from ..."

"Louisiana," Damon finished the sentence.

"Yeah." Lucien gave him a quizzical look. "How'd you know? Did you already get this info?"

"No." A chill ran up his spine, and he looked away. "Bubba was part of the red wolf pack that kidnapped Ava. After I got her back here, I went out looking for him. Even though Barrett told me not to." He shrugged. "Turns out I didn't need to. I never found hide nor hair of him again. I went through every bit of intel we had on Louisiana and every red Were. Bubba up and vanished like smoke."

"Shit."

"Shit's right." Damon narrowed his eyes. "How the hell

did Texas let him in as a Guardian since he clearly is a red wolf."

"They claim that he said he was escaping out of Louisiana jurisdiction. There is no love lost between Texas and Louisiana because of Boudier. So, they let him in the state and when he applied as a Guardian, he was accepted. They said that Bubba was giving Texas good intel on what Boudier was up to. So, they figured they would keep him." Lucien shrugged.

"Did they trust him enough to make him a Guardian?"

"Fuck no. They were only keeping him close until Boudier could be apprehended. In fact, a lot of the intel Barrett had on Boudier the night of the Tribunal actually came from Texas." Lucien crossed his arms over his chest.

"Then Bubba turned on his own Pack."

"According to one of the Guardians Bubba was close to, Bubba actually tried to leave the Pack when it was found out that Boudier was going to be taken to Texas. They said Bubba looked scared as shit."

"Hmmm." Damon rubbed his chin and thought back to his first meeting with the indigent. He'd infiltrated a secret red wolf camp where Ava had been held hostage after they kidnapped her. The red Weres had planned on injecting her with a drug that would constantly keep her in heat. That way, she could have multiple pregnancies, and they could rebuild their dwindling numbers. A female Were couldn't sustain that many pregnancies without harming her body. In the end, it would have killed her.

"Did they say how Bubba got Boudier out?" Damon glared.

"Yeah. He was guarding the cell one night alone and opened the door. Fucker walked right on out of the Compound dressed in regular clothes that Bubba had smuggled into the Compound.

"Where's Bubba now?" Damon felt his heart pounding in his chest like a drum. When he found Bubba again, he was going to rip his fucking liver out and shove it down his throat.

"Can't find him. He disappeared the same night too." Lucien cocked his head. "They don't believe that they are traveling together."

"Why is that?" Damon jerked his head at his Guardian.

"Because when Boudier was spotted at that truck stop, they didn't notice anyone with him. So, either Bubba is on his own ..."

"Or Boudier has already put a silver bullet in his head," Damon finished Lucien's thought.

A roar of a Harley tore down the street. Damon narrowed his eyes as Ryker passed them on his Harley.

"I thought he just came off a shift. Shouldn't he be sleeping?" Lucien asked.

"He should. But try telling Ryker that." Damon narrowed his eyes at his disobedient Guardian.

"Ryker's different. He was really close to Barrett. I think they might have been BFFs." Lucien shoved his hand through his hair.

"I don't think Barrett ever had a BFF." He looked at Lucien. "I mean, isn't that against the code of Pack Master or something? Remain distant. Remain aloof."

"I don't know. But if that's a requirement, then your ass is nailing it, bro." Lucien smiled and slapped him on the shoulder.

"Asshole," Damon muttered. He ran his hand down his face. "I'm going to need another Were to try to find Bubba.9

"I'll do it," Lucien offered. "I'd rather Jaxon stay close to Ginny and in the state of Arkansas. With her pregnancy and all that has happened, he needs to be around for her."

"Yeah, he does. While Ginny did inherit her dead

husband's estate, I don't feel comfortable letting her go back to Louisiana just yet."

"I don't think she does either. Jaxon told me she wants the house and everything in it listed for sale ASAP."

Damon studied Lucien. "She doesn't want anything in the house? No family heirlooms?"

Lucien rubbed his chin. "Well, Jaxon did say that her mother gave her the silverware as a wedding gift. But since it was her mother that stabbed her in the back with a fork, Ginny's not feeling very sentimental toward her family. Any of them."

"I can get the lawyers to liquidate the estate if that's what she really wants. But I need to talk with her first," Damon said. Ever since Ginny had left her home after killing her abusive husband, she'd kind of kept to herself. He could relate to that. When he first came to the Arkansas Pack, he was more of a loner than he liked to admit. His reasons were different than hers, so he wasn't sure if talking to her would make a difference. But he had to try.

"I'll let her know before I head out." Lucien nodded. "Anything else?"

"I'll text you a photo of Bubba. I think I'm the only one of the Arkansas Pack that has met him and knows what he looks like."

"Any advice?"

"Yeah." He turned and looked at Lucien. "He may be big, but he's clumsy and can't take a hit. Remember that if you encounter him."

Lucien grinned. "Will do." He walked back to his motorcycle and straddled his Harley.

Damon watched as his Guardian drove away, wishing he were the one going on this mission.

CHAPTER 24

"The shipment of food isn't going to make it here in time before the next snowstorm." Barrett addressed Helen and Jacey. He had called them into the bar after they closed Saturday night.

"But I thought you said it would get here by Monday afternoon." Helen propped her hands on her hips. "I guess we'll just serve alcohol and no food. Customers are not going to be happy with that."

"Then they'll be really pissed when the liquor runs out." Barrett forked his fingers through his hair.

"What?" Helen's eyes grew wide.

"The shipment of alcohol isn't going to make it here either. They are both stuck in Denver. They know how bad the road conditions up the mountain to Silverton are so the truck driver thought it would be a waste of time to even try. I'm closing the bar Monday too. I'll go first thing in the morning with my trailer and get the food and the alcohol. I'll try to make it back Monday if the weather holds up long enough for me to make it back up the mountain."

"Are you crazy?" Helen frowned. "If they won't make the

149

trip up the mountains, what makes you think you can make it up? You should just close the bar until the truck delivers everything." She shrugged.

"And if I don't make any money this week, I can't pay you, Helen. I know you need the money."

Helen's eyes misted over. He hated to tell her business in front of Jacey, but sometimes Helen was too stubborn for her own good. She never looked out for herself. Always looked out for others. The old woman reminded him of another older woman he used to know.

She blinked back the tears. "I've always made it before, Barrett. Don't worry about me. Besides, I don't think you should be going down the mountain alone."

"I'll go with you," Jacey said.

They both turned and stared at her.

"What?" She shrugged. "It's just a quick trip to Denver. Load up supplies and drive back, right?"

"The roads are dangerous. I don't think …" Barrett narrowed his eyes.

"I didn't ask if it was dangerous. I know the risks. Besides, it would be better if it were two of us going. That way if something does happen along the road, one of us can go for help."

"I don't …" He didn't like putting her in danger.

Helen pursed her wrinkled lips. "I would feel better if you were not alone. And Jacey is right. If something happens like car trouble, then the other one can go for help."

He scowled at Helen. "You're not helping. You are supposed to be on my side," he muttered.

"I am on your side. You may be my boss, but I'm always going to look out for you. Like one of my own." She lifted her chin.

He cut his gaze at Jacey. "Are you sure you want to go? It could be dangerous."

"Absolutely." She nodded enthusiastically. "Besides, if I don't get out of Mena's for at least a couple of days, I'm going to go crazy."

"I thought you liked her." Barrett frowned.

"Oh, I do like her. But I don't like her house. It feels creepy. Even in the daytime. I think because its old. I feel like something is watching me."

"Honey, the only thing watching you in that old house is the ghost of Mena's dead husband." Helen laughed.

"Are you serious?" Jacey's eyes grew wide.

"A few years ago, Mena brought in some crackpot who claimed to talk to the dead. Rumor was she was trying to commune with her dead husband to find out where he hid some old oil bonds." Helen laughed.

"But I thought Mena was rich. I mean she's always dripping in gold and diamonds. I think she must sleep with them on." Jacey frowned.

"Honey, half of her jewelry is costume, or so I hear." Helen leaned in to whisper, despite there being no one else in the room.

"Did she talk to her husband's ghost?" Jacey asked, wide-eyed.

"Well, that medium charged her a couple thousand dollars and claimed that the dead husband told him to look under the floorboards in their bedroom. Poor woman took a crowbar and pulled up every piece of hardwood flooring in that entire house. For nothing. When she tried to contact the medium to complain, his number had been disconnected." Helen shook her head. "The rumor is that even though the medium was a quack, he inadvertently let some evil spirits in that house."

"Helen. I'm sure that's not true." Barrett shot the waitress a glare.

"Well, that's what people have told me. They say that

sometimes they wake up and their covers are snatched off by some invisible spirit." Helen narrowed her eyes. "Have you had that happen, Jacey?"

"No." Her face paled.

"Helen," he warned.

"Guests have also said that they've been woken from a sound sleep by someone moaning. They report seeing someone standing at the foot of their bed."

"Helen, you're not helping. Sounds like a bunch of bull-shit to me," he growled.

Helen's eyes grew wide. "I assure you I have heard it on the best authority that there have been some paranormal activities in that place."

"Don't you need to be getting home now?" He scowled.

She shrugged. "Just trying to help." She looped her purse strap over her shoulder and walked to the exit. She put her hand on the door and turned. "If you do find yourself with some paranormal activity in that house, get you some holy water and sprinkle it over the room. Hang some garlic around the windows and sprinkle salt around your bed." She lifted her hand in a wave and headed out the door.

"Ignore her." Barrett turned back to Jacey.

She nodded but didn't say anything.

He stepped closer and rested his hands on her shoulders. She looked up into his gaze.

Those caramel-colored eyes always seemed to make his heart skip a beat and his stomach hot. He wasn't used to experiencing those feelings, and he wasn't sure the cause.

"You're not buying into all that crap Helen was spouting, are you?"

"Of course not." She forced a smile on her face, but she wasn't fooling him.

"Jacey?"

"Look, I don't believe in ghosts. But something weird is

going on in that house. It feels weird, heavy. I don't how to explain it. At night, I sleep with a light on because I feel like someone is watching me."

His hands slid down her shoulders. He'd watched her room from his window before he went to sleep. How could she have sensed that? It was far enough away that he never really saw anything in the room. Just the light.

"Maybe it's just a car driving by. I mean, you don't see anyone, do you?"

"No. But I feel like whoever is watching me is waiting."

"Waiting for what?" He cocked his head.

"Waiting to hurt me." She looked away but not before he saw the fear flash before her eyes.

"Did you feel like this before the … hunters?"

"No."

He relaxed. "I think you're having some leftover trauma over what happened. That's perfectly normal. You were captured at night, and now at nighttime you feel vulnerable." He leaned in closer. "Would you say that's an accurate description?"

She nodded.

He pulled her into his chest. She didn't fight him, and he felt her body shiver against his.

She pressed her hands to his lower back and sunk into his chest.

Her body trembled against his as he held her, resting his chin on the top of her head. His heart ached for her, but at the same time his chest swelled with an enormous feeling that she needed him.

A surge of wanting to protect her at all costs welled inside his body, and he tightened his arms around her. He wasn't sure how long they stood there like that. But something between them shifted. Something he couldn't understand.

Ever since the day she walked into his bar, he knew she

was different, and he'd tried to keep his distance from her. He couldn't offer her much in the way of transparency. She had been hurt before by her former mate, and she wasn't the kind of female that would tolerate a relationship with a male who only gave her half-truths.

He shivered. Just thinking about Jacey and a relationship scared him out of his mind.

She sniffed and finally pulled out of his embrace. "Sorry about that."

"Don't ever apologize for being vulnerable. That's what brings out the best part of us," he said, looking into her caramel gaze.

She cocked her head and stared up at him. "How is it that you have never mated?"

The question shocked him. "I never wanted to." He'd said those words to his Guardians time and time again. Now he wasn't sure why it was hard to admit it to her.

She gave him a small smile. "I don't blame you. Mating will make you weaker than you ever knew. It can also destroy you in ways you didn't know." She walked over to wall and took her coat off the hook. She shoved her arms into the sleeves and picked up her bag.

"Ready?" he asked.

"Yes."

He opened the door leading out the back and let her out first. He headed for his Jeep, but she put her hand on his sleeve and stopped.

"Do you mind if we walk?" She gave him an uncertain look.

"You don't mind the cold?" He knew her Were blood ran hotter than a mere human, but he still couldn't stop being concerned for her well-being.

"I could actually use the fresh air. I got hot cooking all night," she admitted.

"Let's go then." He changed direction and headed half a mile down the street to Mena's.

"If you don't mind, I'll come inside."

She cut her eyes at him.

"I didn't mean it like that." He cleared his throat. "I meant to just have a look around the room and see if I can find what's making you uncomfortable."

"Barrett, you really don't have to." She ducked her head into the collar of her coat and shoved her hands in her pockets.

"It's okay to ask for help you know," he said.

Her head jerked up, and she arched her brow. "That's actually good advice. You might try taking it on occasion."

He snorted. "I'm horrible at taking my own advice."

She laughed, the melodic sound echoing into the dark night. It made his chest feel lighter.

"Are you warm enough?" He saw her shiver and regretted not taking the Jeep.

"I'll warm up when we get inside," she assured him.

"Come here." He opened his jacket up.

She hesitated.

"Look, it's just an offer of warmth, not roses and candle-light," he said.

"That's good. I've never gotten roses so I won't know what I'm missing out on." She grinned and snuggled into his side. "You're like a walking heater." She sighed.

His body tightened and ached. Her scent was suddenly all around him, and he didn't really think he'd ever smelled anyone that smelled so fucking good.

He tightened his hold on her.

His breathing increased, and his heart thudded against his ribs. He felt the temperature of his blood rise, and his body was aching with lust so strong, he thought he wasn't going to be able to control himself.

What the fuck was wrong with him? He'd never reacted to a female like this before. When that witch and that fairy raised him from the dead, had they done something to his soul too?

He growled.

Jacey stopped walking and stiffened. "What's wrong? Do you see something?"

He shook his head. "No. Just got a lot on my mind," he lied. It wasn't his mind that was making him act like this. It was definitely something south of his zipper.

They came to a stop at the steps of Mena's Victorian house. The older home looked like a child's dollhouse with all its white decorative trim against the maroon siding.

The snow clung to the steep rooftops and dormers, making it look like the perfect Christmas getaway for lovers.

What the hell was wrong with him? He was going on and on in his head like an idiot.

If he ever got ahold of that fairy and that witch, he was going to make them wish they'd never brought him back from the dead.

Jacey stepped out of his embrace and dug around in her purse for the key to the front door. Mena made sure all her guests had a key to their rooms as well as the front door. She didn't want to be interrupted from watching her old movies just to let someone inside.

"Are you sure you don't mind looking around my room?" Jacey stuck the key in the front door and turned the lock. She opened the door and stepped inside.

She looked at him as if waiting for him to say he had changed his mind. He knew going into her room was a bad idea. But he couldn't let her down. Not now.

"No trouble at all." His voice sounded harsh and raspy in his ears. He hoped she hadn't noticed the change in him. The last thing he needed was to get involved with someone who was clearly not looking for any kind of relationship. Even if it was sex.

He knew, looking at her full lips and soft body, that sex with Jacey would be on a whole other level. It would be beyond mind-blowing.

"Are you alright?" She cocked her head. "You look like you're in pain."

"I'm good." He brushed off her concern, embarrassed that someone he barely knew could read him like a book.

He was in pain, alright. Pain from having blue balls.

He swallowed hard and stepped inside the house.

He looked around at the elaborate antique furniture situated in the room and family photos on the walls. A feeling of nostalgia washed over him. He'd once had a life that had family photos. Way before he was Pack Master.

Since he'd moved to Arkansas, the contact with his family had been few and far between. He'd left the family on bad terms when he refused to mate with one of the Council's daughters. Zena had been beautiful for sure, but he knew he didn't want her as a mate. Hell, he didn't want anyone as a mate.

When he refused, his family and the Council had transferred him to Arkansas to serve as Pack Master there. He had not been allowed to speak to his family and had accepted his lot in Arkansas.

He'd made a new family. He didn't even know if his own family knew he had died. A brother he always gave a hard time to and a sister he adored.

Now he'd been uprooted once again and lost his Arkansas family.

For once, just once, he wanted to have what he wanted. And fuck the rules and fuck everyone else.

She pressed her finger to her lips in a symbol of hush and waved with her hand for him to follow her up the stairs.

His footsteps were heavy on the carpeted stairs despite his attempts to be quiet. He tried his best not to look at her ass, but he was male, after all. And she had a really good ass. The best ass he'd ever seen.

He took a deep breath and let it out slowly.

They reached the top, and he followed her down the hallway to her room.

Something felt off. He stopped and looked at a closed door.

"My room is down here." She pointed and frowned.

He inhaled deep. The faint coppery scent of danger hung in the air. "Whose room is this?"

"It's empty." She shrugged. "I think that's where that guy, Charles? Was staying."

"Charles." The one he'd scared off from Jacey. He knew he didn't like the guy. That's why he smelled something off. When a dangerous human leaves a place behind, their intent sometimes stays behind. Charles' intent with Jacey had not been good.

Barrett had known it from the start.

"He didn't come back, did he?"

"No. I'm the only one staying here." She walked to her room and stuck the key in the door. She turned the knob, and the door swung open. "Come on in."

He walked in behind her.

Jacey's smell was all around the room, wrapping around him like a sensual blanket.

He shoved off his jacket and ran his hand down his face. He needed to get a grip.

He walked over to the windows and looked over his shoulder at her. "Do you ever open these windows?"

"No." She shook her head and worried her lip with her teeth. "Do you see anything?"

"No." He looked out and all he saw was the dark night.

They were too high up for anyone to climb up and look through the window. He tried opening one. They were all locked from the inside. "They're locked, and it's too high for someone to be looking in here."

He walked around the room and didn't notice anything out of the ordinary. He pointed to the fireplace. "Do you use that?"

"I haven't. I wasn't sure how to work it." She sat down on the bed. "I've been meaning to ask Mena, but she's still asleep when I get up. I keep forgetting to ask when I get home."

He squatted down in front of the fireplace and turned the gas valve on. He pressed the ignition and held it down for a while. He looked over his shoulder at her. "I'm making sure the gas is primed in the line. If you're not sure when the gas has last been used, it's a good idea."

He turned back to the fireplace and hit the ignition button. The fireplace ignited, and flames danced in the ceramic logs.

A delighted laugh bubbled out of her. "Thank you so much." She stood up and walked over to the fireplace. "I've always wanted to sleep in front of a fire."

His mind went wild with images of her naked, lying in front of the fire while he kissed his way down her beautiful body.

"Thank you." She leaned up on tippy-toes and gave him a hug. His arms went around her waist, and he held her to him.

She pulled back, her hands resting around his waist and looked up in his eyes.

Her eyelids were heavy, and her breathing increased.

Instead of breaking away, she ran her hands around his back.

He shivered.

"I know that this is against the rules ..." she whispered.

"Fuck the rules." He could smell her arousal, and he was

lost in her sweet, sweet scent. "Jacey, I'm having a hard time here."

"I can feel it." She arched against his erection. He growled.

"I don't get close to anyone. It's part of who I am," he said.

"And I'm not looking for forever. I'm enjoying getting my own life back." Her pink tongue darted out and swiped across her lips.

"You got to stop doing that."

"Doing what?" she asked innocently.

"That thing with your tongue. Listen, I'm only a gentleman to a certain extent," he groaned. "Don't make me do something that we will both regret."

"I'm tired of living life by the rules and doing things that are expected of me. For once, I just want something for me. I want to be selfish," she said.

"Tell me what you want."

"I want to be kissed. Really kissed. I want to know when you're kissing me, you're not thinking of anyone else."

"That's the easy part." His voice was hoarse. "The hard part is stopping at your lips." He leaned his head down, and her breath caught in her throat. "You want me to kiss you, and that's something I've thought about for a very long time. But I'm not going to stand here and say that's all I've thought about doing with you, Jacey. I may be a lot of things, but a liar is not one of them."

She swallowed as the room filled with his naughty words. Indecision weighed heavily in her gaze.

"What do you want, Jacey?" He clenched her clothes in his hands, holding on to his restraint. With every breath he inhaled her scent, the scent that was making him wild with lust.

She licked her lips and held his gaze. "I want you to kiss me."

He growled low, his entire body shaking with lust.

He bent his head, covering her mouth with his. His tongue plunged into her mouth, tasting her scent, her vulnerability, her sweetness.

She moaned and opened her mouth wider, letting him plunder her with a greedy abandonment.

This was no gentle kiss. It wasn't the kiss she deserved or needed. It was the kiss that he needed, wanted. Hard and wild.

She tasted better than she looked which was saying something. He'd dreamed of this since she walked into his life, and the reality was better than anything he could have ever imagined.

His hands tightened on her hips as he kissed her hard. He pressed his erection into her stomach, and he swallowed her soft moans with his mouth. His body begged for something more. Something that involved less clothes. He wasn't sure how much longer he was going to stay in control of his instincts.

Her hands slid up his arms. When she reached his shoulders, her fingers found their way into his hair, and she held on as she kissed him back with the same urgency he felt.

"Fuck," he murmured, dragging his mouth to her neck. "You taste fucking beautiful." He buried his face in the crook of her neck and bit down softly.

"Oh, God." She moaned, clinging to him and panting. She shivered in his arms and ground against his erection. "Don't stop."

He cupped her face between his hands and forced her to look at him. Her bedroom eyes had his heart skip a beat and her panting had him wishing they were on a deserted island, away from everything and everyone.

"I want to do more than kiss you," he said.

"Then do it," she said breathlessly.

"Are you sure?" He regretted having asked. He didn't want

her to change her mind. If she did, he was going to jump face-first into the snow to cool off his body.

"Yes."

"How far do you want to go?" Fuck. What was with his conscious tonight?

"Far enough." She blinked, and he could see the indecision was right back in her eyes.

He nodded and tried to swallow. He wasn't sure how far he could go with her without going all the way.

But for her, he'd do anything.

CHAPTER 25

*J*acey couldn't stop the butterflies from thumping against her stomach.

She'd never been kissed the way Barrett had kissed her. Not even her mate had kissed her like that. She'd never been as turned on as she was right now.

She wanted him to rip her clothes off and take her right there in front of the fireplace. But she wasn't brave enough to ask. She'd been rejected before. She wasn't about to put herself out there to be rejected again.

He kissed her, his tongue delving inside her mouth. God, he tasted hot and spicy and sexy.

She really hadn't intended on this happening.

But it felt too good to make her stop.

She ran her hands down his chest feeling every ripping muscle concealed under his shirt. She found the hem of his T-shirt and slid her fingers underneath, touching bare skin.

He groaned at her touch.

She touched every defined, heated ab as she trailed her fingers up to his chest. His amazing body was hard as stone.

She wanted to feel his body next to hers. She grabbed the hem of his shirt and tugged it up.

He held her gaze and then shoved the shirt off his body in one move.

Breathing heavily, she let her gaze lower to his bare chest. His muscles were illuminated by the firelight. He looked like a Greek god sent to earth to pleasure her.

He grabbed her hand and pressed it to his chest, pulling her closer. His intense gaze held her rooted to the floor, unable to form a coherent thought in her mind.

He held her gaze as he slipped his free hand under her shirt. His fingertips traveled up her spine leaving behind shivers in their place.

She wanted him to touch her everywhere. And she wanted to feel his hard body against hers. She needed it like she'd never needed anything before.

She stepped back and grabbed her own sweater. She tugged it over her head and tossed it on the floor.

His eyes darkened, and his breathing grew heavy. He was as aroused as she was.

He stepped closer and touched a finger to her lacy pink shoulder strap. She thought her heart was going to explode with such an innocent touch, and she was glad she'd bought all new panties and bras a week before she had left Mississippi.

She had wanted to start over from scratch. She couldn't think of a better way than with lingerie.

"Beautiful," he said as he ran his finger down to the swell of her breast. His gaze followed his finger. His fingers caressed her nipple through the lace. She moaned.

He dipped his head, covering her mouth with his. She forked her fingers through his hair, pulling him closer and kissing him deep. She sucked his tongue into her mouth. His growled.

She didn't care. She needed this. She needed him.

His hand went around her back. She felt the release of her bra. He skillfully tugged the bra off her shoulders without breaking the kiss.

He held her close, her nipples rasping against his chest in a sweet torture.

He bent and picked her up. She held his mouth to hers as he walked over to the chair behind the fireplace and sat.

"I need to see you better." His deep voice had her trembling inside.

His hands were strong yet gentle as he cupped her cheek and kissed her. She couldn't stop the desire flooding through her body and down to her core. Her body was on fire.

He nuzzled her neck and licked the sensitive flesh. Chills ran down her spine as she ached and arched to get closer to him.

"Barrett," she breathed out his name and dug her fingernails into his muscled flesh.

He lifted his head. "Say my name. I want you to say my name when you come."

Her face heated at his wicked words yet she wanted him too much to stop him. He could say anything to her right now as long as he kept touching her.

He bent his head and captured her nipple between his lips and sucked. She almost came then. She reached between their hot bodies and grabbed his erection through his jeans.

"Jacey." Her name was but a curse whispered on his lips.

She gripped him harder as he sucked greedily on her sensitive nipples.

She fumbled with his jeans until she finally unbuttoned them. She unzipped him and dipped her hand behind the zipper.

His cock jerked in her hand, and he hissed, trying to control his pleasure.

She liked that. She liked that they were both so out of control that they would probably burn each other up in the fire.

"Not yet. You're going to make me come too fast." He grabbed her hand and moved it away from his cock.

She didn't care. She wanted him like this.

"Let me have a little fun first." He grinned, and it should have scared her. But it didn't.

His hand went to her thigh and slowly slid between her legs.

Her eyes drifted shut.

"Jacey, look at me," he commanded.

She obeyed and held his gaze, despite the overwhelming need to squeeze her eyes tight.

"Do you like that?" His fingers caressed her through her jeans.

"Yes," she whispered as she tried to keep her eyes open.

"Keep your eyes on me." He commanded. His fingers found the top of her jeans and he gently slid the zipper down. Slowly and torturously, his fingers dipped behind her pink lace panties just above her clit.

"Don't stop."

"I'm not planning on it." He dipped his head and took her mouth. His fingers mocked the caress of his tongue against hers. She clung to him and released a moan.

He broke the kiss and looked at her. He removed his hand and shoved her jeans down her hips. She kicked them off. His eyes roamed down her near naked body, and he growled.

"I want to taste you and watch you come under my tongue." He gently pushed her back in the chair until she was sitting. He grinned and knelt in front of her.

"Keep your eyes open. Even when you come."

"I don't think I can."

"You can. I want you watching me while I eat you." He

spread her legs with his hands and gazed up her thighs to her panty-clad pussy.

Her entire body was on fire, and she wasn't sure how long she was going to last.

His hand slid up her thighs and cupped her. "You're so fucking wet."

She moaned and bucked into his hand.

He bent his head and kissed her panty.

"Oh, God, Barrett."

"Shush. Mena will hear you and think you need help." He dipped his thumbs on either side of her panties and tugged. The sound of lace ripping echoed between her ears.

"Those were new." She wasn't sure why she said that. It just popped into her head.

"Then don't wear panties around me. Ever." His dark gaze drifted down to her bare pussy. He rested her legs on either side of his shoulders and grinned before burying his mouth against her wet flesh.

She bucked and grabbed his hair. His tongue flicked and licked across her clit, and she couldn't stop moving. She fisted her fingers into his hair, holding his mouth against her.

She dropped her head. He lifted his head and scowled. "Look at me."

She craned her head to the side, watching him dip his head back between her legs.

He held her gaze as he licked her sensitive flesh.

"Barrett." She felt her body tense and then go limp as her orgasm washed over her in a tidal wave. She barely held her eyes open as she came, but a promise was a promise. Barrett didn't stop looking at her as he finished her with his mouth.

Trembling in the aftershocks of her passion, she cupped his cheek.

She reached for him and grabbed his dick in her hands.

He held her hand and looked into her eyes. "I just meant for this night to be about you. I don't expect you to …"

Her eyes widened, and she looked down at his hard erection. "Do you not want me to touch you, Barrett?" Maybe she had misread him.

"More than anything, but …"

She slid from the chair until she was straddling him. His face was still wet from her juices, and she went in for a kiss.

He kissed her back, tightening his hold around her waist. She pulled back and tried to slide down his body, but he held her tight.

"I need to repay the favor." She grinned and looked down at the top of his cock sticking out of his jeans.

"I'd rather you kiss me." He touched her cheek. She leaned into his hand.

Something lonely hung behind his eyes. Something she'd never seen him wear.

She bit her lip, contemplating her next move.

"It doesn't seem fair. You used your mouth on me; I want to use my mouth on you."

"Then kiss me while you do this." He squeezed her hand around his cock, and he groaned.

"We'll do things your way this time." She grinned and wrapped one hand around his neck while the other grasped his cock.

CHAPTER 26

*B*arrett's heart clenched at Jacey's touch. His heartbeat drummed so hard and fast, he thought the organ was going to explode out of his chest like a missile.

"Sit back." Her voice was husky and sexy. As vulnerable as he'd seen her, he liked this take-charge attitude she was giving him.

He smirked. He'd have to give her orgasms more often.

He turned and eased back in the chair. He followed her gaze to where his erect cock sprang out of his jeans and rested against his stomach. Her tongue darted out and licked the corner of her kissable mouth.

He let out a low growl.

He reached out and pulled her down into his lap. He wrapped his hand around the back of her neck. Her warm breath on his cheek and her heavy panting against his chest made him impossibly harder.

"Touch me." He guided her hand to his cock. He hadn't taken his jeans off, and now he wished he had for better access. But he couldn't. He knew that if he was completely naked, he would be making love to her until the sun came up.

He didn't think she was ready for that.

She moved her hand behind the zipper and grabbed the base of his hard cock. She squeezed, and he nearly spilled his seed in her hand.

She pressed her mouth against his, kissing him slow and deep as he worked her hand up and down on his hard erection. She went slow, tortuously slow, stretching out the pleasure.

She pulled back, breathless and beautiful. Her gaze held his, never wavering except to dip down to his cock and then back to his eyes.

He thrust against her hand and groaned.

She said nothing but spoke with her eyes. Lust, desire, and need saturated the air.

The room quickly grew humid, and soon a thin sheen of sweet covered their bodies.

"Jacey," he whispered her name in the night. She lifted her gaze to his and wrapped her free hand behind his neck.

He needed more. He needed to touch her. He dipped his head and sucked her nipple into his mouth. Her breathing increased, and she writhed in his lap. He lifted his head and slid his hand between her legs.

"You're still wet. For me." He needed to claim her in every possible way. Yet that was impossible. They were living in the moment. He knew better than anyone right now was all they had.

His finger slipped inside her tight flesh. She moaned and looked into his eyes.

She moved her hand faster on his cock, and he slid his finger in and out of her wet heat, their bodies moving as one.

She spread her legs wider for him and pressed her wet mouth to his. He kissed her back, drowning in a wave pool of desire and pleasure that was threatening to take them both under at the same time.

"Barrett," she whispered against his lips and looked at him.

She moaned, and he quickened his movements with his fingers. She was close to losing herself to ecstasy.

Pleasure gathered low in his stomach and streaked through his spine. He pressed his head to hers and growled as their frenzy gathered force.

"Oh, God." She moaned and shivered as her orgasm spread through her beautiful body.

Her pleasure set off his own. He growled as his seed spurted from the tip of his cock and landed on his jeans. She didn't stop stroking him until he was dry.

Exhausted and spent, they collapsed on the chair. He gathered her in his arms and held her close. She snuggled into his warmth and sighed with contentment as she settled against him.

"What just happened?" she whispered against his neck.

He shivered at her warm breath and wrapped her tighter in his arms.

"I think *we* just happened," he said quietly. He didn't have a smart comeback or something witty to say. He knew he should keep things normal and casual. But something shifted between them; something came apart. He knew the minute he stepped into her room, they were never going to be the same again.

"That was … mind-blowing," she said.

He kissed the top of her head and inhaled her scent. God, she smelled so good.

Like home, and peace. Like she belonged to him. Nothing he'd ever felt before.

He wasn't sure how long they stayed like that. Her breathing became slow and deep and regular. He glanced out the dark window.

They were safe in the mountain where the past couldn't find them and the future didn't exist.

He snuck his arms under her legs and stood. She stayed asleep, her head resting on his shoulder. He tugged down the covers and gently laid her in the bed. He tucked the comforter and sheets up to her neck.

She looked like a princess, asleep and waiting for her prince to kiss her and waken her.

He rubbed the area over his heart and frowned.

She made his heart ache.

He was no prince. He was stuck between hiding out and existing.

He went over to the fireplace and turned it off. It had put enough heat into the room and he knew the sun would be up in a few hours.

He zipped up his pants and tugged his T-shirt on over his head. He picked his jacket up off the floor. He carefully closed Jacey's door behind him.

He lingered in the hallway for a few minutes, staring at the closed door.

He shook his head and made his way down the stairs and out into the night. He made sure to lock Jacey's room and the front door before he left.

He looked up into the night sky and inhaled deep.

Tonight, he'd felt alive, something he really hadn't felt since coming back from the dead.

The hair on the back of his neck stood at attention. He turned around and clenched his fist.

But saw no one.

He forked his fingers through his hair.

It wasn't fear of something hiding in the dark that had him on edge.

It was the fear of wanting something that he could never have.

* * *

HE CROUCHED against the tree from where he was watching the large Were leave the Victorian house. He looked so out of place here, between the elegant house and the snow clinging to the trees. Werewolves preferred the humidity of the South. That's why there were so many in the Southern states.

He narrowed his eyes on Barrett. How the hell was that motherfucker still alive? Was he something other than Were? He lifted his nose and inhaled deep.

As if sensing the movement, Barrett turned and scanned his surroundings.

He watched until Barrett relaxed and headed back to the shitty bar he'd come out of earlier.

Barrett must have gotten slow. He would be really pissed if he knew that he was being followed. Ever since that hot little female showed up on the mountain.

He turned his attention back to the dark Victorian house. Not a single light was on. It would be the perfect time to pay her a little visit. No doubt from the scent of sex surrounding Barrett, the female would be up for a little sexual game.

He took a deep breath and laid his head back on the bark of the tree.

It wasn't time yet, he had to remind himself. He had to wait. Wait until the perfect moment.

Then he would make Barrett pay.

CHAPTER 27

*J*acey tightened the belt on her robe and swiped some toothpaste on her toothbrush. She hummed a favorite song while she brushed her teeth.

Despite only getting a few hours of sleep last night, she'd woken up with the sun.

She had never felt better.

She washed her face and shoved her toiletries in the small bag and looked up in the mirror.

She smiled to her reflection.

Her eyes were bright, and her skin glowed.

That's what great sex does for a girl.

A laugh bubbled out of her.

She had to ride with Barrett today to pick up supplies for the bar and grill. She bit her lip.

Her heart picked up pace, and suddenly she couldn't wait to be in the Jeep with him for hours. Her body warmed just thinking about it.

She pressed her hands to her heated face. "Get a grip, girl. It's not a date, and there's not going to be any sex … of any kind. This is business." She moved her hands and looked at her reflection.

One night with Barrett and they hadn't even had sex. Yet her body was craving him like a drug.

She could only imagine what sex would be like with the male.

She took a deep breath and grabbed her things. She stepped into the hallway and shivered. She wished she could tell Mena to turn up the air. But she didn't want to make the old woman mad. She was living fairly cheap, and she was grateful for that. It would give her time to build up her money.

She shut her door and plopped her toiletry bag on the bed. She opened the closet and pulled out a pair of black jeans and a red sweater. She wished she had some cute boots to go with the outfit, but her winter boots were more functional as far as keeping her warm.

Besides, this was for work. Not a date.

She took her time curling her hair in front of the mirror over the dresser. She carefully applied some makeup and swiped her lips with some cherry-flavored gloss.

She stepped back and admired herself.

She glanced at the time and noticed it was only seven o'clock. She had time for some coffee before Barrett picked her up.

She walked into the kitchen and headed straight for the coffeepot. Thank God, Mena always set the timer on the coffeepot. The last thing she wanted to do was wait on her coffee to brew.

She took a sip and sighed. Perfect.

A note in elegant but shaky cursive sat next to the coffeepot. Jacey picked it up and read the words.

"Coffeecake in the fridge. Please help yourself."

As if on cue, her stomach let out a rumble.

She pressed her hand to her stomach and opened the white refrigerator. A cake resting on a stand and wrapped in a good amount of plastic wrap sat in the middle of the rack.

She carefully pulled out the cake and set it on the kitchen counter.

She began the tedious task of unwrapping the plastic from the cake. If Mena was going to pick up a new job, the woman should go into the moving business. With her wrapping skills, she would never have anything broken on a cross-country move.

When she finally pulled the last piece of plastic wrap away, she looked down at the cake. It was a cinnamon crumb cake and smelled wonderful.

She pulled open some drawers and found a knife. She opened the cabinet and grabbed a small plate. She cut herself a small piece and set it on the decorative china with tiny vines around it.

She snagged a fork out of the drawer and took her plate and coffee to the dining room.

She eased into one of the antique chairs and looked around the room. She noticed the fireplace, wishing it were lit. She took a sip of her coffee and looked around the room.

The ceilings were coffered with dark beams contrasting with the white ceiling. The three large windows that formed a bay were decorated with a plush, red curtain that pooled at the floor. The walls were covered in dated wallpaper in a tiny floral pattern. Though it wasn't her style, she thought it made the room cozy. The table itself was large with matching chairs and a buffet which sat along the wall. There were paintings of flowers and landscapes along the wall, and an old-fashioned crystal chandelier hung above the middle of the table.

It looked like something out of a dollhouse.

She picked up her utensil and took a bite of her cake. The

taste of butter and cinnamon burst on her tongue, and she smiled.

It was perfect.

Exactly what she needed after the kind of night she had experienced.

She took her time, enjoying the cake and the coffee. She looked at the time on the grandfather clock out in the hallway and noticed it wasn't even eight yet.

She couldn't wait any longer. She hurried upstairs and grabbed her coat and bag. After locking her room, she headed downstairs. She headed out the front door and inhaled the crisp winter air.

She didn't normally like cold air, but today was different.

Today, she seemed to appreciate the different smell of the air.

Today, she was beginning her new life.

She smiled and walked down the road to the bar and grill.

She walked back behind the building and carefully made her way up the slippery steps. She raised her hand to knock on his door and froze.

What if he was still asleep? What if he didn't want her barging in on his privacy? What if he …

Before the next question came to her mind, the door flung open and Barrett stood there. His wet hair brushed his large shoulders, and he frowned when he saw her. He was barefoot and wearing nothing but jeans.

Her body heated at the sight of him, and she dropped her hand.

"Sorry. I was up early and thought I'd save you the trip of coming to pick me up." Her gaze drifted down his muscled chest to the zipper of his jeans. Realizing she was sounding like an idiot, she jerked her gaze up to his face.

She felt like a fool. She'd assumed wrong, and now she was the ass.

"I can come back …"

She didn't get to finish. He grabbed her elbow and pulled her inside the warmth of his apartment.

He held her gaze and slammed the door shut.

Her heart thudded in her chest. She'd never had a male look at her the way Barrett was looking at her. Purposeful, possessive, predatory.

"I was just about to get my shirt on and pick you up." His voice was dark and hoarse. And he was standing way too close for her to catch her breath.

"Oh." It was the only thing she could think to say. He'd had his hands and mouth all over her body last night, and she was acting shy. She wished the floor would open up and swallow her. She wasn't good with the flirting thing.

He took her hand and led her into the kitchen. Her eyelids fluttered at his touch. Such a simple touch had such an effect on her.

"I made coffee." He pulled out a stool at the kitchen counter, and she sat.

She was already on edge being near him. She didn't know if she needed to up her caffeine intake.

He pulled a mug out of the cabinet and filled it. He set it in front of her before pouring himself a cup.

He grabbed his cup and nodded toward the bathroom. "I'll finish getting ready and then we can leave."

"No rush," she said, looking at him over her coffee cup.

She watched him as he went into the next room. He moved with the grace of a lion, every muscle bunching with each purposeful movement.

He was powerful, and dangerous, and beautiful.

She was so out of her league when it came to him.

"I've got to hook up the trailer before we go. It will be easier coming down the mountain than going up." He stuck his head out of the bathroom and stared at her. "You sure you want to come?"

Her mind totally went there, and she blushed. She cleared her throat and nodded furiously. "Absolutely. I think it would be good for me to get off the mountain for a little bit." She gave a small smile.

He nodded and ducked his head back into the bathroom.

"Have you had to do this before? Go get your own supplies," she asked and took another sip of the coffee. He made better coffee than Mena.

The first couple of nights she'd stayed at Mena's, the older woman made really good coffee, but lately it was stronger almost bitter. She was almost tempted to add some creamer to make it tolerable.

Maybe she would pick up some coffee as a gift for her landlady.

"No. I never ran out of supplies before." He stepped out of the bathroom with a skintight, black T-shirt covering his muscled torso. "You're the reason I'm out. People love your cooking. They could take or leave mine."

She laughed. "Well, you cooked a decent breakfast."

"I'm a male." His eyes grew serious. "We have to know how to cook breakfast. It's part of what you learn at man camp."

She barked out a laugh. That brought a grin out of him. For the first time since she'd met him, he seemed to be at ease. Like he was almost enjoying himself.

"You need to smile more."

"I do?" He arched his brow.

"Yeah. It looks good on you." She slid off the stool and carried her empty coffee cup to the sink. She turned on the water and rinsed out the mug.

He came up behind her and wrapped his arms around her waist. He nuzzled her neck, and her eyelids shuttered close.

"I think you're the reason for the smile," he murmured against her neck. He pressed his lips to the sensitive flesh in the crook of her neck.

She trembled.

She needed to get a grip. She was starting over, and she didn't need to get involved with some super-hot Were who could melt the panties right off her. She had to focus on her future.

She took a breath and steadied herself. She set the cup in the sink and turned.

Her breasts brushed against his chest. She bit her lip and held in a moan. She lifted her gaze to his face. His dark-blue eyes were staring down at her, his pupils dilated.

He wanted her. She could smell his desire.

She wanted him just as bad.

"I suppose we should get going." She forced the words out, even though she didn't mean them. She wanted to strip off her clothes and then his and stay in bed doing all sorts of wicked things to each other.

He sighed and nodded. "I guess we do." He stepped back, giving her space.

It felt more like a void, and she didn't like it.

He turned and grabbed his keys off the kitchen island.

He held out his hand and nodded toward the door. "After you."

CHAPTER 28

*A*fter hooking up the small trailer to the Jeep, they pulled onto the mountain road.

Barrett took his time, part of him wanting to drag out the trip with Jacey as long as he could, the other part knowing he should just hurry up and get the trip over. Getting close to her was dangerous. But at the same time, he couldn't deny he just wanted to be near her.

He reached for the dash and turned up the heat and then aimed the vents at her. He saw her shiver, yet she hadn't complained of being cold. He was hot as fuck, but he would suffer so she would be comfortable.

"I'm fine. You don't have to turn it up." She looked over at him and smiled.

"I might be cold," he lied. A bead of sweat gathered at his temple. He tried to ignore it.

She reached over and wiped the sweat off his head and turned her finger to him. "Really? Are you sweating ice crystals?"

He shrugged. "You looked like you were cold."

"I'm not. I'm pretty hot actually."

"Thank fuck." He grabbed the window handle and rolled down the window. A cold blast of winter wind hit him in the face.

She laughed and rolled down her own window.

It didn't even bother him that she'd laughed at him being uncomfortable.

"Are you going to be able to make it back up the mountain pulling that trailer?" She motioned over her shoulder.

"Probably not," he said.

She jerked her head in his direction. "Then why are we bringing it?"

He grinned. "Because I'm going to leave it in exchange for a bigger truck." He let his gaze leave the snow-covered road for a few seconds to look over at her.

"I have a friend in Denver, Alfred, that has a bigger vehicle. He still needs to get around, and there's not much hauling room in the Jeep. I hooked up the trailer for him."

Her lips made a silent circle of understanding. Then she frowned. "Why didn't he just deliver everything up the mountain himself? That way he's not out his vehicle and you get your supplies."

"Because he hates the mountains." Barrett studied the road. The snow was coming down harder in long rows of white sheets. He wondered if they were going to get everything loaded tonight and be able to make it back up before the roads iced.

"Yet he lives in Colorado," she murmured.

He chortled. "He doesn't hate Colorado. Just hates the mountains." He shrugged. "He never really has said why. I never asked him. Figured it was none of my business." Besides, if he got too comfortable with Alfred then he would start asking questions about Barrett's past. He couldn't afford to go down that path.

"Is he a Were?"

Barrett frowned. "No. But he's not human either. Or at least he doesn't smell human."

"Where did you meet him?"

"Ryker hooked me up with him …" As soon as the words left his mouth, he knew he'd messed up.

"Is Ryker a Were?"

He looked straight ahead, the hair on the back of his neck standing erect.

"Barrett, after last night, I'm pretty sure we're past the point of being cordial." She looked out the passenger side window.

Last night. The image of her naked and in his arms had been burned into his brain and tattooed on his heart.

"I'm not trying to be elusive, Jacey," he said softly. "I'm just a very private person."

She turned and looked at him. "I know." She shrugged. "I hope you know I wouldn't tell your business to anyone. It's not like I have any friends here." She faced the front and swallowed. "Actually, it's not like I have any friends at all."

"You have me." His chest burned. Good God. What was wrong with him? He sounded like some love-sick teenager.

She cut her eyes at him. A slight smile brushed across her beautiful lips.

"I mean," he cleared his throat, "it's just that you're not alone." He tightened his grip on the steering wheel. "I know what it's like to be alone. To think you have no one in the world. I know what it's like to start over with nothing and no one from your past. It's hard at first, but as each day passes, you fall into a routine and a pattern. Soon, you'll forget all about your other life because you'll be too busy living your new life."

"Have you done that? Forgotten your old life?" she asked softly.

"Not yet." A deep sense of sadness washed over him. A

sadness he couldn't explain. "But there's always tomorrow."

* * *

"I DON'T WANT you riding the Harley. Not in your condition." Damon narrowed his eyes at Ava.

She stood in front of his bike with her helmet tucked under her arm and glared.

"Why not?"

"Because you're pregnant," he countered.

"And? Pregnant women ride Harleys all the time. Plus, I'm a Were so I'm tougher." She lifted her chin in a defiant stance.

"Ava …"

She held up her hand, and he stopped talking. "Don't start, Damon. I'm tired of doing nothing but eating everything in sight. I want to go on a ride. It doesn't have to be a long ride; a short one will do."

"Ava," He raked his fingers through his hair and stared at her over his handlebars.

"You're just going to the office, right?" She propped her other hand on her hip and waited for his reply.

"Yes, but …"

"It's only a ten-minute drive from the house to the Compound. I know that Ginny is over there with Jaxon. I can catch a ride back in her car." Her face fell a little. "Please?"

He growled, and he already knew Ava was going to win this argument. Hell, she won every argument.

She didn't wait for him to answer but shoved the helmet —his requirement after he'd learned she was pregnant—on her head and walked over to him.

She grinned as she rested her hands on his shoulders and slowly crawled onto the Harley. In her condition, it took her a little longer than usual.

She wrapped her arms around his waist and bent her

mouth to his ear. "Now, see? Isn't this nice? Just like old times before I got fat." She nipped at his ear.

Shivers of pleasure raced up his spine. He was already getting hard.

"You are going to be the death of me, female," he growled.

She slapped him on the shoulder. "Don't say things like that. And please don't say that around any of the Guardians."

He looked over his shoulder and frowned. "Why not?"

"Because I think they are a little spooked since Barrett's death. It doesn't hurt to be a little superstitious where we Weres are concerned."

"Oh, hell. They better not start acting like a bunch of pussies," he growled.

Ava laughed near his ear. "I can't begin to imagine your big, bad Guardians acting like a bunch of pussies."

That pulled a smile out of him.

"Hold on." He started the engine, and the Harley roared to life and rumbled under his fingertips. He tightened his grip and pulled away from the house.

He loved their little house on the outskirts of Little Rock. After Ava's original house had been bombed by some rogue red wolves, she had rebuilt on the same land. It wasn't much, just a couple of acres, but it was wooded and had a great sunset view every night.

Their own private oasis.

Since taking on his new role as Pack Master, he was here less and less, instead sleeping at his old room in the Compound. He needed to be close until they could catch Boudier and make sure justice was served where Barrett was concerned.

He relaxed and increased his speed on the road. The rush of the cool wind and the scent of Ava had him breathing in deep. This felt right and for the briefest of seconds, everything was right in the world.

The ride was over too soon for his taste. He angled his bike and turned into the Arkansas Guardians Compound. He slowed his speed as he drove down the street. Braxton was talking to Jaxon on the sidewalk, and they both stopped whatever conversation they were having when they spotted him. They both gave him a respectful nod.

He wanted to laugh. Never in a billion years had he, Damon Trahan, expected to become Pack Master of Arkansas.

Yet here he was.

He pulled into the parking spot in front of the Compound and killed the engine. He toed down the kick-stand and waited for Ava to dismount first.

"See," she said as she tugged her helmet off her head, "that was fun, wasn't it?" She gave him a devastating grin.

"It could have been longer," he admitted. Since assuming his new role, the only time he had the chance to ride his Harley was on the way to work. He missed the days when he could take off and ride with the wind at his back, pushing him along to some unseen destination.

"I've got time." She grinned.

"Unfortunately, I don't." He looked over her shoulder as Jaxon and Braxton walked toward him. They didn't look happy, and he could feel his senses on high alert.

She followed his gaze and nodded.

"Hey, Damon, Ava." Braxton nodded.

"What's up?" Jaxon said in greeting.

"I was about to say the same thing to you." Damon stuck his hands in his jeans pockets and faced his Guardians.

"I see that you men have some work to discuss so I'll just leave you to it." Ava pressed her lips to Damon's cheek in a quick kiss and then looked at Jaxon.

"Is Ginny here? I was going to catch a ride back with her if she didn't mind," Ava said.

"She is." Jaxon nodded over by the grove of trees near the side of the Compound. "She actually wanted to speak to Damon first."

"Sure. Not a problem." Ava nodded toward the bakery near the end of the street. "I think I hear some chocolate cookies calling my name." She patted her stomach and walked in the direction of the bakery.

"Tell Ginny to come in and I'll speak to her in my office." Damon nodded. He turned and headed into the Compound.

He had unlocked his office and eased into the large chair behind the desk. A few minutes later, there was a soft knock on his door.

"Come in," he said.

The door opened. Jaxon was there with Ginny at his side. Jaxon smiled at his mate and motioned for her to enter the room. He followed behind.

"Sit." Damon nodded to the chair opposite of him.

"Sit, sweetheart," Jaxon encouraged. Ginny blinked and eased into the chair.

When Ginny had first come into the Arkansas Pack after murdering her evil ex-husband, she was thin, too thin. But now, under the protection of Arkansas and the love of Jaxon, she had gained weight and looked like a healthy mother-to-be.

He noticed her hand went over her protruding stomach in a protective gesture. She was pregnant and would give birth before Ava, if the doctor's calculations were correct.

"How much longer?" He nodded at her stomach.

"Eight weeks." She sighed. "But I feel like she's ready to come out now. I can't sleep more than two hours at a time before having to get up to go to the bathroom."

He laughed. "Yeah, Ava too. Except after she goes to the bathroom, she makes her way into the kitchen for a snack … or two."

This brought a smile to Ginny's mouth.

"Thanks for seeing us, Damon," Jaxon said from his position behind Ginny.

"Of course." He looked from the male to Ginny. "Jaxon said you wanted to talk about your inheritance from John."

She paled at the mention of her dead husband. "I think I have a buyer for the house in Shreveport. They like the price and the fact that all of the furniture is included."

"Are you sure you want to do that? I've been told that the furnishings inside the house are valued as high as the house itself."

"I'm sure." She rubbed her stomach. "I'm hoping to close in a few days, and I was wondering if Jaxon could go with me." She looked up at him. "I know with everything going on and trying to find ..."

"Your father," he added.

Her expression hardened. "We might have the same DNA, but that's all we have in common. He's no father of mine."

"I understand." Damon nodded. He didn't mean for his words to come out so harsh. He was just in a hurry to get a thousand things done. But a good Pack Master would know better than that. A good Pack Master would listen. Like Barrett would listen to his men.

"I didn't mean anything by it. Your allegiance to the Arkansas Pack has been proven a thousand times over. Forgive me."

Her eyes widened at his words. She looked up at Jaxon.

He smiled encouragingly as he gave her shoulder a squeeze.

"I need to go sign the papers and make sure the money is transferred to the correct account." She looked away for a minute as if lost in thought. "Apparently, he had more money than anyone knew."

"He did come from a very wealthy family."

"Yes, but the amount we are talking about is beyond what we originally thought." She looked up at him under her lashes like she was embarrassed.

"How much exactly?"

"In the neighborhood of twenty-five million," Jaxon answered.

"Fuck," Damon breathed out. Jaxon caught his gaze with a narrowed look.

"Sorry, Ginny," Damon said quietly.

She laughed. "Jaxon has said worse."

"Hey." Jaxon feigned hurt feelings. Damon knew better. He'd never seen the Were so happy.

"Congratulations, Ginny. Looks like you won't ever have to worry about money." Damon smiled. After the hell Ginny had been through with her abusive husband and sadistic father, she deserved all the happiness money could buy. And then some.

She licked her lips and looked from Jaxon to him. "I know. And I don't really care about the money." She shrugged. "I mean it's nice and all but doesn't mean anything to me. I'm going to donate a large amount to SKYLAR'S HOME. What she's doing for abused girls is fantastic."

"That is very generous of you. Thank you." Damon nodded. The female was still thinking of others even after all the horror that had been done to her. Jaxon better appreciate it. "And Jaxon is free to take you to Shreveport to sign the papers and settle the estate. You said it won't be for a few more days." He looked at Jaxon. "I'm hoping by then we'll have Boudier."

"Damon, there's something else." Ginny rubbed her stomach and blinked rapidly.

"What is it?" He leaned forward, his hands placed on the flat surface of his desk.

"If John was worth this much money, then my father would have had access to the funds."

"What do you mean?" Damon cocked his head.

"Well, in exchange for me marrying, my father wanted John McGregor to fund his empire."

"Empire?" Damon snorted.

She flushed, clearly embarrassed by having such a sadistic father. "Yeah. At least that's what he called it. I really think he was more than just a psychopath. I think he was evil, evil all the way to his marrow." She shivered and wrapped her arms around herself.

Jaxon rubbed her shoulders. "Ginny, that's all behind you now."

"Is it?" She looked up over her shoulder at Jaxon. Damon watched the interaction with trepidation. "Edward Boudier is missing. And until he's caught, no one is safe." She glanced down at her stomach.

"You are safe. He won't hurt you again. I swear it." Jaxon knelt beside her and took both of her hands in his. He pressed reassuring kisses to the backs of both her hands.

Damon shifted in his seat. It was too intimate a moment for him to be a spectator.

Ginny smiled at Jaxon with an eternity of love in her eyes.

Damon was glad the two had found each other after a tortuous start. They both deserved each other and a lifetime of happiness. But Ginny was right. No one was safe until her father was captured and made to pay for his sins with his blood.

Ginny tore her gaze away from Jaxon and looked at him. Her smile was gone and in its place was an expression of sadness.

"The reason I'm even bringing this up is if I have inherited twenty-five million dollars, then my question is, how much money does my father have if John paid him half of what he made every single year."

"John paid your father half?" Damon arched his brow. "That's an ungodly sum of money, and I can't imagine anyone handing over half of their income."

"Well, it wasn't for nothing." She studied the ground for a second before meeting his eyes. "My father had convinced John that when the time came, Edward was going to make John the next Pack Master. Whenever John brought it up, Edward said he was waiting until his retirement was fully funded and all his debts paid."

"Did your father have any debts?" Damon had been advised of the obscene amount of money Boudier had left behind in assets of cash, antiques, and even an offshore account in the Bahamas.

"Debts?" Ginny snorted. "My father made it a point never to be in debt to anyone. He always wanted to be the only one pulling the strings. He had no debt. I think he was just saying that to keep the money rolling in."

"That fits Boudier's M.O." Damon nodded. A shiver ran down his back, and he looked at Ginny.

"And that's why I think whatever money John gave him is hidden. I think he put that somewhere under a different name. Until the right time," Ginny's voice went low.

"Right time for what?" Damon already knew the answer. But he still had to ask the question.

"The right time to make us all pay." Ginny swallowed hard.

"There's no proof of any of this." Jaxon gave Damon a look which spoke volumes.

"Thank you for telling me all this, Ginny." Damon stood and walked around the desk. "I appreciate your honesty."

She nodded, and Jaxon helped her to her feet.

"I need to talk to Damon. I'll call you later." Jaxon

wrapped her up in his arms and kissed her on the lips.

"Okay." She smiled and nodded. "I'll head over to the bakery and give Ava a ride home."

"Thank you, Ginny." Damon nodded his appreciation and watched as she shut the door behind her.

"What do you think?" Damon asked Jaxon.

"It makes sense why we can't find him. If he's got enough money and resources, he can stay hidden until he's ready to be found," Jaxon said.

Damon brushed his hand down his face and sighed. "I don't get Boudier. If I were him and I had the money you and Ginny suspect he has, I would be living somewhere outside the United States. Like Mexico or hell, even Europe. It doesn't make sense for him to stay."

"Boudier is psychotic. He's not meant to make sense. Because Barrett took him down, Boudier is out for blood."

"Yeah and Barrett's dead." Damon looked up at Jaxon and frowned. "And the closest thing he would ever have to getting revenge on Barrett is getting revenge on Arkansas."

Jaxon nodded and looked toward the door that Ginny exited.

"I won't let him hurt anyone else, Damon. I've got too much to lose. I'll see that fucker in the ground before he comes for Ginny." Jaxon aimed his hate-filled eyes at Damon.

Damon knew the Guardian was still holding on to guilt of Barrett's death. Barrett had traded his life for Jaxon's. And Damon had been the one to carry out the execution through the series of events.

"He's going down. I'm going to make sure that bastard pays. I'm done with this Tribunal bullshit. Once I get my hands on him, there won't be anything left," Damon snarled.

Boudier had hurt too many to continue living. If it was the last thing he did, he would hunt the ends of the earth for the Were and rip off his head.

CHAPTER 29

*T*he ride to Denver was hours long but still too short for Jacey. It had taken hours but with Barrett the time had flown. She'd enjoyed being with him in casual conversation, and she wasn't ready to come back to reality.

"Are you hungry?" He looked over at her with those intense blue eyes.

Her stomach warmed and vivid images of last night flashed behind her eyes.

"Yes." Her voice came out more like a croak, and her throat was dry as dust.

"We'll grab lunch before we head over to the warehouse." He turned onto a busy street. Jacey noticed how all the females walking along the sidewalk did a double take when they spotted Barrett.

A tall brunette in expensive, fuzzy boots and a faux fur vest over a black turtleneck stopped long enough to give Barrett a sexy look.

If Barrett saw her, he didn't show he noticed her. Not in the way she wanted him to. A slight scowl crossed her perfect features when he didn't give her a second glance.

Jacey grinned.

"What?" Barrett stopped at a red light and turned to look at her.

"Huh?" She jerked her head to the passenger side window and pretended to be studying the Christmas decorations.

"I saw that. You were grinning. Why?" He cocked his head in amusement.

"No, I wasn't." She shook her head and glanced over at the red light. The red light flashed to green. Yet Barrett didn't move.

"It's green." She pointed at the light.

"I'm not moving until you tell me why you were grinning." He didn't take his eyes off her.

A horn blared behind them, and she turned in her seat. Her heart beat fast, and she jabbed her finger at the light.

"It's green. You can't just sit here." Her voice rose an octave on the last note.

"I can, and I will." He leaned toward her and grinned. His blue eyes were full of amusement.

"Ugh. Fine." She shot him a scorching glare. "I just thought it was funny that you didn't acknowledge that female that was trying to get your attention." She crossed her arms over her chest and huffed. "Can we go now?"

He grinned and eased away right before the light turned yellow.

* * *

BARRETT DID his best to hide his grin. And he was failing miserably.

So, Jacey had been watching his reaction to the human. And she apparently liked that he didn't respond to the flirt.

He had never really shown that many women interest, least of all humans. He enjoyed their company when he had the time. But when he was Pack Master, finding the time to release his sexual urges had been few and far between. That job had kept him hopping like the Easter Bunny on Easter Sunday.

He pulled the Jeep into the parking lot behind the restaurant in Denver. The parking lot was starting to fill up with early lunchtime customers so he made sure to pick a spot where he could get out rather easily.

"I hope you're hungry. This place has the best steak." He jumped out of his side and jogged over to her door. She had already opened the door and hopped out before he could make it over to her side.

"I won't ever turn down a steak. Especially one that comes highly recommended." She gave him a grin.

His stomach warmed and something squeezed inside his chest. He absently reached up and rubbed his palm over his pec and frowned.

"Everything okay?" Her brows slammed together, and she stepped closer.

The feeling in his stomach intensified.

"Just feeling weird."

"Oh, I hope you're not getting sick." Concern stretched across her stunning face, and it made his symptoms worse.

"Yeah." His body ached, his heart seemed to race, and his temp was elevated. It sounded a lot like the symptoms for the flu. Except Weres never got the flu. He shook his head and nodded toward the restaurant. "Let's grab a seat while there's still one available."

He had taken the extra cash that Ryker had left him for emergencies. He reasoned to himself that eating was an emergency. He knew better. He wanted to impress Jacey with a nice restaurant.

He opened the door, and a blast of warm air hit them. She smiled and shrugged out of her coat as the hostess quickly showed them to a booth in the back. He watched her reaction to the place.

"Not what I expected." She slid her gaze away from the upscale steakhouse with linen tablecloths and cozy candles lit in the center of the tables. The low lighting illuminated the brick walls and hardwood floors, wrapping the restaurant in a cozy and intimate feel.

"Let me guess. You were expecting peanut shells on the floor and country music."

She gave him a guilty grin and nodded slowly.

He let out a laugh. "That's okay. I'm been underestimated before."

She held up her hand and gave him wide eyes. "Not that I expected you to be cheap, it's just this is so …"

"Unlike me?" He arched a brow.

"No." She shook her head. "Expensive. It looks like someplace you would take someone on a date. Not just a casual lunch." She looked around.

His stomach dropped. She was right. This was way too nice. And as much as he liked being with her he knew that he needed to stay at a safe distance. Getting close to Jacey was bound to have him spilling secrets.

"It's going to be a long day so eat up," he said gruffly and picked up his menu.

He snuck a glance at her and noticed how her face seemed to fall. Shit. He'd gone and said the wrong thing again. He didn't need to give her the wrong idea.

Fuck.

"So, what do you suggest?" She peeked over her menu at him.

"I usually get the T-bone." He met her gaze and cocked his head. "But the filet is amazing as well."

"Then that's what I'll get." She set the menu down as the waiter came over and filled their water glasses.

"Can I get you both a cocktail?" The young male waiter smiled at both of them, but his gaze lingered a little too long on Jacey.

"I'll just have water," Jacey said and looked over at Barrett.

"Sweet tea," Barrett stated.

"I'm sorry we only have unsweet tea."

"Of course, you don't." Anything north of the Mason-Dixon line stopped serving sweet tea. "I'll have bourbon on the rocks."

"Very good. An appetizer to start?" the waiter asked.

Barrett looked at Jacey. She shook her head.

"No. But I think we're ready to order." Barrett picked up both menus and handed them to the waiter.

"The lady will have the filet, medium rare," he cut his eyes at her to make sure he had gotten her order right.

She smiled and nodded. "Sounds perfect."

"And for the side?" The waiter hovered his pen over his order pad.

She looked at him. "Whatever you suggest."

"She'll have the twice baked potato and the green beans." He looked at her and waited.

She smiled and eased back in her chair, seeming to be satisfied with her order.

"And for you, sir?" The waiter finished scribbling and turned to him.

"T-bone, medium rare. With the same sides."

"I'll put this order in and have that drink right out to you." The waiter turned to leave.

"Actually, bring the lady a glass of your best merlot," Barrett said.

"Very good." The waiter smiled and hurried away.

She gave him a guilty grin.

"Don't worry. Your metabolism will burn it off faster than you drink it."

"Thank you. I really wanted a glass but didn't want to seem like a lush." She sighed.

He laughed. "You couldn't seem like a lush if you tried." He shrugged out of his jacket and rested it on the seat of the booth. "Besides, I couldn't bear to see you ruin that steak with a glass of water. That would be a horrible pairing."

"You're right." Something flashed across her expression. Her eyes lit up when the waiter returned with their drinks.

He placed them with effortless precision in front of them before quietly disappearing.

He watched as she picked up the crystal wineglass by the stem. She lifted the glass to her lips and inhaled the scent of the wine. She'd done this before.

"So, you like wine? I was just guessing when I ordered it for you. I hope you don't mind."

"Not at all." She smiled. "I've never had anyone do that before. It's nice to feel taken care of." She blushed and then took a sip.

He took a drink. The smooth taste of the bourbon coated his tongue and slid down his throat.

"How's the wine?"

"It's the best wine I've ever tasted." Her eyes sparkled.

He laughed.

"No, I'm completely serious. My ex only let me buy beer. He'd never let me get wine." She lifted the glass and smiled. "This is a treat."

He gripped the glass in his hand. "Why wouldn't he let you buy wine? Did he have something against it?"

"He said he didn't want to waste money on it. He said if I wanted to drink, then I should drink beer like him. Because it's cheaper." She wrinkled up her nose. "I can't stand beer. Smells and tastes awful."

"So, what did you drink?"

"Water." She took another drink and let her gaze wander around the room.

Anger curled in his stomach. "I take it he was the one who controlled the money."

She looked back at him and nodded. "He paid all the bills, and I kept the house. He said that's how it worked."

"Did you ever want to go to college?"

"I did. But we married right out of high school." She shrugged and a thin sheet of sadness rested against her face. "He said he didn't want a mate or wife that wasn't going to be home. He had very strict ideas about what a marriage looked like."

"Well, it seems pretty fucking one-sided to me." He growled low.

"You're right. At the time, I didn't see it. My parents have been together forever, and my mom never worked outside the home. She always seemed happy. I guess I was trying to find that for myself." She sighed.

"What would you do if you went back to college?"

Her eyebrows shot up, and she leaned back in the chair looking at him. "Wow, I'm not sure." She placed her hands in her lap. "Right now, I feel like I'm just trying to survive. I don't know if I should indulge in delusions of grandeur."

"Why not?" He took a drink. "Everyone has goals, plans for the future. It's what keeps us going."

"What are your plans?" She cocked her head. The way she was staring at him with those gorgeous caramel eyes had his defenses down.

"My plan is to make The Mountain Top Bar and Grille successful. Make a little money and then move on." It was as honest an answer as he could give under the circumstances.

"So, you don't plan on staying in Colorado?" She took another sip of her wine.

"I think I was the one asking you about your plans." He

grinned. "I know when someone is trying to turn the conversation around on me."

She sighed and studied her wine. "I don't know. When I was a little girl, I thought about going into nursing. But now I'm not sure."

"So, what are the things you enjoy doing? If you find what you enjoy doing, then that's what you should try to make a career out of."

"Well, when I wasn't cleaning the house, I was cooking. I was planning on making a cookbook with recipes I had come up with over the years. I told Jeremy about it, but he said it was a stupid idea."

"Your ex is an asshole. And if I ever see that fucker, he'll wish he were dead." Anger pulsed through his veins.

"Wow. Don't hold back how you really feel." She giggled.

"Sorry." He looked around to make sure people were not staring at him. Luckily, they were in a snug corner where only a few people were seated.

"You're right. He is an asshole." She shook her head and stared over his shoulder like she was looking into her past. "I'm surprised it took me so long to figure him out."

"Growing up in a small town, you were conditioned to see things a certain way."

"Yeah, you're right. My mom and dad adored him. Even after he told me he wanted a divorce and to be unmated, they said it was my fault that he wasn't happy."

He growled and clenched his fingers into fists.

She looked up at him with surprised eyes.

"That's bullshit. You don't depend on someone else to make you happy. If he wasn't happy, it was his own fucking fault. And he's an idiot." This time, his words caught the attention of a couple of businessmen in suits who gave him a look.

He didn't care. Anyone that would throw Jacey away was a fucking idiot.

"You're right." She leaned back in her seat and studied him. "And if truth be told, I wasn't happy either." She lifted her hands palms up. "I mean, I think I was more comfortable with the routine of it all than anything. When he came in that day and shook up my world, I was scared. I didn't know what was going to happen to me or what I was going to do. I had depended on him to keep me in a house and have a roof over my head." She crossed her arms and shook her head. "I won't ever make that mistake again."

They settled into silence.

"You know, I'm still thinking about that cookbook. I mean I have a lot of recipes. Some I've never even made because Jeremy liked the same old thing and never wanted to try anything different."

"You should do it then. You can make whatever you want, and we'll try it out on the customers." Barrett took another sip.

"Really?" She pulled a face. "I mean your customers are quite different than, let's say, customers in here." She looked around at the elegant surroundings.

"Jacey, people are people. If the food's good, they'll eat it. Trust me," he said.

A smile blossomed and bloomed on her beautiful face, and he knew from the look she was seriously contemplating it.

"So, after publishing a cookbook, where do you see yourself?" he asked.

She let out a melodious laugh and held up her hands. "Hold on a second. I haven't even done the cookbook yet."

"I know but you need to stay one step ahead. Set another goal."

"Hmm, well, let's see," she looked up dreamily to the ceiling. "I suppose after a successful cookbook, I would find someone to share their life with me. One maybe two kids with a house in the country."

"No suburbs?"

"Absolutely not. I want enough space to get out and run." She gave him a look.

"I like it." He grinned. He could envision Jacey in that place, a large house set in the middle of a sprawling countryside maybe with rolling hills with woods as far as the eye could see. He could see her running around the front yard chasing two little blonde-haired children that looked like her and a dog yapping at her heels. Probably a lab.

What he couldn't envision was the male with her. The thought made him a little sick.

"Here we are." The waiter appeared with their food and placed their food in front of them.

"Would you be needing anything else, sir?" the waiter asked.

"No, thank you," Barrett said.

The waiter nodded and left them to eat their meal.

CHAPTER 30

The door to his office flung open and slammed into the wall hard. Damon looked up and scowled at the intruder. Every Guardian in Arkansas knew better than to barge into the Pack Master's office without an invitation.

"Colorado," Jayden said with his hands on his hips.

"What?" Damon scowled.

"Boudier. He's in Colorado," Jayden repeated. A scowl covered his face, and he was breathing heavily. "We have a positive ID of him crossing over the Colorado state line."

"You sure?" Damon stood.

"Yes."

"Colorado is a long way from the South. Not a lot of werewolves live in Colorado."

"Which makes it the perfect place to hide." Jayden nodded.

"Maybe." Damon picked up his cell phone. "I need you to get all the Guardians we have available and drive out to Colorado."

"How soon?" Jayden asked.

"Now. Have them fuel up and get their asses on the road."

He punched in some numbers on his cell phone as Jayden closed the door behind him.

"Hello?" The gruff voice of his Guardian came over the line.

"Ryker, we just had a positive id on Boudier. He's in Colorado," Damon growled out. "I need you to head that direction now. I'm sending the rest of the Guardians as soon as they're gassed up."

"Damon ..."

"For fuck's sake, Ryker, just do what you're told," Damon snarled. He cut the call and slammed his phone down on the massive desk. His patience with Ryker was gone. Ryker was becoming more and more unpredictable by the day. Mourning for Barrett was over.

The time for his justice was now.

* * *

"Fuck, fuck, fuck!" Ryker growled. A female coming out of the gas station avoided eye contact and gave him a wide berth as she made her way to her minivan.

He pulled out the nozzle from his gas tank and rested the hose back on the pump. He was cold from riding. He was in Kansas, near the Colorado state line, heading to check in on Barrett since he couldn't get in touch with him.

Now this. Boudier was spotted in Colorado. Which meant he knew or probably suspected that Barrett was alive. Or maybe Boudier was just getting as much distance between him and the South as humanly possible. The hair on the back of his neck stood on end.

No. As much as he wished that was the case, he knew deep down in his soul that it wasn't.

Now getting to Colorado was even more urgent. He had to get to Barrett before Boudier did.

The question was how the fuck did Boudier find out Barrett was alive and in Colorado?

He narrowed his eyes. The only other person that knew about Barrett besides himself and Celeste was Ella.

"That fucking witch." He ground out between clenched teeth. He knew he couldn't trust that fucking Witch of Yazoo City. He should have known better.

He dialed The Mountain Top Bar and Grille and when no one answered, he called Barrett's cell phone. It was the one number he never called. He never wanted it to be traced back to Barrett. But now it didn't matter.

He ended the call when no one answered. He hopped on his Harley and started the engine.

They were running out of time.

CHAPTER 31

"That was so good." Jacey smiled and glanced over at Barrett across the cab of the vehicle. "The best meal I've had since I got to Colorado."

"I wouldn't say that." He looked over at her and turned onto the next street. "Your cooking is amazing. Professional quality." He looked back at the road. "I can see you running your own restaurant."

She blushed at his compliment. It was probably the highest compliment she'd gotten in her whole life.

"You really think so?"

"Absolutely," He gave her a stern look.

"I'm not so sure I'd like to run a restaurant. Cookbook, yes. I've always loved to write so that would be right up my alley." She glanced out at the window. "I can't believe how much snow is coming down." She looked back at him. "Do you think we'll get back up the mountain?" She gazed out the window at the gray clouds hanging heavy in the sky.

"We'll make it back. Alfred's truck will make it through anything." He grinned. Her heart flip-flopped in her chest, and she fought the urge to stare at his handsome face.

After a few more turns through the charming city of Denver, the scenery began to change. Instead of upscale boutiques and restaurants, it was warehouses and industrial buildings.

Barrett slowed his speed and pulled into a driveway of a large warehouse. He pulled around back and parked near a large cyclone fence that had razor wire at the top.

"Is that normal?" She pointed at the fence that looked like something around the perimeter of a prison.

"For Alfred, it is. He's as paranoid as they come. Crazy, old badger thinks someone is going to break in and steal his shit."

Jacey pulled a face. "Does he have something worth stealing in there?"

"Don't let the look of it fool you. He's an ex-Army Ranger and has been collecting military memorabilia for years. He won't let me see what's in there, but I'm told it's worth quite a fortune."

"Ah." Men and their toys. She would never understand.

A man in his early thirties wearing coveralls and a dingy baseball hat came out from the loading hut. "Can I help you?" he called out and wiped his hands on his thighs. He stuck a red bandana in his hip pocket.

"Looking for Alfred. I need to borrow his truck." Barrett rested his hands on his hips.

"Alfred isn't here. He went over to Colorado Springs yesterday. Said he would be back late tonight." He walked over and held out his hand. "I'm Jim, by the way. I work for Alfred doing odd jobs and holding the fort down when he isn't here."

Barrett accepted and shook Jim's hand. "Barrett. Alfred lets me borrow his truck from time to time."

Jim nodded and glanced over in her direction.

"This is Jacey. She's with me." Barrett's tone went low and

deep, and even though the male was human, he clearly got the message that she was off limits.

"So, he'll be back late?" Barrett looked away, and she could tell he was thinking.

"Tell Alfred I'll be back tomorrow." He pointed at the Jeep. "I'm going to leave the trailer here, if that's okay."

"Fine by me." Jim gave a nod. "What time you want me to tell him you'll be back?"

"Daybreak. Maybe before." Barrett nodded, turned, and walked back to the Jeep. Jacey followed his lead.

"So, what are we going to do between now and tomorrow?" she asked.

"I'm not driving back if that's what you're asking."

"But what about the bar? It will have to be closed another day." She worried her lip with her teeth.

"Jacey, it's just a bar. What will one more day hurt?" He gave her a reassuring smile.

She walked around to the passenger side and opened the door. She welcomed the warmth of the Jeep's cab and despite her temperature running higher than a human's, the weather in Colorado was not to her liking.

She preferred the South.

She watched Barrett through the rearview mirror as he made quick work of unhitching the trailer. Within a matter of seconds, he was sliding into the driver's seat.

"Have you had the chance to explore Denver?" he asked as he started the engine and put the Jeep into drive.

"No. When I landed, I went straight to a motel and began looking for jobs." she admitted. "Today I feel like I'm seeing it for the first time. It's a beautiful city."

"You should see Aspen. It's gorgeous." he said with a smile on his lips.

"You've been?"

"Yes, but it's been a while. Used to go there on family winter vacations," he said with a faraway look in his eyes.

"Sounds wonderful." She sighed. "I've always dreamed of going someplace where it snows for a vacation. Skiing, sledding, snowboarding. I think I'd like to try that."

"Don't forget the wine by the fire." He smirked.

"I think that would probably be my favorite part." She smiled.

"I know it's my favorite part," he admitted.

She laughed.

They drove through the city of Denver with Barrett pointing out Christmas decorations on the different streets and storefronts. She smiled as groups of families walked down the sidewalk, wearing hats and mittens, with hot cocoa in their hands. It looked ideal.

Barrett turned into the entrance of a high-rise hotel and slid out of the driver's side.

He went around the Jeep and opened her door. A valet promptly arrived at his side.

Barrett turned and spoke to the valet in hushed tones. She wasn't sure why they were here, but she found herself looking at the windows of the boutiques next door.

"Jacey." He appeared at her side. Her heart fluttered a little.

"What are we doing here?" she asked.

"I figured we would spend the night in Denver and get up early to get supplies in the morning. That will give us enough time to tour the city and have dinner."

She blinked. "But I don't have enough money to stay here."

"It's my treat." He took her gently by the elbow.

"But I didn't pack any clothes, either." She looked up at him.

"Jacey, please, don't worry. I'm kind of the reason you're

in this predicament. You were kind enough to come with me, and now we are going to be stuck for the night. The least I can do is buy you something to wear."

His kindness touched her. "Barrett, you really don't have to do that." She rubbed her arm and looked around. She gathered from the bellhops, valet, and doorman, this hotel was going to cost a fortune.

"I know. I want to." He waved his hand toward the door. "Let's check in. Then we'll decide on the rest."

The doorman smiled and opened the door for them. She smiled back and thanked him.

She stepped inside the hotel. A large fountain sat in the middle of the lounge where strains of beautiful piano music spilled out from the hotel restaurant. There was a fireplace along the wall where people had gathered, sipping what she assumed was hot coffee in steaming mugs. She walked over to the fountain while Barrett went to the registration desk. Underwater lights in shades of blue and green shone against the colorful koi swimming back and forth.

One of the double elevators dinged open, and a woman dressed in black leather boots over black jeans stepped out into the lobby. She was stunning with flaming red hair and a body with curves. Her ample bosom stretched the white sweater she was wearing within an inch of its life.

She caught Jacey looking at her and narrowed her gaze and lifted her chin as she walked out of the hotel with the valet at her beck and call.

Jacey looked at the ground. She didn't belong here. Now she was sure of it.

She turned, ready to tell Barrett she wasn't going to stay. And instead plowed face-first into his large chest.

"Are you okay? I didn't mean to run into you." He held her elbows gently and looked into her eyes.

She blinked back the tears starting to burn the backs of her tender eyelids.

"I'm fine. It's my fault I didn't see you." She studied the floor.

When she looked up, he was staring at her strangely. Had he realized his mistake? Did he figure out she didn't belong here either?

"Come on. Let's go see the room and then we'll go check out the sights in Denver." He laced his fingers through hers.

The gesture made her cheeks turn red. And her stomach warm.

They walked together hand in hand as they got on the elevator.

"What floor, sir? Madam?" The bellman asked politely.

"Fourteenth," Barrett said.

"Very good, sir." The bellman pressed the button in his white-glove-covered finger and faced straight ahead. Jacey watched him on the ride up and not once did he blink.

The elevator dinged.

"Fourteenth floor, sir, and madam," the bellman said crisply.

They got out and by the time the doors slammed shut, she snorted.

"They actually pay someone to push a button?" she asked and laughed.

"Yes. People will pay for pretentiousness." He grinned. He walked a few feet and held out the key card, pressing it against the door. The lock flashed green, and he opened the door.

"Ladies first." He held the door for her.

She sobered. What the hell was she thinking? She couldn't spend the night in a bed with him. If she did, there would be no going back. She knew herself well enough to know she wouldn't refuse to sleep with him. She was supposed to be finding herself and her independence. Not trying to get her itch scratched.

But oh, did he know how to scratch an itch.

"Jacey?" Barrett frowned.

"Yeah, sorry." She forced her feet to move and walked across the threshold of the door. She wasn't going to embarrass herself by telling him she couldn't sleep in the same bed with him when he'd had his face between her legs just last night.

The room was large and was part of a suite. There was a large L-shaped couch that faced the large screen TV on the wall and a desk. The windows were floor to ceiling and had a wonderful view of the city and the snow falling outside.

She glanced in the next room and spotted a large bed. One large bed.

"Sorry. The front desk said that their two-bedrooms were all booked for the night. Some kind of convention in town. This is all they had," he said.

"It's fine," she said and froze. Why had she said that? It wasn't fine. It wasn't fine at all.

"There's a mini fridge under the cabinet by the TV if you want something to drink. I'm going to check on something at the front desk. I'll be back shortly." He headed out the door, leaving her alone in the room.

She peered into the bedroom. While the bed was a king-sized bed, it was still too small to share with Barrett and keep things casual. He was a big Were and filled half the damn bed up with just himself. She couldn't imagine being in the bed all night long and not touching him. It just wasn't physically possible.

She ducked back into the living area of the suite and opened up the mini fridge. She grabbed an ice-cold bottle of water. She opened it and took a nice, long drink. Things were happening too fast, and she needed time for them to slow down so she could think.

She walked over to the window and looked out. Snow falling gently to the earth in a display of quiet strength made her long for a fireplace, a glass of wine, and a good book.

She finished off the water and tossed the bottle into the trash. She had only a few more minutes before Barrett would be back. She headed into the bathroom to splash some water on her face and cool down her body.

CHAPTER 32

"*I*s that jacket warm enough?" Barrett tucked two fingers underneath the collar of Jacey's jacket, testing the thickness of the material.

"It's very warm." She arched her brow. "Why do you ask?"

He cocked his head and zipped her coat up to her chin. He then pulled the hood over her head. The hood didn't stay but fell back against her shoulders.

"That's not going to work. You need a hat that will stay on your head." He frowned and looked around. He spotted a boutique inside the hotel. "Stay right here," he commanded and walked into the store. In less than a few minutes, he bought the hat he'd spotted on display in the window.

He hurried back and pulled the white knit hat with a pink rose on the side on Jacey's head.

"What are you doing?" She frowned and batted his hands away.

"Making sure you will be warm," he stated and glanced down at her boots. Her boots. "Are those boots warm?"

"OMG, you sound like a mother fussing over her five-year-old." She propped her hands on her hips and glared. "Why are you asking all these crazy questions?"

"Because we are going to see the city, and I don't want you to be cold."

"I'm not going to be cold."

"Are you sure?" This time it was him who arched a brow.

"You're acting very weird." She reached out and touched his head with her palm. "You're not getting sick, are you?"

Every time she touched him, his stomach did flips. Maybe he was getting something. But he was pretty sure it wasn't an illness.

He ducked away and shook his head. A familiar roar of an engine made his chest expand. That sound always did that to him.

He looked back and slowly grinned. "It's time."

"Time for what?" she asked.

He turned just as a brand-new Harley Davidson V-Rod pulled up to the door. "That."

"The Harley? But it's snowing," she said.

"Pretend like you're sledding." He grinned. "Don't you like motorcycles?"

"I've never been on one," she admitted, but there was a sparkle behind her eyes.

"Never?" He frowned. "That is an absolute crime. Everyone should have at least one ride on a Harley Davidson before they die."

She grinned.

"Are you up for it?" He cocked his head.

Her grin grew on her face, making his chest expand with some unfamiliar emotion he'd never felt. "Absolutely. Is it yours?"

"No. I just rented it for the day. I figured there was no better way to see Denver than on the back of a bike." He took her hand, and they walked outside to the sleek-looking machine.

"You must be Barrett?" The man, wearing insulated riding coveralls, climbed off the bike and shook Barrett's hand. "You know we don't get many rentals for motorcycles in the winter." He shivered and looked between Barrett and Jacey. "Are you sure you two want to do this? I've got a Mustang I can rent you that's nice and warm." His gaze lingered a little too long on Jacey for Barrett's taste.

"We are absolutely sure," Jacey answered and stepped up to the bike to admire the lines and chrome.

The guy nodded and unstrapped the helmet hooked on the back seat and handed it to Barrett. "I only brought one helmet. I can call the office and have another one brought over right away."

"No need," Barrett answered. "I don't need one. As long as that one fits Jacey."

He took the helmet out of the man's hands and handed it over to her. She grinned and pulled the helmet over her head. Barrett pulled the shield down in front of her face. "You're going to want to keep that down to keep the wind and snow out of your eyes."

"But I really think you'd enjoy your riding experience if you had a full-face helmet." The man frowned. "You'll freeze to death if you don't have something on your head."

Barrett reached in his back pocket of his jeans and pulled out a knit hat. He slid the warm material over his head. "This is all I need."

"Well …" The man looked like he was going to argue. Barrett didn't have time for this bullshit. He needed to get on the road and enjoy his time with Jacey. As short-lived as it would be.

"What time do I need to have this back?" Barrett fixed the

strap under Jacey's chin and jiggled the helmet. It was a bit loose but not by much. He tightened the strap a little more. And then pulled some leather gloves out of his pocket and held them out to her.

"Where did you get those?" She took them and pulled them on over her slender fingers.

"At the same place I bought that fuzzy-looking hat for you." He pulled out a second pair and slipped them on. He fisted his fingers, ready to feel the motorcycle underneath him.

"I can pick it up any time before seven," the man said with his hands on his hips.

"Perfect. See you then." Barrett climbed on the bike and waited for Jacey to climb on behind him. He'd never ridden with a woman on a motorcycle before. He'd always preferred to ride alone. It was the one thing that he always kept just for himself.

She wrapped her arms around his waist and laid her head against his back. He smiled to himself as he started the engine. The motor roared to life, and several people turned to stare.

They all probably thought it was too cold to be out riding a bike in the middle of winter while it snowed. He didn't care. They wouldn't understand. They were mere humans.

The adrenaline in his veins pulsed as he eased forward and checked traffic. When it was clear, he turned the motorcycle onto the street. The gentle snow hit his face and cheeks, melting into his fevered skin within a fraction of a second.

The roar of the engine and the feel of the freezing wind had his blood pumping hard. Jacey tightened her hold on him. He nearly groaned, liking the feel of her against him.

He turned down street after street, taking his time and showing her the delights of Denver. The traffic lights were decorated in red and green boughs of evergreen and large, colorful ornaments. The flickering streetlamps were tied with big red bows and decorated with bits of holly. Store windows had each been meticulously decorated, careful not to leave one square inch bare.

He turned out of the business district and headed toward the residential area of the city. Here, the traffic was slow and unhurried, and he took his time driving down each street and looking at the decorated houses.

He stopped at a stop sign and looked over his shoulder. "How are you doing? Hanging in there?"

"I'm good. But I really thought you'd go faster," she said near his ear.

"Faster?" He grinned. "Hang on tight."

He pulled out onto the street and increased his speed. The whine of the engine sent pulses of energy through out his entire body. She giggled near his ear as she clung tighter.

Traffic slowed ahead, and he glanced around. He increased his speed and wove in and out of traffic with expert skill.

Peals of laughter from his rider had him increasing his speed even more.

If it had been any other female, they would have been screaming in fear. Not Jacey.

He headed out of town. Once on the highway, he opened the Harley up, letting the speed take them where it would.

They had nowhere to be, and no one knew who they were. In this moment, they were both free.

Half an hour later, he felt her begin to shiver behind him. He turned on the exit ramp and pulled up to a gas station. Killing the engine, he got off first.

"You're starting to freeze." He lifted the shield from her helmet. Her caramel-brown eyes stared back at him in amusement.

"A little. But I want to ride more," she said, taking his hand and letting him help her off the V-Rod.

"Go inside and grab a coffee. I'm going to gas up, and I'll be in there in a second." He worked the strap loose off her chin and pulled the helmet off her head.

"Okay." Her cheeks were rosy, and he knew if he touched them, they would be cold.

She didn't seem to mind though. She headed into the building and over to the coffee station. He turned his attention to the gas pump and pressed some buttons.

While he gassed up the bike, he watched Jacey inside. He noticed the men turn and give her a second look, yet none had enough balls to walk up to her.

Good. He would hate to have to kill someone today.

After filling up, he headed inside. He walked over to where she was sipping on a hot cup of what looked like tea.

"No coffee?" He arched his brow.

"Nah, I thought I'd have some hot chocolate instead." She held up the cup for him. "Want to try it?"

His fingertips brushed hers, and her pupils dilated at the simple contact.

He lifted the cup to his lips and took a sip. The hot, sugary, sweet chocolate coated his tongue and slid down his throat.

He smiled and handed it back to her.

"It's good."

"It's perfect. Especially for a day like this." She turned and gazed out the window. The snow falling in sheets gave a silence to the world outside.

He headed over to the cashier and paid for both the gas and the hot chocolate.

He walked back and stood beside her, watching out the window as the snow fell. It wasn't exactly romantic, but he would take whatever he could when it came to Jacey.

After she finished her hot chocolate, they both headed out of the store and into the snowy weather. He fixed her helmet on her head and started the bike.

This time, he took his time getting back to the hotel.

CHAPTER 33

*J*acey looked up at the bathroom ceiling. She dipped her fingers into the bubble bath and sighed. She wasn't sure of the time, but she knew she should be getting out pretty soon or else she was going to resemble a prune.

After they returned to the hotel, Barrett stayed downstairs to take care of the payment on the Harley they had rented. He'd told her to go upstairs and get warm in a bubble bath.

She didn't argue. She'd loved riding with him but after an hour, she began to feel like a popsicle.

She heard the door open to their room and froze.

"Jacey?"

"Yeah." She grabbed a towel and scrambled to her feet. "I'll be out in a minute."

"No rush," Barrett called out through the closed door. "I'm going to grab a shower in the other bathroom and get ready. I've got some clothes for you to wear tonight. I'm putting them on the bed."

"Okay." She wrapped the towel tight around her naked body. "Thank you."

She stepped out of the tub and headed to the sink. She looked under the sink for a hairdryer and froze. A pretty gift basket wrapped with a pink ribbon sat in the middle of the shelf. She picked it up and set it on the marble bathroom counter.

She fingered the gift card attached to the ribbon.

"To Jacey Miller. Please enjoy!"

Barrett. He must have set this up when we were riding, she thought.

She smiled and unwrapped the ribbon and cellophane.

Inside were lipsticks, eye shadow, and every kind of cosmetic a girl could want.

It wasn't cheap either. This was the high-end stuff. The stuff she could never afford.

Her heart seemed to swell inside her chest. As gruff and big as he was, Barrett was the most thoughtful male she'd ever met in her life. He was too good to be true.

She took a deep breath and pulled out the hairdryer and stopped. She needed to grab her clothes while Barrett was in the shower.

She opened the door and peered out. She heard the water turn on in the other bathroom and hurried out with the towel still around her body.

She stopped short.

Lying on the bed was a fire-engine-red wrap dress with expensive heels in a beautiful shade of nude. Beside the dress, a single red rose.

Jacey Miller had never swooned a day in her life. But now she was very close to it.

* * *

BARRETT STEPPED out into the living area and froze. Jacey turned from gazing out the darkened window when he entered.

"Wow," he breathed. "You look amazing."

"Thank you." She gazed down at her dress. "You look pretty handsome yourself."

He wiped his sweaty palms on his slacks and straightened the vest he wore over his black button-up shirt. It felt like ages since he'd had an opportunity to dress up. He didn't even mind the fact that he'd used a good chunk of the emergency cash tonight.

"Thank you for the makeup and the dress and well, everything," she said under her lashes. "You really didn't have to do that."

"I know. I wanted to do it."

She nodded and looked back out the window. "I'm guessing you have someplace special for us to go tonight?"

"Yes. I've made reservations at a restaurant. It's one you'll like."

"So, no more riding in the snow?" She quipped with a grin.

"Not today, at least." He held out his arm. "Are you hungry?"

"Starving, actually. Which is weird." She tucked her arm in his and looked up at him. "After all that food I ate at lunch, I shouldn't be hungry."

"That's a good sign. It means you're enjoying life." He looked down at her and opened the door to the hallway. He stepped aside so she could walk through first.

Her scent hit him dead in the chest as she brushed past him. His body hardened, and he fought to keep it under control.

He walked over to the elevator and pushed the button.

The elevator dinged immediately, and the doors opened.

They stepped inside, and the bell man quickly pushed the button.

Barrett rested his hand on Jacey's lower back.

It felt like an eternity until the elevator doors opened into the lobby.

"Are we taking the Jeep?" She looked up at him. His heart nearly stopped in his chest.

She'd used dark-bronze color on her eyes which accentuated their natural caramel color. Her long, dark eyelashes blinked slowly as she waited for him to answer. She'd never wore lipstick, but tonight she'd swiped her full lips with a pretty pink color which seemed to simmer under the lights in the lobby of the hotel. She wore no jewelry, hell, she didn't need to, she was a jewel herself, and the dress fit her curves like a dream. He looked away and noticed that every male in the room had turned to look at her.

He picked up her hand and wrapped his arm around her body, leading her outside. "Actually, no."

She looked up with him with wide eyes. He smiled. "I wanted to drink tonight so this way we don't have to worry about a sober driver." He winked.

She laughed. The sound went straight to his heart.

He held out his hand. She blinked and took it.

"Again. Thank you." She looked up at him. She shook her head. "All of it must have cost you a fortune. I'm not sure how I'll ever repay you."

"You already have," he said.

"What?"

"You already have repaid me. By your presence. Here tonight. That's all I need." He tore his gaze away from her and trained it straight ahead as they walked. He was afraid if he continued to look at her, she would see the truth. That she was his weakness, his point of vulnerability.

She stopped and squeezed his hand. He turned and

looked at her. "For everything. I feel like I've gone from losing everything in my life to finally finding myself. You made that possible by giving me a chance at a job that I had never done before. If it hadn't been for you, I'm not sure what I would have done."

"You would have survived without me. You're a very strong woman, Jacey." He frowned, looking at her. "I hope you know that."

She shrugged as if she really didn't believe him.

"The hotel's restaurant looks nice." She stopped at the restaurant entrance in the lobby.

"We're not eating at the hotel. We are going out. It's a European restaurant, and it has the best wine in Colorado."

"Do you carry that wine at your place?" Her eyebrows shot up.

"Do you think anybody at the bar would be able to afford it?" he deadpanned. "That would be a no. But I do keep a bottle on hand for a rare occasion."

"Oh yeah? Like what?" she asked.

A few seconds passed, and he cleared his throat. "Well, that occasion hasn't happened yet. But when it does, I'll have the wine."

She touched his arm and laughed. "You're really funny, you know that?"

He frowned. "No one has ever told me that before."

They'd called him a hard-ass, bastard (when they thought he wasn't listening), and stubborn. But never funny.

They stepped outside the hotel into the cold air. They walked a block before getting to their destination.

He opened the door to the elegant restaurant and let Jacey walk in first. He walked up to the hostess and leaned over to give her his name.

"Right this way, sir." The hostess carried two menus with her as she showed them the way to their seats.

Jacey didn't seem to notice the heads she turned as she followed the hostess. But Barrett did. He scowled at every mouth-breathing human who dared look in her direction. They quickly got the hint and looked the other way.

Barrett pulled out Jacey's seat for her and then sat opposite her. The table was located in a quiet corner just as he requested when he made the reservation.

The flicker of candlelight from the center of the table enhanced the ambiance of the romantic place.

The hostess handed them their menus and quietly left.

She took the linen napkin and unfolded it before putting it in her lap. He did the same and looked up as the waiter approached their table.

"Good evening, sir, madam, I am Rafe. I'll be your waiter this evening." He gave a slight bow. "Can I start you off with a cocktail or perhaps a bottle of our wine?" He passed Barrett the wine and spirits menu.

He opened it and quickly found the wine he wanted. "We'll have a bottle of this, please." He handed the menu back.

"Yes, sir." The waiter's face brightened. "Very good, sir. Can I start you off with an appetizer?"

"Yes. We'll start with the Moulard Duck Foie Gras Terrine," he stated.

"Excellent choice. I'll put that in and get your wine." He gave another short bow and headed off in the direction of the kitchen.

"Foie Gras?" She lifted her eyes. "I've never had French food before."

"It's good, trust me. You'll take one bite and fall in love."

She wrinkled up her nose. "I'm not so sure."

The waiter appeared with a bottle of wine. He held it out for Barrett's inspection, and he nodded his approval. Rafe then began uncorking the bottle. The cork came out with a resounding pop. Rafe poured a little into a glass. Barrett swirled the dark-garnet liquid around in the long-stemmed wine glass and lifted it to his nose and inhaled. He took a sip.

"Perfect." He held out the glass for him to fill.

Rafe then filled Jacey's glass.

"Have you decided what you would like to order?" he asked, looking at them both.

Barrett looked at Jacey, making sure she wanted him to order for her. She nodded and sipped happily on her wine.

"For the second course, we'll both have the Butter Poached Maine Lobster."

"Excellent choice, sir." Rafe smiled and quickly excused himself.

"How's the wine?" He looked at her over his glass.

"Wonderful." She smiled and relaxed back in the chair. It was the most unguarded he had seen her, and he was glad he splurged for the expensive wine.

"This place is beautiful." She looked around at the elaborate floral arrangements around the room.

"Thank you for bringing me here." She looked back at him. "I've never been somewhere so nice." She looked around and placed her hands in her lap. "You've been here before?"

"Yes. It's been a while. Many years ago, in fact. When I was younger. My family liked to vacation here in the winter. My mom loved the food. So, my father made sure to bring us here."

"Oh. Where do your parents live?" she asked.

He looked away. He'd told her too much. Way too much.

"They used to live on the East Coast. But they were both killed in a plane crash."

"Oh, God. I'm so sorry, Barrett. I didn't mean to pry." She reached across the table and touched his hand.

"It's okay. It was a very long time ago."

"Do you have any more family?"

"A brother and sister. But we're not close anymore." He took a sip of wine and studied the inside of his glass. His stomach ached a little as he thought about Addison and Edgar. Ever since coming back from the dead, he'd been thinking about his siblings more and more.

"I'm sorry."

"Don't be. Things happen." He shrugged. "That was a very long time ago." A time before he became Pack Master of Arkansas and the biggest responsibility he had was which vacation home he was going to stay at. He'd been young and foolish and had disappointed his family in ways that mattered most.

Now it seemed like a lifetime ago.

Rafe magically appeared with their first course. He refilled Jacey's water glass. "Enjoy." Then he disappeared back toward the kitchen like an apparition.

"They are actually really good." He put some of the delicacies on her plate before serving himself.

She speared one with her fork and carefully placed it in her mouth.

Her expression changed from unsure to pleasure. When she finished chewing, she looked at him with wide eyes. "That was good."

"I told you so. You act like I'd feed you something gross." He snorted and ate one for himself. The rich taste of butter and garlic burst on his tongue.

"It's not what I expected at all." She ate another one and sighed.

"Glad I could introduce you to the finer things in life." He grinned. "But if you think this is good, wait until you try the main entree. It's amazing."

"And the dessert?" She arched her brow.

"It's to die for."

CHAPTER 34

While Barrett paid the bill, Jacey stepped outside to wait for him.

The blast of cold air felt good on her skin. After eating such an extravagant meal and drinking all that lovely wine, she welcomed the fresh air. She wrapped her arms around herself. The snow had stopped falling, leaving behind a fresh white blanket on the ground.

"Hey, sweetheart, you cold?" A rough voice behind her sent chills up her back.

She turned around and dropped her hands to her sides.

Two men in jeans and a winter coat leered at her. She could smell beer on their breath, and she knew they were drunk.

She didn't answer them but looked back inside to see if she could spot Barrett. One of the men stepped in her line of vision, obstructing her view.

"Excuse me." She tried to step around him to go back toward the restaurant, but he grabbed her arm.

"That's not very nice. Where are your manners, little Southern girl?" He grinned down at her.

A low rumble erupted behind the man as Barrett came barreling out the restaurant doors. He plowed into the man holding her and knocked him away.

"You don't ever fucking touch her, do you understand?" Barrett stepped in front of Jacey, becoming a wall between her and her aggressors. Fear beat like a drum in her chest.

"I don't see a ring on her finger so that means she's free," the man smirked.

Barrett plowed his fist into the human's face, sending him hurling to the ground. The other man looked like he was coming to his friend's aid until Barrett rounded on him with a look so lethal it could kill. The second guy stepped back.

"You broke my fucking nose," the guy on the ground cried out.

Jacey looked around, and by this time a small crowd had gathered. The hostess in the restaurant had stepped outside.

"What's going on out here?" The older gentleman with graying hair and a suit looked at Barrett and then the guy on the ground.

"He broke my fucking nose," the guy cried out.

The manager looked at Barrett and scowled.

"He put his hands on Jacey." Barrett glared. He looked like he was ready to fight the manager too.

"Is this right?" The manager looked around Barrett at her. "Did he touch you?"

"He did. I was trying to walk back inside, and he started to harass me." She put her hand on Barrett's arm. She could feel the muscles bunching under the material of his clothes. His anger was palpable.

"Aren't you going to do something? He broke my nose!"

The manager narrowed his gaze to the man on the ground. "Then I suggest you don't put your hands on ladies. And if you don't get your sorry carcass away from the front of my restaurant, I'm going to call the police."

"Look, asshole, I have rights … " The guy on the ground started to stand and face the manager, but his friend stepped in front of him.

The manager narrowed his eyes and pulled out his cell phone. "I'm calling the police."

"Let's go, man. Before he calls the cops. We can't afford that." The second guy mumbled under his breath.

She looked over at the two men, and it hit her. She knew where she'd seen them before.

Her legs buckled. Barrett caught her before she hit the ground.

"Are you okay?" he asked, his face creased with concern.

"Yes. Just lightheaded," she lied.

"Let me call a taxi," the manager of the restaurant offered.

"No, I'm fine. I need the fresh air." Jacey reassured him.

"Are you sure?" Barrett stared down at her.

"Yes."

He wrapped his arm around her tightly and they hurried back to their hotel. They didn't speak and when they reached the hotel, they headed straight for the elevator.

The bellman greeted them and pressed the button for their floor.

When they got off on their floor, Barrett cradled her face between his hands.

"Are you okay?" He leaned into her, his eyes full of worry.

"Yes. It's just." She licked her lips.

"What?"

She looked him in the eyes. "Barrett, I'm pretty sure those guys were the ones who tried to trap me when I was a wolf."

* * *

THEY GOT BACK to the room, and it was all he could do not to jump in the Jeep and go looking for those guys. But Jacey was still shaken, and she didn't want him to leave. He saw the fear brewing behind her eyes.

Instead, he ran a bubble bath for her so she could relax. He promised that he wouldn't leave.

He paced the living area, looking out the window at the lights in downtown Denver. He opened the sliding glass door and stepped outside into the night air.

The temperature had dropped considerably, and he unbuttoned his shirt, needing to feel the cool wind against his skin. His shirt whipped in the wind as the cold air stung his chest. He lifted his head to the dark sky and let out a frustrated growl.

He shouldn't have left her by herself. He should have made her wait inside with him. He should have protected her better.

If something like this ever happened again, he knew in his soul he'd kill for her.

He dropped his head to his chest as realization settled over him like a thick blanket.

She was his mate.

He'd known it all along, but he'd tried to convince himself otherwise. Now it wasn't going to end well for them. He couldn't be with anyone. He was supposed to be dead.

She wasn't looking for a mate. She was looking to find herself.

He looked up over the city as the lights twinkled before him. How had it come to this?

Shaking his head, he stepped back inside. He walked over and peered inside the bedroom.

Jacey was curled up in her robe, asleep on top of the bed.

He headed into the bathroom to get ready for bed. When he came out, he curled up on the bed next to Jacey, pulling her into his arms.

* * *

BARRETT WAS up early and showered before Jacey rolled out of bed, before she realized he had slept by her side the entire night.

She yawned and covered her mouth with her hand. "You should have woken me."

"I was just about to do that," he said. She looked better today. More like herself. Gone was the fear in her eyes, replaced by calm reassurance.

"I'm going to head downstairs and pick us up some coffee and something to eat to take with us."

"I'll be ready by the time you get back." She crawled out of bed and tied her robe around her.

His body tightened, and he really wanted to see what was on under her robe. Not that he didn't already have carnal knowledge.

He headed for the elevator.

When he got to the first floor, he went over to the in-house restaurant and put his order in for two fresh coffees and some pastries to go.

He headed over to the front desk.

"May I help you, sir?"

"Yes, I need to use your phone. My cell phone died, and I forgot to bring my charger," he said.

"Of course." The man at the front desk provided a landline phone for him and moved away so he could speak in private.

He dialed the only number besides Ryker's he had memorized.

"Hello?" Helen answered.

"Helen, it's Barrett."

"I have been worried sick to death about you and Jacey,"

she said. "When you two didn't return yesterday, I nearly called the cops."

His gut tightened. "Well, I'm glad you didn't." He did not need the attention of the police on him. He was supposed to be a dead man.

"Look, I'm calling to say that we had to spend the night because I couldn't get the truck yesterday. I'm headed over there today to pick it up and the supplies. Which means we'll be closed another night.'

"Want me to drive over and put a sign up saying why?" Helen asked. "They're going to want to know why we're closing."

"I don't give a rat's ass what they want. The roads are bad enough as it is. Don't you dare go out in this weather to hang up a note as to why we're closed. They'll figure it out. Besides, I can't imagine why anyone would come out in weather like this anyway."

"To drink. When people get the itch, they'll do whatever," she stated.

She wasn't wrong.

"Anyway, I just called to let you know we'll be headed back today and for you to take the day off," he said. People were starting to filter in the lobby and get a little noisier.

"Thanks for letting me know, honey. I'll see you guys tomorrow." She ended the call.

Barrett replaced the receiver on the cradle and met the register's gaze. "Thank you."

"Any time, sir."

He headed back to the bakery and picked up his order. He took a long drink of his black coffee and sighed. They had a long day ahead of them. He needed all the coffee he could get.

CHAPTER 35

$\mathcal{J}$acey was still nibbling on her strawberry cheese pastry when Barrett pulled up at the industrial building they had visited yesterday.

"Don't rush. I'm just going to talk to Alfred before changing vehicles. You'll have time to finish your breakfast." He grabbed his coffee cup and slid out the Jeep.

The younger guy that they'd met yesterday came out from the open hull of the loading dock. He nodded in greeting when he saw Barrett. Barrett returned the gesture.

She took a sip of her coffee and sighed.

Watching Barrett walk across the parking lot in his tight-fitting jeans and sage-green jacket had her stomach doing somersaults. He moved with expected grace for someone his size, and his beauty was unlike any she'd ever seen.

An older man walked out with a long, white beard, trucker hat, and a scowl. He saw Barrett and spit a stream of tobacco on the cold ground. He held out his hand, and Barrett took it.

They talked for a little bit then Barrett nodded over his shoulder at his Jeep and then pointed to his trailer they had parked off to the side. The old man nodded and then Barrett jogged back toward the Jeep.

He opened the door, slid inside, and started the engine. "Make sure you take all your stuff out."

"So he's letting us borrow his truck?" She finished her coffee and tossed the empty cup in the paper bag with the used napkins.

"Yeah. I have to bring it back in a week, which works out well. It doesn't have me rushing to bring it back to him tomorrow." He pulled the Jeep next to the trailer and put it in park. He got out, and she followed.

She grabbed the bag of trash from breakfast and wadded it in a ball. She opened the door to the back seat and grabbed her duffle bag full of the items Barrett had bought for her during this trip. He even hung up the dress she'd worn last night so it wouldn't get wrinkled.

She was continuously astounded by his generosity. He was not like any male she'd ever been around.

"Let me hold that." He walked over to her side of the Jeep and took the duffle bag and hooked the strap on his broad shoulder. He took her hand in his and walked over to the building.

A loud roar sounded from inside the building and the garage-style door went up. Out shot a very large truck with an enclosed trailer attached. It looked like one of those moving trucks except larger, and it was painted in camouflage.

"What is that?"

"That's what's going to save our ass and our supplies." He grinned back at her.

"Will it make it up the mountain?" She eyed the truck with suspicion. "If the delivery truck won't make it up, what makes you think this one will?"

"It'll make it because it has a larger engine, and the tires are specially made for snow. It used to be an old Army vehicle but Alfred has repurposed it to haul supplies and stuff."

"And stuff? Do I want to know?"

"Probably not." He tugged her with him as he walked to the truck. The old man scrambled out of the cab and landed in front of them. He eyed Jacey with a suspicious look.

"Alfred, this is Jacey. She works for me at the bar and grill. She volunteered to help me get supplies." Barrett gave the introductions.

"Nice to meet you." He held out his hand. She took it. His grip was firm but not too hard, and his expression softened a little. "You are too pretty to be doing a lot of manual labor." He shot Barrett a dirty look.

"Relax, Alfred. She's not going to be lifting anything." Barrett glared.

"Good," he gruffed out a reply. "Nowadays, men don't treat women like ladies anymore." He shook his head and looked at her. "If he gives you any trouble, you let me know, okay, honey?"

She fought a grin and looked up at Barrett. "I'll do that."

Alfred handed the keys over to Barrett and patted the door. "Be careful with my girl here." He cut his eyes at Barrett "You know I don't lend my stuff to just anyone."

Barrett let out a long-suffering sigh. "I know, I know. I appreciate it. And I'll take care of your truck."

Alfred nodded and headed back in without so much as a goodbye.

"Is he always like that?" She looked at Barrett.

"Usually much worse. You caught him in a good mood today." Barrett nodded to the truck. "You ready to go?"

"Yes. I made sure to get everything out of the Jeep." She held up her ball of trash. He took it and tossed it into a nearby trash can.

He walked her around to the passenger side of the truck and opened her door. She climbed in, and he shut the door behind her. She looked around at the wide cab. The large console in the middle of the bucket seats was dusty from lack of cleaning.

Barrett climbed in and glanced over at her before he put the truck in drive.

"It shouldn't take long to load, and then we'll head home," he said as he turned onto the street.

She nodded and looked out the passenger side window.

Home. It didn't feel like home to her, but it didn't feel like a strange place anymore. She knew it had more to do with Barrett.

It should have frightened her. It didn't. She knew she needed to be focusing on being more independent and not leaning on him so much. Being vulnerable is what got her into this situation to begin with. She'd been too dependent on her ex, and he used her weakness against her.

As much as she was entranced and drawn to Barrett, she knew that they wouldn't last.

Love never did.

Once they got back up the mountain, she would have a long talk with him and set some boundaries.

It would be best for both of them, despite the pain in her chest.

CHAPTER 36

"*E*veryone needs to sit down and have a glass of wine," Ava ordered. She had invited all the females, including Granny, over to her house for a girls' dinner. After Damon and the Guardians headed out to Colorado to find Boudier, they had all been worried. She thought dinner would be a welcome distraction.

"You and Ginny can't drink. And it makes me feel guilty to drink in front of both of you." Haley eyed her glass of white wine. "Maybe I shouldn't drink either."

"Ginny and I are preggers. The rest of you aren't. Besides, I also have chocolate-covered salted caramel. So, I'm not missing out on the wine," Ava said with a bright smile. She opened a large rectangle canister filled with treats and showed the ladies.

"Yes, I'll definitely take one of those," Ginny said, nearly licking her lips.

"Well, I'm drinking. I am definitely not going to feel guilty," Catty announced. She took a big drink of her red wine and smiled. "And I'm having chocolate." She snagged a piece and popped it into her mouth. She sighed with appreciation. "That's really good, Ava."

"Thanks!" She smiled. "I got it at the candy shop by the Riverwalk."

"I'm with Catty. I need a drink. This is the only time I get to drink, when I'm away from the Bella Luna," Kate said and eased into a chair, cradling a glass of white wine.

"I thought you have wine night every night with your guests," Skylar said, taking a piece of chocolate-covered caramel.

"Oh, the guests get wine. But lately the clientele I'm getting seem to be big drinkers. There's usually no wine left for me." Kate shrugged. "It's probably for the best. Work has been crazy. Every month has been filled. I've had to hire some help."

"Is that who's watching the B&B while you're here, dear?" Granny asked, pouring
herself a liberal amount of wine in a glass.

"Maria. She's a friend of Beau's, and she's an amazing cook. She's divorced and needed the extra income. I'm grateful to have her," Kate said.

"Well, we're glad you're here, dear." Granny patted her leg and eased onto the couch.

Ava looked around the room and tried to ignore the silence that settled among the women. Catty cocked her head and was eyeing her with suspicion. Haley was glumly studying the inside of her wine glass. Ginny was nibbling on a chocolate and avoided eye contact. Kate was the only one enjoying her wine.

Skylar stood up and sighed. "Fine. I'll ask since no one else has the balls to do it."

"I have the balls to do it," Catty said and then waved her

hand in the air, "but you should ask. I'm tired of being the one badgering everyone all the time."

Skylar rolled her eyes at Catty and turned to Ava. "So, what's the update? How close are the Guardians to getting Boudier?"

Ava stuffed another caramel in her mouth and shrugged. "I don't know," she said with a mouthful of chocolate.

"Ava, you're the wife of the Pack Master. Surely you know something." Catty narrowed her eyes at her.

"Geez, Catty, stop looking at me like that," Ava scowled.

"I can't help it. It's my attorney cross-examination look." She glared harder. "It's what makes the criminals tell me everything."

"Well, I'm not a criminal," Ava shot back.

"Did they catch him yet?" Haley looked up from her wine.

"Ugh. You guys. You're not even supposed to know they went to Colorado." Ava gnawed on a fingernail. "If Damon finds out I told, he's going to be angry."

"Easy, honey," Granny reassured. "No one is telling Damon anything. It's just, you know we are worried about our males. Just don't want to see anything happen to them."

"I know. I know." Ava rubbed her stomach and eased into a chair. "To answer your question, no. They haven't caught Boudier yet. But they are close."

"I'll be glad when this whole thing is over with," Catty said and took a long drink of her wine. "I feel like once Boudier is dealt with, then we can all get on with our lives."

Silence swept the room, and everyone turned to Ginny.

Ginny looked up from grabbing another piece of chocolate. "Please stop looking at me like that. You know I've already stated my opinion on the bastard."

"But he's your father, Ginny," Haley said quietly

"He may be my biological father but believe me when I say, he has never been nor will he ever be my father. I have more reason to want him dead than any of you." She shrugged.

"We just don't want to hurt your feelings, Ginny," Skylar said softly. She reached over and squeezed her hand.

Ginny smiled. "I know. And I trust that Damon and the Guardians will get him. In fact, I hope they kill him instead of bringing him back for a Tribunal. No good will ever come of Edward Boudier walking this earth."

Ava nodded. On that point, she could agree.

* * *

IT TOOK LESS time to load the truck than he thought possible. The owner of the shipping company offered to load the truck for Barrett with his forklift. Barrett was glad for the help. The sooner they left the sooner they could get back to Silverton.

The snow had started to fall as they drove back. The tires had hit some slick patches but with his skillful driving, he'd kept the truck on the road.

For the majority of the drive back, Jacey had slept, her head pressed against the window. He'd snuck glances at her time and time again and was grateful she couldn't see him staring at her.

She stirred and lifted her head. She looked over at him and gave a lazy smile as she stretched her arms over her head. "Why didn't you wake me? I'll never sleep tonight."

He grinned. "I figured you needed the rest."

"Wow, how close are we to home?" She looked out the window as if trying to see some invisible sign. Up here, there were none. Up here, there was anonymity.

"Be there in about five minutes."

"Wow. I really slept too long." She shook her head and

grabbed her water bottle in the console. Before they left he'd gassed up and grabbed waters for both of them.

"You'll have a lot of energy for helping unload all this stuff," he joked.

"Yes. I can't wait to try out my new recipes for the bar this week." She grinned, and her eyes sparkled with excitement.

A little while later, they were pulling up at the back of the bar. A fresh batch of snow had fallen on the cold earth, and the trees were trembling with ice. It was beautiful.

He killed the engine. "I'll unlock the back door, and we can start unloading the supplies. You have your gloves, right? It's going to be cold."

"Right here." She held up the set of insulated gloves and zipped up her coat to her chin.

He nodded and headed to the back door. He quickly unlocked it and opened the door. He stepped inside and flipped on the switch. The phone at the bar began to ring. He turned to ignore it but waited. What if it was Helen? She was probably calling to see if they were back yet. That woman worried too much. She was going to end up dropping dead of a stroke.

He turned and yelled over his shoulder. "I'll be right back. Got to catch this call."

He jogged into the bar and grabbed the phone.

"Hello?"

"Barrett, where the fuck have you been?" Ryker nearly yelled through the phone. "I've been trying to reach you since yesterday. You're not answering your cell phone."

"My cell died, and I had to go into Denver to pick up supplies. I just walked back in the door." Barrett lowered his voice when he heard Jacey come into the kitchen. He headed toward the front door of the bar with the cordless phone and stepped out onto the porch so Jacey wouldn't overhear.

"Jesus, Barrett. Do you know what's been going on? I've been trying to warn … "

A deafening explosion sounded behind him, knocking the windows out of the bar and knocking him off the porch into a bank of snow. Heat welled up behind him, and he felt like he was on fire.

He rolled over on his back. His ear ached, and white noise rang in his head. He blinked at the massive ball of fire engulfing his bar.

Jacey.

He scrambled to his feet, his heart lurching in his chest. She was still inside.

"Fuck!" he screamed and ran back into the bar now completely engulfed in orangish- red flames. He yelled and called her name as the smoke and fire bit at his lungs. No answer.

He ran into the kitchen, holding one arm up to try to see something, anything that looked like Jacey.

Fire licked and crawled up his back, and he could literally feel the flesh melting away from his bones.

Maybe the explosion had knocked her outside? Thoughts raced through his head as pain cut away at every exposed nerve ending in his body.

He raced out the back door and out into the cold night.

Lying still on the snowy ground was Jacey. He hurried to her side and knelt on the ground. The cold snow brought relief to his burning flesh.

Jacey stirred but didn't open her eyes.

She's alive. Everything will be okay. Everything has to be okay.

Voices filled the street in front of the bar. He glanced over his shoulder as neighbors pulled up in their trucks to see the fire. Someone yelled for someone to grab some hoses and try to put out the fire. He knew it wouldn't be long before they discovered them in the back. How would he explain being burned so bad yet still coherent?

He slid his arms under Jacey and fought back a growl. Ignoring the pain in his back, he stood and ran into the cover of the woods.

CHAPTER 37

*J*acey grimaced at the pain shooting through her brain like fireworks. She opened her eyes and looked up at the burned figure hovering above her.

A terrified scream escaped her lips.

"It's okay, Jacey." Barrett's gravelly voice came out of the burned man's body. He stood up and stepped back. "It's me. Barrett."

"Oh my God. What happened?" She scrambled to a sitting position, forgetting about her own pain.

"There was an explosion in the bar. It knocked me off the front porch. I thought you were inside so I came into the kitchen looking for you. Are you okay? Are you hurt?" he asked.

"I'm fine. You're the one that's hurt." She was shocked that he still had the ability to stand let alone be concerned about her.

"I can take the pain. I've done it before." His voice was taut like he was barely holding on.

"Why are we in the woods?" She could see the bar burning through the trees.

"People were gathering. I figured it would be easier to leave than have them see me like this and wonder why I'll be healed in a day or two." He shrugged. He let out a hiss of pain.

"I don't know what happened. I didn't turn anything on in the kitchen. Not the oven or the stove. I stepped out the back door and heard something that sounded like ticking. The next thing I remember is a loud sound and getting thrown to the ground. I guess it knocked me out."

"Do you have your phone?"

"Yes, I think." She fumbled in her coat pocket and produced her cell phone. She held it out. "I would think someone has already called the fire department."

"You said you heard a ticking. Ticking equals a bomb. I'm not calling the fire department. I'm calling someone who can help." He punched in some numbers and held it up but away from his ear.

"A bomb just went off in the bar. I need help. Meet us at Mena's."

Barrett ended the call and handed the phone back to Jacey. "We need to get to Mena's without anyone seeing us. Can you walk?"

"Of course, I can walk." Her chest squeezed tight. "I should be the one taking care of you. My God, you're ... " She slammed her hand across her mouth. Just looking at him hurt her chest. The flesh was literally melting off his face.

"We need to get going."

She nodded and forced back her tears. She needed to stay strong for him.

"Stay in the woods. We can get into Mena's through the back entrance."

"What if she's locked the back door?" She looked at him.

"She never locks that back entrance."

It seemed like forever as they made their way to Mena's. He didn't complain, but she could hear him groan with each footstep he took. She didn't dare look at him because she knew if she did she would start crying.

They snuck in through the back door, careful not to make a sound. The TV was off, which was weird. She didn't have time to dwell on it. She headed upstairs to her room and waited for Barrett to follow.

She pulled the key out of her jeans pocket and unlocked her door. He stepped inside, pain splayed across what was once his burned face.

"Tell me what to do? Tell me how to help you." She begged.

"Go turn the shower on. As cold as you can get it." The words slipped out between his gritted teeth.

She hurried to the bathroom and turned on the shower. Sticking her finger under the running water, she waited until it was like ice. She turned, but Barrett was already behind her in the small bathroom.

"I need you to help me get my clothes off," he said through gritted teeth.

She knew it took a lot out of him to ask for help.

She moved behind him and froze. The back of his shirt had melted into his skin.

"I need you to take it off, Jacey, so I can heal," he said. He reached over and grabbed the sink. "Please."

Nausea rolled over her. To help him, she was going to hurt him.

She gritted her teeth and reached for the shredded shirt and slowly pulled.

He didn't make a sound even though she could see his muscles tensing as she pulled the shirt away from his burned flesh. When she was done peeling his shirt away, his body was left a bloody mess.

He turned around and nodded. "I can do my jeans. I'll be out in a while. I just need to stand under the cold water."

She nodded and shut the bathroom door behind her. She pressed her back against the wallpapered wall and slid down to the floor. Hot tears streamed down her face and soaked into her shirt.

After about twenty minutes, she stood and cracked open the door. She peered inside. "Barrett?"

"Yeah," he breathed out.

"Feel better?"

"Not really." His voice was tired, weary.

"I don't have any medicine, but I can see if Mena keeps anything downstairs."

"See if she has vodka. That would be better at killing the pain." He stepped out of the shower and slowly picked up a towel. The lower half of his body wasn't as burned as his chest and back. He tucked the towel around his waist.

"Go wait for me in my room." She hurried downstairs. She no longer cared if she woke Mena up or not. She rummaged through the cabinets in the kitchen until she found the liquor.

"Thank God." She grabbed the bottle of vodka and hurried back upstairs.

Barrett stood in the middle of her room.

"Here." She rested her hand on his unburned waist and handed him the bottle. "Drink this and lay down."

"I can't lay down." He unscrewed the top and turned the bottle up, swallowing a liberal amount.

"Then sit down. Please," she begged.

He finally nodded and headed over to the chair. He sat on the edge, careful not to rest his burned back against the chair. He took another long pull on the bottle before easing back into the chair.

A long minute later, his body relaxed, and she knew he was falling asleep.

She took the bottle out of his hand and placed it on the floor. Grabbing a pillow off her bed, she put it behind him and eased him back. He flinched but didn't fight her as he drifted off into a sleep he so desperately needed.

She stood back. His werewolf blood would heal him. But it would take at least a week. Until then, she was going to take care of him.

* * *

RYKER'S GUT TWISTED. After getting disconnected from Barrett and then getting a call from him on an unknown phone about a bomb, he knew they were all in deep shit. He was almost up the mountain but apparently not in time. If he'd just been there ten minutes earlier, he might have stopped the bomb. He couldn't fail Barrett again. He didn't bring him back from the dead just to see him back in the ground.

"Fuck," Ryker growled at the crowd of people standing in front of the burning bar. The fire department was on the scene, trying to hose down the building and keeping the rubber-neckers from getting too close. A few were taking videos on their cell phones.

"Fucking losers." He turned into the driveway at Mena's and put out the kickstand before killing the engine. He jogged up the steps and looked over his shoulder to see if anyone was watching. They were all too busy preoccupied by the fire. Even Mena was standing there off to the side. Even from behind he could see the brightly colored muumuu hanging out from under her large winter coat. She'd pulled her fur-lined hood over her head to keep the snow from getting her hair wet.

Good. The less people who saw him the better.

He eased inside the house and looked around the first floor but didn't see Barrett.

He headed upstairs, taking them two at a time. He stepped into the hallway and spotted a dim light shining from under a closed door. He inhaled deep.

Barrett's scent was all over this place. But it was different, off.

"Barrett?" He headed down the hallway to the closed door and pushed it open.

He froze when he saw a female sitting on the bed, watching Barrett sleep in a chair.

He turned his glare on the girl. "Who the fuck are you? And what did you do to Barrett?"

The female jumped up from the bed and stepped between him and Barrett.

"Don't you come one step closer to him." She picked up the vodka bottle sitting on the floor.

"Or what? You going to drink me to death?" he snorted.

She glared and threw the bottle as hard as she could at him. He tried to duck, but the end of the bottle caught him on the side of his head, cutting his temple.

"Fuck," he cried out and touched his fingers to his head. He pulled his fingers back. They were coated with blood.

"Look, I don't know who you are, but you stay away from Barrett." She spread her arms like she was ready to take him on in a full-out fight.

He would have laughed if he had the time.

"I don't know who you are, female … "

"My name is Jacey. I'm with Barrett." She lifted her chin definitely.

He froze. "Wait. What do you mean you're with Barrett?" He narrowed his eyes.

"I mean I'm not leaving his side. Until I find out who blew up the bar," she countered.

"So, were you with him when it happened?" Ryker cocked his head. He knew women, and although she tried to take his head off with a bottle of vodka, he didn't feel like she was a mastermind when it came to bombs.

"I was in the back, unloading the supplies for the kitchen." She shook her head. "Wait, why am I even telling you this. How do I know you're not the one who planted the bomb?"

"Because Barrett just called me not an hour ago to come pick him up." He looked her up and down. "I'm guessing he used your phone to call from."

She walked over to her coat and dug out her cell phone. She pulled up the last call and showed him the screen.

He nodded and then looked back over at Barrett. "Was he inside when the bomb went off?"

"No, on the porch." She looked down at the floor and blinked. "He came back in because he thought I was still inside."

"Shit," Ryker murmured. "Well, we can't stay here. We have to get moving."

"But Barrett needs rest."

He looked up at her and glared. "Look, lady. If Barrett stays here, then he'll be dead before dawn. The person who planted that bomb thinks he's dead, but if he stays here, then everyone will know he's alive. And that includes the killer."

CHAPTER 38

*B*arrett felt a nudge on his elbow, and he scowled. His body felt heavy, and he wasn't ready to wake up. Not yet.

"Barrett, get up." A deep but familiar male voice had him on alert.

He forced his eyes open. Hovering over him were Jacey and Ryker. He blinked, and the night's events came flooding back to him.

"Ryker." He stood and held out his hand. Ryker froze.

"What's wrong?" He looked from him to Jacey.

"Barrett, look in the mirror. Your skin is almost healed," she said softly.

He walked over to the mirror over the dresser and looked at his reflection. His chest was completely healed from where the fire had burned his flesh. There was a small area over his right eye that was still scarred, but it actually looked like it would heal too. He turned and looked at his back in the mirror.

"What the hell?" He studied his healed skin in the reflection of the mirror. He had suffered the worst of the burn on his back where his shirt had melted into his skin. Now there wasn't even a hint of a scar. "How is that possible?"

"I don't know. Maybe it has something to do with when we brought you back." Ryker scratched his chin. "Remind me to ask that Fae."

"Fae?" Jacey looked from Ryker to Barrett with wide eyes. "You actually know the Fae?"

"Yes. Well, one in particular," Ryker answered. "She did us a favor."

"I heard they weren't very friendly to our kind." Jacey crossed her arms over her chest.

"Well, I don't really care what you heard, female," Ryker spat out. He turned to Barrett. "What I want to know is who is this? And how do we know we can trust her?" He jabbed his finger in Jacey's direction.

Barrett's anger flared. He rounded on his Guardian and growled low and deep. "Don't you ever talk to her like that again, and if you want to keep your finger, you better fucking move it."

Ryker dropped his hand and glared. "Holy shit. Not you too. First Damon, then Braxton and Jayden. Then that fucker Zane got the itch followed by Lucien and Jaxon. I don't know what the hell kind of water you are drinking but keep that shit away from me."

Barrett glared. Ryker knew without saying it that Jacey was Barrett's mate.

"I don't have time for this, Ryker. We need to find out who set that bomb." Barrett rolled his shoulders, letting the tension drain off his back.

"Well, if you had kept your cell phone charged, you would have known to be on the lookout. I've been fucking trying to call you since yesterday."

"What are you talking about, Ryker?" Barrett rested his

hands on his hips. He noticed that Ryker cut his eyes over at Jacey.

"You can talk in front of Jacey."

Ryker glared and then let out a sigh. "Edward Boudier escaped out of Texas. In fact, they have tracked him to Colorado."

"Fuck." He let the word out on a low growl.

"Wait. Boudier? The former Pack Master of Louisiana?" Jacey frowned. "Why would he be headed to Colorado?"

"He's coming to finish what he started." Ryker pointed his finger at Barrett. "He's coming to make sure Barrett Middleton is dead."

* * *

"BARRETT MIDDLETON. You said your name was Barrett Midland." Jacey licked her dry lips. Nausea washed over her in a rush, and she stumbled back against the chair he'd been sitting in.

Her legs buckled. She eased into the chair.

"Jacey, I'm sorry. I couldn't tell you my real name … I was supposed to be …"

"Dead." She looked up at him. "I know. When the Pack Master of Arkansas sacrificed himself for his Guardian, it was all the werewolf community could talk about. Especially in Mississippi."

"You're from Mississippi?" Ryker cocked his head.

She ignored him and glared at Barrett. "You lied to me."

"Jacey, I had to." He pleaded with his eyes.

"Enough!" Ryker held up his hand. "We don't have time for this lover's quarrel bullshit. Boudier is near, and we need to get the fuck out of here before he finds you." He pointed his finger at Barrett.

"Jacey comes with us." Barrett stated.

"Oh, no. I'm here to make sure you are safe. I don't even know who she is. She could be working with Boudier for all we know," Ryker stated.

Barrett took two steps and punched Ryker in the face. Ryker grunted and stumbled back but kept his balance. He rubbed his chin and glared at Barrett.

"We are not leaving Jacey. If Boudier set that bomb then that means he's been watching us, and he knows Jacey is with me. That means he'll try to hurt her to get back at me." He glared. "Jacey comes with us."

"Fuck it!" Ryker growled and threw his hands up. "Fine. The girl can come."

By the look on his face, Ryker wasn't happy about her coming along. And neither was she.

"We need to take your Jeep," Ryker said.

"I left it in Denver. I borrowed a bigger truck to haul my supplies in."

Ryker froze. "Big enough to haul my Harley?"

Jacey couldn't help but feel a little left out as the two large males talked amongst themselves, like they had forgotten she was in the room.

"Yes," Barrett said. "We need to head away from here and go someplace that is secure."

"All your property was turned over to Damon upon your death. You don't have any properties left," Ryker stated.

"Not me. But someone else I know does." He held out his hand. "Let me see your phone."

Ryker dug his cell phone out of his jacket and handed it to Barrett.

Barrett punched in a few numbers and waited.

"It's Barrett Middleton. I need another favor, from you this time, not your wife. I need a secure place in Colorado." Barrett rested his hand on his hip as he spoke. He glanced at her and gave her a reassuring smile, like everything would be okay. Jacey didn't feel confident in that at all.

"Great. Thank you." He handed the phone back to Ryker.

"Who was that?" Ryker frowned.

"Eric Nordstrom. We have a place. Near Aspen. Secluded. Minimal staff which he will send away as soon as we arrive. It's in the mountains so it's hard to get to. Plus, it's loaded with cameras all over the place."

"Great. Now all we got to do is retrieve your truck and load up my Harley," Ryker said.

Jacey got up and walked over to the window. She smiled. "Well, if you want to get the truck, now is going to be your best time." She turned and looked at both of them. "The fire department just moved it out from behind the back of the building and parked it right outside Mena's."

"Grab your coat and bag, and let's go," Barrett stated. He stopped and looked down at his naked chest and towel wrapped around his waist.

"I've got a second pair of clothes in my saddle bag. You can change in the snow," Ryker snorted.

Jacey grabbed her stuff and hurried out into the hall. She raced down the stairs with the males right behind her. The hair on the back of her neck stood up, and a chill raced through her.

She opened up the front door and raced out. She stood by the passenger side door and waited while Ryker dug out some clothes for Barrett to put on. A few seconds later, he was jogging up next to her.

Damn her heart. Her body betrayed her and warmed at the sight of him in dark jeans and a black T-shirt. He didn't have a jacket, but he didn't look like he was freezing either.

"When we get to Aspen and are alone, we need to talk," he said, stuffing his hands in his pockets.

"Yes, we do." She opened the door and turned around. "I'll sit in the back seat while you and Ryker sit up front. I'm sure you two have a lot of catching up to do." She tugged open the door and climbed inside.

CHAPTER 39

*I*t took over six hours to make it to the house in Aspen. Ryker barely said a word the entire time. Barrett knew Ryker was mad.

Ryker would just have to get over it. Barrett was more concerned about the situation with Jacey.

He knew how she must be feeling. To her, he had lied, and that was something she would never be okay with. She'd told him that right from the beginning.

He'd screwed up royally.

He looked up at the house looming in front of them.

"Shit. That's big." Ryker parked in the circular driveway and killed the engine.

"I wouldn't expect anything less from Eric Nordstrom." Barrett opened the door and climbed out.

Dawn was just breaking over the mountains and the outdoors lights were still on, illuminating the brick and wood mansion.

Jacey slid out of the truck and slammed the door behind her. She stepped up beside him and gazed up at the house.

"You know the guy who owns this?" She tore her gaze from the house to him.

"You could say that."

"He must be a multimillionaire." She looked back at the house.

"Billionaire," Ryker said as he passed them to go to the back of the truck to unload his Harley.

The large wood and wrought iron front doors opened, and an older woman walked out and greeted them with a smile.

Barrett jogged over to the entrance and held out his hand. "I'm Barrett Middleton. You must be Nancy. I'm assuming Eric told you I was coming."

"Yes, sir, he did." She smiled wide and looked past him to Jacey.

Jacey walked over to them. "Hi. I'm Jacey Miller."

The older woman smiled. "I'm Nancy. I'm the caretaker for Mr. Eric." She looked back at Barrett. "I have stocked the kitchen with food so you shouldn't have to leave the house for at least a week. After that, look in one of the large freezers in the basement. I always keep a month's supply of casseroles and dishes in there as well."

"Thank you so much. I really appreciate this," Barrett said. He glanced over his shoulder as Ryker walked his Harley out of the back of the truck. He lowered the kickstand and parked the motorcycle beside the truck.

"If your friend is ready, I can give you all the tour," Nancy said.

Barrett turned and motioned for Ryker. Ryker sighed and took his time getting to the front door.

"I'm Nancy, the caretaker for Mr. Eric," she addressed Ryker.

"Ryker." He stuck his hands in his jeans and gave the older woman a greeting in the way of a nod.

Barrett cut his eyes at the Were. He had half a mind to knock Ryker on his ass for being so damn disrespectful.

Nancy didn't seem to take offense. Instead, she opened the door and waved them all in. "I'll give you the tour and answer any questions you might have before I leave."

"I hope we're not putting you out. This was kind of short notice," Jacey said softly. Barrett's heart softened at Jacey's generous heart.

"Not at all. Mr. Eric has made reservations for me in Vail at the Four Seasons. He says it's part of my Christmas bonus this year," Nancy said joyfully. "I couldn't ask for a better boss."

"No doubt," Barrett said. His dealings with Eric had been years ago while he was in South Carolina, and it had been strictly business. Some found the man cold, but Barrett always felt like Eric didn't trust people, that maybe they were always after him for his money. Barrett could empathize with that.

Ryker closed the door behind them as they stepped inside. He glanced around, noting the expensive wood paneling along the walls and coffered ceilings with large beams.

"This is the foyer, and if you want to do something outside and need warmer gear, just press this panel right here." Nancy pressed the third panel, and it slipped back like a pocket door, revealing a closet with winter coats and boots.

"Wow, that's clever." Jacey nodded.

"Now if you'll just follow me." Nancy turned to the right. They found themselves standing in a large living area with a stone fireplace that reached all the way up to the thirty-foot ceiling. There were two seating areas with two sets of couches, one facing the fireplace and one facing out the large floor-to-ceiling windows. The fireplace is wood burning. There is plenty of wood already cut on the back deck if you need it. If you run out, there is more wood out by the shop which is that smaller building off to the side of the main house. The shop has ski equipment, snowmobiles, some ATVs, along with a couple of cars and trucks. But we never take the cars out in this weather."

"Right through here is the kitchen." Nancy didn't stop walking as she talked. She must have known they had traveled all night and were ready to relax.

The kitchen was just as luxurious as the rest of the house. Commercial-grade stainless-steel appliances with white quartz countertops streaked with black. The large kitchen island had stools for seating and a large kitchen table by the large windows with a breathtaking view of the snow-covered mountains.

She showed them the two bathrooms downstairs, one near the kitchen and the other near the garage entrance.

They followed as Nancy led them into the dining room with the large table big enough to seat sixteen people. She showed them the indoor gym and the door connecting the six-car garage. She walked them back into the living room and opened the large glass doors that led out to the massive outdoor living area with a full-sized kitchen, seating area, two fire pits, and a heated infinity pool.

Next, they headed up the massive staircase from the foyer that led upstairs to the seven bedrooms.

He watched Jacey's expression as she looked from a massive bedroom with a spectacular view to a massive bedroom with a view of a running creek.

There were six more bathrooms upstairs, each attached to the bedrooms.

"The only thing I've not shown you is the wine cellar downstairs." Nancy smiled. "There's a small staircase behind the kitchen that leads to it."

"By the bathroom?" Jacey asked.

"Yes. That's the very one. If you take that staircase, you'll be in a hallway. If you go right, you'll enter the wine cellar. And if you go left, that leads to the theater room. Feel free to help yourself to the popcorn maker and the candy."

"You should be more worried about us drinking all the wine," Ryker muttered.

Nancy laughed. "Oh, my dear. I don't think that's possible. There are over two thousand bottles down there."

"Really?" Jacey's eyes went wide.

"Yes. And please help yourself to any of the wine. Mr. Eric gave me instructions to tell you to make yourselves quite at home." She looked up at Barrett. "Is there anything else I can show you while I'm here?"

"No, thank you, Nancy. You've been a tremendous help." He smiled. "I'm sure you are eager to start your vacation in Vail."

"I've never stayed at the Four Seasons before." Her eyes shined. "It's going to be a real treat." She walked toward the front door and pulled a key out of her pocket. "This is the key to the safe room. It's in the basement too. To be honest, I'm never in there. We've never had any trouble with a break-in, probably because we're so far hidden in the mountains. The only time the alarm went off was when a bear was trying to get in the house."

"A bear?" Jacey's voice waivered.

"Oh, don't worry, dear. They're in hibernation now. You won't see any bears." She looked back at Barrett. "Mr. Eric says when you go inside, you'll see the cameras and their locations. If you need to monitor your surroundings. Oh. And there is another set of keys to the house and the large garage in the safe room as well. Mr. Eric said if you had any questions about the security system to give him a call."

"I will. And thank you again, Nancy, for all your help. We really appreciate it." Barrett smiled.

"Enjoy the house and enjoy your stay." She smiled and grabbed the handle to her carry-on bag. The handle telescoped out, and she rolled the bag out the front door and toward a small Toyota truck parked off to the side.

Barrett closed the door and frowned. "Where did Ryker go?"

"He said he had to make a call." Jacey shrugged and walked into the kitchen. He followed behind her.

"We need to talk," he said.

"No shit." She whirled around, her eyes full of anger. "You let me open up to you about my private life and in return you lied."

He looked at the ceiling and measured his words. "It was never my intent to hurt you, Jacey. But I was …"

"You were supposed to be dead." She cocked her head.

"Are you disappointed?" he deadpanned.

"I'm disappointed that you lied to me. I thought you were different. I thought you …" Her slender throat worked as she swallowed.

"Cared?" He stepped closer. "Of course, I care. More than you know. But if I told you who I was, who I really was, then it would put you in danger."

"I'm in danger anyway!"

Her words found their mark. His chest ached with the resounding truth.

"I know. I'm sorry." He grimaced. "If I could take this all back, I would."

"So, you are the Pack Master of Arkansas." She looked at him like she was meeting him for the first time.

"I was the Pack Master. Damon Trahan is my successor."

"Yeah. I heard about that." She walked over to the window and crossed her arms, looking out over the mountain scene in front of her. "So why did you fake your death?"

"He didn't," Ryker answered from across the room. "He

sacrificed his life, fell off a cliff with a silver knife in his heart."

Barrett shot Ryker a warning look to stay out of the conversation.

"But you should be dead." Jacey frowned, trying to comprehend what they were telling her.

"He was dead," Ryker answered.

"Ryker ..." Barrett warned.

Jacey held up her hand. "No, I want to hear what Ryker has to say. He seems to be the only one here not afraid of telling me the truth." She looked at Ryker. "Barrett was dead?"

"Yeah. I didn't know that Barrett was going to sacrifice his life for Jaxon that day ..."

"Jaxon?" She frowned.

"The Guardian that Boudier wanted dead. Edward Boudier brought a Tribunal against Jaxon. He wanted Jaxon's life in exchange for the murder of his wife and son-in-law."

"Jaxon didn't kill either one of them. Ginny Boudier did. In self-defense."

Jacey nodded. "I heard that Ginny's mother stabbed her with a silver fork to keep her from leaving her abusive husband."

"She did. They fought, and her mother fell against some silver antlers on the wall, killing her instantly. Jaxon came in to get Ginny and that's when the husband showed up. He tied to kill Jaxon, and Ginny ended up killing him too."

Jacey shivered and wrapped her arms around herself. "Ginny had an abusive mate?"

"She was forced to mate with him by her father. They were not true mates. As you know, a true mate would never hurt his female."

Something flickered across her face. She looked up at him. "So, you sacrificed yourself for Jaxon."

Barrett said nothing.

"Yes, he did," Ryker answered. "The blood debt was paid when Barrett died. But with a little help from our neighborhood witch, Ella, and some Fae magic, we were able to bring Barrett back."

"Wait. Are you talking about the witch from …?"

"Your neck of the woods, yes." Ryker stated.

"But how?" Jacey asked.

"Ella worked some blood magic to keep Barrett barely alive until Celeste could get there. She's a very powerful Fae, and it's her husband's house we are standing in. Celeste was the one that healed him." Ryker spread his arms.

Surprise blossomed across Jacey's face.

"And now that Boudier knows that Barrett is alive, he's not going to stop until he makes that a reality. For good this time." Ryker snorted. "And I'm short a fairy and a witch which makes it important that Barrett stays alive."

"Oh, God." Jacey's hand flew to her mouth, and her legs buckled. "Boudier won't quit until he finds you."

"I don't care about that," Barrett growled. "What I do care about is the fact that if anyone else finds out that I'm alive, the Council will try to force the blood debt again."

"Meaning Jaxon isn't safe. He could still be put to death," Ryker stated. "You may be pissed off about him lying to you, but he has bigger problems like keeping his Guardians alive."

"Ryker, enough." Barrett growled.

"Fine. I'm going to put my Harley out in the garage." Ryker stormed out the front door.

Barrett went to Jacey and knelt by her seat. "Jacey, I'm so sorry. I never meant to hurt you. Truly, I didn't."

"I know. It's just." She shook her head and waved him away. "So much has happened over the last two days, and I'm exhausted." She pressed her hand to her temple. "I just need some time to process all of this."

"I understand." His head did, but his heart didn't stop aching. Hurting her was the last thing he wanted.

"Pick any bedroom you want. I'll get your stuff out of the truck." He turned and headed outside, his heart heavy and his soul tortured.

CHAPTER 40

*J*acey sat up in bed with a start. Her heart pounded like a jackhammer, and she sucked in deep breaths.

She tried to remember the dream that had her body on alert, but already the images were fading like wisps of smoke.

She looked around and realized where she was. She took a deep breath and relaxed back on the bed. After Barrett had brought her stuff in, she'd chosen a bedroom at the end of the hallway. It was a master suite with a fireplace and a little sitting area at the foot of her bed. She ran her palm across the lush, light-blue comforter that lay across her legs. The walls were covered in a lovely shade of cream wallpaper, and the large furniture was obviously expensive.

Whoever this Eric Nordstrom was, obviously had a lot of money.

She threw back the comforter and stood. Her feet touched the cold hardwood floor, sending a shiver through her. She raised her arms over her head and stretched her sore muscles. She felt like she'd been beat up.

Emotionally, she had been beat up. Too much had

happened in such a short amount of time for her to compre-hend everything. She walked over to the window and pulled back the curtains. It was getting dark outside, and dusk would soon be swallowed up in the darkness.

She glanced over at the bedside clock. Seven o'clock.

She'd slept the entire day away.

Her stomach growled, and she pressed her palm to her abdomen. She'd not eaten since lunch the day before.

She glanced down at her bra and panties, the only thing she'd worn to sleep in. She really wanted a shower before she headed off to find something to eat.

She padded into the bathroom and turned on the water. She stood and looked around at the white marble bathroom. Everything, the floors, the countertops, the shower, even the large soaking bathtub was made out of white marble striated with black streaks. It was streamlined yet elegant.

A large, white, fluffy robe hung on a hook on the bath-room door. She could wear that until she had time to wash her clothes.

She grabbed a towel and a washcloth from under the bathroom sink and hung it over the shower. She tested the temperature of the water with her fingers and stepped inside the shower.

She stiffened under the sting of the hot spray. Soon her muscles relaxed, and she lifted her face to the water. She held her breath, letting the water wash away the unshed tears still hiding behind her eyes.

Barrett. Every time she thought of him she wanted to cry.

Part of her understood why he hadn't told her the truth. She could understand why he had lied. But the other part of her, the part ruled by her heart, was cut to the core with betrayal.

Tears slid down her face and mingled with the water. Emotionally, she didn't know where her soul started and

Barrett began. In such a short amount of time, she'd given him her heart and now she wasn't sure what she should do.

She'd heard tales of Barrett Middleton when she lived in Mississippi, of how he was one of the youngest Pack Masters ever to take power. There was a mystery surrounding him, and a lot of the werewolves didn't know whether to like him or be afraid. At least that's what she'd always been told.

Jack Welbourn had never said a bad thing about Barrett. From rumors around Mississippi, the two Pack Masters were close like a father and son might be. Every Were in Mississippi had always had a healthy respect for Jack and his opinion. Therefore, Barrett Middleton had been respected by the Mississippi Weres.

She'd heard rumors of how strikingly handsome Barrett was, how he could have any woman he wanted. It was also rumored he'd never mated because he had and never would find a mate. That he was cursed somehow.

She never put much stock in curses but after hearing how he'd come back from the dead, she was starting to change her stance on the subject.

Now Boudier was after him. Edward Boudier was the most hated Pack Master ever to walk the earth. When she was still living at her parents, they never would let her cross into Louisiana not even to New Orleans for Mardi Gras because they were afraid of Boudier.

Now he was loose, and no one was safe from his revenge.

She rubbed her hand over her heart, trying to erase the unease building up behind her rib cage.

Something was coming for them. Something bad. And she wasn't sure they would survive this time around.

* * *

RYKER PUSHED his plate across the kitchen island and sighed.

He might not like Jacey or trust her, but the female could cook like nobody's business.

"Do you want some more?" Jacey looked over at him from the stove. She held up her spatula and waited for his answer. "I can make another hamburger."

"He's already had two." Barrett scowled from his seat at the kitchen island. He had finished up his second burger, and he still looked pissed. At who, Ryker wasn't sure.

"I'm good." He held up his hands but kept his gaze on Barrett.

Barrett narrowed his eyes.

Ryker groaned and gritted his teeth. "It was good. Thanks for cooking." That was as much gratitude as he was going to show Jacey.

"How hard was that to say?" She looked at him, unfazed by his gruff manner.

"Harder than you know." He snorted. He had to give it to the female. At least she wasn't intimidated by him.

"I've baked cookies, but they need to cool." She nodded to the cookie pan sitting on the table.

"What kind?" He eyed the sheet and felt his mouth water. He was stuffed, but he never turned down dessert. Never knew when today might be your last so he never deprived himself.

"Sugar cookie and peanut butter."

Fuck. He headed over to the table and snatched one of each off the pan. He bit into the sugar cookie and moaned. The cookie nearly melted on his tongue.

"That's good." He ate the rest and then tried the peanut butter. He groaned. It was even better. "Are these the break and bake kind?" He looked at her. He was going to have to stockpile these and keep them in the freezer.

"No. I made them from scratch." She wrinkled up her nose in offense.

"Really?" He wondered if she were trying to win him over with her cooking skills. If so, he was going to have to stay strong. He would not let her break him.

"Ryker is a sugar addict. You keep these out, there won't be any left." Barrett snatched up three of the sugar cookies and two of the peanut butter. He glared at Ryker while he ate.

"Here, don't you want one?" Barrett handed her a sugar cookie.

She gave a sheepish grin and shook her head. "No when I was making them, I kind of ate some of the dough."

"Is there any dough left?" Ryker eyed her. He loved cookie dough better than cookies.

"Yes." She narrowed her eyes in warning and pointed her spatula at him. "But I'm saving it for tomorrow."

"Since you cooked, we will do the dishes," Barrett offered.

"What?" It was time for Ryker to wrinkle up his nose. "I don't do dishes."

"Are you sure?" Jacey looked between them and gathered up the three plates and put them in the sink. She'd already cooked and eaten by the time he and Barrett came downstairs. She'd told them both to sit down, and she cooked them some hamburgers without asking if they were hungry. She probably knew Ryker would refuse, which he would have out of conviction.

"Yes." Barrett narrowed his eyes at him. "We'll do the dishes."

"Alright, well, I'm going to …" A pounding on the front door had both the Weres pulling out the guns from the back of their jeans. Eric Nordstrom had a lot of weapons in the safe room, and Ryker and Barrett had helped themselves.

"Stay here." Barrett looked at Jacey. "Stay out of sight." Barrett looked at him, and they both moved in sync toward the front door.

Ryker looked at the camera by the front door but couldn't get a clear visual of the front door. He looked over at Barrett who was standing behind the door with his gun aimed at the door.

"I can't see. Whoever it is knows there's a camera here and is covering it with something."

Another round of pounding sounded on the door.

"Open it," Ryker said to Barrett. "I've got a full clip and so do you. We can take out whoever it is quickly."

Barrett nodded and reached for the handle. He unlocked the door and tugged it open.

"Don't fucking move!" Ryker growled as he aimed his gun at the target on the other side of the door with his finger on the trigger. He saw a very angry Damon standing on the other side.

"Put that fucking gun away, Ryker," Damon thundered. Braxton, Jayden, Jaxon, Zane, and Lucien stepped forward, flanking their new Pack Master.

Ryker let out a held breath and shoved the 45mm behind his back in the waistband of his jeans. "Fuck, Damon. You could have warned me. I almost shot you full of silver."

"I'm not that easy to kill." Damon narrowed his eyes and then looked over Ryker's shoulder. Damon went still, his eyes went wide, and he visibly paled.

Ryker shoved the door open wide and stepped aside. "Guess there's a lot of explaining to do."

CHAPTER 41

"What are you doing here?" Barrett's stomach dropped. He looked at each of his Guardians in the eyes. His gaze settled on Damon. A myriad of emotions washed over Damon's face. Grief, shock, relief.

"I called Damon after the bomb went off," Ryker retorted. "I needed to let them know what's going on."

"You just put them in danger," Barrett thundered.

"They're already in danger. Any Guardian from Arkansas is." Ryker turned on Barrett. "If you think Boudier is going to go away after he kills you, you are wrong. He'll take his time picking every one of us off. We need to be ready, and we need to be prepared."

Ryker was right.

He let his gaze wander over the men he once ruled over. The look of shock on everyone's face rocked him to his core.

"Turns out I'm not as dead as everyone thought," Barrett deadpanned.

Damon blinked and looked down, his face a mixture of pain and betrayal.

"You look like Barrett." Jayden shoved past Damon and stepped inside. He invaded Barrett's space and leaned in and sniffed Barrett's neck. "Smells like Barrett."

"Get off me, asshole." Barrett shoved Jayden in the chest.

"Sounds like Barrett too," Jayden said excitedly.

Zane stepped in and took Barrett's head between his palms. His eyes were watery with grief. His expression hardened and then he pulled Barrett into a tight hug.

Barrett hugged his friend back, swallowing back the hurt he'd caused all his men.

When Zane let go, Braxton stepped up and gave a little grin. Barrett shook his hand but that wasn't enough for the Were. Braxton pulled him into a hug.

Jayden was there to greet him when Braxton let go. He hugged him tight.

"Jayden, if you start humping my leg, I'm going to kick you in the nuts," Barrett gruffed. He wasn't built for all this emotional upheaval.

Jayden laughed and pulled back.

"Good to see you Barrett," Lucien held out his hand. And pulled him into a quick but hard hug.

Jaxon stood in the doorway, eyes wide and mouth open. He looked even more upset than Damon to see him alive. With good reason.

Barrett forked his fingers through his hair. "Jaxon, I'm sorry. I know this means that you're not safe now."

Jaxon rushed him and grabbed him by the collar, his expression intense and full of anguish. "You're alive."

"Yeah." Barrett cleared his throat. "I'm sorry about that."

"Are you fucking kidding me? You're alive. This is amazing." Jaxon hugged him hard. The Were was trying not to sob.

Barrett hugged him back. "You're not mad?"

Jaxon pulled back and looked into Barrett's eyes. "Are you fucking kidding me? Why would I be mad?"

"Because the blood debt won't be paid now." Barrett gritted his teeth.

"I don't care about that. The fact that you were willing to die to save me was more than I could ever ask. I'll willingly face whatever price, even if it costs me my life to have you alive."

Barrett swallowed hard. Now it was his eyes that were burning.

Jaxon swiped at his eyes and looked away. Barrett looked at Damon who had not moved since he arrived.

"There's a lot that I need to know," Damon said quietly.

"There's a lot that I have to tell," Barrett answered.

"Great. Now that the Hallmark movie moment is over, can you pussies please follow me into the kitchen? We can talk over coffee and homemade cookies," Ryker said.

Barrett was the last to step into the kitchen, and when he did, he had all eyes on him.

"What's going on?" Jacey stopped when she entered the kitchen. She looked at Barrett.

All the Guardians were studying her intently. "Who is this?" Jayden finally asked.

"Jacey Miller." Barrett stepped between them and obstructed their line of vision.

"And she's …" Zane asked

"She's none of your concern," Barrett growled.

All the eyebrows on the Guardians shot up but none asked anything else.

"Are these friends of yours, Barrett?" Jacey stepped up beside him and rested her hand on his arm.

He looked down at her, and his chest ached. "Yes."

She nodded. "Well, in that case, I'll make some more cookies." She walked over to the oven and turned it on.

"Want me to get the cookie dough?" Ryker asked.

"No. You leave the cookie dough alone." She narrowed her eyes at him. Barrett bit his cheek to stop laughing.

"Fine." Ryker growled and waved his hand toward the expensive coffeepot. "You assholes are making your own coffee. I am not doing it." He headed over to the kitchen table and snapped up a handful of peanut butter cookies before Jaxon could grab one.

"Jesus, Ryker. Don't be a fucking pig," Jayden groused.

Ryker glared at Jayden. "You're lucky I didn't lick the whole tray."

Braxton and Zane laughed. Barrett's chest felt light, something he'd not felt since he'd come back from the dead.

"Enough." Damon looked around the room and walked over to the window and looked out.

The room grew quiet, and everyone settled own. Barrett could tell the Guardians were confused. They were conflicted over being grateful that he was alive and being loyal to their new Pack Master.

Damon turned around and looked at him. "You're alive. So why don't you start with how that's possible."

Barrett nodded slowly. "I want to say that the night I died, I was ready to do that. That's why I put Damon as my successor." He looked at Damon who swallowed hard.

"I want to apologize for forcing you to attack me that night, Damon. I know that you never would have done that if I didn't do something drastic."

"That's why you pretended to attack Ava." Damon filled in the rest.

"Yes, and I'm sorry for that."

"I know. Ava said that you asked for forgiveness that night before you died." Damon propped his hands on his hips and glared. "So, tell us how you're alive."

Barrett cut his eyes at Ryker.

"Well, that's kind of my fault." Ryker chewed thoughtfully on a cookie. "After that witch lied for Boudier at the Council, I found her before she could leave. I was hoping she had some magic for bringing someone back from the dead."

"You knew Barrett was going to die?" Damon cocked his head.

"No. That was as much a surprise as anything. I was going to try to bring Jaxon back." He leaned back against the wall. "Anyway, the witch told me to fuck off and that she wasn't helping me do shit. But after it was Barrett who fell off the cliff, she changed her mind." He smirked. "Apparently, she's got a thing for our Pack Master."

Damon bristled. Jacey turned and narrowed her eyes.

"Former Pack Master," Barrett corrected. He didn't need the tension between him and Damon. He had bigger issues at hand.

"She hightailed it down to the bottom of the cliff and dragged him to a hidden cave."

"Ella brought Barrett back?" Lucien asked.

"Not exactly. Here's where it gets complicated." Ryker took another cookie and shoved it in his mouth. He took his time chewing, forcing them all to wait.

Just like Ryker to irritate everyone in the middle of an emergency.

"Get on with it!" Damon thundered.

Ryker sighed. "Fine. I had already called Celeste Nordstrom when I found out about the Tribunal."

"Who's Celeste Nordstrom?" Jayden asked.

"She's the wife of Eric Nordstrom. The owner of this house. And she's Fae." Barrett scrubbed his hand across his face.

"Fae? So, when did we start cavorting with the Fae?" Zane scowled.

"When her mother called and asked me if I could send

some help up to Vermont. That's where I sent Ryker. To help out."

"Battling an evil fairy queen and her demons is a little more than helping out," Ryker deadpanned. "You make it sound like I went to help with a bake sale."

"Yeah. Ryker would be horrible helping with a bake sale. He'd eat all the profits," Jacey muttered.

Barrett smiled and turned. She didn't bother looking up as she placed more cookies on the cookie pan for baking.

Ryker glared at her but didn't respond.

"Celeste flew in the night of the Tribunal. I brought her back to the cave. Ella had enough blood magic to stop the decaying process but not enough to bring him back. She'd also made sure to dig out any silver left in his body."

"So, Barrett was dead?" Lucien narrowed his eyes. "Like legit dead?"

"Totally legit." Ryker pushed off the wall, seemingly bored with the whole conversation. "Once Celeste got there, she brought him back from the dead. Apparently, she can heal people by ... touch." He shrugged. "I stayed in the cave with Ella, taking turns watching over Barrett. Since the damage was so severe, it took him a long time to heal completely. When I felt it was safe, I snuck him out under the cover of darkness and drove him as far away as I could get. Which in this case turns out to be Colorado."

"Why didn't you tell me?" Damon advanced on him.

"Because it's safer for all of you, especially Jaxon, if I'm dead." Barrett looked at the Were. "Ryker did the right thing not telling you. He was protecting you, all of you."

The room grew quiet.

Zane cleared his throat. "So does this mean you're the Pack Master?"

"No. That title remains with Damon. I think the best thing to do is forget you saw me and go back to Arkansas."

"We can't." Damon shook his head. "Boudier is here."

"I know. He bombed my bar." Barrett scowled. Ryker cleared his throat. "Sorry, he bombed Ryker's bar."

"We saw that." Braxton said. "We tracked Boudier up to the mountain and saw the damage he did."

"According to what we found at that Victorian house down from your place . . ." Damon was cutoff.

"What house? Are you talking about Mena's?" Barrett's gut twisted.

"Yeah. That's the one. We tracked Boudier to that house. The old woman who owned the house was murdered and put in a freezer in the basement. Looks like she'd been dead a while."

"But that's not possible." Jacey looked at them and visibly paled.

"Yeah. I saw Mena watching the fire last night. I saw that stupid muumuu she always likes to wear." Ryker stilled.

"Did you see her face?" Damon cocked his head. "When was the last time you actually saw her?"

"I saw her from behind. I didn't see her face. She had a coat on and the hood pulled over her head. It was snowing." Ryker's eyes darted from each of the Weres.

"I was staying there. I usually got off work late, so I didn't see her. But she always stayed up late watching movies. I could see the light from the TV under her door. And when I got up in the morning, I didn't see her because she always liked to sleep in."

"So, the last time you saw her face to face was . . ." Damon questioned.

"The day I moved in. She said she didn't like people bothering her and that she would leave out some coffee and something for breakfast. She said it was a pretty relaxed house."

"That's what we thought." Damon looked from Jacey to

Barrett. "We think Boudier had tracked you to Colorado. He had someone staying at Mena's, a guy named Charles who is one of Boudier's hired thugs. He tells Boudier that he found you. Boudier arrives the day after Jacey starts staying at Mena's. The timeline suggests he sees Mena's as the perfect place to set up so he can watch you. So, he kills Mena the day he arrives and pretends to be her."

"Oh, God." Jacey covered her mouth with her hand. "Edward Boudier was living in the house with me the whole time?"

"Yes," Damon said.

Barrett reached for Jacey and pulled her into his chest. "It's okay. You're safe now."

"Boudier will realize that there isn't a body in that bar. He probably already knows this. And he's on his way to find you, Barrett. And he will hurt and kill anyone you care about." Damon's eyes landed on Jacey.

Barrett tightened his hold on her. She was trembling in his arms. She was terrified, and he felt exposed. Protecting her was the only thing he wanted to do.

"He's not going to hurt you. I won't let him," he murmured in her hair.

He looked up, and every one of the Guardians were looking at him with stunned expressions.

"What?" Barrett growled.

"Holy shit," Jayden murmured.

"Hell just froze over." Braxton cocked his head.

"What are you assholes talking about?" Barrett shot back.

"We're talking about you finally finding your mate." Lucien grinned and stuck his hands in his pockets.

"Did you know about this Ryker?" Jayden asked.

"Yeah. So?" Ryker took another cookie and popped it in his mouth.

All eyebrows shot up.

"And you're okay with Barrett finding his mate?" Zane arched his brow.

"It's none of my fucking business. Why should I care?" Ryker shot back. "Besides, she makes damn good cookies." He took the last one off the plate and strode out of the room.

CHAPTER 42

*J*acey headed up to her room while the rest of the Arkansas Guardians talked to Barrett.

Stunned. Confused. Horrified. Terrified. Just some of the emotions cresting and crashing through her body.

A soft knock at the door forced her to turn her gaze away from the window.

"Can I come in?" Barrett asked from the other side of the closed door.

"Sure." Her heart jumped in her throat. She smoothed her hair down and did a quick check of her reflection in the mirror.

The door swung open, and he stepped inside. The room seemed to be swallowed up by his presence.

"How are you feeling?" He shut the door behind him for privacy.

"I'm better. She rubbed the back of her neck and studied the floor. "I can't believe I was staying in a house with a dead body in the basement. No wonder I felt creeped out the whole time I was there."

"Your instinct was right." He shook his head. "I should have picked up on it. Should have sensed something. You were in the house with a psychopath the whole time." He shoved his fingers through his hair and sat down on the bed.

"That's not your fault." She stepped closer.

He jerked his head up. Pain echoed through his handsome features. "Are you kidding? This whole thing is my fault. Boudier is after me. And anyone I care about, which includes you."

Her face heated, and her stomach did weird things, making her feel like she was riding a rollercoaster.

"I guess we need to talk about the elephant in the room." He cocked his head and looked up at her. He patted the spot beside him on the bed.

Her stomach warmed. Sitting on a bed beside Barrett was a dangerous idea.

She walked over to him anyway and sat.

"I don't think I'm your mate, Barrett." She finally said the words that made her heart ache.

"Is that what you feel?" His voice was harsh, rough.

"It doesn't matter what I feel."

He jerked his head toward her. "How you feel is the *only* thing that matters." His intense gaze burned her to her soul.

She looked away. It hurt too much to look at him.

"Barrett, you are a Pack Master. I'm a girl from Mississippi who never had any kind of money or influence. I'm not even in the same league as you." She looked at him and blinked back her tears. "That's why it doesn't matter. That fact that I love you doesn't matter. I could never be your mate. You need to mate with someone within your station."

"You love me?" He cocked his head, and there was gentleness in his eyes. It was a look she'd never seen on him.

She threw up her hands and shook her head. "After all that I just said, you latch on to those three words."

"Those three words are the only words that count." He cupped her cheek and pushed a loose strand out of her eyes.

Her heart ached and burned at the same time.

"I love you, Jacey."

She blinked but not in time, and a tear rolled down her cheek. She tried to look away, but he held her still with his gentle hand.

"I knew you were my mate the second you walked in my bar." He smiled. "I tried to keep my distance with you, but it was hard. And that one night in your room," he laughed softly, "that was pure hell not to make love with you."

"Then, why didn't you?" She frowned.

"Because I didn't want to force you into mating with me if you didn't love me."

"I love you, Barrett, but I still can't mate you. You deserve someone . . ."

"Stop! His expression hardened. "If you say you are not my equal one more time, I'm going to lose it."

"Barrett, you know as well as I do Pack Masters mate with royalty, with females who have an elite bloodline."

"It's an outdated system. And its bullshit." He cocked his head and studied her. "Did you know that I'm originally from Charleston, South Carolina?"

"No. How did you become Pack Master of Arkansas? Usually the Pack Masters are chosen within the state, within a family line."

"I was in line to be Pack Master of South Carolina. The Pack Master wanted me to marry his daughter, Olivia, and in exchange I would become Pack Master. He was getting up in age and had children late in life. He wanted his daughter settled and someone to pass the Pack Master title on to."

"Why didn't you do it?"

"Because I didn't love Olivia. And I didn't believe in marrying for political gain or leverage. Those are people's lives we are talking about. My father found out I refused and banished me from South Carolina. He had some pull with the Southern States, and there was an opening for the Pack Master in Arkansas after the former Pack Master passed away." He stood and walked over to the window. "I was forbidden to come back to South Carolina even for my father's funeral."

"Barrett, I'm so sorry. Surely he forgave you before he died."

"I don't know. He died in an airplane crash as he was headed to Mississippi to meet with Jack Welbourn." He shrugged, but she could see the pain behind his eyes.

"I resigned to spend my life in Arkansas. After my death and subsequent resurrection, my priorities changed." He walked toward her slow and unhurried.

"I don't give a shit about rules and propriety. I don't care what people think. And I sure don't care about marrying some blue blood." He shook his head. "Since I have been resurrected, I've walked around living in the shadow of who I was. Now, since I met you, I've never been more alive. And I know, now more than ever, what I want. And what I want is you."

She had time to take a breath before his mouth was on hers. She gasped. Her body tingled in all the right places. She dug her nails into his shoulders, clinging to him as his tongue snaked inside her mouth. Her heart swelled with love.

He finally pulled his mouth away and looked down into her eyes.

"You are mine," he said, sending her heart soaring. "You were always meant to be with me."

She lifted on tiptoes and pulled his head down to hers, pressing her lips against his.

A knock at the door had him cursing under his breath. He

pulled away and glared at the door as if he were considering killing the offender on the other side.

"Barrett, we need to talk." She recognized Damon's voice and let him go.

"We're not done here," he said, looking at her with tenderness.

"I know." She nodded and stepped away before she jumped him where he was.

He gave her one last look before walking over to the door.

Left alone in the room, she stared out the window. She knew that Barrett was her mate. She'd been afraid of admitting it before, afraid of being disappointed and let down. But not now.

Now she knew what she wanted. And she wanted him.

CHAPTER 43

*B*arrett closed the door and stepped out into the hallway. Damon put his hands on his hips and stared at him. "We can talk in the room down the hall." He walked toward the farthest room and stepped inside. He closed the door behind Damon.

"I want you to keep the Guardians around to make sure Jacey is safe. Boudier will hurt her to get back at me."

Damon frowned. "Our loyalty is to you, Barrett. She's not even a part of the Arkansas Pack."

"She is mine. That makes you loyal to her as well." Barrett leaned into Damon's personal space and growled.

Damon narrowed his eyes, and then his expression relaxed into that of amusement. He let out a laugh. Damon never laughed.

"What's so fucking funny? This is serious." Barrett wanted to punch him in the face.

"It's fucking hilarious to finally see you find your mate. You are the one Were that swore never to get mated, and now you've found her and you're a mess." Damon rubbed his chin and studied him. "It's actually really funny."

Barrett walked over to the window and stared out. "I guess this is how you felt when you found Ava?"

"Yeah. And you can understand how pissed off I was that you were showing her so much attention when you showed up in Louisiana."

Barrett snorted and turned around. "I have no idea why you thought I was flirting with her. You came unglued."

"No shit." Damon walked over to a chair near the window and plopped down. "When you see a male, any male showing an interest in your female, you come unglued."

Barrett swallowed hard and turned back to the window. The icy winter scene in front of him seemed so peaceful, romantic even. But the situation was anything but.

"I had no idea it would feel like this." He rubbed his stomach. "Was beginning to think I had the flu."

"Ah, how the mighty have fallen," Damon smirked.

Barrett turned and shot him a glare.

"Not judging. We've all been there." Damon studied him. "We will protect you and Jacey. I've already called Jack Welbourn, and he's going to be sending some of his Mississippi Guardians."

"Did you tell him I'm alive?" He frowned.

"The cat's out of the bag, Barrett. You won't get it back in now." Damon shook his head.

"I know." He studied the ground. "I need a favor."

"Sure." Damon stood and propped his hands on his hips.

"I want to marry Jacey."

Damon's eyebrows shot up.

"In case something happens to me, I want all the wealth that I have to go to her. I want it to go to her in case something happens. I want her to be financially secure, so she doesn't have to worry about money."

"So, she said yes to marrying you?" Damon asked.

"Not yet. But she will."

Damon nodded thoughtfully and cocked his head. "I thought all your wealth as Pack Master went to me."

"I'm not talking about that. That is yours by right, and I don't want that back. I'm talking about my family inheritance. From South Carolina."

"I thought they disowned you when you came to Arkansas."

"I kept my family inheritance." Barrett froze. "Wait. How did you know that?"

"When we held a memorial for you, Edgar and Addison showed up."

'You had a memorial for me?"

"Of course. We had been putting it off until we found and recovered your body. Ryker had wanted to do it right after the Tribunal, but I wanted to wait. I should have known he was hiding something."

"Don't fault Ryker for lying about all this. He was doing what he thought would protect the Pack." Barrett sighed.

"I know. I don't hold any bad feelings toward the guy. I actually respect him more for what he did. Out of everyone, I was surprised he had the foresight to bring you back."

"He's a good Were to have on your side." Barrett narrowed his gaze. "But being around him for weeks on end was a pain in the ass. That one will never mate. No one will put up with his bullshit."

"At least one of us is safe," Damon deadpanned.

Barrett snorted.

"I'll make the arrangements for the wedding." Damon opened his mouth and froze.

"What? Just spit it out," Barrett stated.

"I'm glad you're not dead." Damon's words were scratchy, and the large male's gaze tightened.

Emotion welled in Barrett's throat. He didn't want to be a pussy and cry. But Damon's words meant a lot to him.

Before he could speak, Damon took two steps and embraced him in a hard hug.

Barrett hugged him back. When they pulled away, they eyed each other.

"I'll make the reservations for the wedding. You need to talk to your female and prepare her. She might be your mate, but a woman never likes to be told what to do," Damon smirked, walked to the door, and opened it.

No doubt. He might know Jacey was his mate but trying to get her to agree to such a drastic life changing decision was going to be hard as hell.

* * *

JACEY SNUGGLED down in her coat and looked at Barrett over the fire pit on the back deck. It was dark and only the light of the fire and the lights from inside the mansion lit up their side of the mountain.

He'd asked her to follow him outside so they could have a space to themselves to speak privately. She wasn't sure what he was going to say, but she knew it wasn't good. He looked as nervous as a cat in a room full of rocking chairs.

"What? Just say it." A shiver ran through her body. "You're making me nervous."

He stopped pacing on the other side of the fire pit and aimed his gaze at her. "Why don't you sit down."

Shit. This was bad.

She eased down on the lounger in front of the fire pit. Despite the fire and her warm coat, she couldn't stop shivering.

He walked around the fire pit and sat next to her. He picked her up hand and looked into her eyes. She swallowed hard.

She hated to admit that having him sit so damn close to her made her heart do funny things.

"I want you to marry me," he finally said.

"You what?" All the air whooshed out of her lungs, leaving her struggling to catch her breath. Surely, she'd misunderstood. Or just hadn't heard him correctly.

"Jacey, I want you to marry me." He narrowed his eyes a little like he was trying to convince her to say yes with just one look.

She jumped up from her seat and swung around. "You cannot be serious."

"I'm perfectly serious." He stood.

"We don't even know each other." Not to mention he was the Pack Master of Arkansas.

"But you are my mate. I know that now. I think I've known it all along," he shoved his hand through his hair. "I just didn't want to admit it."

Reality crashed into her. "Well, as lovey as this proposal is, I politely decline your invitation." She lifted her chin and wrapped her arms around her body like a shield.

"Ugh. I'm making a mess of this, aren't I?" he grimaced.

"You could say that." She took a step back and glared.

"You need to understand the importance of marrying me. It's for your own good." He cocked his head.

"My own good? Are you kidding me?" She took a deep breath before she said something she would regret. "Barrett, I came to Colorado to start over, to finally get the life that I've always wanted. I want to live out my dreams and being married to someone who will tell me what to do doesn't fit in my picture." She turned and walked over to the railing. Her heart thudded in her chest like a drum.

"You don't understand," he said.

"Oh, I understand perfectly well. You think I'm your mate, and you think we should get married." She frowned.

"Although I'm not sure why, if you really thought I was your mate, you would even care about getting married? You know as well as I do that Weres aren't required to marry. That's human tradition."

"By marrying me, it will give you protection."

"Protection from what? Boudier is after you, not me."

"That's where you're wrong. Boudier is after you too."

She froze. "What?"

"Boudier will hurt me anyway he can. He has been watching you so that clearly means he's going to try to hurt you, or worse, before he comes to me. He knows that if something happens to you, it would devastate me."

Her heart swelled a little. "Really?"

"Of course. Do you know how much you mean to me?" He took a step forward.

She wasn't sure of anything anymore.

"Listen. By marrying me, you will have the protection of my Guardians. They are willing to lay down their lives for you."

She shook her head. "I don't want anyone to do that for me. I didn't ask anyone to do that." She licked her lips. "If I just left, went some place north like Alaska …"

"It would not matter," Barrett said finally. "Boudier would come for you first. Then me. If you stay here with the protection, you are safe. A lot safer than you would be out on your own."

She opened her mouth and then slammed it shut.

"You need to think about your family as well, Jacey."

"My family?" she jerked her head up at him.

"Yes. Boudier will go after your family too. But if you marry me, I can let Jack Welbourn know, and he will give your family Guardian protection."

Her knees nearly buckled. She'd not thought of her mother and father. Although they'd practically disowned her after her breakup with her mate, they were still her parents.

"There's more." Barrett took a deep breath. "I know that you didn't want this. I know you truly wanted to live your life and not be tied down. I also know that you are my mate. I would never ask you to mate me if that's something you truly don't want to do. But by marrying me, you will get the protection you need. It's a lot easier to get divorced than get unmated."

Her heart fell and shattered in her stomach. So, he really didn't want to stay with her either.

One more male had found her lacking.

She swallowed her pride and blinked back the stinging tears. She turned and gripped the metal railing so he wouldn't see any escaped tears.

"I'll marry you, Barrett. But once this is over, we will divorce. You will go your way, and I'll go mine." She didn't wait for him to answer but quickly headed into the house.

CHAPTER 44

*B*arrett waited near the altar of the small, white chapel. Ryker had managed to find the small church buried deep in the mountains. The Were had not only managed to procure a minister, but he'd also gotten the appropriate paperwork needed for the ceremony in record time. Out of all the Guardians, Barrett had figured Ryker would be the one to try to talk him out of marrying Jacey.

Surprisingly he had not, instead setting out to get everything ready for the ceremony.

Barrett looked over at the minister and glared. He didn't trust humans, not even ones that proclaimed to be ministers. The minister returned a friendly smile, and Barrett looked back down the aisle waiting for his bride to appear.

"Where is she?" he muttered to himself. Had she gotten cold feet? Had she escaped? Or worse, had Boudier found and kidnapped her?

The last thought had him turning to go check on her, but the minister grabbed his suit sleeve.

"Here she comes now." He patted Barrett's arm reassuringly.

Barrett stared down the dark aisle but only saw Damon. Barrett hurried down the steps and met him halfway.

"Where are you going?" Damon's eyes widened. "Get back up there."

"Where's Jacey?" Barrett looked over his shoulder but couldn't see a thing.

"She had to get dressed, you idiot." Damon slapped him on the shoulder. "You didn't expect to be the only one dressed up for your wedding, did you?" Damon snorted. "Now get back up there by that fat preacher before Jacey sees you and thinks you're getting cold feet."

Barrett took a deep breath, relieved that she was safe and was still getting ready to marry him. He walked back up to the minister who shot Damon a stern look. Apparently, he didn't like being called fat.

"I need someone to stand beside me, right?" Barrett gave Damon a look.

"Are you asking me?" Damon arched a brow.

"No, I'm asking that fucking poinsettia in the back," Barrett deadpanned. "Of course, I'm asking you."

Damon cracked a rare smile and walked up beside him.

"Please refrain from using profanity in the Lord's house," the minister said through gritted teeth.

"You must forgive him, Padre, this is his first wedding," Damon answered.

"And last. I'm sure." The ministered lifted his chin. "Marriage is not something to be entered into lightly."

"No shit. It was hard enough to get the female to agree to marry me in the first place," Barrett groused.

"Language," the minister admonished.

Damon laughed. "She wasn't excited to be Mrs. Barrett Middleton? That's a shocker."

"I was expecting a different response from her when I asked." Barrett stuck a finger in his collar and tugged on the tie. Ryker had tied his tie, and it was choking him to death. Asshole probably did it on purpose.

"Did you bring her roses? Ask her to be your wife by candlelight?" Damon cocked his head.

Barrett looked at the Were. "Where was I going to get roses in this snow?" He turned back to the empty aisle. "I did ask by firelight, that should count."

"Hmm. Knowing you, you probably didn't even ask. You probably told her she was marrying you," Damon said.

Barrett opened his mouth and then slammed it shut.

"You totally did, didn't you?" Damon barked out a laugh. The sound went through the whole church, ricocheting off the walls like cannon fire.

"Fuck off," Barrett growled.

"I've already told you both nicely not to use profanity in the Lord's house. If you two can't …"

Barrett looked down the aisle and sucked in a deep breath. A hush fell across the small chapel, and they turned to see what he was looking at.

Jacey stepped out from the doorway wearing a simple white dress. The silk material melted to every curve of her body. It was sleeveless and curved to fit her breasts perfectly. She didn't wear a veil but had her hair up off her shoulders. She held a small bouquet of poinsettias and what looked like baby's breath. She looked up at the Were on her side and nodded.

Ryker held out his arm, and she stuck her arm in his.

Barrett's gut tightened in rage. He didn't want Jacey touching Ryker, not even for him to walk her down the aisle.

"Easy," Damon whispered near his ear. "Don't make a scene. This preacher looks like he's ready to change his mind and not carry out the ceremony."

Barrett gritted his teeth until he thought they would break off in his mouth.

He heard snickers from the peanut gallery which consisted of Braxton, Zane, and Jaxon. They were sitting in the front row while Jayden and Lucien were keeping guard in various positions around the church.

They'd managed to get the minister to do the wedding at midnight so there would be less of a chance to be seen. They'd made sure of the safety of the place before bringing him and Jacey here under the cover of darkness in one of Eric Nordstrom's Hummers.

Now he was standing in front of a minister with his gaze glued to Jacey as she was being escorted down the aisle by a glum-looking Ryker.

She looked stunning, like the front page of a wedding magazine. His heart raced with every step she took toward him. He couldn't tear his gaze away.

"Who gives this woman away?" the minister asked

"That would be me," Ryker said.

Barrett let out a low growl and shoved Ryker out of the way, taking Jacey's arm. A loud snicker rose up behind him. He shot a glare at his Guardians in the front row.

Barrett barely heard whatever the hell the minster was saying. Instead, he answered when he was supposed to answer and kept his gaze trained on Jacey. He held his breath when it was her turn to repeat the vow. He half-expected her to back out and run down the aisle, but she didn't.

After an eternity, the minister said a final prayer. He didn't bow his head or close his eyes but continued to look at his new bride.

"Amen." The minister raised his head and smiled with relief. "I now present Mr. and Mrs. Barrett Middleton."

A loud chorus of whistling and yells went out into the small space. The minister grimaced, and Ryker shoved some money into his fat hand. The minister thanked Ryker and hurried toward the front door in an effort to get everyone out.

Barrett had no problem with that. He wanted to get out of that place as soon as possible. He wanted to be alone with Jacey.

* * *

JACEY FELT like she was walking in a dream. When she'd accepted Barrett's proposal, she'd never thought they would actually have a wedding in a chapel. She thought he was going to take her into town and find a justice of the peace. But no, she'd had an actual wedding. She knew that Guardians had a way to get paperwork done fast but to get married the same night he'd proposed was unheard of.

Their honeymoon night would be spent in the mansion. With the Guardians stationed around the house like secret service. It was big enough that everyone had their own bedrooms.

She wasn't sure if they even liked her or not. Not that it mattered. As soon as Boudier was captured and dealt with, she would be seeking an annulment. She wasn't going to stay married to someone who didn't love her. She wasn't about to repeat that mistake.

Now back in her room, she stood in front of the mirror, looking at her wedding dress. Ryker told her Barrett had paid for the wedding dress. Yet another thing she'd not expected. He'd also told her that he was walking her down the aisle just to make sure she didn't change her mind.

If Ryker had not stood outside her door while she got dressed, she might have tried to sneak away.

Now she was married to Barrett. To a man who wasn't willing to mate her.

She'd gotten herself into another loveless marriage. The one thing she swore she would never do.

Exhausted, she walked over to the bed and lay down. Maybe this was all a dream.

She closed her eyes. Maybe when she woke up, everything would be okay.

* * *

JACEY WAS LOST in a world of longing. She didn't ever want to leave.

"Jacey."

She knew from the deep, sexy tone who that voice belonged to.

She blinked open her eyes. Barrett was sitting beside her, leaning way too close. He brushed a strand of hair away from her face.

"Jacey, I want to talk."

She smiled, her body still in dream state. She didn't want to talk. She wanted to do something else. She eased up on her elbows and looked at him.

"I know you're tired, but I really want to talk to you."

She watched his eyes dip down to her breasts and then back up to her gaze. She glanced down.

She was in a wedding dress.

It all made sense now.

She was dreaming. She hadn't actually married Barrett, and she was not in Colorado. She was dreaming.

She leaned forward and cocked her head. "You want to talk?" She arched her eyebrow.

He swallowed and nodded.

She eased off the bed and looked down at her dress. And frowned.

"What's wrong? Did you not like the dress?" he asked, standing. "You look beautiful in it."

"It's tight, and if you're going to talk then let me change. It's not very comfortable." She turned and gave him her back.

She felt his fingertips on her back as he pulled the zipper down. The dress went slack, and she held the front up with her hands. She turned and smiled. "That's better."

He cleared his throat, and his face went red. "I'll get you a robe." He did a bad job of pretending to avert his gaze from her as he walked into the bathroom.

"Interesting." She cocked her head. "Since I'm dreaming, I can do anything I want. I can *have* anything I want."

Barrett returned with the silky, white robe and held it out in his hands. She turned her back and dropped the dress to the ground and stuck her arms in the sleeves of the robe. She turned around to face him without bothering to tie the robe.

Her body warmed. She could smell his arousal.

She dropped her hands to her sides, letting the robe gap enough to see the front of her white lace panties and the soft curve of her breasts.

She watched as he let out a slow growl and curled his fingers into fists at his sides.

Now this was fun. Making Barrett want her. And since this was a dream, it didn't matter if they had hot, wet sex. In dreams, there were no consequences.

She walked over to the tall, silver ice bucket holding a bottle of champagne. She turned and pointed. "Why don't you open that. It's been a long time since I had champagne." Years actually. At a family wedding. She couldn't help but wonder if champagne in a dream would taste different than champagne in reality.

She bet it did. She bet it tasted a lot sweeter.

"Sure." His voice was hoarse and deep. It sounded very

much like the night when he'd gone down on her, making her come so hard she nearly fainted.

He quickly popped the cork on the frosty bottle of champagne, sending a bubbling stream onto the floor.

"Fuck," he mumbled.

"Not yet," she muttered.

His head jerked up in her direction, and she nearly laughed at the look on his face.

"What?" he asked.

"Just pour. Then we can talk." She walked back over to the bed and sat.

He poured the sparkling liquid into two fluted glasses. He walked over to the bed and handed one to her.

"Thank you." She tipped the glass to her lips. The cool bubbles burst on her tongue, and she sighed in pleasure.

She looked up at him and patted the space beside her on the bed. He sat. She looked down his chest. He'd rid himself of the jacket and tie as soon as they had gotten into the car. He still wore the white shirt, but it was unbuttoned about five buttons. He'd changed into jeans which hugged his lean hips and showed off his impressive bulge.

She finished her champagne and placed the glass on the bedside table. She turned to talk to him, and her robe gaped open, showing him her full breast.

His gaze dipped to her bare breast, and his pupils dilated.

She smiled to herself.

She tucked her legs underneath her and looked at him straight on. Her robe gaped with each breath she took, promising him a view of her nakedness. She tossed her hair back and leaned a little close to him.

"So, tell me, what is it you want, Barrett?"

* * *

BARRETT WASN'T sure what he expected when he went into Jacey's room. But he certainly didn't expect her to be half-naked and looking at him like she wanted to eat him.

After the wedding ceremony, they had been rushed back to the mansion by the Guardians. There had been no reception afterward. There hadn't been time to plan one so everyone had gone off to their own bedroom. Ryker had ribbed him about the likelihood of Jacey not allowing him into her bed. He'd come to her tonight to talk to her. To tell her how much he really loved her.

Now he was finding it harder and harder to talk about anything. Her scent, her arousal, and her beauty stunned him. It made him want to do whatever she wanted.

Now he knew why Weres mated, and how deeply the bond was. He wanted to mate with Jacey, but he knew it had to be her idea. Not his. He wouldn't pressure her to do anything she would regret.

"You seem nervous." She bit her bottom lip and crawled closer. He fought the unholy urge to flip her onto her back and pound his desire into her body until they were both drenched with lust.

He cleared his throat and forced himself to focus. "I want you to know that I take our marriage vows very seriously. I know this whole thing is very sudden ..." His words grew slow as he watched her lean forward and trail her finger down the front of his shirt. His body ached with desire so strong, he thought he just might shift into wolf.

She put both of her hands on his chest and shoved him backward onto the bed. She straddled him.

His cock hardened and lengthened. His breathing increased. His heart pounded so loud he thought he might go deaf.

Jacey looked down at him. She frowned and cocked her head. "You know this is very odd."

"Well …"

"You're not usually this talkative in my dreams," she whispered.

His eyes widened. "Wait. Jacey, this is not a dream." His heart fell.

Ignoring his words, she leaned down, her mouth inches from his. "In fact, your mouth is usually busy, occupied doing other things."

His hands grabbed her hips. She smiled and ground down on his cock.

"Fuck …" Her hot heat scorched him though the denim of his jeans. All he wanted was to be inside her right now.

"Jacey, you're making this hard . . ."

"That's the idea. Making you hard so you can make me wet," she purred. She swung open her robe, revealing her bare breasts and white, lacy panties.

She was more exquisite than he remembered. Lust poured through his body until all he wanted was to be inside her. He growled. He didn't know what had gotten into her, but he liked it. He liked her open and wild.

Before he could get another word out, she had slammed her mouth down across his, kissing him hard and firm. Hard as a rock and all self-control gone, he cupped her face and kissed her back, his tongue thrusting into her mouth, tasting, claiming, and wanting nothing less than all of her.

She moaned against his mouth, deepening the kiss. She sucked on his tongue.

She was sexy as fuck, and he never wanted his mouth off her.

She dug her nails into his shoulders, clawing as she ground her lithe body against his.

He had to be sure. He had to be positive that this is what she wanted.

He wanted the choice to be hers.

Grasping her shoulders, he pulled her back and looked into her caramel-brown eyes. ,

"Jacey, are you sure you want to do this? I need to know because it's going to be hard as hell to stop."

"More than anything, this is what I want," she moaned and leaned forward.

"I need to tell you something else," he said. He wanted to make sure she knew that he was giving her everything. Every piece of him that he had.

"What?" She frowned.

"I love you. Since the day I saw you. I want to mate you. Now and forever, I want you to be mine." The words came out harsh.

Her expression softened, and her pupils dilated. "I love you too."

It was the most precious gift he'd ever been given in his whole life. It was something he would never take for granted. He knew he would protect her with his life.

He cupped her face between his hands. She leaned into him. Their bodies heated as they pressed against each other.

Her fingers slid to the buttons on his shirt. She pulled back, breaking the kiss.

Leaning back, she slid both hands into his shirt. Keeping her gaze on him, she gripped the shirt and pulled. The sound of ripping and the sight of buttons flying in the air made him even harder.

"My turn," he murmured. He slid his hands inside her robe and shoved it off her shoulders and onto the bed. Reaching for her, he pulled her down, covering her mouth with his. Their hot tongues slid across each other in a wicked dance of desire.

She moaned and moved her mouth to his neck. He fought the urge to flip her on her back and bury himself in her sweet body. This was their wedding night, and he wanted to make it special for her.

She trailed kisses down his neck to his chest. Her hot mouth closed around his nipple and sucked. She nipped at his flesh with her teeth, and he hissed at the pleasure coursing through his veins.

She kissed her way down his stomach, as her soft hair caressed and tickled his flesh. When her hands found his zipper, he groaned. She quickly worked his jeans free and tugged them off.

"Jacey," his voice sounded hoarse in his own ears and was barely audible over the pounding of his heart. "Sweetheart, I don't think I'm going to last much longer if you keep touching me like that."

She looked up at him with a wicked twinkle in her eyes. "Like what?" Her tone, innocent and playful, did not match the desire in her eyes.

She grinned and palmed his erection. He gripped the sheets in a white-knuckled hold.

Her eyes widened with lust as she pumped his straining erection. Each stoke of her soft hand had him arching off the bed into her palm.

She bent her face to his thighs, pressing her mouth to the corner of his hip.

She kissed his flesh until she was mere inches away from his erection. She spread his thighs apart. She bent her head and licked her way across his balls, sending electric desire shooting up to the tip of his cock.

"Fuck." He tightened his grip on the sheets.

She palmed his cock and licked him from top to bottom, taking her time and making him growl in sexual frustration.

His balls tingled and tightened with his impending orgasm. He quickly pulled her away and flipped her onto her back.

Hovering above her, he stared into her eyes.

"I wasn't finished," she pouted.

"You get your pleasure first." He grinned down at her. He took her mouth with savage lust. She'd opened up the beast inside, and now it couldn't be caged.

He grabbed her panties in his hands and tugged, ripping the thin material in two and tossing them to the floor.

He dipped his head, and his mouth found her taut nipple. He sucked the pretty pink bud in his mouth. She moaned and cradled his head close.

Since he'd met her, he secretly wondered if and when they did have sex, would she be able to handle his aggressive sexual side. She was everything feminine and delicate, and he didn't want to scare her. He needed to go slow. But now, tonight under the glow of the fireplace and the heat of their bodies, he knew their first time wouldn't be slow.

He needed to get inside her and mark her as his own.

He needed to make sure she would never belong to anyone else.

He licked his way done her flat stomach to the inside of her leg. He brushed his mouth against her satin skin.

He crawled between her thighs. She moaned and moved her hips toward his mouth. He grinned and placed his hand against her silky mound. His thumb brushed her clit. She bucked her hips upward.

She was hot and wet and ready for him. But he wanted to get the first orgasm out of the way. He needed to be inside her a long time before she came again. He wanted it to last.

He hooked her legs over his shoulders and bent his head. He licked his way up her wet entrance to her clit.

"Barrett," she moaned and grabbed his head.

He growled and flicked his tongue across her pussy, teasing and taunting her. He looked up between her legs to find her staring at him, a mixture of lust and love.

He continued to taste her sweetness, licking it up and savoring her scent on his tongue. She was his own personal candy. The one scent he would always crave and never betray.

She bucked her hips against his mouth as he licked and sucked her clit. Her breathing turned to a pant, and her eyes were completely dilated with pleasure.

"Barrett, please," she begged.

He liked her like that. Bare and begging for him to give her what she needed.

His body grew tight and hard, and he couldn't wait any longer to be inside her body.

He sucked her clit into his mouth and pressed his face into her wet heat.

Jacey arched and cried out as her body went limp. He continued to work her over with his mouth while she rode out her orgasm against his mouth.

After she'd finished, Barrett climbed up her body and positioned himself between her legs.

Looking into his eyes, she reached up and pulled his face to her and kissed him.

He growled and thrust inside her body.

She gasped as his large erection filled her body. She knew he was big, but she wasn't sure he would fit.

Painful pleasure shot between her hips, and he looked down at her.

He stilled, giving her time for her body to accommodate his large erection.

"You're tight," he moaned as a single bead of sweat rolled from his temple onto the pillow.

"You're really big," she said, gasping.

"Don't move." he said through gritted teeth.

"I need to." She bucked her hips upward. "It feels too

good." Whatever pain she'd felt was now melting away into warm bliss.

He moved his hips against hers in slow, methodical strokes. Each motion sent delicious shivers through her body from her head to her toes.

"I wanted to go slow for our first time. But I don't think I can," he admitted.

"I don't want slow. I just want you."

Looking down, he cupped her cheek and covered her mouth with his. His hips pistoned in long, deep strokes into her body, sending sparks of intense pleasure through her body.

She let out a moan, deep in the back of her throat. He trailed kisses from her mouth to her neck, kissing and licking the sensitive flesh there.

She wrapped her legs around him as he powered into her, his hard cock filling and pleasuring her at the same time.

Their bodies were wet with sweat from their heated lust. He raised his head and looked down into her eyes.

"Come for me." he commanded deep and dark.

It was all she needed to send her into her second orgasm. She tightened her legs around him and felt her body begin to tingle between her legs. Pleasure poured like warm caramel from deep in her stomach and streamed through her body.

She turned her head and bit down on his shoulder, digging her nails into his flesh as she came hard and fast.

He growled and thrust harder and faster, fueling his own orgasm. He bent his head and bit down hard as he came inside her body.

Exhausted, he collapsed onto her, and she cradled him to her body. He lifted his head and smirked. He shifted his weight and pulled her into his chest as he gathered her into his arms. She smiled as she snuggled into his body, curling a thigh around his masculine legs.

He placed his finger under her chin and lifted her gaze to him.

"I don't know what I would do if I ever lost you," he murmured. His eyes were intense and full of love.

"Then don't let go of me," she sighed.

"You're lucky if I ever let you out of this bed, wife." He grinned.

"I like the sound of that." She smirked.

"What? Not ever getting out of bed?" He kissed her softly.

"I mean the wife part," she moaned. "But I do like the bed part too."

He pulled her onto him until she was straddling his hips. She kissed him and rubbed her body against his until he was rock hard again.

This time when he slid into her body, they took their time, memorizing and savoring each other's bodies until the early hours of the morning.

Jacey never wanted to wake up.

CHAPTER 45

*J*acey stirred. She opened her eyes and frowned. Lying on her pillow was Barrett with his arm wrapped protectively around her naked waist.

She was still dreaming. It was just a different part of a dream. She smiled, studying his face. Even in his sleep, she couldn't deny the pull of wanting him all over again.

She slipped out of his hold and grabbed his button-up shirt off the floor. She shoved her arms through and made her way to the kitchen. Grabbing a bottle of water from the fridge, she headed back to the bedroom but movement out the large windows caught her attention.

It was snowing. She walked up to the window and gazed out as the moon illuminated the scenery. Pine trees were decorated in a white garland of flakes, and the ground was a soft blanket of white. She bet if she walked outside, it would be completely silent, the snow covering up any sounds of nature.

"Jacey."

She turned at the sound of his deep voice.

He was standing in the doorway wearing his jeans. He

hadn't bothered to zip them, and his stomach muscles rippled as he walked over to her.

Wrapping his arms around her waist, he stared out at the wintery scene before them. She leaned back against him and sighed. "Isn't it beautiful?"

"Not as beautiful as you."

She laughed and turned in his arms.

His gaze drifted down the front of her body. She didn't button up the shirt.

She reached out and trailed her fingertips across the muscle that veered into his jeans. Looking into his eyes, she slid her hand inside his pants.

He hissed at her touch, and she tightened her hold on his hard cock.

He slipped his skilled hand inside her shirt to fondle her breast. He gently plucked her nipple. A moan slipped out of her mouth.

"Feel good?" he whispered near her ear.

"Anything you do feels good."

He covered her lips in a searing kiss, and suddenly his hands were everywhere, touching and caressing.

"I want you now," she moaned and shoved his jeans down his hips. He kicked his jeans off.

He grabbed her ass and lifted her off her feet. She wrapped her legs around his waist. He leaned her against the wall and positioned his erection at her entrance.

He thrust, entering her in one swift, sweet motion.

Her head fell back, and she moaned as he pumped inside her, his fevered mouth on her neck.

"Tell me that you're mine," he growled. "I need to hear you say the words." His hoarse voice skidded across her flesh, giving her goosebumps in the most pleasant way.

"I'm yours, Barrett." she cried out as her climax hit.

Groaning, he buried himself deep as he spilled his seed inside her.

They stayed melded into each other's bodies, their heavy breathing the only noise in the room.

"Let's go back to bed." He kissed her gently on the lips and placed her on the ground.

He gathered up their clothes. "Don't get dressed. There's no need." He grinned wickedly and picked her up in his arms and carried her back to their bed.

* * *

JACEY SNUGGLED down into the covers, searching for warmth against the chill. She smiled to herself as she remembered with stunning clarity the dream from last night. She didn't want to open her eyes just yet. She wanted to stay in that sexy haze of desire and love.

She reached up to hug her pillow but instead of softness, her hand met warm, hard flesh.

Frowning, she cracked open an eye.

Her body heated.

It was Barrett.

Her heart slammed into her chest. Her stomach dropped. And then she knew. It wasn't a dream at all.

He lay beside her, one hand splayed across his stomach and the other thrown across his head as if he were blocking out the sunlight.

She needed to ease out of the bed before he woke. She needed to gather herself and think about what had happened and what it meant for them.

"Good morning." His voice had her stilling her movement on the bed.

She said nothing but pulled the comforter up to her chin to hide her nakedness.

313

Every touch of his mouth, every caress of his hand came blaring back in the bright light of day. Her face heated and flushed. She had laid her soul bare, given her body and her heart to him. In return, he had taken and devoured it.

She had confessed her love for him. That was the worst part. That was the part that tore her heart out.

"It wasn't a dream." She covered her face with her hands, too embarrassed to look at him.

He sat up and reached for her. "What are you talking about? What wasn't a dream?"

She pulled her hands away from her face and turned to him. "What have we done, Barrett?"

His expression changed, turned serious. "I don't understand. Why are you so upset?"

"I thought last night was a dream." She stood, taking the comforter with her. She needed to get as much distance from him as possible. She knew what would happen if she stayed in bed with him.

He shook his head and narrowed his eyes at her. "You told me last night you wanted this. That you wanted me."

"I know. That's because I thought it was a dream." She tried to swallow, but her mouth had turned to ash.

"So, you only want me if I'm a dream?" His gaze narrowed.

"Dreams don't have consequences. Reality does." She tried to hold in her tears, but one disobedient tear slid down her cheek.

He stood, ignoring his nakedness. He reached up and wiped her tear away.

"I've never done anything like this before. I don't have random sex. The only male I've slept with was my . . ."

"Husband." He cocked his head. "Which would be me."

"Husband. For now," she said quietly.

"What does that mean?" He touched her cheek, but she

stepped back. He straightened, and the room filled with tension. "Jacey, what do you mean, I'm your husband for now?"

She looked up and said the words that hurt her most to say. But she had to. "Barrett, I'm not naïve. I understand very well that once Boudier is captured and the danger is over, the marriage will be annulled." She looked away. "Or at least it could have been before we . . ."

"Made love? Mated?"

She reached up and covered his lips with her hands.

He pulled her hands away and smiled. "Jacey, sweetheart. We are mated now. After last night, there's no doubt in my mind that we are mated."

"Being mated doesn't last."

"Yes, it does." His eyebrows slammed together.

She gave him a droll look. "Seriously? You didn't just say that." She shoved her thumb in her chest. "You're looking at the one female in all of werewolf history whose mate left her for someone else. Remember?"

Barrett's eyes hardened, and he leaned toward her. "He was not your mate. He never was, and he never will be."

A shiver ran up her spine. Not from fear but from sexual excitement.

He reached for her and cupped her face. "Jacey look at me. I know that things were not done how you would have preferred. The fast wedding ceremony, the lack of a honeymoon. You deserve so much more, and I'm sorry. But I think you're confused about my feelings for you . . ."

A pounding on the door had her jerking out of his hold.

"Barrett! Are you guys up?" Ryker's voice bellowed through the closed door.

"Damn it. His timing sucks," Barrett growled.

He found his jeans on the floor and quickly tugged them on. She tightened the comforter around her like a cocoon.

Barrett walked over to her and caressed her cheek with the palm of his hand. "Jacey, this conversation is far from over. We're going to talk about this, okay?"

She nodded but didn't bother meeting his gaze.

The pounding intensified.

"He's going to knock the door in if you don't open it," she spat out, eyeing the door nervously.

"Are you going to give your husband a good morning kiss before I go kill Ryker?" He crossed his arms over his chest.

She jerked her head in his direction and glared.

"If you kiss me, I'll answer the door." He grinned.

"Ugh. Fine." The last thing she wanted was Ryker busting through the door with her naked under the comforter. She raised up on her tiptoes and pressed her lips to his cheek. At the last second, he turned and pressed his lips to hers.

Her body flooded with desire. Every time he kissed her, he did that to her.

He pulled back and glared at the door. "Let me go see what he wants and then we'll talk."

CHAPTER 46

*J*acey sprinted for the shower the second Barrett left the room. She shut the door and reached for the lock. Groaning, she realized the stupid door had no lock. After last night, he might want a little action in the shower.

She turned the water on and jumped in while it was still cold. Shivering, she washed her hair while the water turned warm then hot. She couldn't make herself relax. She was too busy straining to hear any noise to indicate he was back in the bedroom. Reaching for the razor, she quickly shaved her legs, only nicking herself twice in her haste.

Turning off the water, she grabbed the robe and tied it securely. She opened the door leading into the bedroom and peered inside.

Empty. Whatever Ryker wanted must have been important.

At least it gave her time to dry her hair.

She found the hairdryer in the cabinet and wiped down the mirror before drying her hair. She stared at her reflection while the hot air blew across her wet hair while images of her and Barrett flitted through her head.

She'd been brazen last night. Touching him and tasting him as much as she wanted.

And she was utterly humiliated. She never acted like that in her life. Not even with her ex-mate. But then again, sex with Jeremy had been lacking.

Not with Barrett. Sex with him had been absolutely mind-blowing. Something she'd only read about in romance novels.

Barrett had been aggressive but in a tender way, anticipating where she wanted his hands, his fingers, his mouth.

She looked at her flushed reflection. The heat in her stomach began to grow as she thought about how they'd made love. And how many times. Just thinking about it had her going wet.

"Jacey."

She jumped and spun around at the closed door.

"I'll be right out." She clutched the top of her robe to her chin and spun around to the sink. She quickly brushed her teeth and finished drying her hair.

Making sure her robe was secure, she walked back into the bedroom.

Barrett was at the closet, still only dressed in jeans and pulling clothes out of the closet.

"Are those your clothes?" She pointed to the closet and then cocked her head. "Wait, those clothes were not in there yesterday."

"I had Braxton move my stuff in here before the wedding. Having clothes already here for us when we arrived was something Eric provided without me asking." He turned and looked at her. "I'm sure I'll have to pay him back."

"You certainly have really good friends," she said, tightening her robe. She couldn't drag her eyes away from his body and how his muscles moved with each motion. It was like poetry.

"You have good friends now too." He glanced at her before grabbing a long-sleeved black T-shirt off the hanger and a pair of dark jeans and tossed them on the bed.

Her body warmed and tingled in all the right places. She clenched her legs together, trying to ease the building ache.

"Is everything okay?" She cleared her throat and forced herself to look out the window. The snow was no longer falling, and the morning sun glistened on the white landscape like tiny diamonds.

"It is." He grinned and walked over to her. "Ryker said that Boudier was found on the other side of Denver. He's been captured."

"They have him?"

"Yes, some Mississippi Guardians got the drop on him, He was hiding out in a sleazy motel. They captured him as he left the room. According to a map, he was trying to figure out where we had gotten off to."

Her stomach dropped. "So, we're safe now."

"Yes. We are." He turned back to the closet and tugged out some jeans and a cable knit sweater for her. "Which means we can go down into the city. Ryker and the other Guardians are bitching about how hungry they are. I suggested we all go down into Aspen for breakfast."

He tossed the clothes on the bed and walked over to her. "I know we still need to talk. We'll do that when we get back. Right now, I just want one day with you that's normal. Where nobody is trying to kill us."

She looked at him, and her heart clenched in her chest. He was so utterly handsome, the most handsome male she'd ever seen. She would cherish what they had experienced last night, but she knew she couldn't let him be tied down to her forever. She needed to learn how to live on her own and not depend on anyone else.

"I'm going to jump in the shower." He gave her a quick kiss before he walked into the bathroom.

She nodded and proceeded to get dressed. She had time to grab a cup of coffee and settle her nerves before they left.

Depending on Barrett and loving him too much was going to be her downfall. And she wasn't ready to fail at life again.

* * *

BARRETT USUALLY ENJOYED LONG, hot showers, but with the good news that Boudier was captured and Jacey was officially his mate as well as his wife, he was in too good of a mood to linger.

He jumped out of the shower and gave a quick shake of his head. Water droplets splattered on the pristine mirror.

He toweled off quickly and headed into the bedroom to get dressed. He slid the black T-shirt over his head. He sat on the edge of the bed and put on his black biker boots.

He grabbed his jacket and headed downstairs.

Knowing that Jacey would most likely be in the kitchen, he headed in that direction. He rounded the corner and stopped.

Jacey was standing in front of the large picture window by the kitchen table with Ryker, Jayden, and Lucien circling her. She was cradling a hot cup of coffee between her hands and shaking her head at whatever the Guardians had said.

"Come on, Jacey. Just tell me." Jayden frowned and elbowed Ryker out of his way.

She cocked her head. "Why would I tell you? You'll just eat it all up, and there won't be any left."

"No, I won't. I don't eat that much." Jayden flashed her a pretty smile.

"Bullshit. Jayden can put away twice as much as any Were I've ever met," Lucien snorted.

"I was here first before you assholes showed up. If she tells anyone anything, it's going to be me." Ryker growled at Jayden and then tried to give Jacey a smile. It looked more menacing than charming.

Jacey arched her brow at Ryker and took a step back.

He didn't know what the fuck they were talking about, but he didn't like it.

"What the hell is going on here?" Barrett thundered as he walked toward the group. Jacey's eyes widened at him, and the Guardians had the good sense to take a good three steps back from her.

No one answered so he looked at Lucien for answers. "Well?"

Lucien grinned and held up his hands defensively. "Ryker and Jayden were trying to talk Jacey into telling them where she hid the homemade cookie dough. But she's a tough cookie herself and won't break."

"Haha, Lucien," Jayden scowled. "You're such a kiss ass." He looked at Barrett and gave him a pleading look. "Come on, man. It's just a little cookie dough. Just one little taste. I mean, those cookies were amazing. They reminded me of home."

Jacey's expression softened. "Jayden, you didn't tell me that . . ."

"That's because he's bullshitting you." Barrett narrowed his eyes at Jayden. "Stop trying to play on her sympathy. She's not handing her cookies over."

"Shit. What did I miss?" Damon walked into the kitchen and headed for the coffeepot. Braxton, Jaxon, and Zane were right behind him.

"Ryker and Jayden are in a death battle to get Jacey's homemade cookies," Lucien snorted.

Jaxon let out a laugh. "I figured as much from Jayden but not Ryker." He sobered and gave Ryker his full attention. "Never knew you were a sweet tooth, Ryker. Hell, I've never seen you as much as eat dessert after dinner."

"Fuck off," Ryker groused and stormed over to the coffeepot.

"Yeah, I'm not so sure you guys should be trying to talk Jacey out of her cookies, Barrett's not going to take kindly to sharing." Lucien laughed.

Barrett shot him a glare and stepped in between the Guardians and Jacey.

"Alright. Enough with the smack talk," Damon groused. "I'm starving my ass off."

"I found a great place in town that serves an all-you-can-eat pancake breakfast," Zane said. He looked at Jayden. "They might even be able to fill you up, Jayden."

"I doubt that," Jayden sighed. "But you know what would help?" He cut his eyes at Jacey.

"No. She's not giving you any cookies or cookie dough, and if you bring it up again, I'll gut you myself," Barrett growled.

A snicker rose up from the room as the Guardians grabbed their jackets and filed out of the kitchen.

Barrett turned to Jacey. He knew the guys were joking, but he didn't like it. Was this how he was going to feel from now on now that he was mated?

Barrett picked up her jacket draped on the back of the chair and held it out for her. She stuck her arms in the sleeves and quickly zipped up the coat.

"I'm ready." She looked up at him.

He could feel the tension between them hanging heavy in the air. This was not how he wanted his life with her to start.

He took her hand in his and gave it a gentle squeeze. Jacey was a female who wanted to trust him, but she needed to be shown that what he was saying and his feelings for her were real.

He was just going to have to put his words into actions.

CHAPTER 47

*J*acey entered the cozy, log-cabin style restaurant with Barrett at her side. While the Guardians had ridden together in one vehicle, she and Barrett had driven together in one of Eric's four-wheel-drive trucks. Conversation had been light and not serious. It was exactly what she needed. She didn't want to have an emotional narrative before having to face all the Arkansas Guardians.

"Over here." Braxton stood up from the table near the large stone fireplace and waved them over. The morning crowd was slowly drifting in from the snow outside. And the noise of conversation mingled with the sweet aroma of pancakes and bacon.

Barrett pulled out the chair for her, and she eased into the seat. He sat next to her at the head of the table. Jaxon was seated to her right, and Ryker sat across the table from her. Damon sat at the other end with Braxton, Zane, Jayden, and Lucien filling up the rest of the table.

"We already ordered coffee for both of you," Zane said as he closed his menu.

'Perfect," Barrett said and picked up his menu and studied the options. Jacey took a sip of her water and glanced around at the Weres at the table. They were ribbing each other and joking.

She knew they were more a family than she'd ever had.

How sad was that? She's been born in a nuclear family, given a good life as she grew up, married the Were everyone expected. And when she'd failed in her marriage and basically in her life, her family had disowned her. Even those she'd thought were her friends stopped talking to her.

Suddenly she wasn't that hungry.

She glanced up and found Barrett staring at her intently. She blinked and laid her menu down on the table just as the waitress approached.

"What can I get everyone?" The waitress was young, midtwenties with blonde hair, blue eyes, and flawless skin. She wore black tights with a matching black shirt which accentuated her breasts. She had tall, gray boots that reached up to her knees and a tiny, denim apron wrapped around her waist.

It didn't go unnoticed that she smiled a little too much and stood a little too close to Barrett.

Anger boiled in Jacey's stomach and spread through her veins like gasoline poured out in a stream. She narrowed her eyes at the female and opened her mouth to tell her to step away from Barrett.

Before she could get the words out, Barrett rested his hand on Jacey's thigh. She relaxed under his touch.

"My wife and I will have the all-you-can-eat pancakes," Barrett stated.

"That's what we're all having," Jayden answered for everyone. "And bacon. Bring lots and lots of bacon."

The waitress's gaze dropped to Barrett's hand, and she flushed. "Of course. I'll put this in right away," she stammered before heading back to grab more coffee to refill everyone's cup.

"The waitress didn't know," Ryker snorted.

"Didn't know what?" Barrett looked at Ryker.

"That you two were married." He held up his left hand and pointed to his ring finger. "You don't have a wedding ring and women assume you're single."

"Yeah, Barrett. You have to get a wedding band or else," Jayden said. "Haley said if I was marrying her, I better wear a band."

"But aren't you mated?" Jacey looked at him.

"Oh, yeah. But I wanted to marry her too." Jayden smiled and then looked away like he was picturing the woman he was thinking about. "I want her in every way possible. Mated. Married. You know, forever."

Jacey smiled. She liked Jayden. He might be harassing her for her cookie dough, but he seemed like he truly loved and cared about his mate.

"Yeah, the only one at this table that is not mated is Ryker," Lucien snorted.

Ryker glared at the Were.

"You don't have any interest in being mated?" She looked at the scary Were.

"Nope. I'm happy to have my freedom." Ryker took a sip of his coffee and let his gaze wander over the room. She noticed that his gaze lingered a little too long on one female in particular.

"You sure about that?" Jacey smirked. She glanced over at the female in the corner. "You're looking really hard at that female over there."

Ryker shot her a glare.

Damon barked out a laugh, followed by the other Guardians. "She's got you pegged, Ryker."

"No, she doesn't," he growled and pointed his fork at her.

"No, you don't." He looked back at the female. "She has a nice ass. That's all."

"Right. She's sitting, Ryker. How do you know what her ass looks like?" She cocked her head.

Another round of laughter rose up from the table. The girl in question looked up from her coffee and glanced in their direction.

"Keep it down," Ryker growled. "You are all acting like a bunch of animals."

"Well, technically we are," Jaxon said and smiled as the waitress set down a plate piled with pancakes.

They were all too busy eating pancakes to talk much over breakfast. Jacey had to admit it felt good to be around the Guardians.

When they were done, they left the restaurant and stepped out into the bright sunlight.

"So, what's the plan?" Braxton asked.

"Since Boudier has been captured, there's no need for us to stay here," Damon said, slipping on his sunglasses. "It's too late to head back to Arkansas now. We'll head back in the morning."

"In the meantime?" Braxton waited for an answer.

"Everyone can have the day off. To do whatever." Damon said.

"Finally," Jayden sighed. "You've been working us to the bone, Damon."

"Your lazy ass needs to be worked to the bone." Damon gruffed.

Jacey grinned.

"I want to go skiing. I've never been," Lucien said.

"I'd like to see that. Your big ass on the bunny slope," Zane snarked.

"Bunny slope, my ass. I want the black diamond run." Lucien crossed his arms.

"I'll bet you one thousand dollars that I can ski better than you." Jayden held out his hand.

"Challenge accepted." Lucien shook Jayden's hand. "And I won't even feel bad about taking your money."

"You guys coming?" Braxton looked at Barrett.

"We'll be there later. We've got something to do first," Barrett took her hand in his and slid on his sunglasses.

"Catch ya later." Ryker nodded.

She watched the Guardians all pile up in the Hummer they'd driven down from the mountain and pull out onto the street.

She looked up at Barrett. "So, what are we going to do?"

Barrett tucked her arm into his. He started down the sidewalk lined with stores, coffeehouses, and boutique-type stores. "We, Mrs. Middleton, are about to take care of some business."

CHAPTER 48

*B*arrett took Jacey's hand in his as they walked down the sidewalk. He missed the touch of her skin on his but was glad the gloves were keeping her hands warm.

Peace and contentment settled in his chest.

For the first time in a long time, he felt like he was home. With her at his side.

"I'm assuming you have a particular shop you want to stop at?" Jacey cut her eyes up at Barrett.

"I do. I want to introduce you to an old friend." Barrett looked down at her. A smile settled on his lips.

They walked farther, looking at all the shops along the way. When he spotted a familiar gold sign sticking out from the storefront a few feet away, he quickened his steps.

He stopped in front of the jewelry store and opened the door, letting Jacey enter first.

The familiar scent of the store washed over him, a memory of his past.

Jacey's eyes widened at the amount of diamond jewelry housed in glass cases in the upscale store.

"What are we . . ." Before she could get her question out, an older gentleman in his late sixties walked out of the back of the store. His smile widened when his gaze landed on Barrett.

"Barrett! How very good of you to come see your old friend, Gianni!" He grabbed Barrett in a tight hug. He released him only to kiss him on both cheeks.

"I see you haven't changed old man," Barrett chided.

"Just a little bigger around the edges." Gianni patted his rounding stomach and laughed. "It's my wife. She keeps feeding me with too much Italian food and wine."

They laughed, and Gianni's gaze landed on Jacey. His eyes widened. "And who is this lovely young lady?"

"Gianni, I'd like to introduce Jacey, my wife." Barrett pulled her to his side.

The old Italian's mouth dropped open. He blinked a couple of times. Slowly, his smile grew until his face split into a huge grin.

"Jacey, this is Gianni Bertolli, a close friend of the family."

Jacey smiled and stuck out her hand in greeting. Instead of shaking her hand, he cupped her face. "Jacey. What an honor it is to finally meet the woman who holds Barrett's heart." He bent and kissed both cheeks.

Jacey's face went red, and she ducked her head. "Thank you, Gianni. It's very nice to meet you."

"You chose well, Barrett. Never have I seen such beauty and such evident love between two people." Gianni stepped back.

"Thank you." Barrett took her hand and raised it to his lips, kissing the back of her knuckles. "My wife is very modest and doesn't realize how beautiful she truly is." He stared down at her.

Gianni stiffened and shook his head. "Then you must tell her every day, all the time. Until she believes it." He waved his hands in the air, emphasizing his point. "That's what I do to my dear wife, Bella. I tell her every morning and every night how beautiful she is."

Jacey grinned.

"Hold on to her my friend, for I daresay you will not find another diamond among pebbles." Gianni grinned. "May God bless you with an abundance of beautiful children."

Jacey frowned as Barrett grinned.

"Now tell me, do you have something special you can show my wife?"

Gianni's eyes lit up. "I have just the one." He disappeared into the back, leaving them alone. Barrett trailed a finger down her cheek and kissed her gently on the lips.

"Ah, it is so good to see young people so in love." Gianni announced and walked behind the counter. He set down a box on the glass.

They walked over, and Gianni opened the box.

It was a V-shaped necklace set with diamonds and sapphires. At the tip of the V was a large diamond. The entire thing was set in platinum. Sitting on either side of the necklace was a pair of matching sapphire earrings.

"It was made in my hometown in Italy. Custom made. Not another like it in the world."

"It's breathtaking," Jacey breathed out.

"Smart woman, Barrett. This one has an eye for quality. You are right to marry this one. Not just beautiful but smart too."

Jacey blushed at the compliment.

Barrett nodded. "Yes, you are right. And I don't plan on letting her go."

Jacey fidgeted under his words and looked away.

"Now can you show us something in the ring department?" Barrett cocked his head and held up his bare ring finger.

"Ah. Of course." Gianni glanced down at Jacey's hand and noticed she didn't have a ring either.

Jacey turned to him, her eyes wide. "Barrett, you don't have to buy me a ring," she whispered.

"Of course, I do. You're my wife. Besides, I need a ring too." He cocked his head. He knew she was doubting his faithfulness to her. So, he was going to have to prove it.

Gianni stepped over to the wedding bands and pulled out a tray. He took his time until he found what he was looking for.

A slow smile crossed his face. "This. This wedding band is fit for a queen. It's platinum. The engagement ring is ten carat diamonds with diamonds and sapphires around the band.

Barrett watched Jacey's stunned reaction. Her lips parted as she stared down at the glistening diamonds set before her. He knew she probably never had anything this expensive in her life.

"How much is it?" She looked up at Gianni.

Gianni shrugged. "What does the price matter to Barrett Middleton's wife?"

"But …"

"Why don't you try them on?" Barrett said.

She nodded, and Gianni picked up the rings. He held them out to Barrett. "Why don't you do the honors since you are the husband?"

Barrett took the rings. He held Jacey's hand in hers and slid the wedding band on first and then the engagement ring.

They were a perfect fit.

She inhaled deep, and her eyes widened as she held her hand up to the light. The diamonds and sapphires danced under the lights. "It's absolutely gorgeous. I don't think I've ever seen anything so beautiful in my life."

"Oh, I have," Barrett said softly, staring at his wife.

Jacey jerked her head in his direction. Their gazes locked.

Barrett forced himself to look back at Gianni. "Do you have something in platinum for me?"

"It just so happens there is." Gianni smiled. "Diamonds or no diamonds?"

"No diamonds," Barrett stated. In his line of work, he'd just knock them off.

"I'll get them rung up for you right now.' Gianni smiled and headed into the back of the store.

"Perfect." Barrett turned back to Jacey and smiled.

"Barrett, I can't let you buy these for me. There's no telling how much they cost." Her eyes widened. She started to take them off, but he grabbed her hand. He carefully slid the rings back on her finger.

"The money doesn't matter to me. Do you like them?" He frowned.

"Of course. They are stunning." She glanced back at the rings.

"Good. When I said our vows, I meant them. Until death do us part. And when I mated with you last night, I meant it." He kissed her gently on the lips. "You're mine now and forever. Those rings are just to let everyone else know you're taken."

CHAPTER 49

They stepped out of Gianni's store and onto the sidewalk.

"I can't believe you did that." Jacey looked from her dazzling ring up to Barrett. "I can only imagine what this has cost."

"Stop worrying about the money." He cocked his head. "I wanted to buy it for you because you deserve it. And I love you."

Her chest melted, and it took all she had not to sigh and sink into his strong arms.

How she longed to hear those words and yet she couldn't bring herself to say them back to him. She knew if she did, she'd lose herself in Barrett forever.

"Jacey?"

The distinctive male voice from her past had her stomach crashing to the ground. It couldn't be.

She turned slowly and came face to face with her ex-husband and mate.

"Jacey, what are you doing here? Are you following me?" Jeremy narrowed his eyes at her.

"Following you? Why the hell would I follow you?" Anger flooded through her, and she wanted to knock that arrogant tone out of his voice with a well-deserved slap. How dare he think she was following him? She let her gaze drift to the well-endowed female to his side.

It was Wendy. Jeremy's new mate. The one he'd left her for.

"We've not met," Barrett growled low.

"I'm Jeremy, Jacey's ex-husband." Jeremy propped his hands on his hips and lifted his chin.

"I'm Barrett. I'm Jacey's husband." A lethal grin was etched into Barrett's face.

Jacey jerked her head toward Barrett and stared.

He'd actually told Jeremy he was her mate and husband.

"You're her what?" Jeremy asked. His eyes widened, and his mouth pumped open like a fish.

"Her husband. And of course, mate *for life*." Barrett wrapped his arm around her and held her close. "We came to Aspen to get married. It was a beautiful ceremony."

She sank into his warm chest and wrapped her arms around his waist. She liked the way he took up for her and protected her. It was something she could very well get used to.

Wendy grabbed Jeremy's arm. "We're here on a romantic getaway." She looked straight at Jacey as if she were staking her claim.

Jacey snorted. She could keep Jeremy. She certainly didn't want him back.

"Wait, what do you mean married?" Jeremy finally found his voice and sputtered. "You can't do that."

"Why not? She's single and free to do anything she likes." Barrett picked up her hand and kissed it. "I'm honored that she would even consider me worthy to be her mate."

"When did this happen?" Jeremy demanded to know.

"Last night." Jacey straightened her shoulders. She held out her left hand for them to see. The large diamond on her finger glittered under the sun. It was almost blinding.

Wendy's mouth tightened into a jealous line.

Jacey had never felt better.

"Barrett, Barrett!" They turned to see Gianni hurrying out of his shop toward them.

"You forgot this." Gianni handed Barrett a small box wrapped in white paper and a red bow. "You wouldn't want to forget your gift for your new bride, would you?"

"Thank you, Gianni." He stuck the gift in his jacket pocket and watched the old man walk back into his store.

"What is that?" Jacey eyed his pocket. Realization hit her. It was the same box that held the diamond and sapphire necklace. "Barrett, you didn't buy that necklace, did you?"

"What if I said yes?" he smirked, giving her his full attention.

"But it must have cost a fortune." She shook her head.

"I would only buy you the best. Besides, money is no object." He bent his head. He covered her lips with his in a blistering kiss. Her body went warm and fuzzy, and she couldn't help but sink into his arms.

"Are you ready, sweetheart?" Barrett reached for her hand.

"Yes." She couldn't help but smile as she laced her fingers through his.

Barrett shoved his sunglasses on and ignored Jeremy and his new mate and continued walking down the sidewalk.

"You didn't even say goodbye," she laughed.

"He's lucky I didn't punch his face in," Barrett said gruffly and pulled her closer into his chest.

"What did you think about her?" She looked up at him to gauge his reaction.

"I think Jeremy's an idiot. For choosing her over you. He

must be going blind." Barrett looked down at her and stopped walking. "What do you think about your ring?" Do you like it?" Even though he was wearing sunglasses, she could sense he was really concerned about her opinion.

"Like it? I love it." She shook her head and held out her hand. "It's beautiful, but it's too much Barrett." She looked up at him.

"It's not too much for you." He pulled her close and bent his head. "They are still watching."

"Why don't we give them something to look at then?" She wrapped her arms around his neck and kissed him hard. When she felt his hands on her ass, she wished they were back at the mountain mansion with nothing to interrupt them.

When he pulled back, she was breathless, and her heart was racing.

"Have you ever been skiing?" he asked with a smile on his lips.

"No."

"You'll love it. It's almost as satisfying as shifting and running in the snow." His eyes widened wickedly.

She let out a laugh. This felt right. Even if they wouldn't last, she was going to enjoy the moment. It was all she had with him.

CHAPTER 50

"So, what did you think?" Barrett looked at Jacey from behind his goggles and stuck his ski poles in the snow. They were standing in their rented ski gear at the bottom of the snow-covered mountain that they'd just skied down.

Jacey's face broke into a wide grin. "That was scary. And exciting." She threw her head back and laughed.

"Want to go again?" He pulled her into his arms and gave her a quick kiss. She looked gorgeous in her white ski gear and furry, white hat.

"On the bunny slope? No. I want to try the ..."

"The triple black diamond?" Lucien skidded to a stop on his snowboard beside them. He pulled up his goggles and grinned.

"Yeah. That sounds fun," Jacey said with excitement.

"Hell, no. You're not ready for the triple black diamonds. Those are the hardest runs and should only be attempted by experts." Barrett frowned. No way was she going to go down something so dangerous. He glanced down at Lucien's snowboard.

"An expert like Barrett," Lucien stated. He followed Barrett's gaze down. "When's the last time you snowboarded, brother?"

"A few years." He loved snowboarding even more than skiing.

"You can snowboard too?" Jacey gave him a look of appreciation.

"I used to." He used to do a lot of things he enjoyed. Before duty called him to a life of sacrificing what he wanted.

"Here." Lucien bent down and took off his board. "I'll stay with Jacey so you can snowboard."

"Nah." He didn't want to leave her.

"What's the hold up?" Braxton skied to a stop in front of them, sending a small spray of snow into the air.

"Barrett is going to snowboard while we stay with Jacey." Lucien grinned broadly and held out his snowboard.

"No."

"What's the deal? We going again?" Damon skied up to them with Jayden, Jaxon, and Zane behind him.

"Barrett's going to snowboard." Braxton grinned.

"No, I'm not," he stated.

"Why not? You're not pussing out, are you?" Jayden gave him a horrified look.

Barrett growled and stepped closer to the Guardian. "What did you say, Jayden?"

The other Weres took a step back.

Jayden blinked. "What? I mean I understand you not wanting to get hurt on your honeymoon. Plus, you've been dead. I'm sure that takes a toll on your psyche. Better to stay safe and all that."

"Give me that fucking board." Barrett snatched the snowboard out of Lucien's hand and headed back to the ski lift.

"But that's the wrong ski lift, Barrett. That's takes you up to where they are setting up for the X games," Jayden called out.

Barrett turned and shot his Guardian a look. "I know."

* * *

"This is going to be the shit." Lucien grinned from ear to ear.

"Is this legal? I mean, are they going to just let Barrett on the course?" Jacey looked up at the Were. She'd been escorted over to the sectioned off part of the mountain by the Guardians. She looked up at the starting line.

The course was steep with a ramp part of the way down. Barrett had taken a snowmobile to the top. He stood at the top and strapped his snowboard to his feet.

"This is Aspen. The games won't be starting for a few more days so they won't mind if he tests the course." Lucien crossed his arms over his chest.

She swallowed and looked back up at Barrett. "But that looks really steep. Not to mention the ramp. I thought he was just going to snowboard down."

"Barrett isn't known for doing anything easy," Ryker stated. He looked down at her. "Don't worry. He knows what he's doing."

She bit her lip. She couldn't help but worry.

Hard rock music blared through the tall speakers set up along the course. All the Guardians lined up on either side of her, eyes trained on Barrett.

"Watch this shit," Lucien said.

She didn't dare take her gaze off Barrett's large figure.

His eyes met hers. He smiled, slid his googles over his eyes, and took off.

He snowboarded agilely, moving his board side to side as he picked up speed down the course.

She forgot to breathe as he hit the ramp and launched himself into the sky. He flipped through the air, his body twisting and turning in complete revolutions. He stuck the landing and skidded to a halt in front of them, spraying Jayden with snow.

"Dude, that was awesome." Jayden wiped the snow from his face. "What's that called?"

"Switch Frontside Triple Cork 1440," Ryker answered for him.

"How the hell did you do that?" Jayden asked.

"I was expecting you to do the Double McTwist 1260." Lucien shrugged. "But what you did was even better."

"Wait, how does Lucien know this lingo?" Zane frowned.

"Because like Barrett, Lucien grew up a rich kid. His parents could afford winter vacations to ski resorts." Ryker snorted. "Unlike like the rest of us."

Jacey swallowed. Ryker was right. Barrett was different than any of them.

And he had the pedigree to prove it.

"Give me my board back. I want to try it." Lucien took the snowboard out of Barrett's hands and headed up to the top.

The rest of the Guardians clapped Barrett on the back and congratulated him on his skills before scattering to do their own thing.

"So, what did you think?" Barrett looked down at her intently. "You haven't said much."

"I'm impressed. You must have been coming here for years."

He shrugged. "I prefer snowboarding to skiing. It's almost like shifting and running through the snow."

She arched her brow. "Really? Think you could show me?"

He grinned broadly. "Of course. Let's go rent some boards, and we'll get started."

CHAPTER 51

"*D*id you get enough?" Barrett looked at Jacey across the cab of the vehicle.

"I think I've found my new favorite hobby." Her eyes sparkled, and her face was a pretty shade of pink from snowboarding for hours.

"You picked it up really quickly. I am very impressed," he admitted.

"Do you think next time you can teach me some of your snowboarding tricks?" She grinned.

"Ah. No." He lost his smile.

"Why not?" She frowned. "Don't think I can do it?"

"No. I know you can do it. But I don't want you to. It's too dangerous." He wanted her protected at all costs. Even if she didn't like it.

"I can't believe it's only two o'clock. It feels like it should be a lot later." She sighed and rested her head against the passenger side window. She tucked a strand of silky, blond hair behind her ear and crossed her arms over her chest. "I'm exhausted."

"No doubt. Not only did you snowboard for the first time

today, you also skied. You'll probably sleep great tonight." His body tightened as he thought about tonight. Would she be too tired to make love?

"I saw some ground beef in the freezer. I think I'll make some chili for dinner. And some homemade bread." She turned her head, her eyes unsure. "Do you think the Guardians will be okay with that?"

He started to tell her not to worry about cooking, that he would make the men get their own food. But he knew from the look in her eye she wanted to do this. She wanted them to like her.

Instead he told her the truth.

"They will love it as much as they love you."

* * *

"THE MEAT IS ALMOST COMPLETELY THAWED. ONCE I brown it, I can start on the chili." She looked at Ryker and Jayden across the kitchen island. She hid her smile as she continued to dice peppers on the chopping board. She scooped up the tiny bits of green and dumped them in the stainless-steel bowl with the chopped onions.

"God, it smells good." Jayden rubbed his stomach and eyed the fresh bread on the kitchen table. No sooner had she pulled the bread out of the oven than Ryker and Jayden had bounded into the kitchen like two lions looking for a gazelle.

"It will take less than an hour." She narrowed her eyes. "I thought all the Guardians were supposed to be having a meeting with Barrett."

"We are," Ryker stated and crossed his arms.

"But I'm just so freaking hungry," Jayden moaned.

"Ugh. Fine. If I give you both some cookies, will you get out of my way?"

"Yes," they said in unison.

She grinned and opened an overhead cabinet. She pulled out a box of Raisin Bran. She watched the faces go from disgust to surprise when she pulled out a plastic container out of the box.

She opened the lid and gave them each three cookies.

"That's where you hid the cookies." Jayden stuffed one in his mouth and nodded. "Pretty smart. Thanks, Jacey." Satisfied, he headed out of the kitchen.

Ryker held the cookies in his hand and stared at them. "You do realize you'll have to move them now."

"I have several places you won't even think to look," she shot back.

He looked up and gave her a slight grin. "Don't try me. Bet I can figure it out."

She arched her eyebrow as she pulled out a skillet and placed it on the stove. When she turned around, Ryker was still there, uneaten cookies in his hand.

Tension stretched between them in the room, and suddenly the opulent kitchen grew smaller.

"Is there something you want to talk to me about?" She crossed her arms and cocked her head. She wasn't going to let him or any of the other Guardians intimidate her. She was stronger now and she could hold her own, no matter what happened between her and Barrett.

"Will you fight for him, or are you going to walk away?"

It was the last question she expected out of stoic, hard-ass Ryker.

"Is that any of your business?" She uncrossed her arms and lifted her chin. "Ryker, I know you don't like me. And I know that you feel like you have to protect Barrett. You are the one who brought him back from the dead."

"Well, technically, it was that Fae, Celeste." He waved his hand in the air and looked away.

"But you are the reason he is here today," she said softly.

Her heart dropped, thinking Barrett could have ended up dead.

"I will always protect him," Ryker stated.

"So will I." She rested her hands on the kitchen island and looked at the intimating Were. "Ryker, technically I am mated to Barrett."

"And married," he added.

"I don't know how much of my past Barrett has told you, but I was once mated before ..."

"With some asshole in Mississippi who wanted the mate bond broke. Jack Welbourn complied."

"Yes." She frowned.

"Barrett told me about it before the wedding. He told me you never wanted to get married or mated again."

She looked away.

Ryker took a step closer. "I don't know about mating. I've never mated, nor do I ever plan on it."

She sighed.

"But I do know that Barrett loves you, and I've seen the way you look at him. You love him too."

She jerked her head toward him.

"I may be an asshole, but I protect those who are my family. You are Barrett's mate, and you are now my family."

She blinked back the sting of tears in her eyes. Her own biological family had rejected and abandoned her. Yet she found a stronger family.

"What I'm saying is you don't need to be afraid that Barrett will reject you, like that last asshole. Barrett is nothing like him. Plus, he's not an asshole. At least not to you." Ryker cocked his head. "Don't be afraid of your future with him and don't measure it with the experience of your past. I predict you two will be very happy with a houseful of children."

His words blossomed the hope in her chest. She took a

deep breath in and focused on the present. Ryker was right. It was time she left her past behind and moved into her future with Barrett.

She walked around the counter and grabbed the plastic container of cookies. She placed the cookies in his palm and smiled. "Thank you for that, Ryker."

"Anytime." A smile hovered on the corners of his mouth. "And thanks for the extra cookies. I'll be sure to rub it in Jayden's face." He walked out of the kitchen.

She gazed out the window at the mountain range before her. She closed her eyes and took a deep breath. She was taking charge of her happiness. And she was willing to take risks, especially where Barrett was concerned.

A brief knock on the door interrupted her thoughts. She opened her eyes and walked to the door to see which Guardian had gotten locked out.

She reached for the handle and opened the door. "Who got locked out this time?" she laughed.

A figure dressed in a thick winter coat had his back to her. He turned just as she laughed.

Her stomach dropped. Something was off. Not right.

His hand shot out. He sprayed her in the face. Pain spread across her face and mouth. She dropped to her knees in agony. His hand clamped down over her mouth before she could scream and alert the others of the danger.

She struggled, kicking her feet and clawing at his hand. He shoved a needle into her neck.

Fear turned into hopelessness as she lost consciousness.

CHAPTER 52

"**W**here have you been?" Barrett scowled as Ryker sauntered into the room.

"Getting cookies." Ryker shrugged and stuffed another cookie into his mouth.

"Hey, how did you get more cookies than me?" Jayden narrowed his eyes on Ryker.

"Jacey gave them to me. She must like me better than you." Ryker chewed thoughtfully.

"I highly doubt that. I'm the most likeable guy here," Jayden argued.

"You sure about that?" Braxton grinned.

"Okay, most likeable besides you, Braxton," Jayden conceded.

"You ladies finished, or do you want to braid each other's hair before we start the meeting?" Barrett growled. He looked over at Damon and shook his head. "A few months under your leadership, and they all turn to pussies."

"Well, not all. Zane, Ryker, and Lucien are still hard-asses. Like yourself," Damon snarked and stole a cookie out of Ryker's hand.

"Let's get to it, shall we?" Barrett propped his hands on his hips and looked over at Jaxon. "What's the update on Boudier? Are they still holding him in Denver? 'Cause if they are, we can just drive over there now and handle justice ourselves."

The Guardians growled low in agreement.

Jaxon pulled out his phone and hit some keys. He frowned. "The last email I got was a few hours ago. Nothing new since."

Someone's cell phone rang, and everyone reached for their pockets.

"It's mine. "Lucien grinned and swiped his finger across the screen. "Hello?"

Barrett watched intently as Lucien's expression melted into a mask of blackness.

"How long ago?" Lucien demanded through the phone. The room grew silent, and Barrett could hear his own heartbeat.

Lucien ended the call and met his gaze. "Boudier escaped. He killed two Guardians holding him in Denver, and no one knows where he is now."

Nausea rolled up in the back of Barrett's throat. His heart seized. He looked over at Ryker. "Where's Jacey?"

"She's downstairs in the kitchen. Cooking." Ryker eyes narrowed.

Barrett bolted out of the room with the other Weres right behind him.

"Jacey," he called out as he rounded the corner into the kitchen. The stove was on, and the skillet of ground beef sizzled unattended. He headed into the pantry. The space filled with food and glassware was empty of Jacey. His heart dropped.

"She's not in the house." Ryker hurried into the kitchen.

His face was pinched, and his tone was low. "Me and Damon have searched the whole house."

"Maybe she's outside," Barrett said. White noise built inside his head until he was dizzy with fear. Something was wrong. Bad wrong.

"I've sent Jayden, Jaxon, and Lucien out to search." Damon propped his hands on his hips. "Maybe she needed some air and went for a walk."

Barrett's world tilted. He grabbed the wall for support. "She wouldn't go for a walk. She was talking about how tired she was after skiing all day."

"Don't start worrying just yet. Wait until the other Guardians get back," Damon said calmly.

The front door opened, and Barrett jerked his head up. Lucien, Jayden, and Jaxon walked into the kitchen. Lucien met his gaze.

"She's not outside, is she?" He already knew the answer.

"No." Lucien cocked his head. "But we found a set of prints and a set of tire tracks that don't match any of our vehicles."

"Boudier," Barrett growled. He hurried out the kitchen to the front door. Damon grabbed his arm before he could get out the door.

"Wait, Barrett."

"He has her. I can't do nothing. I have to get her back." Barrett shook off Damon's hold and glared at the Were.

"I understand, and you will. But you know as well as I do that Boudier is setting a trap. You can't rush after her without a plan. He won't hurt her until you are there to witness it. If I know that deranged psychopath, he wants an audience." Damon narrowed his eyes.

He knew Damon was right, but everything inside of him was shaking to go after his mate.

"Fuck it. Hurry up and come up with something. You've got twenty seconds before I leave this house," Barrett thundered.

After that, heaven itself would not separate him from finding Boudier and ending his sorry life once and for all.

CHAPTER 53

*P*ain splintering through her head woke Jacey. She grimaced as she reached up to touch her forehead, sure she would find warm blood on her fingertips. She held her hand up to her face and grimaced.

No blood.

She blinked, her eyes growing accustomed to the dark space that smelled of mothballs and dust. She eased up off the small cot where she was lying.

Thick fear coiled around her neck. She wasn't in the mansion. From the looks of things, she was in an abandoned cabin. From the scent of arousal, she wasn't alone either.

"I never thought he would find a mate. But he did. Much to my delight," a dark male voice crept through the cabin.

She jerked her head to the corner of the room. A figure dressed in a thick, black coat stepped forward.

Edward Boudier.

"I take it by the look on your face, you know who I am," Edward sneered.

"Where are we?" She forced her feet under her and glanced around. The cabin was small with only a front door

351

and a boarded-up window. She couldn't see out, and no one could see in.

"We are not far from your boyfriend."

"You mean my mate." She narrowed her eyes and fisted her hands at her sides.

A slow smile slid across his lips like a lizard. "Mate. Even better."

"What do you want from me?" Her heart hammered in her chest.

"From you? Why, you are nothing but a means to an end my dear." He pressed his back into the door and crossed his feet at his ankles.

There was finality in his words. She had to get out, get away. If Barrett found her, she knew that Boudier would kill him.

"Ah, there it is." He spoke slow, his voice like molasses.

Chills ran down her backbone.

"There what is?"

He pushed himself off the door and took a step toward her. "The sound of fear in your voice. You know that today will be the day your life will be forever changed, don't you?"

She blinked. Nausea rolled into the back of her throat.

He cocked his head. "You know, I was really upset that those wolf hunters let you get away." His eyes hardened. "If Barrett hadn't shown up and attacked them, I would have had you days ago."

"You sent those humans? To trap me?" Her voice and her legs trembled.

"I did. Before I made myself at home at Mena's, I was watching you from a building across the street. The owners had shut the restaurant down for the winter, so I broke in and made myself at home upstairs in the attic. I was waiting for the opportune time to take you while Barrett wasn't looking. I had posted those two hunters nearby, hoping to catch you in your wolf form. When I saw you sneak out of Mena's to go for a run, I knew I had my chance."

"Barrett showed up before they could take me."

He gritted his teeth. "He always ruins everything."

She tried to swallow the fear she was choking on. "So, what are you going to do now? Wait until Barrett gets here and kill us both?"

His expression relaxed. "You're getting ahead of yourself, my dear. Once Barrett arrives, I'll have those men outside capture him. They'll kill all of his Guardians and then when that's done, I'll shoot him with a silver bullet to the stomach."

She gasped.

"Oh, don't worry. The silver won't kill him, at least not at once. He'll suffer while it poisons him to death. And while he's writhing in pain, I will force him to watch while I mate with you. After that, he'll never want you again. I'll make you watch as he dies and then …"

"You'll kill me." She lifted her chin despite the desperation and hopelessness clawing in her chest.

"No. I'll let you go. I'll make sure everyone knows of how you were shamed while Barrett watched before he died. You'll be forced to walk this earth while every Were will turn their back on you and look upon you with scorn. Hell, they might even kill you for disgracing your mate, Barrett."

She shook her head. "I'd rather be dead."

"I know but you need to live a little, long enough to suffer. Don't worry, I'll prolong your pain." He smiled and rubbed his hands together. "And I'll do it when you least expect it."

"You truly are evil." She took a step back.

"And you are about to know more pain in one day than your whole life. I can't wait until Barrett takes his last breath. That fucker has caused me more trouble than any other Pack Master." He rubbed his neck.

"Barrett has more honor than any Pack Master I know. You kill him, and you'll start a war with all the other states."

His eyes lit up. "And all the other states will learn to bow down to me. I'll kill their Guardians until they relent and pledge their fealty to me."

"You don't have the power to do that." She lifted her chin.

"I have the money to do it. I can buy all the power I need. I already have the Red Wolves in my pocket. They have been wanting a war with the humans for years now. They want every human wiped off the face of the earth until there are only Weres. I'll give them their war in exchange for forcing the other states to hand over their control to me. When this is over, I'll rule the whole United States."

"You're crazy."

"You keep saying that, like it's true. The fact is I was born to be the leader of this world. And I plan on making that happen."

She shook her head. This could not be happening. She would not let it happen.

"Barrett will come for me and when he does, he will kill you."

"Let him try." He grinned manically. "He will fail."

CHAPTER 54

"We are losing daylight." Barrett hit his hand on the steering wheel and growled. His stomach clenched with anger and fear.

She was gone. And he knew who had her.

As soon as they realized Boudier had taken Jacey, the Guardians had loaded up into two vehicles and followed the fresh tracks in the snow. The only ones who were not in the vehicles were Jaxon and Lucien. They had shifted into wolf form and headed out ahead of the trucks. They could cover more of the unstable ground than the vehicles could handle.

They quickly realized the tracks were not from tires. Boudier had wisely made his way up the mountain in a vehicle with tracks versus tires.

"What if . . ." His words trailed off in his aching throat. He never felt as helpless as he did in that moment.

"You keep it together, Barrett. We will find her before Boudier can do anything," Damon commanded. "Don't you go passing out on me."

Barrett looked across the cab of the vehicle. Damon's eyes were cold and hard. He had the look of a leader.

Barrett nodded. "You're right." He sucked in a deep breath and slowly released it. "Boudier will make sure I'm in front of him before he hurts her. Before he kills me."

"Boudier won't get that chance," Damon nearly growled. "That fucker is going down once and for all, and there will be no fucking Tribunal."

"You're right. There won't be one." Barrett narrowed his eyes and kept his gaze ahead.

He was going to be the one ripping Boudier's head from his body, and he would be the one ending his life. Boudier had been a thorn in his side for too long.

Now he fucked with the wrong Were. By taking Jacey, Boudier just signed his death warrant. By the end of the day, Boudier would no longer be walking the earth.

"Stop!" Damon yelled and pointed out the windshield. "There's the truck. Looks like that fucker got smart putting those tracks on his wheels."

"He knew we would follow and needed to get ahead of us," Barrett growled. He was out the door in a flash.

Damon followed.

He grabbed the handle of the four-wheel-drive and opened the door. Empty. But the scent of Jacey washed over him like a waterfall. He could still smell her fear.

"He couldn't have gone far." Damon stopped beside him. Lucien, Jaxon, and Braxton gathered around.

They scanned the wooded area near the top of the mountain.

"There's no way he could have gotten far. We are near the top of the mountain," Barrett narrowed his gaze.

Lucien came tearing out of the wooded area in his large wolf form. He skidded to a stop in front of them.

Jaxon was right behind him.

Zane pulled out their clothes from the vehicle and threw

them on the snow. Lucien and Jaxon shifted into their human bodies, their fur disappearing into their flesh. They both crouched in the cold snow as they adjusted to their transformed bodies.

"What did you see?" Barrett demanded. The blood in his veins throbbed. He needed answers or else he was going to tear off up the mountain to find them himself.

Jacey.

Boudier had Jacey.

Fear and desperation mingled together until he nearly choked on the taste of it.

He'd never experienced such hopelessness before. It tasted a lot like death.

"There's a shack half a mile through those trees." Jaxon stood and shook off the snow. He arched his back, unconcerned with his nakedness before grabbing the clothes off the snow-covered ground. "From the smell of it, Boudier's not alone."

"What?" Barrett's heart sunk to his knees. Who could Boudier have on his side?

"Yeah." Lucien tugged his jeans up over his lean hips and zipped. "Smells like red wolves."

"Fuck," Barrett growled and turned toward the tree line. The urge to find Jacey consumed every cell in his body. He started for the tree line.

"Easy." Damon grabbed his arm and halted his steps. "We need a plan."

"I need to get Jacey." He glared at the Were.

"You need to save Jacey," Damon growled. "He's expecting you to run in there in a rage. He wants you to do that. And when you do, he will kill you."

What Damon said was right. But his heart didn't want to hear it.

"Barrett. I know how it is when your female is being held hostage. I know you want to run in there, get her out, and burn the fucking cabin down with Boudier inside." Damon squeezed his arm. "I know because when those red wolves had Ava, all I wanted to do was kill every one of them." Damon gave him a nod.

"What stopped you?" Barrett's voice cracked with the pent-up emotion.

"You did." Damon said softly.

The Weres grew silent.

"Me?" Barrett blinked.

"Yeah, motherfucker. You think I wanted to have my ass handed to me by you if I disobeyed? You have always been our leader. You have always kept us safe, even in the midst of danger." Damon shrugged. "Even when we didn't want to listen to you and did our own thing."

Lucien chuckled.

"And right now, you are letting your emotions for Jacey get the best of you. Now you need to let your Arkansas Guardians help you. Let us back you up. Like you've backed us up a thousand times before." Damon stared at him.

Barrett blinked.

"Barrett" Jaxon squeezed his bicep, "What Damon says is true. Let us help you get your female back. We won't fail you, but we have to be smart about it."

"Yeah, man." Jayden rubbed the back of his neck. "Trust us. We don't want anything to happen to Jacey."

"Fucking straight," Ryker growled.

Everyone turned to look at the Were.

"What?" Ryker snarled. "I mean who else is going to make those dope-ass cookies."

"Well, it sure won't be Ava," Damon stated.

Everyone laughed.

Barrett studied the ground for a second before looking up at his Arkansas Guardians.

"I can't live without her," he simply said.

"I know, brother." Damon looked at him. "I know."

CHAPTER 55

*J*acey's heart lurched. She was trapped with Boudier and no escape in sight.

She knew Barrett was coming for her. She also knew Boudier wasn't alone. She'd seen him speak to someone at the door briefly before shutting the door and closing her off from the rest of the world.

She dragged her gaze from him to the small boarded-up window.

"Don't even think about it." His voice had her jerking her attention back to him. "It's nailed up good and tight. I made sure to bring you where there's only one way in and one way out. I want Barrett to know I hold all the keys."

Nausea rolled in her stomach. He was right.

Helplessness swirled in her stomach. This was it. This was the end of her life.

She's been dealt a horrible hand in life, been betrayed and lied to, and when she finally found love, her life was to be snatched away before she even had a chance to experience happiness.

"I hate you." The words spilled out of her like water. She lifted her gaze to his.

His eyes seemed to sparkle with her venomous words. "Hmm. I like that. I like that a whole lot." His mouth curled into an evil grin. "Now I'm not sure who to torture and kill first. Barrett? Or you?"

She narrowed her eyes. "Just kill me now, your sadist fuck."

"Now, now. You know I can't do that. When I put on a performance, I prefer an audience." He nodded toward the door. "And as you know, my audience isn't here yet."

She had to force Boudier's hand before Barrett found her. If she was still alive when Barrett found her, Boudier would make Barrett watch as she was killed.

She pushed off the wall and ran straight for Boudier. A look of surprise streaked through his eyes before they hardened to snake-like slits.

He grabbed her and tackled her to the ground. She landed hard on her side, the air knocked out of her lungs.

He laughed as she struggled to suck air into her oxygen-deprived lungs.

"This is going to be so much fun," he chuckled manically. He wrapped his hand around her throat and squeezed.

Her throat ached, and tears streamed from her eyes. Anger turned to panic and then to fear.

She clawed at his hand. Her gaze met his for a minute before everything started going dark.

He released his hand from around her neck. She sucked in a deep breath, air burning as it made its way down her sore throat. She wheezed and coughed at the pain.

He stood and looked down at her, his face emotionless. "I can see why Barrett chose you. You are very beautiful. But you are also a woman, which means you are weak and can be broken very easily. Like a china doll." He sneered and turned away.

"I'm stronger than I look." Ignoring the pain in her throat, she pushed herself up to her feet. Ready to face him.

He glanced over his shoulder and laughed. "No, you're not." He spun around and kicked her hard in the chest.

She flew through the air, pain spreading through her chest. Her head hit the wall, and she slid to the ground in a heap.

The last thing she saw was Boudier's evil smile as he slid a knife out from the back of his pants.

CHAPTER 56

"There are three guards on either side of the cabin. The back is facing a cliff right off the mountain so there's no way up or down that side," Lucien stated.

"Boudier is expecting us to hit him straight on," Barrett said. His chest clenched so hard, he thought his heart stopped for a minute. He looked back at Damon from the cover of the tree line. "Have you heard from Jaxon? He was supposed to call ten minutes ago. The longer Jacey stays inside that shack, the more danger she is in."

Barrett had called in a favor to Alfred before they even left the house. Alfred might be human, but he had connections to the military, and they needed all the manpower they could get.

"I can't wait any longer. We need to move." Barrett looked at his men. "This is different than anything we have ever faced. More dangerous. I can't ask you to risk your life for me or my mate. Half of you are mated. And I will understand if you want to turn around so you can live another day."

"Fuck, Barrett," Ryker growled. "You think I brought your ass back from the grave just to let you or your female die?"

"Yeah, man." Zane nodded. "You've already sacrificed everything for the Arkansas Guardians. We aren't going to let you down."

"Right." Jayden looked offended. "I mean we're not pussies, dude."

Barrett's throat tightened. He blinked back emotion welling up behind his eyes.

"We are in this with you." Damon clapped his hand on his shoulder. "We'll get Jacey back. You need to have your chance at happiness."

Barrett looked around at his Guardians. The look of determination was etched in each and every face.

"We will follow you into death," Lucien stated. They all nodded.

It was the last thing he wanted for them. But it was the one thing they were all going to face.

* * *

"Do you hear that?"

Jacey looked up at Boudier from the floor. "What?"

"It's the sound of death coming for you. And that mate of yours." He grabbed her elbow and snatched her off the floor. "I want you to see this. Witness how all those fucking Arkansas Guardians will die."

He flung open the door. The cold air slapped her in the face. She sucked in a breath, and the bitter wind stung her lungs.

"I have way more men than Barrett does. He's outnumbered, and he knows it." He cut his eyes at her. "Yet he'll still come. And they will follow him because they are sheep."

"They are loyal. Something your Guardians don't possess," she hissed.

"I rule my Guardians with an iron hand. It's the only way

to keep those wolves under control. Besides, have you seen how many men I have on my side?"

She swallowed hard and glanced around outside. The sun was kissing the horizon, eager to disappear for the day. The sun cast its rays on the blanket of snow covering the ground. The tree line surrounding the cabin was thick and dense. She blinked. And that's when she saw movement near the trees.

Boudier whistled and a line of large red wolves stepped out from the shadows of the trees. Jacey gagged as their rank odor hit her nose.

"Let Barrett get to the cabin. I want to make sure he sees his female die," Boudier called out. "As for the other Guardians, go after them now. Make sure you kill them all."

The wolves nodded their heads in understanding and then stepped back into the shadows.

"You won't win." She glared at him.

He squeezed her arm hard. She tried to wrench her arm free from his iron-clad grip.

"You are ruled by your heart. And now because of you, so is Barrett. Love is weakness. And because of Barrett's weakness for you, he will die."

She looked away, tears in her eyes. She vowed to herself in that moment that she would do whatever it took to save his life.

CHAPTER 57

*B*arrett heard the growl of the red wolf before the animal broke through the trees and headed straight for him. Dozens of other red wolves followed behind.

He forced his body to shift, letting the wolf inside come to the surface. He leaped through the air, knocking the red wolf to the snowy ground and sunk his teeth into its fur. The wolf howled and bucked Barrett off. Barrett took a meaty chunk of the wolf with him.

The red wolf writhed in pain and howled in anger. Barrett spit the bloody flesh to the ground, marring the white snow. Barrett turned to see his Guardians in their wolf form fighting the reds. They were outnumbered four to one, yet his Guardians didn't seem to care. They fought like wolves possessed. The scene seemed to unfold slowly before his eyes.

Braxton had one red wolf by the throat, pinned to the ground. Three other reds came up behind him and sunk their teeth into his back and legs.

Zane was circled in reds. But he was quick. When one attacked, he quickly fought him off and battled the next.

Lucien had two reds on the ground. He had one pinned down with his large back foot while he tore out the throat of the other one.

Jayden was circled by five reds snarling and biting at him. Jayden lunged and managed to get his mouth around the neck of the one nearest to him. Barrett barely heard the crack of the red's neck breaking in the battle.

He cut his eyes in Damon's direction. There were six red wolves piled on top of him. Damon growled and sprang up out of the pileup. The wolves were not deterred. They lunged for him at once, each baring their teeth.

One red growled and bit Damon near the throat. But Damon was quick and knocked the red wolf off and proceeded to land a death bite on its neck. Damon ripped his throat out. A small fountain of blood spurted into the air.

Six more red wolves lunged at Damon.

Barrett growled in anger. He ran hard at his enemies. He flung his body at two reds, knocking them to the ground.

They were strong, but he was stronger. He jumped and landed on one's throat, crushing his windpipe. The red struggled to breathe. Barrett wasted no time. He sunk his teeth into his neck and ripped out his throat. Barrett turned to fight the other red, but the wolf was backing away. He glared at Barrett through his wolf eyes and launched himself at Damon.

Barrett looked around at the fighting. The closest Guardian to him was Lucien. More reds had piled on Lucien, biting and clawing at him like a pack of wild animals.

Barrett plowed into the group, knocking reds off Lucien and biting at their necks.

He managed to kill two and then moved on to help Zane.

Every time he killed one red wolf, the other red wolves

would back away from him and turn their attacks on the Guardians.

He blinked. Then it hit him. Boudier didn't want him dead ... yet.

He wanted to make sure that Barrett was alive so he could watch as Boudier tortured her.

Fuck.

He looked over at Damon who was busy making hamburger out of two red wolves.

Their eyes met. Damon nodded in the direction of the cabin.

He was telling Barrett to go save his female.

His chest clenched. His men needed him here, to fight with them. But Jacey needed him as well.

Damon growled and nodded again, telling him to go.

It was the hardest fucking choice of his life.

The scream of a female tore through the fight. Barrett growled.

Jacey.

He bolted through the woods and toward the cabin.

CHAPTER 58

*B*oudier stood in the doorway of the abandoned cabin. He had Jacey in front of him, his arm wrapped around her neck, using her like a shield. Blood was dripping from her neck.

Barrett skidded to a stop a few yards in front of Boudier. He growled. And looked at the face of his enemy.

"I can see why you favor this female so much, Barrett. She tastes so sweet." Boudier's face slid into an evil grin.

The fucker had bitten her.

Red hot rage exploded inside of him. He threw his head back and howled.

"Shift back or I'll kill her on the spot." Boudier's smile slipped.

Boudier knew that Barrett could kill him quite easily in his wolf form. Boudier was thinking that with Barrett in his human form, the fight would be more evenly matched.

Boudier was wrong.

Barrett forced his wolf back inside and shifted into human form. He stood from his crouched position in the snow.

Boudier's gaze traveled over his body and then hardened.

"How did you escape the Texas Pack?" Barrett asked. He knew he should keep Boudier talking. He knew Boudier. The asshole loved to talk about himself.

Boudier grinned. "I had help from that red wolf, Bubba. He was trying to keep his nose clean but when I saw him in Texas, I told him he was going to help me, or I was going to get my men to kill his mama. You'd be surprised what some people will do for their mama. Bubba was one of the red wolves that had kidnapped Ava. After Damon rescued her, Bubba vanished. I found out later he had sought out a Guardian position in Texas. Said he wanted to walk the straight and narrow."

"Damon tried to track down Bubba after Ava was returned to Arkansas. He was going to find him and kill him."

"Tell him to get in line." Boudier's expression hardened. "After he helped me escape, he managed to get away from me. I had to enlist the help of some other red wolves to track you down. And I did. All the way to Colorado." He nuzzled Jacey's ear. She grimaced and tried to pull away. "Imagine my surprise when I realized you had found someone. Your mate."

Barrett's gut tightened. Despite being nude in the snow, his whole body was hot from the anger inside.

"I paid two hunters to find me a female wolf. I told them the area where I had spotted one." He stuck his tongue out and licked the side of Jacey's face. "I would have had her too, if you hadn't come along."

"Is that why you set the bomb?" He took a step closer, his gaze trained on Boudier.

"I set the bomb to blow her up. I knew she worked in the kitchen and would sometimes come in early. I wanted you to watch as she burned up in that building."

"But that's not what happened." Barrett shrugged and took yet another step.

"No, it's not." He narrowed his eyes. "When they didn't find a body, I realized that both of you had gotten away with that asshole Ryker. With a little help from my red wolves, they figured out where you had headed. So, I ended up taking her myself. Just to make sure no one fucked it up again."

"You want me. Let her go and you can kill me." Barrett held his hands out at his side.

"You make it sound so simple, Barrett. I want so much more than that. I want the blood debt that I am owed that was never paid. I want to see Arkansas fall and the Guardians die. More than that, I want to see the anguish on her face as I peel the skin from her pretty little face." Boudier pulled out a knife from behind his back.

Barrett's gut clenched. He only had seconds to respond.

"No!" He sprinted toward them just as Boudier pressed the knife to Jacey's throat.

A loud whirl seemed to come out of nowhere. For a second Barrett thought it was the sound of his desperate heart.

Boudier's expression changed, and his eyes widened. He heard the sound too so it couldn't have been coming from Barrett.

Barrett reached Jacey just as the familiar staccato sound of gunfire emanated from the back of the cabin.

The cabin began to shudder on itself as gunfire drilled into the dilapidated structure. Barrett shoved Jacey into the snow and covered her with his body. Boudier looked around, trying to figure out where the gunfire was coming from.

Rising above the cabin from the backside of the mountain was Lorcan and Brutus, the Louisiana Assassins, in a Black Hawk helicopter.

"You motherfucker! I own you!" Boudier screamed.

Lorcan grinned and gave him the one-finger salute. Brutus aimed the weapon at Boudier.

Boudier scrambled in the cabin to take cover.

Barrett stood and grabbed Jacey by the hand. "Run." He pulled her with him toward the cover of the tree line. Deafening gunfire exploded behind them. He ran fast, pulling Jacey with him. They were almost at the cover of the trees.

Suddenly, Jacey slowed.

"Don't stop running. We're almost there!" he yelled over the noise.

"Barrett?"

Something in her voice had him turning toward her. Something wasn't right.

She stopped and grabbed her stomach. His gaze dipped to her fingertips. Blood spilled out like a burst waterline. She looked up at him, eyes wide, face pale.

She collapsed. He caught her before she hit the snow. He looked up at the cabin. Boudier was crouched in the doorway, a gun aimed at them, a satisfied smile on his face. He mouthed the words "silver bullet."

Brutus launched a Hellfire missile toward the cabin. The building exploded into fire. The front door collapsed, trapping him inside. Boudier's screams of pain echoed in the mountains.

Barrett looked down at Jacey. "Let me see."

He pulled her hands away from her stomach and lifted her sweater. The bullet was buried in her stomach, and he could tell by the scent it was silver.

"I have to get it out, okay?" He met her eyes.

"I'm sorry. I should have ... run faster," she whispered. She reached up and caressed his cheek with bloody fingertips.

"Don't you think about leaving me, Jacey." His voice broke, and he wiped his eyes before he looked at her wound.

"This will hurt but once I get it out, you will heal and be okay."

If the silver bullet was left in, it would slowly poison her. But once he got it out, she could heal herself quickly.

He barely noticed the other Arkansas Guardians running up behind him and gathering around. He was focused on digging out the bullet.

"Boudier shot her." Barrett swallowed the lump in his throat.

"Barrett." Damon put his hand on his shoulder.

"I need to get this out. If I get it out, she will be okay. She can heal herself." He finally gripped the metal, pulled it out, and tossed it on the ground.

"Barrett." Damon squeezed his shoulder hard. "She's not breathing."

Barrett's heart stopped in his chest. He looked into her face. "No, she has to live." He bit his wrist and poured his blood into her mouth. She didn't swallow or move.

"Let me help her, Barrett. I know CPR." Jaxon knelt on the other side of her.

Jaxon didn't wait for permission but started pressing on her chest with his hands and breathing into her mouth.

Barrett growled.

"Let him help her, brother," Damon said. "Jaxon is well-trained. I know you don't like another male touching her, but he's just trying to help."

Barrett let Damon move him away while Jaxon worked on Jacey.

Lorcan landed the Black Hawk not far from where they stood. He, along with Brutus and Ryker, exited the aircraft and jogged over to where they stood.

Ryker knelt on the other side, holding pressure on where the bullet had entered. "She's not breathing."

The animal inside Barrett broke free from Damon, and he

rushed over to the still body of Jacey. Anger and pain and desperation welled up inside of him.

Blind agony welled inside of his chest. He pulled Ryker's handgun out of his holster and aimed it at Jaxon.

Lucien, Zane, Braxton, and Jayden all took a step back. Lorcan and Brutus held their ground.

"Fix her now," he demanded.

"Hold up, Barrett." Lorcan took a step forward. "Jaxon is helping her. Besides, we all know you wouldn't shoot your own Guardian."

"Fix her now. You said you could fix her." Barrett kept the gun trained on Jaxon.

Jaxon looked up but didn't stop performing CPR. "I'm trying. She's lost a lot of blood, not to mention the bullet was silver."

"Fuck this," Ryker growled, ignoring the gun over his head. He jogged over to the Black Hawk and pulled out a box. He jogged back over and began to apply the defibrillator pads to her chest.

"Clear." Jaxon stopped chest compressions, and Ryker sent a round of shocks to her heart.

"Give me the gun, Barrett." Damon stepped up beside him.

Barrett met his gaze. His whole body felt numb. Blindly, he handed over the weapon to the Were.

"I have a pulse," Jaxon announced. "Lorcan get that Black Hawk ready, and we can transport her to the nearest hospital. Brutus, go get the stretcher out of the chopper."

"There's a stretcher?" Lucien asked.

"The whole back is set up like a hospital helicopter," Ryker stated. "Apparently, Alfred is a bit of a paranoid old fart. Said he is ready for war."

"Yeah, well, right now, Alfred is my new best friend,"

Jaxon said. All the Weres bent down and picked up Jacey and gently placed her on the stretcher.

"I've got the coordinates for the nearest level one trauma hospital. Jaxon rides in the back, and Barrett can ride in the front," Lorcan stated.

Barrett shook his head. "I'm riding in the back."

"No. You're not." Damon stepped up. "Jaxon needs the room to work back there. Besides, all you would be doing is getting in the way."

Barrett watched as Lorcan and Brutus carefully lifted the stretcher and all the Guardians followed them to the Black Hawk. The scene of how reverently and gently they were caring for Jacey shook him to his core.

"She is one of ours now, Barrett." Damon cut his eyes at him. "We will protect her with our lives."

He couldn't speak but nodded. If he said a word, he was going to break down like a fucking pussy and weep. And one thing he wasn't was a pussy. Especially in front of his men.

CHAPTER 59

*L*orcan landed the Black Hawk on the hospital's landing pad. He'd managed to radio the hospital and tell them he was bringing in a gunshot wound. The look on the faces of hospital staff as they rushed out to the Black Hawk was comical.

At first, the doctor was giving Lorcan a hard time about procedure and protocol and how he couldn't land a Black Hawk on the helipad. When Brutus aimed the fifty caliber gun at him, the doctor shut up really quick and ordered the staff to get Jacey inside and stabilized.

Barrett followed them inside, refusing to leave Jacey's side until they rushed her into surgery. The nurses tried to get him to wait in the waiting room, but he refused. He stood at the restricted door, waiting.

He rested his back against the wall and waited. Seconds turned into minutes which twisted into hours.

"Barrett?" Damon headed down the hall to him.

"She's in surgery. I don't know how long it's been." He swiped his hand down his face and frowned at the dried blood on his hand.

Braxton, Zane, Jayden, and Jaxon followed behind Damon.

Braxton pulled out a bandana from his back pocket and held it under the water fountain. He turned to Barrett. "Here, man, you need to wipe your face. You look like a bloody version of Braveheart."

Barrett took the bandana and rubbed his face with it. "No wonder every nurse that has passed by has asked me if I need medical attention."

"Ryker went with Lorcan and Brutus to return the Black Hawk to Alfred," Damon said. "He certainly proved to be a great ally to have."

"Yeah. Glad he was willing to help. He's pretty fucking stingy with his equipment," Barrett stated.

A nurse in green scrubs and a smile made her way over to them. "Sir, are you the husband of the gunshot victim?"

"Yes. Is she okay?" His stomach dropped.

"They are still working on her. The surgeon said it's going to be a while before the surgery is over. He has instructed me to offer you," she cut her eyes to the ground of large dangerous-looking males, "and your friends a special waiting room."

"A special waiting room?" Zane arched his brow.

"Well, yes. It's private. And there's a phone in there. The surgeon will call with updates during the surgery." She smiled encouragingly.

"It's because we're big and scary, isn't it?" Jayden cocked his head.

She looked at him and blinked.

"Be honest." Braxton crossed his large tattooed arms and grinned.

"Yes, honey. It is." She sighed. "You guys are scaring all the patients and staff just standing out in the hall. We've already had two nurses complain that you guys look like a biker gang ready to go on a shooting spree." She gave Braxton a wink. "I, myself, like a big, manly biker."

Braxton lost the smile and straightened. "I'm taken."

"We'll take the room. We really appreciate it." Damon nodded.

The nurse smiled and led them down a series of corridors until they came to a windowless room. It was fairly large with a TV, red wall phone, and three couches. There was a refrigerator near a small table which held a coffeepot and paper cups.

"Will this room still be available after Jacey gets out of surgery?" Jaxon asked. "If she ends up in ICU after surgery, I know the policy is no one is allowed to stay at the bedside. Barrett's not leaving the hospital, and neither are we."

She nodded. And then glanced at the papers in her hand. "Honey, it looks like the hospital bill will be paid in cash and in full. You guys can do whatever you want. This room will be available as long as his wife is here." She closed the door behind her.

"You don't have to stay." Barrett eased onto the couch.

"Why would we leave?" Jayden frowned and sat down beside him.

"You need to get back to Arkansas, to your mates." Barrett looked at Jayden and then the rest of his Guardians. Ryker slipped into the room and grimaced.

"Yeah about that." Ryker rubbed the back of his neck "Looks like Granny and the rest of the females are on their way here as we speak."

All eyes turned on him.

"How'd that happen?" Damon growled.

"Look, dude, you need to answer your phone. Ava has been trying to reach you." Ryker narrowed his eyes at Damon.

"I've been a little busy," he retorted.

"No shit. Haven't we all?" Ryker deadpanned. "They are on their way so gird your loins."

Jayden snorted.

Barrett eased back into the couch and sighed. It was nice to have his men around him right now. He glanced around at the motley group. "Thank you all for risking everything for Jacey."

"Of course. She is your mate. Which makes her our family," Braxton said.

Everyone nodded in agreement.

Barrett looked over at Jaxon and grimaced. "Jaxon, I owe you an apology. I'm sorry for pulling that gun on you."

"You owe me nothing." Jaxon shrugged and smiled. "Besides, you already died for me once. I wasn't going to let you lose her. I was going to make sure she survived."

"Well, I helped too, you know," Ryker glared.

"Yes, yes, Ryker. We know you did." Zane eased onto the couch.

Ryker walked over to the coffeepot. "If I got to be stuck in this small-ass room with you idiots, then I'm going to need something stronger than coffee."

The phone rang, and Barrett jumped up to answer it.

"Hello?" He held his breath as the surgeon gave him a quick update. He remembered to thank the doctor before hanging up.

"What did he say?" Jaxon asked.

"He said that she had lost a lot of blood. He was surprised that the bullet was out but said that it helped that it was because there were some traces of poison around the area."

"So not only did he shoot her with a silver bullet, but he coated it with poison. Motherfucker." Damon ran his hand through his hair.

"That's not all. She was shot in the spleen. He had to take out the spleen due to continued hemorrhaging. He said that people live full lives without spleens all the time so he's not worried about that. He is worried about the poison and her recovery. He's going to clean up the wound and stabilize her before taking her to ICU. He wants to leave her on the ventilator for a few days and keep her in a medically induced coma."

"That's actually good." Jaxon stood and looked at everyone. "That will give her body time to heal. Since she's a Were, she'll heal twice as fast."

Barrett breathed out a loud sigh. "I hope you're right, Jaxon."

"I am. I have a good feeling about this." Jaxon nodded encouragingly.

"Well, I have a feeling that someone better go out and get some fucking Starbucks," Ryker grimaced. "Cause this hospital coffee is shit."

Everyone laughed.

CHAPTER 60

"They're going to let me see her. I can only stay for ten minutes." Barrett hung up the phone and looked at the Guardians who never left his side.

They all nodded, and Damon stepped up to him. "Want me to go with you?"

Barrett's stomach tightened, and he blinked. "Thanks, brother. But I need to do this myself."

"Can we see her?" Ryker asked, his voice oddly low.

Everyone looked at him. "What?" He glared. "I know you pussies are wondering the same thing. You're just too scared of Barrett to ask."

Barrett managed a smile. "They'll let me take one person with me. This first visit I need to have her all to myself. I'm sure you all understand."

The Guardians nodded.

"There are three visitations a day. Decide who wants to go with me to the next one." Barrett opened the door leading out to the hallway. A man in green scrubs and a surgical hat stood in the hallway. He was older, probably midsixties and had a weary look on his face.

"I'm assuming you are Mr. Middleton, Jacey's husband?" He cocked his head and held out his hand. "I'm Dr. Reynolds."

"I am." Barrett accepted it. "How is she?"

"She is stable. The surgery took longer than I expected. I wanted to make sure all the hemorrhaging had stopped before I sewed her up. As you know, I had to take out her spleen. The bullet pierced it, and there was no way to save the organ. She's lucky. If she had been hit in any other organ, she would not have made it."

Barrett nodded.

"She will be in ICU for at least a few days. I want her to stay intubated and on the ventilator. She will be given medicine in her IV to keep her sedated and not moving. I want her to rest completely. She's not out of the woods yet." Dr. Reynolds cocked his head. "I don't suppose you have the bullet she was shot with, do you?"

"No. I dug it out." He leveled his gaze at the doctor.

"Interesting. The bullet was coated in poison. I'm running some blood tests to determine what it was."

"When you get the results, I want to be notified." Barrett curled his hands into fists.

The doctor nodded and met his gaze.

"Mr. Middleton, I'm not sure you are aware of the law. Anytime a gunshot or stabbing victim comes to the hospital seeking help, I am required by law to notify the police. Not to mention the fact you flew her here on a Black Hawk helicopter, fully armed."

"I know." He didn't really give a rat's ass about getting in trouble with the law. All he had to do was make one call to the government, and they would cover all this shit up.

"Here's what I know, Dr. Reynolds. I know that my wife is fighting for her life right now. I knew I had to get her to the hospital fast. I would have stolen a Harriet jet if it would have cut out some time."

Dr. Reynolds nodded in understanding. "I'm going to bet that when I do report this to the police, I'll have the FBI crawling all over the place."

"And the CIA and whatever bullshit initials they have," Barrett said. "Now I want to see my wife, if you have all the answers you need."

Dr. Reynolds nodded. "Follow me." He led him down another maze of hallways to an elevator. Once inside, the doctor pushed the third-floor button. When the doors opened, he followed him. Dr. Reynolds keyed his badge to the ICU, and the doors flung open. Inside was row after row of rooms with glass doors. The scent of old blood, antiseptic, and hopelessness hung heavy in the air. The nurses were bustling from room to room, touching IVs and recording something in the laptop computers.

"Even though we've placed her in a medically induced coma, she can still hear you, Mr. Middleton. I encourage you to talk to her." Dr. Reynolds walked inside the room and motioned for Barrett to follow him.

He braced himself for what he would find.

Jacey looked so small and so pale in the bed. A large tube was shoved down her throat and was connected to a machine near the head of the bed. Multiple IVs were stuck into her arm, marking her perfect skin. A monitor with bright lights revealed her fast heart rate and low blood pressure.

"This is Megan, Mr. Middleton. She is Jacey's nurse for the night. She's here until seven."

Megan turned away from checking the IV bag and gave him a warm smile. She was petite with short, brown hair and brown eyes.

"You look so young." Barrett frowned.

She gave a little laugh. "Thank you. I'll take that as a compliment. But I just turned thirty."

"Megan is one of our best nurses. She's been working in ICU ever since she got out of nursing school," Dr. Reynolds said. "Even our residents go to her for advice."

"Don't worry, Mr. Middleton. Mrs. Middleton is my only patient tonight. I will be spending all my time focused on her," Megan said.

"Don't worry, Mr. Middleton. I'm also on call tonight so if there are any changes, Megan will call me." Dr. Reynolds studied the IV and glanced at her vitals.

"We'll step out and let you spend some time with her." Megan smiled and touched his arm reassuringly.

His eyes widened. "What if I touch something and mess it up?"

"You may be big, Mr. Middleton, but you won't mess anything up." Megan smiled. She walked over to the bed and pulled back the covers revealing Jacey's arm. She pulled up a rolling chair and patted the back. "Sit here and you can hold her hand. I'll be right outside. I can monitor everything on the monitors out there."

Megan followed Dr. Reynolds outside to the nursing station. Barrett looked back at Jacey. He eased over to the bed and sat carefully in the chair. He reached over and picked up Jacey's hand.

"Sweetheart. It's Barrett." He trained his eyes on her face. "You're going to be okay."

The only sound in the room was the rhythmic noise of the machines trying to keep her alive.

He swallowed back the emotion in the back of his throat. "You should have seen the look on the staff's face when we landed a Black Hawk at the hospital. I think the doctor nearly shit himself. I think they thought the hospital was under attack with all those missiles loaded on the chopper."

Helplessness sank into his bones, weighing and pulling him down. He couldn't help her.

He swiped a hand across his eyes and wrapped her small hand in his. He bent and kissed her fingertips. He noticed she still had dried blood on her hand where she'd grabbed her stomach when she'd been shot.

"All the guys are here. They wanted to see you, but I told them they were going to have to wait. So, you need to get better so they can visit." His voice cracked, and a tear rolled down his face. "I'm not leaving without you, Jacey." He laid his head on her hand and let the tears flow.

"I can't lose you when I just found you." His tears and desperation soaked into the sheet. "I love you."

A sharp beep echoed in the room. He lifted his head off the bed. Megan and Dr. Reynolds ran into the room.

"Mr. Middleton, we need you to leave," Dr. Reynolds said as he started pushing buttons.

Two more nurses rushed in with a rolling cart. He stepped back to get out of the way.

White noise filled his ears, and he couldn't make sense of what was going on. One nurse grabbed him by the arm and tugged him out of the room. He barely heard her say that he had to leave because Jacey was crashing.

What did that mean? Was she dying? Was she leaving him?

He was rushed out of the ICU, left alone in the hallway.

Nausea rolled in his stomach, and he looked around for a bathroom. He quickly spotted one and hurried inside. He barely made it.

CHAPTER 61

$\mathcal{B}$arrett made it back to the private waiting room. When he walked in, all the Guardians stood.

"They said she was crashing and made me leave." His voice cracked.

The room was painfully silent as he made his way over to the couch and sat. He buried his face in his hands.

"I don't know what to do." His voice came out broken like his soul.

"What about that Fae?" Jaxon looked at Ryker. "Call her and tell her to get her fairy ass down here."

"I've tried. I can't get in touch with her." Ryker raked his fingers through his hair.

"What about the poison that was coated in that bullet? Do we know what it was? If we know then we can find a cure," Braxton said hopefully.

"The doctor said the tests aren't in yet." Barrett studied the floor.

"Fuck that shit." Jayden headed for the door. "I'm going to the lab to tell them to hurry the fuck up."

"You're going to get us kicked out of here, dumbass," Zane growled.

"We landed a fully armed Black Hawk on the helipad. If they've not kicked us out yet, then we're probably good," Ryker snorted. "I'll go with him."

"We'll be back." Jayden and Ryker shut the door behind him.

"Lucien and Zane, call up those Louisiana Assassins and see if they have insight into what that poison might be." Damon placed his hands on his hips. "They were with Boudier for years, so they would know the kind of crazy shit he was into."

"On it." Lucien and Zane headed out the door.

"Braxton and Jaxon, I just got a text from Ava. They aren't far from here. Apparently, they flew into Denver a little while ago. They rented a car. Can you meet them downstairs?" Damon asked.

"Sure thing." Braxton nodded.

Once they were alone, Damon sat beside Barrett.

"I can't help her. I feel helpless not to find a way to help her," Barrett admitted.

"I know. When it's your mate, you would do anything for them. And now, you feel like you can't." Damon squeezed his shoulder. "She is in the best trauma hospital in Colorado, hell, in the Midwest. I checked the credentials of her doctor, and he's the best there is."

Barrett nodded. "I promised to protect her, and I broke that promise." He cut his eyes over at Damon. "There is nothing Jacey hates worse than a liar."

Damon glared. "Listen to me, you stubborn asshole."

Barrett jerked his head up. He's never been spoken to that way in his life.

"You are not a liar. You did do everything in your power

to protect her. Boudier got off a lucky shot. But he got his in the end," Damon growled.

The door opened, and they both turned.

Standing in the doorway were the three Assassins: Lorcan, Brutus, and Killian. They were all dressed in their uniform of black and wearing sunglasses, despite being inside.

"You won't have to worry about Boudier anymore. The cabin exploded when the Hellfire missile hit it. What was left ended up sliding off the mountain." Lorcan cocked his head.

"Good." Barrett nodded. "Although I will regret not taking his fucking head off myself."

"I feel you there," Brutus grunted.

Damon nodded for them to come inside. They shut the door behind them.

"Did you get a call from Lucien?" Barrett asked.

"I did. I told him that we were headed back to the hospital to talk to you. I think my brother and Zane were going to pick up some food for everyone. They should be back soon." Lorcan eased his large frame onto the couch. Lorcan and Lucien were twin brothers and had been at odds for years. But recently, they were on the same page when it came to Boudier.

Brutus, with his buzz cut and stern expression, took up residency against the wall and crossed his arms. Killian poured himself some coffee. Killian looked more like a rock star with his longer hair and smirk. It was easy to forget he was one of the three deadly werewolf Assassins.

"This coffee sucks," Killian grimaced.

"It's hospital coffee. It's supposed to suck," Brutus grunted.

"What do you know about the poison?" Barrett cut to the chase.

"I know that Boudier liked to keep wolfsbane around. He

would poison those he thought were going against him. That guy was paranoid as fuck," Lorcan admitted. "From what Lucien told me, the bullet was extracted by you, and the doctor removed your female's spleen. That would have only left trace amounts in her bloodstream. It takes a large amount of wolfsbane to kill someone." Lorcan cocked his head.

"Well, it's something. She was stabilized out of surgery and now she's . . ." Barrett's voice drifted off. He couldn't bring himself to say the words.

"Is your female Were?" Brutus asked.

All eyes turned on him, and the room grew silent. Killian paused the cup to his lips and looked from Barrett to Brutus.

"What the fuck kind of question is that?" Barrett stood and curled his fingers into fists.

Brutus pushed off the wall and unfolded his hands.

Lorcan stood between the two Weres. "You'll have to excuse Brutus. He wasn't raised with any manners." He glared at the Assassins.

"Wait a minute," Killian put his coffee down. "I think I'm getting where Brutus is going." He looked at Barrett. "Remember when Boudier stabbed that Were with a silver knife coated with wolfsbane at dinner?"

Lorcan nodded. "Yeah? So?"

"The Were didn't die a slow death of poison, remember. It was fast. He went into cardiac arrest. Boudier was pissed because he wanted to watch him die slowly."

"Right." Lorcan looked at Barrett. "He was a Were, but he had a mixed bloodline. His mother was Fae while his father was Were."

"I assure you that Jacey is Were. I can smell it on her." Barrett glared.

"Yeah, but what about you?" Damon asked. "I saw you cut your wrist and give Jacey blood."

"My blood is from a pure line of werewolves traced all the way back to England. I discovered when I was a child that my blood had accelerated healing properties. Six times that of a normal werewolf. Both my mother and father were Were. Besides, as you recall, I gave Lucien blood too and nothing happened," Barrett stated.

"Yes. But that was before you died and came back to life," Damon said. "You said a Fae brought you back. She didn't give you blood, did she?"

"She did." Ryker stood in the doorway. "And that witch did some kind of blood magic on him to keep him alive until the fairy could get there."

"Well, if she's got my blood and Fae blood, shouldn't that be healing her quicker? Not making her sicker?" Barrett asked.

"Her body is trying to adjust to having Fae blood inside of her." Lorcan nodded. "Her body has a choice to accept it or reject it."

"Fuck." Barrett's knees buckled, and he sat back on the couch. "I've killed her."

The phone rang. Barrett looked up, his throat dry.

Damon grabbed the phone. "Hello?" He turned his back to Barrett.

Barrett held his breath. Seconds ticked into eternity. He waited.

Damon hung up the phone and turned around. He met Barrett's gaze.

"Her heart stopped, and they had to shock her a couple of times," Damon said slowly.

"Oh, God." Barrett felt the hope drain out of him like air out of a balloon.

"They got her back. She is stabilized now." Damon squeezed his shoulder.

Barrett looked up and nodded. She was still with him. She was still alive.

"It looks like your female is fighting, Barrett," Lorcan said.

Barrett nodded. "She's strong, and she's a fighter."

"Then she will pull through just fine." Lorcan nodded.

"Yes, she will." Barrett sighed. He frowned and looked up at the Assassin. "How did you three get to Colorado so fast? And how did you get in that Black Hawk with Ryker?"

"When we found out that Boudier had escaped Texas, we tracked him to Denver. It was there we ran into Ryker getting the Black Hawk from Alfred." Lorcan shrugged.

"You know Alfred?" Barrett cocked his head.

"Don't we all?" Killian grinned.

"Anyway, after a few minutes of deciding who was going to pilot the chopper . . ." Lorcan rubbed his jaw.

"He means, after Ryker and Lorcan argued over who was going to fly followed by a couple of punches thrown." Killian smirked.

"Lorcan got in a cheap shot," Ryker growled and glared at the Assassin. Killian lost the smile and went back to drinking his crappy cup of coffee.

Barrett stood and held out his hand. "I appreciate the help."

Lorcan took it. "Anytime. I'm glad I was part of putting Boudier in the ground. That fucker won't hurt anyone ever again."

Barrett walked over to Brutus and shook his hand and then Killian's.

"What are your plans since Louisiana is without a Pack Master and Boudier is dead?" Damon asked.

"We will stay in Louisiana. Help keep the peace and hopefully give the civilian Weres some hope. Once they put in a Pack Master, I guess we will see what our next steps will be.

If they put another asshole like Boudier in, then we all might be joining Arkansas." Lorcan grinned.

"We would be proud to have all of you," Damon stated.

"We will keep that in mind." Killian lifted his cup in a salute. "Right now, let's get Barrett's female well."

Barrett nodded. Jacey had a long fight ahead of her. And he would be with her every step of the way.

CHAPTER 62

*A*va, Kate, Skylar, Haley, Catty, Ginny, and Granny all showed up at the hospital armed with bags and bags of Chinese takeout.

"I can't believe you're alive." Granny had tackled Barrett the second she entered the waiting room. She wouldn't let him go as she cried and patted his chest, as if making sure he was real.

"I couldn't tell anyone," he said softly. He looked at the females looking at him like he was a ghost. His gaze landed on Ava.

"Ava, I owe you an apology. I'm sorry I put you in that situation."

"You did it to force Damon to kill you. I see that now." Ava's eyes watered. "You did
it to save Jaxon."

He nodded.

Ginny launched herself at him. He stiffened. It wasn't until he felt the sobs and her arms wrapped around him that he realized she wasn't angry.

She stepped back and looked up at him. "Thank you. For

saving us." She grabbed his hand and put it on her stomach where her baby was growing.

He fidgeted, uncomfortable at the intimate contact. Jaxon growled but didn't move.

"You saved us all. Jaxon, my baby, even me."

He nodded and let his hand fall from her stomach. He wasn't used to all the attention.

"We brought food. We figured everyone would be hungry." Granny's gaze landed on the three large Assassins standing along one side of the wall. "We brought enough for everyone."

"Thank you." Lorcan nodded.

All the females started piling food onto plates and handing them out to the Weres. Granny handed Brutus a plate.

"Thanks," He said low and deadly.

"You're the one they call Brutus." Granny narrowed her eyes.

"I am." He cocked his head. "You're Jayden's grandmother. The one that sells sex toys."

"Yep, that's me," she said brightly.

"Jesus, Granny," Jayden chided. "Stop acting like it's a great thing."

"Watch your language, Jayden. Besides, what's wrong with making fat stacks of cash?"

Killian snorted. She leveled her gaze on him. Barrett couldn't help but notice Lorcan easing toward the door.

"You're Killian." She handed him a plate that Kate had passed to her.

"Yes, ma'am. I am." He gave her a devastating grin. Barrett shook his head.

"I heard you're the ladies' man of the Assassins." Granny wiggled her eyebrows.

Lorcan took another step toward the door.

"So, my reputation precedes me, does it?" His smile widened. "I like it."

Lorcan had his hand on the doorknob.

"Not so fast, Lorcan." Granny spun around, causing a gray curl to fall down over one eye.

Lorcan froze and slowly turned.

To Barrett, Lorcan looked a little green.

"I remember you. And I think you remember me." Granny grinned.

"Wait. Have you met Lorcan before?" Jayden stopped eating and looked up from his plate.

"Oh, yeah. I remember you." Kate crossed her arms and stared. "You came to the Bella Luna looking for Braxton."

"Lorcan." Killian stared. "You don't mean to tell me that Granny was at the B&B with those writers that tried to molest you."

The room grew quiet, and Lorcan turned bright red. "That's not what happened."

"Of course it's not. Lorcan was going to help us do some research for a BDSM book that author was writing." Granny lifted her chin in the air.

Brutus choked on his chow mein noodles, and Killian laughed. "That's not what he said."

"Shut up, Killian." Lorcan glared.

"Lorcan said they were vicious females who tried to fondle him." Brutus cracked a rare smile.

"I never said fondle."

"There might have been a whip, but there was definitely not fondling." Granny glared at Brutus.

"For the love of all that is holy, stop talking, Granny." Jayden grabbed his stomach. "I think I'm going to be sick."

The room erupted in laughter.

"Lorcan, tell us again what those big, bad writers were going to do." Killian wiped the tears from his eyes.

"Fuck off, Killian." Lorcan grabbed the doorknob and headed out the door.

"I'll go after him," Lucien said.

"No. Let him go." Brutus chuckled. "He's not used to getting ribbed. This is good for him. Builds character."

Barrett looked around the room, amazed at how far they had come. The Assassins who had once tried to kill his Guardian Braxton were now eating a meal together, all bad feelings gone.

Peace settled over him for a second. Jacey was stable and was still fighting. After they got through this, he was never going to take one day for granted.

$\mathcal{T}$hat morning before the sun came up, Barrett stood in the middle of the waiting room and looked at the scene. All his Guardians, minus Ginny and Jaxon as well as Damon and Ava, were still in the room. The men had slept upright on the couches while their females slept curled up in their laps. Lucien and Catty were curled up on the floor with a pillow and a blanket. Even Granny had fallen asleep on the couch.

Ginny and Ava had wanted to stay too, but Barrett insisted the males get a room since they were both pregnant.

Brutus had stayed while Killian and Lorcan had gotten a hotel close by. They had already made plans to take turns with Barrett at the hospital.

The scene moved him more than he could express with words.

There was a soft knock on the door. Barrett walked over just as Megan, the nurse, peeked in.

She took one glance around the room and motioned for him to come out into the hall.

He shut the door behind him. "Is she okay? Is something wrong?"

She gave him a smile. "She's doing good. Better than good. I came to get you so you can sit with her."

"Really?" His heart thudded in his chest.

"Absolutely." She smiled and led the way back to ICU.

When he stepped inside the unit, the scent of antiseptic hit him. But this time he could smell another scent.

Jacey.

He followed Megan to the room. She nodded for him to enter. She went to sit at the nursing station with the other nurses.

The room was dim and only illuminated by the machines surrounding Jacey. He glanced up at the monitor. Her heart rate was steady, and her blood pressure was good.

He eased over to the bed and sat in the rolling chair. The tube was still in her throat, but she didn't look as pale.

He sat and gently picked up her hand.

"Jacey. It's Barrett." He squeezed her hand. "They say you can hear me. I'm not so sure. But I am sure of one thing. I love you very much. I don't ever want to be parted from you ever again. I want you to know that I can't imagine a life without you in it. Please don't stop fighting. Please don't leave me."

He bent his head and kissed her fingertips. They were clean. Megan must have given her a bath sometime during the night when she thought Jacey was strong enough to handle it.

He sat back and looked at her hand in his. She was so tiny compared to him. The bones in her hand were fine and elegant, while his were large and strong.

But they fit each other.

He grinned to himself. He once thought being mated made one weak. Now he knew it only strengthened him.

Her hand tightened around his.

He blinked and shook his head. He must be delusional from lack of sleep.

But when he saw her fingers move against his, he realized what he was seeing. He looked up at Jacey's face.

Her eyes were open, and she was looking at him. Suddenly, the ventilation alarm went off, and Megan came running into the room.

"She squeezed my hand," he said.

Megan's eyes grew wide when she saw Jacey was awake. "I can't believe she's awake. She was given a large amount of sedation to keep her still." She pushed some buttons on the ventilator silencing the machine. She went to the door and ordered the secretary to call Dr. Reynolds.

"Is everything okay? Do I need to leave?"

"Actually, stay." Megan leaned over the bed and looked at Jacey. "Mrs. Middleton, I know you're scared, but you are in the hospital. Your husband is here. Right now, you have a tube down your throat helping you to breathe. I want you to try to relax, okay?" She looked at Barrett. "I want to see if Dr. Reynolds wants to take the tube out of her throat. I don't want to give her any more sedation until I hear from him."

Barrett nodded. He brushed the hair out of her face. "Sweetheart, try to relax, okay? You were hurt, and they had to put a tube down your throat to help you breathe. Try to slow your breathing down a little, okay?"

Jacey looked directly at him, eyes wide and alert. She seemed to understand what he was saying because her breathing grew slow and steady.

"What's the update?" Dr. Reynolds hurried through the door. He looked at him and then at Jacey.

"She's very much alert. Even with all the sedation," Megan stated. "She's gotten amazingly stronger throughout the night, and I believe she's ready to be extubated."

Dr. Reynolds listened to her lungs with a stethoscope. He looked at her vitals and then nodded. "You're right, Megan." He turned to Barrett. "See. I told you Megan was the best."

"If you'll just step out of the room so we can get the tube out, that would be great," Megan said.

He nodded and stepped outside. He noticed the other nurses giving him curious stares but none said anything.

"Mr. Middleton, you can come inside," Megan said from the door.

Barrett turned and headed into the glassed-in room.

He looked at the bed. Jacey was sitting up. Her eyes were heavy, but she was alert.

"Jacey?" He hurried to the bed and grabbed her hand.

"Barrett." Her words came out hoarse, and she winced as she spoke each syllable.

"Her throat is sore from having that tube down her throat. It should go away in a day or so," Dr. Reynolds said. He leaned over the bed. "Jacey, how do you feel?"

"Thirsty." She winced.

"I'll get some ice chips and see how she tolerates them."

"How is your pain? Do you need some more pain medicine?"

She shook her head. "No. I don't like how it makes me feel."

Dr. Reynolds nodded and looked at him. "She's doing remarkably well. While you were out of the room, I glanced at her wound. There's no redness or sign of infection. Her vitals are strong. The lab results showed the poison as unknown."

Wolfsbane wouldn't show up. Barrett knew that, but Dr. Reynolds didn't.

"She's healing at an incredible rate. She's going to be our miracle patient." Dr. Reynolds smiled at her.

Her Were blood. Mixed with his. Plus, a whole lot of prayer.

"Thank you. For everything you've done." Barrett held out his hand to the doctor.

"She did the getting better part." Dr. Reynolds smiled and shook his hand. "I'll give you two some privacy." He shut the sliding glass door behind him and Megan.

Barrett stepped closer and picked up her hand. "Are you hurting?"

"Just my throat." She blinked slowly. "You look like you've not slept in a week."

"I couldn't sleep until I knew you were going to be okay. It's not been a week. Just a very long night."

Jacey frowned. "What about Boudier?"

"Dead." Barrett sat and kissed her hand. "Lorcan hit the cabin with a missile, and Boudier burned up in the fire."

"Good. He won't come looking for you again," she said weakly.

"You scared me. I thought I was going to lose you." He pressed her hand to his cheek. Her skin against his made his heart ache.

"I'm tougher than I look. I'm from Mississippi, remember?" She gave him a ghost of a grin.

His heart exploded with hope. She really was going to be alright.

"I need to tell you something." He glanced over his shoulder, making sure they were alone.

She frowned. "What is it?"

"When you were shot on the mountain, I thought I was losing you. I bit my wrist and gave you my blood."

"I don't understand. You're a Were. Not a vampire. Your blood wouldn't have healed me."

"My bloodline is pure. From a royal lupine line. I discovered when I was child that my blood could accelerate healing. I thought by giving you my blood, it would speed up your healing process." He took a breath and looked away. "What I didn't know until Ryker told me was when I was brought back from the dead by Celeste, she actually gave me her blood."

"Fae blood? So, I have Fae blood too?" She swallowed.

"Yes. That's why your heart stopped. Your body was trying to reject it." He shook his head. "You almost died. And it would have been my fault."

She reached over and caressed his cheek. "But I didn't die. And if you hadn't given me your blood, I would have died. You saved me, Barrett."

He nuzzled her palm. He had no words. He rested his head in the crook of her neck and inhaled her scent. "I love you."

"I love you too," she said softly.

"I don't want to leave this room. I think they are going to have to call security to try to remove me."

She chuckled and then grimaced. He lifted his head and frowned. "You need pain medicine."

"No. I'm just sore. Do you think you can help me sit up?"

"Let me ask the nurse if it's okay." He walked over to the door and poked his head out. He caught Megan's gaze, and she walked over. "She wants to sit up."

"Let me change her dressing first and then we will sit her up in the chair."

"Thank you." For once, he knew everything was going to be alright.

CHAPTER 64

*J*acey recovered quickly and was soon moved to a room. She'd always been a quick healer but with Barrett's blood, she was almost vibrating with power.

She was shocked at all the visitors that came into the room. All the Guardians stopped by and so did the Louisiana Assassins. They each brought either a small bouquet of flowers or a balloon.

Even grouchy Ryker brought her a stuffed animal.

She began to feel a little overwhelmed when Granny and the rest of the females stopped in to see her.

"Go get something to eat, and I'll sit with Jacey." Granny patted Barrett's arm.

"I'm not hungry," he growled.

"It's okay, Barrett," Jacey assured him. He hadn't left her side since she woke up. "In fact, I'd love it if you'd get me something other than hospital food." She pulled a face.

"What do you feel like?"

"I could eat a cow." She sighed.

"Hamburger it is." Barrett grinned.

"And a milkshake?" she asked hopefully.

"Of course." He bent down and kissed her lips. Her stomach warmed. "I won't be gone long."

She nodded and turned her attention to Granny when he shut the door behind him.

"I can't believe all the flowers and gifts." She looked around the room.

"I know I can barely move with everything in here." Granny laughed. She pulled up a chair close to the bed and sat.

"I'm sure the nurses will be glad when we all leave."

"Oh, yes. I think they are trying to figure out if we are a biker gang or somehow connected to the mafia." Granny grinned.

Jacey laughed.

A knock at the door had them both turning. Ava poked her head in and smiled. "Mind if I come in?"

"Come on in." Jacey waved her in. "We sent Barrett to go get me a hamburger. And hopefully something for him to eat too."

"I know. Me and Damon ran into him in the hallway. I sent Damon with him." Ava came in and rubbed her stomach.

"I'm getting some coffee from the nurses' station. Anyone want some?" Granny stood.

"Ugh, no. Not that stuff." Ava wrinkled up her nose.

"You young whippersnappers are so used to your Starbucks and lattes. You don't know how to drink real coffee anymore." Granny huffed and headed out the door.

"Sit." Jacey motioned to the chair that Granny vacated.

Ava eased into the chair and stared at Jacey.

"What?" She patted her hair. "Does my hair look that bad?"

"No, silly. I'm just looking at you because you are

Barrett's mate. You are one in a million. You are his miracle."
Ava smiled brightly.

"I don't know about that." She ducked her head.

"Oh, believe me. I know." Ava nodded.

There was a soft knock on the door. Catty poked her head in, and Ava waved her in.

"I'm bringing the whole crew with me." Catty laughed as Kate, Ginny, and Skylar followed behind her.

"We brought chocolate." Ginny held up a bag of Twix and grinned.

"I wanted to bring wine, but I was outvoted." Catty scowled.

"There will be plenty of time for that once we go home." Ava laughed.

"Home. I like the sound of that." Jacey sighed and leaned back against the pillows while the chocolate and gossip were passed around.

* * *

WITHIN DAYS, Jacey was well enough to travel back to Arkansas with Barrett. He had hired a private plane and flown them back in style. Because of Barrett being alive, an emergency Tribunal with the Council was called with all the Southern Pack Masters in attendance.

Jaxon stepped up and admitted that since Barrett was alive, the blood debt still needed to be paid. He was willing to pay the price. But it was unnecessary. All the Pack Masters stood and said they would no longer back a Council that would inflict death upon an innocent Guardian. It was agreed that Arkansas had bled too much already.

The Council agreed and admitted they had been hasty in siding with Boudier. They canceled the blood debt owed by Jaxon.

The Council stated that the Pack Masters needed more control, and that they should decide what to do about leadership in Arkansas.

Damon agreed that Barrett is the rightful Pack Master of Arkansas. He agreed to hand over control back to Barrett. But Barrett refused.

Lorcan and Lucien offered a solution. They both thought that Barrett should be Pack Master of Louisiana since the position was vacant.

He was also told how much he would inherit of Boudier's estate. Close to two hundred million dollars. Lorcan, Brutus, and Killian pledged fealty to Barrett.

* * *

Three Months Later

JACEY FINISHED DRYING the wine glass and put it back in the cabinet. She glanced around the newly redecorated kitchen. She was glad that they had sold Boudier's house and bought another nearby. This house was more her style, and there were no ghosts to remind her of Boudier.

She looked out the window and frowned at the torrential downpour. She wished Barrett would hurry up and get home. The weather service had predicted a tropical storm to hit New Orleans in another hour.

Unease snaked up her spine. She had never been afraid of storms, but tonight felt different. Maybe she should have convinced Barrett to evacuate.

Tap, tap, tap.

She looked out the dining room window and spotted the low-hanging branch like a finger tapping. The lights flickered and then went out. She grabbed the lighter out of the drawer and lit a couple of candles.

"Where are you, Barrett?" she whispered to herself. She picked up the cell phone to dial his number.

When he didn't answer, she put the phone down.

A loud crash rattled the house. Jacey screamed and grabbed a candle. She turned toward the sound. A branch poked through the living room window. In the dark, there was something else. A monster in the shape of a human.

Fear coursed through her veins. Standing in front of her was Boudier with half the flesh on his face peeled away, exposing the muscle of his jaw and teeth. He reached a burned hand toward her. She stepped back and screamed.

"You are supposed to be dead."

"I wasn't killed in the cabin when it went up in flames, you stupid bitch. I jumped off the cliff of the mountain. Red wolves found me to keep me alive ... only to torture me. They said I was of no use to them anymore. They poured liquid silver on my skin to keep me from healing from the burns." He snarled at her.

"How did you get here?" She knew she had to keep him talking to buy time. Maybe Barrett was on his way home. He had to be.

"I escaped when one of them left a knife out where I could reach it. I got loose and cut all their heads off for what they did to me." His eyes shifted, changed into something dark, something evil.

"I made my way back to my home and guess what I discovered. That motherfucker, Barrett Middleton, is Pack Master over my state. He sold my beautiful historic house to a bunch of old-ass ladies. Barrett has taken everything from me. My house, my position, the loyalty of my Guardians. And guess what, bitch? Now I'm going to make him pay. I'm going to take you."

Boudier lunged at her with the knife. Before she could move, she heard a low growl behind her.

Barrett launched through the air in wolf form. Boudier screamed as Barrett landed on top of him. Boudier plunged the knife into Barrett's chest.

She screamed in the dark.

Barrett bared his teeth and clamped down on Boudier's throat. He ripped his throat out and tossed the bloody tissue onto the floor.

Lorcan and Brutus rushed into the room.

Lorcan grabbed Jacey. "Are you okay? Did he hurt you?"

"I'm okay."

Brutus pulled out his gun and put two bullets in Boudier's chest and one in his head. "I don't think he's coming back from that."

"How did you know to come?" Jacey looked at Lorcan.

"Barrett said he had been trying to call you. When he couldn't get ahold of you, he told us to go over and make sure everything was okay."

"The phones were busy because the system is overloaded with everyone calling." Killian came into the room. "I checked the perimeter. Boudier was alone. I didn't find anyone else."

"He stabbed Barrett." Jacey's gaze landed on the puddle of blood on the floor. White stars danced behind her eyes. Her knees buckled.

"Easy." Lorcan grabbed her before she could hit the floor.

Her eyes closed, and the voices drifted into silence.

CHAPTER 65

"I am Pack Master, and I want to see my wife," he thundered at the doctor in charge of the Louisiana Werewolf Compound.

"We're not finished bandaging you up, Mr. Middleton." The elderly doctor taped another piece of tape on the bandage. "I've already checked her out, and she's fine."

Barrett brushed his hands away. "I don't care about being wrapped up like a fucking mummy." He looked around. "I want to see my mate. Which room is she in?"

The doctor sighed and pointed to a room in the corner.

Barrett threw him a glare. These Louisiana Weres needed a lot of instruction when it came to how he ran things. He made his way to the room while the medical staff parted like the Red Sea.

He opened the door and found Jacey sitting on the edge of the bed. She looked up at him and smiled. "You're okay."

He took her in his arms. "Of course, I am. It takes more than a knife in the heart to kill me. I mean, I've been dead before so I should know." He hugged her tight. "I'm more worried about you."

"The doctor ran some tests on me to make sure everything was okay." She pulled back and looked at him.

"He told me you were fine. Lorcan said you fainted. It must have been all the excitement." He kissed her forehead. He couldn't stop kissing or touching her. He needed to make sure she was alright.

"Then he didn't tell you everything," she said quietly.

He pulled back and looked in her eyes. "What do you mean?"

"I fainted because ... I'm pregnant." She looked at him under her lashes.

"You're ..." His heart lurched in his chest. "Pregnant?"

"Yes." She patted his chest and took a deep breath. "I know we had not talked about having children, and I understand that you might not be okay ..."

"You're pregnant," he said again. He liked the way those words sounded on his lips. His gaze dipped to hers. He covered her mouth with his, kissing her long and deep and thoroughly.

When he finally pulled away, he stared down at her with all the love he had in his heart.

"So, you're okay with this new development?"

"I'm going to be a father. And I am mated to the only female I have ever loved. A few months ago, I thought everything had been taken from me. I walked through hell, and now I'm on the other side. Everything I lost has been given to be ten times over." He kissed her again. "I'm more than okay with having a baby with you."

She smiled and hugged him tight. "Good. And just so you know, twins seem to run in my family."

He pulled back and looked at her. Then laughed. "As long as you and the babies are healthy, I'm okay with twins."

He brushed her hair away from her face. "I love you, Jacey. And I can't wait to see what the future holds for us."

The End

ABOUT THE AUTHOR

Jodi Vaughn is a USA Today best-selling author of over twenty five paranormal romance and contemporary romance novels. She loves writing novels where good always overcomes evil and sometimes the heroine saves the hero.She lives in Northeast Arkansa with her family, three dogs, and two very fickle swans who travel the neighborhood in search of greener pastures.

Sign up for her newsletter at her website jodivaughn.com to keep up with upcoming events, releases, and the latest news!

ALSO BY JODI VAUGHN

The Vampire Housewife Series
Lipstick and Lies and Deadly Goodbyes (book 1)
Merlot and Divorce and Deadly Remorse (book 2)
Bullets and Booze and Dead Suede Shoes (book 3)
Aces and Eights and Dead Werewolf Dates (book 4)

Werewolf Guardian Romance Series
Her Werewolf Bodyguard (book 1)
Her Werewolf Protector (book 2)
Her Werewolf Defender (book 3)
Her Werewolf Champion (book 4)
Her Werewolf Hero (book 5)
Her Werewolf Valentine (book 6)
Her Werewolf Mate (book 7)
Her Werewolf Alpha (book 8)

Veiled Series
Veiled Secrets (book 1)
Veiled Enchantment (book 2)

Somewhere Texas Series
Saddle Up (book 1)

Trouble in Texas (book 2)

Bad Medicine (book 3)

Somewhere in Paradise (book 4)

Cloverton Series

Christmas in Cloverton

Lost Without You (book 1)

Lost All Control (book 2)